FALLING FROM HIGH PLACES

JAMES MCGETTIGAN BOOK 2

JOHN HAYDEN

Library of Congress Control Number: 2021907880 Names: Hayden, John

Title: Falling From High Places

ISBN: 978-1-7356187-4-6 (paperback)

ISBN: 978-1-7356187-5-3 (Epub)

DEDICATION

In memory of Fergus, one of life's great listeners.

ACKNOWLEDGMENTS

To readers of ACT of GOD, who enjoyed James McGettigan as a protagonist and urged his return, I offer my appreciation and thanks.

CHAPTER 1

I was about to risk my own life. Every man should possess the right to risk his own life, in order to preserve it.

Has it ever been said about a man, who throws himself out a window to escape a fire: He was guilty of attempted suicide? What would have caused a French philosopher to defy death in such a way? I'd bet he was never accused of murder.

A different Frenchman said: *False opinions are like false money, coined first of all by guilty men and thereafter circulated by honest people who perpetuate the crime.*

I'd been a victim of false opinions.

I made no claim of being guiltless.

***

The District Attorney for the Cape & Islands District of the Commonwealth of Massachusetts occupied offices on Main Street, in Barnstable. Somewhere around twenty prosecutors plied their trade—punishing the guilty—under his guidance, if not his thumb. In a room reserved for Grand Jury testimony, I stood at a podium opposed by Stephen Lincope, one of those prosecutors. Lincope used a fancy lectern finished, as it had been, with some gleaming chemical preservative. His carried a seal, whose gold leaf lent a distinguished appearance. Mine was shopworn. Lincope's shining lectern announced with precision whom was hunter and whom was prey.

Twenty-three of my peers sat in swivel-backed chairs, gazes alternating between the combatants: a State empowered gladiator and me, today's luncheon course.

Deirdre Collins, my criminal attorney, wasn't present, her ethereal camaraderie guaranteed by advice she'd given, in increasing decibels, over the prior several days. Deirdre considered me either a great fool or subject to suicidal tendencies. Since Deirdre didn't know me well, it was possible she hadn't considered the additive probability of those two options. Deirdre recommended I accept indictment as a foregone conclusion.

"A Grand Jury will indict a ham sandwich," she'd proclaimed. It seemed improbable my $750/hour legal representative was the originator of such a pithy comment, but she continued without brooking interruption. "Dead solid certainty we get an acquittal, if it goes to trial. Their case is bullshit. You'll be fine, when it's over."

Deirdre's assurances endeared her to me, although I was cautioned by hard-earned evidence she would fight-on to the last drop of my blood—real or economic making no difference. Deirdre never defined what *fine* meant in her world and hadn't explained why, if the outcome of a trial was a finding of innocent, this District Attorney was so insistent upon an indictment. My innate skepticism screamed the DA was similar to other politicians: he was for sale. Not directly, perhaps. Indirectly, the methods for influencing an elected official were myriad. The sum and substance of our attorney-client conversation had been—targets of Grand Juries didn't testify unless they were stupid.

Except when they did.

Strategy can be defined as the science and art of employing political, economic and psychological forces to afford maximum support towards meeting a goal—most often winning. Strategy was differentiated from tactics by being premeditated and rehearsed. I had a strategy. It had been premeditated, but not with Deirdre.

"Please state your name for the record."

Lincope was in his thirties, close enough to the age of my children as not to matter. His reputation conformed to a bright, well-prepared rising star. Not a lifer in the DA's office, not by a long shot. A promising ADA may well have wondered how this dogshit loser found its way onto his calendar, and whom he offended to make it so.

McGettigan made eye contact with Grand Jurors, standing before them in a timeworn gray suit, black loafers, white button down and solid blue tie cinched short of throttling me. I told them, "I used to be James McGettigan: husband, father, engineer...all in all a man who lives quietly, works hard and, by most of society's inadequate measures, is more good than bad."

Lincope, caught unprepared for a witness to wander off in a direction other than the gallows, snapped, "Don't be cute." With a glance at his Grand Jury, he realized his icy superiority had slipped. "Answer what you're asked."

Cape Cod year-round residents shared one almost universal characteristic; rebellion against authority was feasible, if such authority was applied with too much enthusiasm.

"Address?" Lincope had just begun the pro-forma portion of my testimony, and his fish was vomiting the hook and lure.

"My wife died two and a half years ago. Cancer..."

"The Grand Jury will not tolerate your lack of cooperation, Dr. McGettigan. Address, please?" His insouciant sneer made it clear who was the alpha-dog.

More than one member of the Grand Jury nodded agreement. Most were sullen, remembering their life outside this confined chamber in which the Commonwealth of Massachusetts had imprisoned them. I counted five wearing discontent as an adornment. One squirmed in subdued insurrection. I'd told these Grand Jurors my wife died of cancer. At least six of them appreciated what a life-changing loss felt like.

"Fiddler's Cove Road, in Monument Beach, where I've been a resident for thirty-one years, where my two children grew up and attended..."

My new friend, the ADA, was irritated beyond doubt or question. "The Grand Jury's not interested in your children, Dr. McGettigan."

For the second time, the ADA addressed me by my honorific: PhD in engineering.

Deirdre had assured me this would be the case. "ADAs..." she'd said "...spit out fancy titles, understanding jury members are either suspicious or disdainful of the educated elite."

I walked a fine line. There were more seeds to plant with this jury, but not everything about James McGettigan's immediate past would produce compassion. "My own cancer surgery was a little over a year ago. Followed by chemo…"

Lincope raised his voice. "That's enough."

Outside the security of his protective shield, he advanced towards the jurors. "Dr. McGettigan seems to have trouble with authority. Perhaps this gives you insight into why he's here today." When he whirled around, on his way back to where he began, Lincope missed two of my six sympathizers returning to his fold—as four others hardened their resentment of the Commonwealth's treatment of a taxpayer.

My approach to aging separated the whole of McGettigan into more manageable parts. The Organism was in charge of survival; its pure physical needs must be met. The Organism believed itself a cancer survivor, after surgery and chemotherapy. Emotional outbursts destabilized its functions. McGettigan—I thought of myself in the third person more frequently—planned the Organism's activities. McGettigan was unwilling to call himself a cancer survivor. Long dead ancestors beat a drum of dread and horror—McGettigan liked to think himself above such nonsense—yet he listened to the drumbeat. McGettigan the Foolish was the third member of Me, Myself and I, his presence abhorred by the other two. In-charge of stupidity, a Fool specialized in bad decisions. Until recently, this working separation was somewhat practical, humorous on occasion and guiltless, if not blameless. Now? I wasn't certain I could sustain so many moving parts, nor was I positive how they came to be. James McGettigan was no longer whole and couldn't be the sum of those parts.

Once his podium and microphone were attained, Lincope returned his attention to the accused. "Are you employed, Dr. McGettigan?"

"Yes." McGettigan the Foolish had been prepared to offer several smartass responses.

My business with few exceptions served public officials—Mayors or their sort, who had suspicions. Not their normal, paranoid suspicions centered upon power and re-election, but qualms about physical events. Why had a high school gymnasium collapsed in a snowstorm? How did a Power Plant in Iraq come to be used by terrorists? Suspicions didn't mean a crime had been committed, but it didn't mean one hadn't. For a man who'd spent a career exposing bad men—I drew a distinction between 'catching' and 'exposing'—there was one screaming question to ask: how did I get here?

"Who is your employer?" The ADA had recovered. His foot told another tale—toe tapping, prodded by nerves, as it was.

"James McGettigan died those months ago, at the hands of Donald Hartnett, CEO of BGFH. You know what people call them...Big Giant Bleeping Huge Contracting Corp. He shot me. Not the other way round." McGettigan's eyes fastened on the back row where four nominees for support stared back in shock.

Donald Hartnett had been a billionaire. How many billionaires were charlatans—or criminals? Hartnett had been both those things. On the day McGettigan died, Hartnett had been vindictive, triumphant and a superb shot as he held a muzzle-loading, antique pistol. The pistol was part of an extensive collection owned by Robert Linney, my best friend from childhood, who, suffering from early onset Alzheimer's, resided anonymously in Cuba. Who managed his substantial fortune was unknown to me. Robert's mother, Gwyneth, had been the third person in Robert's private gunroom, when the mammoth lead ball struck my chest. Philanthropy had been no part of what made Hartnett agree to negotiate peace amongst us two. McGettigan's possession of proof positive, ticking towards disclosure on a web site Hartnett couldn't find or destroy, provided his motivation. For Hartnett and McGettigan, it had been the ultimate end game.

"I can have you removed, Dr. McGettigan. You will answer my questions as they're formulated."

McGettigan, during death and resurrection, enlarged his menagerie of self by one. McGettigan's Ghost now offered frequent advice and caustic views of his fellow travelers in life. McGettigan and the Foolish had become a mess in their attempts to manage the Organism—imagine when my therapist heard about the Poltergeist.

I shouldn't have been indicted, if justice was blind, not for the murder of Donald Hartnett. Should McGettigan be indicted for different deaths, ones he contrived, took part in, or caused over the last twelve months? Not an issue for this Grand Jury to deliberate.

"Of course you can have me removed, Mr. Lincope. Should you elect to deprive me of the right to speak, how will light be shed on these accusations. I didn't kill Donald Hartnett. I was unconscious and dying when he was shot. I don't know who shot Mr. Hartnett.

Those are the facts this Grand Jury should hear testimony on. I'm ready to provide compelling testimony…when you're ready, of course."

Since friends and family pestered McGettigan's Ghost interminably, I toyed with posting a laminated advisory in my kitchen telling anyone who was curious: James McGettigan did not cross over, see any crazy bright lights, and returned from wherever death took a man more or less as he left.

Lincope could indict McGettigan and the ham sandwich with little additional effort. If the back-row jurors were annoyed with ADA Lincope, their bravery was insufficient to confront his authority.

Deirdre advised an unacceptable tactic—throw Gwyneth Linney under the bus. As a boy I'd been blessed with a woman who loved and offered understanding apart from my parents. With Robert taken from her by an unforgiving disease, and her husband dead, offering Gwyneth as a substitute executioner of Donald Hartnett would be unthinkable.

Lincope whirled a second time. Frustrated, it was time to pare away the outer layers of this onion and get to the meat.

"Two men go into a room. One comes out in a black, zippered, bag. Who else shot Donald Hartnett dead?" The ADA burned with righteous indignation. "If not James McGettigan, then who? Educate us, please, Dr. McGettigan."

Billy Nichols, my long-time fisherman friend, found me in Robert's secret gunroom. I had a hole in my chest, took breath in an irregular pattern and was unconscious. Hartnett fell where he shot me, with an indescribable wound between his eyes.

"As if God shot him," Billy said, after the Organism returned to post-surgical coherence.

It was where Billy found me, and what I'd held, which gave me pause last Fall—and took my breath away today. Because, while I remembered standing at the opposite end of Robert Linney's massive oak table from Hartnett, and on the diagonal across from Gwyneth, Billy claimed my memory was faulty with categorical certainty. McGettigan was the engineer, Billy the fisherman; who was the better bet to be correct? I'd been, at most, fifteen feet from Hartnett. Six to eight feet from Gwyneth. Why would I have dragged myself, with my last breaths, to where she stood? How had I held an antique pistol, a twin to the one in Hartnett's right hand, as crime-scene photos indicated?

How had Donald Hartnett wound up dead?

Gwyneth Linney stated she fled the room as soon as Hartnett removed a pistol from Robert's elaborate display of antique weaponry. She described terror overcoming her. I would believe her performance, except I'd been there. Her rigid account maintained she saw no gun fired, not by either Hartnett or McGettigan. No other loaded weapon hung in a display covering two walls. No additional weapon was found loaded by police or crime scene technicians.

Robert Linney's presence in Cuba wasn't a matter of public record. Because he hadn't returned home, Robert offered no statement or his expert views vis-à-vis his gun collection.

McGettigan's Ghost could accuse Gwyneth Linney.

I would not.

As for dying, I must've looked for *Her*: the wife, friend, confidant and lover who was once mine, whose loss qualified me to advise my son Patrick on losing his first love to an unrelated murder—advice which consoled my precious boy not the smallest iota. Prodded by the Devil, I'm certain, McGettigan cannot say if he tried to locate the wife who'd been lost.

McGettigan's Ghost guffawed at emotional mumbo jumbo.

With his dad attached to tubes and machines, Patrick had said, "If you'd seen Mom, you would've stayed." It may not have occurred to my beloved son: Mom could have been in an entirely different location than Dad. If I'd been dead in the first place.

Many in law enforcement and the media declared James McGettigan guilty of Donald Hartnett's murder. Among them was United States Senator Warren Harding, Patrick's former employer. Donald Hartnett had many friends, it seemed, now he was in a better place. Better Place was a phrase anointed upon the deceased by those who never knew Hartnett. Yachts, mansions and unlimited resources made the material world he departed quite livable.

EMT's believed McGettigan a goner. Surgeons told me later—I'd been close enough to dead, when they opened me up. They also acknowledged the Organism was lifeless a short time before their efforts produced results. For an unknown reason, made to sound miraculous by the same surgical team, the crude chunk of lead stopped before tearing apart my heart and lungs.

Within days, a San Francisco attorney representing BGFH and Hartnett's estate received a cryptic telephone message. This attorney, when he returned a call from Sandy Watson, my business partner, suggested a meeting to bridge all differences. I would wager Sandy, knowing his inclination towards proper expression, said, "Bite me. Take a look at the web site…come up with the biggest number the Hartnett family and BGFH will stomach…add a zero. Then call again."

Payment had been concluded well before I recovered enough to share in negotiations. Sandy's actions had been rash and immoral, if not illegal. Weighed on a scale opposed by the crimes of Donald Hartnett, Sandy's transgression was the equivalent of a broken taillight. Put to good use the money was, which didn't include McGettigan's enrichment.

Our legal system had been and still was, despite the powerful logic hurled at me by ADA Lincope, stymied. Had there been a crime? If so, who was its victim and who the criminal? The matter hadn't been resolved by ballistics, for bullets and pistols of a particular vintage offered nothing conclusive. Hartnett held one pistol, which on its face appeared to have shot McGettigan. McGettigan held a second pistol, which on its face, appeared to have shot Hartnett. If pistols could talk, Lincope could offer the Grand Jury better evidence.

McGettigan stated, "I'll offer the Grand Jury a theory, backed-up by visual and auditory evidence, using the laptop my attorney requested."

"Evidence of what?" Lincope had prepared a script—a progression of questions to take the jurors on a junket from fairy-dust to cupcakes.

Twenty-three citizens edged forward in their seats. My six best hopes were agitated and excited; this was closer to the confrontations they watched on television. They'd heard the sound bite: McGettigan said Hartnett shot first. McGettigan offered proof. They all wanted to see my magical attestation.

"There is no laptop, Mr. McGettigan. We're not turning your testimony into a sideshow."

Lincope hadn't been briefed by his boss, the District Attorney, who must be the tip of the legal spear aimed at my throat. Whatever drove the District Attorney was irrelevant to this ADA, whose petulant response displeased everyone in the room, including himself.

I honored my bargain with Hartnett's heirs and corporate associates. No information from my web site had reached the public. Hartnett's reputation remained revered, with no attempt by McGettigan to sully it in retrospective.

Who wanted McGettigan tried for Hartnett's murder? A second aim of my charade was to identify such a person, or persons. "If you provide the laptop, my evidence will be absolute...clear to each member of the Grand Jury. Evidence involving..."

"That's enough," Lincope snorted a second time. "Sit down Dr. McGettigan...sit down and remain quiet. Mr. Foreman, please maintain the Grand Jury's decorum...no discussion of this case. Thank you."

Scurrying from the room, he sought a life preserver.

Lincope, upon re-entering the Grand Jury room, wore a blanched expression. "There will be no laptop." He swirled his tongue inside his mouth, trying to eradicate the cotton which had taken up residence. "Dr. McGettigan...what was your firm's gross income last year and from which clients was such income derived?"

The cat was out of this bag.

An arm attached to a woman's body was raised in the Grand Jury's back row. Face fixed in defiance, her fingers waggled seeking attention. Ignored, she raised her voice.

"He's here to provide testimony. As one juror, I want to hear anything to enlighten these events. If there's nothing more than the Commonwealth's claim of whom murdered whom...no real evidence of what happened...you can't expect an indictment."

Some heads nodded. Some didn't. I couldn't count fast enough to determine whether McGettigan had a majority. "My evidence will give the jury..."

Lost control, Stephen Lincope had—not his brightest career highlight. "You're out of order, Dr. McGettigan."

Directed not to let evidence damaging to Donald Hartnett, or BGFH, come into the record, it was reasonable for Lincope to assume—given talk of a laptop and how damaging the content on a web site I created could be to Hartnett's living associates—McGettigan intended a scorched earth policy. Bribery. Murder. Sedition. All resided on Robert Linney's List. The List and its contents, in brilliant color and stereo sound, would scare the bejesus out of men several steps above the pay-grade of the Cape & Islands District Attorney.

How had we all come to this?

Donald Hartnett knew well enough last Fall; McGettigan was prepared to kneel before a powerful King. Hartnett lost key associates to Robert Linney's vengeful morality and lost his private assassin to Billy Nichols' courage. Yet an inexhaustible supply of politicians, Generals, spies, hit-men and ordinary people were available and prepared to do his bidding.

McGettigan saw reality and buckled under its weight.

I'd chosen to construct a deal with the devil to save my children. Choosing my death, in favor of my children's future, was simple. I would make the identical bargain again, though my therapist suggests avoiding those circumstances.

Gwyneth Linney had been wiser than McGettigan, had known Hartnett wouldn't relent, wouldn't suffer the smallest nick to pride. He was, after all, a King. She made a deal of her own. She traded McGettigan's human sacrifice in return for the lives of her family. But all along she'd seen what my vision could not. McGettigan's death would be inadequate tribute. Hartnett wouldn't trade as an equal with an old woman. Hartnett was a tumor on the Linney family's future—requiring Gwyneth to sculpt a more refined excision. Hartnett miscalculated—for Stanley Linney imposed his fanaticism for historic weaponry and shooting on his wife as well as his son.

Gwyneth knew—she would have to kill Hartnett herself.

Gwyneth was clinical. She offered Hartnett a foolproof method for exorcising McGettigan. Hartnett could arrive at Robert's mansion unarmed, knowing she loaded two antique pistols among the dozens displayed with maniacal pride on Robert Linney's walls. They must have been charged with an identical quantity of powder.

But not a full charge.

A full charge would've eliminated any chance of McGettigan's survival. The geometry was clear: She could control only her distance from Hartnett—close enough to kill.

McGettigan was alive for no other reason than the skill of a woman near ninety and blind, unfathomable, luck. I saw her drop the pistol as she ran away in horror; suffering I'd thought from too much dignity to remain and watch a man, a boy whom she thought to be her third son, bleed to death. McGettigan had loved Gwyneth—the

Gwyneth who cared for and shaped James the growing boy—enough to save her from guilt in Hartnett's demise.

Someone continued to seek Hartnett's revenge. Or McGettigan has again miscalculated events and misread intentions.

Several hands were in the air, including those of the Grand Jury Foreman. A full-scale revolt was under way. Either this jury would be allowed to see the evidence claimed by McGettigan or there would be a vote of No True Bill.

What was left for Lincope was to retreat—to run away—to live and fight another day.

I knew the feeling well.

"Mr. McGettigan, you are dismissed." Venality marked Lincope's words. This ADA was confused. He was, in this limited case, a functionary.

I crossed him off my list of the overtly guilty.

While I expected not to be indicted, No True Bill was far from being found innocent. I could be indicted tomorrow, or any other day when suspicion was converted into a ham sandwich.

Years before I encountered Donald Hartnett, I experienced evil up close in the form of a child rapist who subsumed humanity in favor of corporate earnings. The rapist had, indirectly, been McGettigan's first murder victim. ADA Lincope might find it ironic to discover he'd sought to indict the correct man for the wrong crime.

CHAPTER 2

At the GTO's door, my fingers slid over new maroon clearcoat. Months ago the paint, chrome, tires and other parts melted in a puddle of McGettigan's tears, when an explosion ripped apart the multi-million dollar boathouse which belonged to Robert Linney. Explosion was a good word for the aftermath, because it began a crazed period during which Hartnett sought my destruction; a time I thought finished until the Grand Jury arrived on my doorstep.

I'd been arrested and booked. Arraigned and bailed-out. Demeaning had been the intention of the law enforcement community. Their efforts were successful.

The GTO had been restored, but more fragile than once it was.

From Superior Court, the GTO took 6-A towards Sandwich, then Town Neck Road till I wound up on Canal Service Road. At the Cape Cod Canal's southern extreme, where it spilled into Buzzards Bay, the Massachusetts Maritime Academy sat across from my cottage. At its northern extremity, a section of reveted bulkhead was interrupted by an opening to Sandwich Marina, whose ambience was despoiled by the looming bulk of Mirant Power Station. Joe's Lobsters was my target. Sixteen minutes and my lobster was boiled and buttered. Ravenous appetite satisfied, a slow stroll was my intention.

May on Cape Cod can be fickle. The Red Sox season was in full swing. Boston and its suburbs enjoyed new leaves and flowers, but not here. Today hinted at warmth, an azure sky adorned with nary a cloud to scale its height. Tidal flow brought violent eddies close. An estimate of tidal velocity, in a Canal five hundred forty feet wide and thirty-two feet deep, wasn't straightforward. Five knots was the guesstimate made at the Massachusetts Institute of Technology, where McGettigan was listed as an alumnus.

Hunger had warped my point of view; lunch restored perspective. Semi-comatose in the sun, I observed a Mercedes SL Roadster pull in next to the GTO. McGettigan's invoice would provide funds for several of its lease payments. Behind the Mercedes an observer of an anonymous sedan would predict it belonged to a government motor pool. Deidre Collins exited the silver convertible in blissful ignorance of the sedan or its driver. This left two possibilities: The sedan's arrival was a coincidence, or the sedan followed Deidre absent her cooperation.

Short, blonde highlighted hair was cropped in a style with a name. My mind couldn't drag the skater's, or actress's name into clarity. Vibrant smile, eyes laughing and lips glossy pink, little mystery accompanied the news my attorney brought for my pleasure. I imagined her adding hours to my invoice—a bonus for winning was allotted in their discretion by many attorneys. Deirdre wore a tight mauve skirt, but not too tight. A lighter version of the same shade was reflected in a blouse not tucked-in, but stylish while overriding the skirt's waistline. Over her shoulder she'd tossed a tan gabardine blazer. Orange flats replaced earlier pumps.

The driver of the sedan had exited by the time Deirdre was halfway towards me: nondescript except for silver-tipped, sixties shagginess. Middle-aged, tall-ish, dark glasses covering inquisitive eyes, his build was unlike the no-neck linebacker commonly found in the private soldier business. Which the Foolish took as a good sign. None of four parts of me held an ounce of affection for linebackers.

Shaggy-man stared. Was it Deirdre's provocative walk which drew this fixation? Or something quite different? Shaggy, with his boyish hair, made no attempt to hide his interest. Was he waiting? Or plotting?

McGettigan couldn't help his suspicions. In little more than a year, a mostly mundane existence had been marred by three attempts on my life, not counting a knife plunged into my right arm's shark-bite of a cancer scar, or a wire noose around my neck designed to strangle.

"Whatever did you say to those jurors, James?"

A familiar scent floated on the breeze. I was a man who responded to Chanel #5. With little effort it would be possible to think Deirdre sincere.

Her last bottle's liquid, darkened and suffering slow evaporation, sat on a countertop next to *her* sink in our Marsh Landing, Florida home. Except there wasn't a Marsh Landing house, not after Hartnett's assassin blew the bedroom, bath and most everything else to smithereens. Fire took what the explosion hadn't. No Chanel rested on *her* countertop, not any longer.

"Are those tears of joy, big boy? Lincope is apoplectic. All the hounds from television and the papers have called my office, though truth be told they'd have preferred if you'd been handed over in leg irons."

Shaggy-man never moved; his gaze penetrated me, trying to leave the impression of disinterest.

"Have you had lunch, Deirdre?" An empty lobster body and claws illustrated my question. I began to stand, joints creaky under the effort of leaving the past behind.

"I ate." She reached out to pull me the rest of the way.

Her touch was an electric shock. I yanked my hand away and fell on the Organism's rear-end.

Deirdre's touch was nothing amongst the greater concerns McGettigan faced. It wasn't like I was running around on *her*. I've existed in something like blissful ignorance without another woman; never having desired other than what I'd been blessed with. Felt privileged to be *her* husband. She who was smarter and all-round better than *her* mate for life.

"Jesus, James. I'm not molesting you."

Deirdre's voice betrayed annoyance and something else. Anyway, I thought it was something else. James McGettigan hadn't had an exchange even bordering on sexual, with a woman other than my own, for close to forty years—and couldn't determine what this something else was.

McGettigan propped himself up and rose like the ape who stood on hind legs for the first time in recorded history. Was it to further distress me, when she took my hand in hers? Or was seeing life, for everything it might yet be, impossible? James McGettigan wanted what he could never have; he wanted *her* back.

Should I wear a sign?

"Is it so difficult to see me as a woman?" Deirdre Collins was lovely, when annoyed. "How long since she died?"

This was a question of fact; McGettigan ought to be able to drag out an admission.

"Near enough three years."

The Foolish could provide Deirdre with hard statistics: Years, months, days and, with an infinitesimal pause for calculation, the minutes since she took her final breath; since I might have done the same, despite my therapist's claims.

"How long will you keep her on your altar?"

She'd crossed a line I was unprepared to examine, although my children asked much the same in more careful language. I turned to Deirdre and stared, dumbfounded at her intrusion.

"Let me finish. I'm not unfeeling or callous, despite what you think. You're a Neanderthal, James McGettigan. Your wife must have been so special. But you're alive. How can you stand up...go on with life...when you're always kneeling? Would there be some huge harm in sharing a few dinners with me...no expectations, no strings?"

I didn't, no couldn't, answer.

We walked slow. Found ourselves on the northern edge of the Marina. "Do you like boats, Deirdre?" I asked this in a toneless voice, but not an argumentative one.

"I've never spent much time near boats. You must, though?" This wasn't her inner lawyer speaking. This was someone softer.

"How about the Red Sox?"

"Are they the football team?"

Her response strained credibility. This woman lived in Boston by choice—despite winters when even McGettigan, who believed himself a rugged New England seaman, bailed-out from their deprivation.

Finally, she giggled. "We have four seats behind the visitor's dugout."

She meant the law firm, when the royal We was deployed.

McGettigan leaned his back, where one of two tumors had been harvested, against a steel railing which ran the length of the bulkhead. Sturdier than needed, McGettigan laughed at the irony: the railing protected a man the Commonwealth hoped to ship to Walpole State Prison.

Sandwich Marina was tight, its opening to the Canal little more than fifty yards across. Yachts which transited the Canal often tied-up along the bulkhead to purchase fresh fish Joe's was known for.

Growls from large diesels broke a delayed reaction to my experience with the Grand Jury. Big diesels were workhorses; McGettigan had been a workhorse all his life. Work was what Donald Hartnett's death—McGettigan rejected calling it murder—took away. My small partnership now deemed a pariah among politicians who, in the not distant past, stood in line for services not listed in the Yellow Pages.

Diesel noise rising, behind me was a large yacht whose presence was a month too soon for summer. In my mind's eye, the hull slowed as the Canal's opposing current brought her to a stop. It would be critical to get a bow line secured, before she wound up crosswise in an angry, swirling, river within an ocean.

Deirdre's hands clamped my right arm in a death-grip. She turned me towards the yacht as she spoke.

"Someone's in the water."

She pointed as my mind accelerated to match what had occurred. Before conscious thought caught-up, I knew I was going in the water. Several heartbeats were required for the Organism and McGettigan to agree on this decision.

At the most critical competitive moments, elite athletes experienced an odd, higher state of mind: Time slowed to a crawl. McGettigan possessed first hand knowledge of this phenomenon, though in the ignorance of youth hadn't appreciated how a fastball, which from my perspective appeared frozen in slow motion, made a batter's knees buckle and eyes roll upwards into their sockets. Nearing sixty, the very idea of faster or slower was unpredictable. Life would be easier if I knew which was coming when. So to thrust myself, from fifteen feet above the black, cold, Canal wasn't trivial.

I yelled at Deirdre, "Run to the Coast Guard Station. Get help."

Head rotated to examine the yacht, two unaware deckhands worked to secure a bow line a hundred feet from where I stood. Their ambivalence puzzled me, while the Organism's vision kept a pink, gauzy nightgown in its crosshairs. I felt each day of my age, arms outstretched, sucking air into my lungs, as computations were made: How far had the current taken a pink nightgown; was its owner conscious and swimming or under the influence of gravity, salinity and tidal velocity? I'd get but one chance. If I had to dive a second time, my strength wouldn't last—and neither would the woman. Anyone with McGettigan's experience around boats knew— a search on the Marina side of the inlet wasn't a difficult choice. If the pink nightgown were in the main Canal, its owner would be smashed on huge rock, riprap walls.

Peripheral vision noticed white water streaming along the yacht's hull as she gathered rearward momentum, almost as if someone intended to grind McGettigan into chum.

Submerged, I held on as cold sucked oxygen from the Organism's lungs. Eyes pried open in soupy visibility, legs kicked hard to thrust me forward in no more than a guess about a pink nightgown's direction.

A massive shape blotted out what sunlight had been present.

A demonic bass drum changed the pressure in my ears—whoosh, whoosh, whoosh—propellers cavitating as they mixed water and air into death's cyclone. Evade the propellers' suction—no other command to the Organism meant anything.

Pink nightgown disappeared as a concern.

Maintain depth and forward motion became the sole task.

McGettigan believed himself two thirds of the way across the inlet, headed for the PILOT boat. Maybe six feet below the surface and out of range of those propellers, I didn't so much find the woman, as run into her. Compared with my increasing imperative to breathe, her orientation and movement wasn't a high priority.

My hand touched her right shoulder. I planned to turn her, then haul both of us upwards and further away from the propellers. One truth governed: Propellers could kill us, but without soon reaching the surface, we would drown.

However close to dead she may have been, it wasn't enough to keep her right arm from a slashing motion which widened my eyes as a double-edged knife raked my side.

She kicked away in a desultory motion.

Cold prevented me feeling anything. Self-preservation caused me to abandon her rescue. When I broke the surface, gasping in relief, my position was fifteen feet from the opposite bulkhead. The stern of *Marvelous Lady M* sat dead in the water, drifting towards me under the current's influence. Instinct caused the Organism to touch its side, returning with a fistful of bloody saltwater

Coast Guardsmen swarmed their dock; two rigid inflatable surfboats were almost underway. Scissor kicks took me to the massive bulkhead, where I grabbed hold. Both inflatables surrounded the woman. I watched her nude figure dragged from the water.

I was alone. Deirdre called to me from the Coast Guard dock, her words indistinguishable. McGettigan wasn't panicked; cold would retard bleeding. A sense of dizziness extended a whisper of warning: My blood pressure was dropping. This was the last admonition I'd receive.

"Help. Bleeding badly. Help."

Strong hands held my left arm, the one which threw hundred miles per hour fastballs, when the world was thought flat. Dragged like a flopping tuna, McGettigan believed the fish-gods must be laughing—tables turned and other forms of hooey. A Coast Guard kid looked on in horror at what I couldn't yet see, then ripped open and taped a succession of bandages.

A second uniform held a towel against my side. Quite far away, I heard him say, "Hold this while I start an IV."

When McGettigan regained consciousness, we were racing towards the dock as a high-pitched, continuous wail assaulted my hearing. Was it me who made this awful sound?

A male voice, located in the bow, offered a sarcastic opinion. "Whore-shriek."

Just the two words were all I heard, as if a hyphenated epithet contained a dissertation of information. Had I passed-out a second time? No response informed this silent question.

EMTs made a triage assessment of two waterlogged victims to determine priorities for transport: James McGettigan would go first and then the woman whose frenetic departure from *Marvelous Lady M* caused this ruckus.

A massive bandage which encircled my chest from armpit to waist replaced the blood soaked towel. A bag of saline fed my body liquid. I'd gutted my share of fish: to experience the sensation proved what they said about Karma. The woman's blade had cut me from armpit to mid-section—to the bone over my ribs. Throughout preliminary medical attention, whore-shriek continued. I whispered a final insistence.

"She slashed me."

To McGettigan, wrapped in a blanket, her tear-streaked Asian face alternated between the far extreme of emotions. What she felt was plain enough: angry and afraid.

I explained as best I could, when asked by the ranking Petty Officer how a man-overboard situation had gone so wrong. I told him McGettigan's rescue had been unsuccessful due in large part to the yacht's Captain being incompetent; no responsible helmsman would engage propellers in close proximity to underwater swimmers. When my anger exhausted itself, I offered a further opinion: The woman had escaped the yacht, not been pushed or fallen in the Canal by accident.

The Petty Officer's expression showed little deference for my opinion.

No added protest emanated from McGettigan. Because, while I knew nothing of the woman who cut me, I knew the owner of *Marvelous Lady M*.

CHAPTER 3

Prior to the last twelve months, my relationship with hospitals had lain dormant since knee surgeries ended professional baseball dreams. Prior to the last twelve months, my personal relationship with those I investigated for crimes of corruption had been more detached than less. Politicians, who accepted bribes, failed a test of character was how I'd come to view their failings. Construction executives who over-billed, or slipped cash into the sticky fingers of the aforementioned pols, were amoral mercenaries, not murderers. For McGettigan, events of the last twelve months removed all residual sentimentality towards a certain class of individuals: men and women who would do anything to achieve their ends. Hartnett and his crew, members of an over-rated billionaire class, sought to end my miserable existence and perished for their efforts.

McGettigan had learned. Or been taught. I learned how it felt to never sleep. Never relax. Learned to listen as my heart, in the most literal sense, stopped. Learned to know no pity, to beg solitude's end while seeking nothing less. Learned to see the strain of events mark me with deep facial furrows and long, frightful, scars. James McGettigan was now, and I feared would forever be a different kind of human. I was suspicious, distrustful and sometimes melancholy. I reacted in haste with thoughts of violence.

I waited with less and less patience for the past twelve months to recede. I strained to hide my new identity from my children, who weren't fooled. Their mother's genes provided all the necessary tools of observation.

"You've lost a lot of blood, Mr. McGettigan. You'll feel like crap for ten days or so. One look at your chest told me you've had plenty of experience with post-surgical care...so I won't bore you with details. Shouldn't be any permanent issues. Questions?"

"How long till I go home?"

Her snort was informative. "The nurse will get you ready, when we're certain you're stable. Go home. Your wife will take good care of you." No echo of irony kept the doctor's good intentions alive.

It was this altered McGettigan who watched a priest standing outside, uncertain whether to enter. Was he preparing his bag of oils to anoint another traveler to everlasting life?

Not this priest.

This priest was a pariah, and played first base on McGettigan's high school baseball team.

Defrocked, he was an exaggerated figure of the New England underworld and the subject of frenzied legend. Tall, he stooped a little to peer through the door's glass to examine me. His eyes saw through me, looking beyond the IV bag, blood pressure and heart monitors and the rolling tray on which a carafe of ice chips sat within the reach of my left arm. Nicotine colored hair sat astride an oval face unchanged from when Timothy Timilty and James McGettigan served 7am Mass, five days a week, for Father Jackie 'Sparks' McMullen, Chaplain of the BFD and teacher of religion to the junior and senior class. Pouches of skin sagged, making the bottom of his face appear engorged, like a dentist had stuffed his lower jaw with tube-shaped gauze pads. Stretched too tight across his chest, the black cassock was an artifact of a thinner man, one with fewer burdens of conscience. A white Roman collar was over-run by a waddle pockmarked by semi-healed teenage acne.

Timilty's reputation preceded him, although our last meeting had been at high school graduation. By lore and eminence, a visit from this particular priest assured the need of Last Rites, affirmation resting with seventeen murders attributed to him by the media.

A wise man would have been worried.

A Fool allowed his mouth to stay closed and the call button untouched. If Timmy had come to end my life, his odds of success were good whatever action I contemplated.

Graceful movement belied his girth. With one hand he repositioned the room's single chair so his head was close and his hand held mine with reassuring pressure.

"Can you still pray fast, Old Son?"

Years of repetition, disassociated from current events, forced the dead language of the Latin Mass from McGettigan's tight, drawn lips. Sentences ran together, in the manner required to complete Mass in under seventeen minutes with perfect diction—Sparky's minimum requirement for his altar boys.

"Pater noster, qui es in caelis. Sanctificetur nomen tuum. Adveniat regnum tuum. Fiat voluntas tua, sicut in caelo et in terra. Panem nostrum quotidianum da nobis hodie et dimitte nobis debita nostra sicut et nos dimittimus debitoribus nostris. Et ne nos inducas in tentationem, sed libera nos a malo. Amen."

In the manner of conspirators, his hushed voice continued. "Why, Boy-O, did you always get to ring the Offertory Bells for Kyrie Eleison?"

McGettigan absorbed the question. Did this amount to a secret handshake? Or was resolving our mutual history somehow more important forty years after the fact?

"Well, because I had better wrist action...cleaner sound. Your finest hour was trying to play Mr. Tambourine Man with the damn bells during the Kyrie...at Easter our senior year."

I attempted a smile at the memory: every parent throwing a fit; Monsignor Thomas Aquinas Everett, the Headmaster, purple as he rotated his massive ordination ring in anticipation of marking our cheeks with vicious backhands.

"Would you pass the ice chips, Timmy?"

Delicate fingers poured frozen crystals into a paper cup. Stains on those digits, plain to my eyes as the cup came to parched lips, were a close match to his dyed hair. An amalgam of unfiltered cigarettes, nervous sweat and unwashed hair wasn't reflected in his exterior demeanor.

"You took Everett's beating with panache, James. All I wanted was to slit his arrogant, fat throat."

Monsignor T. A. Everett had been a sadist. Short and massive, he was cantankerous and suitable for insolent teenage caricature. His ring's impression in your cheek was an invitation, a penance almost, for our fathers. There was no mistake about the excuse it had been for Timmy's dad—a day after Easter Timmy suffered a concussion and broken wrist. McGettigan wondered what else those days had wrought.

Timmy's next question was droll, as if casual or unimportant. "Whatever happened to you, James? You had the talent. Fenway Park…Yankee Stadium…Chavez Ravine, those dreams were within reach. I've heard things, but I'd rather hear it from you."

It wasn't bells from the Latin Mass ringing in my ears, but our shared psychological drama, perhaps existing nowhere but in my old classmate's mind, which held my full attention. Cat and mouse didn't suit me, a man who was yet expected to dress and transport himself, and eighty-nine surgical staples, home to my cottage. I shut my eyes and provided my version of a lifetime's scripted responses.

"My parents wouldn't let me sign with the Braves, when we graduated. Went to MIT like my father, like a good little boy. Tore an ACL…they didn't know how to repair it back then. Tough to pitch with no ACL. Went to graduate school. Got married. Had kids. She died. Here I am—filleted by some berserk Asian girl after she jumped off a fricking yacht."

Timmy increased the grip pressure in the hand enveloping my own. It was impossible not to wonder—was this pressure pure reflex, or indicative of having received critical information? His head was bowed. Not a word suggested a mocking tone, when he requested forgiveness.

"Confíteor Deo omnipoténti (I confess to almighty God), beátæ Maríæ semper Vírgini, beáto Micháéli Archángelo, beáto Ioánni Baptístæ, sanctis Apóstolis Petro et Paulo, ómnibus Sanctis, et vobis, fratres: quia peccávi nimis cogitatióne, verbo et ópere: mea culpa, mea culpa, mea máxima culpa."

Timmy, when he raised his head, stared through me pleading for a specific blessing, even if forgiveness wasn't mine to convey. McGettigan couldn't grant what this penitent man sought. Though I was content to be a lapsed Catholic, I wouldn't blaspheme the beliefs and rituals of my long dead mother.

Misereátur tui omnípotens Deus (May Almighty God have mercy on you), dimíssis peccátis tuis (forgive you your sins), perdúcat te ad vitam ætérnam (and bring you to life everlasting), was what I said to myself using the voice belonging to McGettigan the Foolish. To Timothy Timilty, I offered the next best available benediction.

"Timmy, I always believed you were a good boy. You were smart about things it took years for me to learn. I believe in forgiveness…and believe you'll find it." Timilty may have been confused by what I said next, but there was a chance it would elucidate earlier hesitation. "For myself, Timmy…I'm not so sure."

With my eyes closed, time was released from its standard measure. My hand was not.

Whether I awoke was no great concern.

***

Three prescription vials accompanied a bowl of broth, crackers and green Jell-O. I watched Timmy twist the childproof cap, remove two opioid tablets, toss them to the back of his mouth and reach for my precious Jell-O to wash them down.

"How about sharing?"

A plastic spoon contained a pill amongst the gelatin's alchemy. "James, you kill Hartnett?"

His simple question was better suited to Stephen Lincope than Timmy Timilty. Timmy and Brendan might not be the most loving of brothers, but without question Brendan was the incumbent District Attorney of the Cape & Islands District. Brendan and Timmy, involved together, suggested my alert level should rise three notches.

"Nope."

"Who's twisting Brendan's nuts?"

Confirmation received, McGettigan's proven assumption about the District Attorney's incentive to persecute brought no enlightenment. Brendan Timilty's search for an indictment had never been based in a quest for justice, just as Timmy's melodramatic interrogation was aimed at the wrong man.

"No idea. Ask Brendan."

"Who'd be on your short-list?"

"Whose side you on?"

"My own, Boy-O, as always."

Boy-O may well be the last endearment heard before a bullet put out the lights in any of his victims soul. Eyes ablaze, he added, "Prudens quaestio dimidium scientiae, laddie." *To know what to ask is already to know half.* Timilty liked riddles.

"Leave me a number, Timmy. I'll let you know, when I know."

Timmy's presence could be distilled from several motivations. If he wanted to know—was McGettigan prepared to forgive and forget?—no refutation had been offered. Was it the answer he'd hoped for? Or was Timothy Timilty recruiting me to an unknown brotherhood.

He patted my shoulder like a real priest, expressing assurance James McGettigan was within Almighty God's care and protection in the next life, if not this one. I was near sleep, when I heard his last remonstration, edged in granite and dipped in rancor.

"This is some twisted shit, James. Think about who's offered you assistance…who hasn't…and who may yet."

The door hissed to a close behind Reverend Father Timothy Timilty (SOJ), his footsteps echoing long after their sound dissipated.

*****

Sunshine warmed a man for whom immersion in the cold of the Cape Cod Canal remained an altered reality. Timothy Timilty's presence in Hospital World had an aura of dislocation—bad verse within otherwise didactic poetry.

John Updike's famous 1960 piece about Ted Williams's last game for the Boston Red Sox—a game for which a very young James McGettigan sat five rows behind the Red Sox dugout—explained what motivated a man who dreamed of glory with a knee full of sawdust. Updike wrote: *For me, Williams was the classic ballplayer…on a hot August weekday, before a small crowd, when the thing at stake was the tissue-thin difference between a thing done well and a thing done ill.* Updike had condensed McGettigan's unfulfilled ambition—how a man performed a task when no one watched or cheered. So it was for a mind replaying events over and over: An Asian Girl, handy with a knife; Brendan Timilty, District Attorney, whose testicles may, or may not, be under duress; A decision by the Grand Jury of No True Bill; Timothy Timilty, SOJ, at my bedside.

Somewhere there were dots to connect.

Napoleon had said about Jesuits: *The aim of this organization is power—power in its most despotic exercise—absolute power, universal power, power to control the world by the volition of a single man.*

Sleep would not come, for a thing done well made unreasonable demands.

CHAPTER 4

Recitation of the past year's harvest underway, I pushed myself to a standing position. One bout with cancer, chopped finely, equaled two scars. Stir in one knife attack and a jagged scar materialized while another, almost healed, became a recurrent reminder. Cracked-open breastbones, brought about by a GSW, allowed marrow to flavor a stew of assassination. Fillet a swimming man with a single thrust—you get surf and turf. McGettigan was breakfast, lunch and dinner.

During all this recent history, McGettigan often refused to carry his cell phone for the very reason he was employing the damn device—invading Amanda's personal privacy.

"Hello, this is Dr. Nocito. If you're in crisis, please get to a hospital. Call a friend. Call the EMTs. But get to a hospital."

Was McGettigan in crisis?

"Mandy…James. I'm at the Town Beach. It stinks to ask, but could you come and talk. Dinner's available, if you like."

A borrowed pickup held an hibachi and a cooler. An antique thermos held tea. McGettigan was careful to put no significant strain on wide staples holding the Organism together, while he lifted the Hibachi onto the truck's leeward side. Charcoal glowed enough light to observe two large, sizzling, chicken breasts. I continued to feel like the Organism could fall into two halves, neither attractive.

Did this mean I was closer to accepting the benefits of therapy?

Her loss had been bad enough. Close to three years later, teetering on an emotional balance beam, falling had been inevitable. I shot a man in the head, in self-defense, after he shot and killed four others.

Therapy helped me admit: Self-defense was a convenient disguise for something else. Acquiescent in the deaths of at least five others, where did lack of prevention fit the scheme of legal or moral responsibility? There were alternatives, although therapy agreed a rational man might be excused for not choosing those solutions under difficult, if not impossible, circumstances. Patrick had been forced to watch a sexual deviate end a lover's life; McGettigan arrived too late to save her. Inexcusable perhaps, his father's private reaction was abhorrent—thankful for the safety of his child but uncaring for parents who lost two daughters in one cataclysmic eruption of malevolence.

Therapy was insufficient. Confession was a much simpler process. Renounce sin. Pay a penance. In my experience, results were sketchy with either method. But I'd rejected the latter and tried the former for a paltry few months.

Stiffness set in. I swallowed three aspirin and added onions, tomatoes and sliced potatoes in a butter and olive oil laden skillet.

Headlights streaked through pine trees on the winding road which led nowhere but here.

Amanda Nocito, went to grammar and high school with my daughter Julia. A scholarship softball pitcher at Stanford, she'd been taught from the age of eight by all three of me. She told anyone who'd listen—McGettigan put her through college. Talent and brains played a big part, but 'thank-you' sounded wonderful when she said it. Her greeting encompassed a hug and few words.

"Why the dramatic location?" No judgment piggybacked on this question.

"Cottage is empty."

"Bullshit, James. Not the reason. Not close to the reason." Mandy sounded much like two other women in my life—so sure they knew what was, or wasn't, propelling me forward or backwards.

"Botched rescue of a girl in the Canal. Had some surgery. Screwed me up some." I pointed and waved at the car, even though the occupant's identity was occluded by the headlight's glare. "Got a date?"

She pushed me half over onto my back. "Don't be pissy. Two kids. Pitcher and a catcher. You know…like it's my turn to pass on what you gave to me." She crossed her arms and stared.

"They hungry?"

McGettigan threw more chicken on the fire. Like all young girls, they viewed me as a relic of Amanda's softball fables.

Between bites, Mandy interrogated me. "Where are the attorneys?" She meant my children.

"Patrick decided to take the job in Africa…with the Red Cross. He was going nowhere here. Wouldn't run for Congress, like he'd said at first. Half the time he wasn't getting out of bed. Each day got worse, if you ask me. Which he didn't."

Patrick and his father were as close as parent and child could hope to be. If Patty blamed me, he'd never made an accusation. Which explained why he had a therapist of his own. How long would it take to get past what happened? Therapy hadn't yet extended a ladder long enough to reach me in a damp, putrid hole I'd manufactured all on my own.

"Julia?"

A furtive grin creased my face—Mandy received the memo. My future President of these United States had always been Julie, but not after Donald Hartnett. Woe to those who failed to comply. As a brand new named partner in a Washington law firm, what male would argue?

"She went with Patrick. To get him settled, she said." I hadn't believed a concocted story. Neither would Mandy.

"Sandy still out of the country?"

"Yup." How short would the catalog, of those who cared about McGettigan, be?

"Billy?" Billy was my fisherman friend of a lifetime.

"In Seattle for Tom's wedding." Tom Nichols was a Massachusetts State Trooper.

I saw it creep into Amanda's electric blue eyes; there were no more names.

"I read the paper…must have felt good not to be indicted."

"Deirdre asked me out to dinner." This was unimportant to my quandary. Disclosure was a diversion.

"Was she worthy?" This scalpel burst any balloon inflated with male ego.

To the girls, she said, "Back in the car, you two. You've been fed. I'll be along in a few minutes and take you home." She turned serious. "How bad are your injuries?"

I pulled up the old Stanford sweatshirt, sent when Amanda first understood college softball would be well within her wheelhouse.

"Well, that's a real doozy. So…which hurt is worse?"

This last bit was the therapist's trademark, deflected questions with no beginning or end.

"Didn't seem like an accident…the girl jumping off a yacht. Screamed like a banshee the entire time. Wanted attention…which would make it harder to kill her. Wasn't an accident, when the yacht backed-down on me trying to get her out of the water."

A puff of wind blew smoke into Amanda's face. "All this you concluded while in the water, trying not to be chewed to pieces by the props…while a tiny Asian girl you never rescued sliced you into Sushi. Sound about right?"

"And while I was in recovery, Timothy Timilty joined me for some chitchat about his brother Brendan. Asked me to forgive his sins." Anyone in Massachusetts knew Timmy courtesy of the Herald, where his life's story was front-page fodder on a recurring basis.

"Was Timilty on the yacht? How else could he have known you were at Falmouth Hospital?"

The benefits of therapy came clearer. I'd fixated on brothers as they related to my pending indictment. Could Timmy have been interested in events involving the Asian girl? Could Brendan's twisted testicles be a ruse?

"Where's the Asian girl now? There must be dozens of cameras at the power plant. Or at Joe's? Or the Coast Guard Station? Find the yacht. You're under employed, James. Do something positive…figure out what happened"

We sat in silence, waiting for more to be said.

"James, tell me why I'm here. I'm gonna take the girls home, if some new investigation's your biggest trouble."

I added the last portion of fuel to the fire's embers. My therapist had told me more than once—it was my job to admit what dragged me into the depths, when a day was done and the ones left to hate each other were McGettigan, a Ghost and a Fool.

"Hundreds of times a day…I ask how can I justify what I did and didn't do? How can I stop Patrick hurting? I suffer in silence, because Patrick wants no instant replay of the worst moments of his life. I've got to accept what I see in his eyes…he's less than he was. And it's my fault." My rambling ended in an inaudible whisper. "What will I say to his mother? For certain she hates me."

"Other than making sure Patrick is loved, which Patrick understands he is, recovery isn't yours to offer. This gruesome place you seem hell bent on occupying is nothing to do with Patrick, Julia or anyone but yourself. Crank it up, James. Cope until you heal, like it or not."

She kissed the top of my head and strode to her car and two young ball-players.

Therapy was, when it worked, the application of truth and common sense.

Crank it up.

CHAPTER 5

Anywhere from Nova Scotia to Florida—*Marvelous Lady M* could have covered thirteen to sixteen hundred miles since her exit from the Canal.

Real time satellite imagery would be ideal, if it was available. A perfect solution would be assistance from Colonel Anton Petrovsky, an intelligence officer at the Pentagon. When I exposed Hartnett's plan to destabilize Iraqi oil sales, Petrovsky marked McGettigan as either a co-conspirator suffering remorse, or a reluctant hero. I'd been neither—and told him so. Whatever he thought of McGettigan as a murder suspect, allowing me to use military satellites was a no-go. This fresh tinge of outlaw, pasted on me by Brendan Timilty, wouldn't be easy to eradicate. Headlines—*McGettigan to be Indicted*—had been front-page banners; failure to indict was relegated to page nine.

Out of frustration or boredom, I listed marinas in Massachusetts, New Hampshire and Maine where *Marvelous Lady M* may have made port.

I put the cellphone on speaker.

Crank-it-up was my intention.

***

Massachusetts and New Hampshire marinas were a flop. To continue a failed effort would be an amalgam of bullheadedness and boredom. A Maine coastline, where McGettigan crewed lobster boats as a kid, was next. I hit the road.

Route 1 split into two branches after passing through Wells. At a spot called Cozy Corners, Maine Rt. 9 wound its way into Kennebunk Beach. After crossing the old-fashioned bridge spanning the river, Rt. 9 continued towards Cape Porpoise, Fortune's Rocks and Biddeford Pool. A right turn on Ocean Avenue completed, the rounded stern of *Marvelous Lady M* stood out through a blowing downpour.

M appeared abandoned. Chick's Marina was deserted as well—most slips empty and no cars parked out front. Further along Ocean Avenue, as homes and Inns got larger, Green Heron was my target for a one-night stay.

Of three large homes with optimal views of Chick's, one showed lights as a gloomy day turned charcoal. Armed with foul weather gear, clutching a thermos of hot tea, the house closest to Chick's, with its wraparound covered porch, was ripe for trespass. A shingled façade provided camouflage against passersby.

To say a watcher had long since tired of the task, was understatement at its finest. Peering into the storm was futile; every inch of the Organism ached. Even the cellphone mocked my failure; it hadn't rung nor delivered a text since leaving Cape Cod. Three days wasted, everything changed when a long, black, limousine slid to a stop. It took a count of five before McGettigan rose from a slouch. Parked with the hood aimed in my direction, the front and rear curbside doors were open before I noticed. Four large men hauled boxes towards the yacht. A telephoto lens revealed nothing more than slickers and rain hats. Long gone now, the limousine might have been a figment of my imagination.

Hidden behind spreading lilac bushes, the GTO was invisible.

No one in their right mind would consider the man crossing the street ill intentioned—too dumb to come out of the rain was a better description.

Marvelous Lady M displayed a custom mahogany boarding ladder for its guests. When McGettigan crossed to the starboard side, facing the river, a passing boat would observe a tall man peering into a gracious interior.

Too tempted would be my excuse, if discovered. "Sorry sir…real sorry…didn't hurt anything…just looking." I'd mutter those words in a hangdog apology. Seven words represented the full extent of my escape plan.

Under *M*'s beautiful blue awning, the door to the interior was locked. All the hatches were dogged down against rain, heavy seas and curious engineers.

No Asian girls cavorted in pink underwear.

On the street, a truck came to a stop.

McGettigan moved further down the float, surgical wound protesting, where an ancient dory bobbed up and down among its brethren. Dropped into the skiff's ribbed wooden bilge, I lay where a mixture of rain and saltwater would soon mix with the Organism's remaining blood. Pounding raindrops diluted noise from their comings and goings. Too nervous to twitch, rolling onto my side for a hurried peek revealed a lone man on the foredeck. No more than a silhouette, an AR-15 rifle hung by his side. Escape seemed impractical unless the guard turned away or departed. If he did either, I could yank the motor's starter-cord and put distance between the yacht and the skiff.

Would the sentry shoot a waterlogged, local fisherman?

McGettigan reminded himself: I know the owner of *Marvelous Lady M,* a woman in her mid-seventies who was, even in these perilous economic times, a billionaire dozens of times over. How could, and why would Meredith Lawrence consent to the use of her prized yacht for criminal activity?

"Nonsense," would be her retort, nose sniffing the superiority of a billionaire's rarified air. A second glance at the rifle brought one true thing into better focus—Meredith was irrelevant in this place at this instant.

A voice floated on the storm from the yacht's stern. The sentry on the bow shook rain from his eyes and turned away. In seconds the skiff glided towards shallow water and the shore. Scurried into the marina's shadow, the muted rumble of diesels overpowered the rain's drumbeat. When I dredged up courage enough to look, *M* was headed downriver to the cold Atlantic. Huddled like a drowning rat, the inventory of things learned during this prideful binge of foolishness required no effort. Nothing about the yacht, its crew or its purpose was elucidated by a man blinded to danger until moments ago.

CHAPTER 6

Three hours sleep seemed enough, when nervous energy drove me into a frenzy of honey-dos. My she placed the list on the fridge, weeks before leaving me with no honey to do for. Today the front porch would have rotten wood repaired, new shingles installed and mahogany floorboards sanded and stained. I stripped off my t-shirt to let sunshine rehabilitate the scabby string of staples.

Behind me a powder blue Bentley convertible rolled to a stop on bleached-white sea shells. Reggie Tucker's purpose was easy to discern—turning James McGettigan's day to shit.

"Looky, looky. Fancy Jimmy Crack Corn workin' with his hands. How the mighty have fallen."

Blonde ponytail, blunt shaped face with bleached eyebrows, scar across his left forehead, he always suggested it was obtained in a woman's bedroom. Tad over six feet, two-forty, muscles grew on top of others, crowding out brain function. Reggie began working for the Solbergs to cure a chronic shortage of cash and stayed even after Jan Solberg, the patriarch and my wife's father, died. Anna, my mother-in-law, thought Reggie slow and steady: Anna was sweet and gullible. And like Ingrid, and Kristian her brother, Anna was wealthy enough from the sale of Jan's electronics company to buy several small countries. So she indulged herself, allowing Reggie to shear the sheep.

Like a wounded water buffalo, Reggie decided to move me to speech by shaking the scaffolding. Not confrontational by historical measure, the altered McGettigan reacted in an unusual way, if you were accustomed to watching James bob and weave to avoid trouble with his relatives, or their servants. Reggie's arrogant face tilted upward to offer stinging commentary about McGettigan, who became fair game for Reggie's third-rate derision the day I buried *her*. As his mouth opened, McGettigan pushed the nail gun into his left eye socket.

Reginald Tucker froze, pose signaling capitulation. Tan faded to chalk, he calculated whether he could disengage before I pulled the trigger.

The Bentley's passenger door opened; for a microsecond my world was upside down. My wife walked a few steps in the direction of the scaffolding and said, with every ounce of entitlement and breeding she possessed, "Enough. You are such a boor, James."

Ingrid's grating voice broke the spell.

Copying her sister's style— light blue cotton shirt tucked into tan capris, long honey shaded hair put up in a twist—was meant to put me off-guard. My heart ached for looking.

Reggie crept away, uncertainty replacing bravado.

Ingrid, hands on hips, demanded, "Get in the car. I need to talk."

Talking to Ingrid was talking to a wall. She wanted what she wanted.

"Tea's in the pot. I'll be a minute or two." Ingrid didn't drink tea.

With the distraction of Ingrid's impersonation removed, one thing was certain: I wasn't finished. Reggie had retreated to the Bentley and held a real gun. He watched me approach, expecting obeisance and apology. The nail gun imitated an effective battering ram. Cascading glass distracted Reggie; he was too slow and wouldn't have shot me anyway. Reggie wouldn't frighten the pinky finger of soldiers-for-hire McGettigan had met, not in a pleasant way, courtesy of Donald Hartnett. Nail gun in his ear, simple language seemed best.

"Stay away, Reg. Beating a murder rap isn't so hard…if your IQ's over fifty. No one would even miss you."

Reginald Tucker's eyes receded into his pronounced forehead.

Theatrics aside, the moment passed with little more than disappointment.

***

Charlie Hamilton saved the lives of my entire family during L'affair Hartnett. Charlie lived by a set of rules acquired during two years as a sniper, alone in Vietnam's jungles. Neither a code nor anything so melodramatic, Charlie's Rules contributed to the changes in McGettigan. Charlie would be disappointed—blowhard threats did not appear anywhere in his rules.

At the kitchen sink, I washed out my tea mug. Talking was easier, if I didn't look at Ingrid.

"What is it you want?"

Sensing Ingrid close, McGettigan felt her hand move in a sensuous motion over my backside. Ingrid was on her third husband and, from what I knew, the first two would take her back in an instant. Ingrid was nothing like my dead wife. Cool, calculating and unfeeling was McGettigan's assessment of the younger sister by twelve years. Her hand continued its invitation.

"Stop."

"Afraid you can't?"

Her lips formed the little pout which had taken her far in this world. She wet them with her tongue.

"Or afraid you can?"

Her fingers picked at those staples as her eyes taunted me. Malicious amusement abandoned, she looked up, transformed by the casual nonchalance of the rich and entitled. Lit an unfiltered cigarette and picked tobacco off her tongue.

"I need you to help Rand. He's in some sort of trouble."

Rand Jellenek, Ingrid's current husband, owned Jellenek Construction Equipment. Delivered by fate to be the perfect accoutrement for Ingrid, I liked him well enough—with the exception of his insane choice of a wife, who screwed any man who caught her roving eye.

"Why don't you leave me alone? Rand is more than capable."

In an instant she seemed distracted, wrapped in a somber haze. Perhaps if I played my assigned part, I could sidestep this soap opera.

"What kind of trouble?"

She shook her hair—the thing some women could do and other women hated them for.

"How would I know what kind of trouble? He doesn't come home. Just lives on the damn job site."

"What job site?" This innocent question tilted me in the wrong direction.

"New Jersey. On the waterfront…some ugly-ass high rise where his cranes crashed. Don't you keep up?" Ingrid tossed her mane for further effect. "Either help him or I'll make you come to the wedding." Ingrid's face transformed as she recognized: James didn't know what wedding was under discussion.

Whoever's nuptials were the subject, Anna must be attending. Anna Solberg was a force of nature like her daughter, my wife, had been. Choosing the lesser of two evils, I succumbed.

"What's Rand's cell number. I'll call him."

Eyes flashed and her mouth hardened as the words squeezed out. "Go see him. Make him tell you."

I watched from the screen door until she reached the car. Face reddened under impeccable makeup, she glanced back at me, unforgiving of the injury to her latest toy. Passing like ships in the night, the Bentley almost collided with a Sheriff's patrol car.

Donny Slater, the Sheriff, was a Townie. In most instances Townie was a pejorative. Like McGettigan's a dick was a pejorative, when used by Donny. We'd known each other more years than made sense for intense resentment; it was the mountain of Solberg money which rubbed him raw. I could tell him my kids inherited their mother's wealth, not me. Telling would make nothing better between us; he described me as a little shit though six inches separated the Sheriff's hair from my chin.

Donny enjoyed arresting me for Hartnett's murder.

I walked to the driveway so as not to offer Donny a moment's hospitality.

Donny climbed out. So did Daniel Bazel, an Assistant US Attorney who, when we last spoke, worked in the Federal Office Building in Newark. Ordinary in every way, our conversations a decade ago had been short and unpleasant. Our lone meeting, in the dank corridors of the Newark PATH station, had been swiped from a 'B' movie about organized crime. McGettigan, in Bazel's wet dream, would have worn a wire broadcasting a particular meeting among certain politicians and me. My answer had been impolite.

"Morning, Donny." It was a forced greeting. "Something you want?"

Well past his physical prime, Bazel grabbed my left forearm and led me a few steps away. He spoke without looking me in the face, as if something over my shoulder caught his attention, but hadn't.

"Rand Jellenek is up to his neck in shit. You should ask Phil Spazutta to yank him out."

No surprise was Bazel's arrival; Ingrid always seemed one step ahead of trouble and Bazel still had a hard-on for Phillip Spazutta, Esq., one of the most powerful political attorneys in the State of New Jersey. Phil and I were friends of a sort, bound together by dead wives and a well honed personal definition of right and wrong: Different definitions to be sure, but honed nevertheless.

When Bazel and I met in an airless subway station, on a stupid hot summer day, McGettigan had already resigned from an assignment rather than be forced into a witch-hunt aimed at convicting Spazutta of corruption. Almost a year ago Phil paid-off what he'd considered a past-due debt, helping me stay alive in the bargain.

"Do you hear yourself, Bazel?"

Bazel poked his right forefinger into my chest, pointing his left in the direction of the disappearing Bentley.

"The little lady's gonna testify against her husband. You gotta keep the Solberg name out of the mud, so not to let your wife's mother suffer the media jackals for nine months of trial. So I'll trade you Jellenek for Spazutta. Wear a wire…get something, anything, puts Spazutta in jail. Voilá. Rand Jellenek pays a fine for the two crane accidents. Everyone goes home happy." Bazel smiled a jackal's grin. "Criminals like you know how to use micro-electronics, right?"

I took the proffered recording device without a word. His intimation a US Attorney played some role in my indictment for murder was the shrieking whore in the room.

CHAPTER 7

GTO parked in a Hyannis lot, commuter flight to Boston left behind, shuttle to LaGuardia on time, McGettigan took a taxi to EWR.

I drove a rental to Phil's office.

"Phil's not here."

"I called before leaving Boston. Phil said he had a free afternoon."

The law firm receptionist's look, hurled my way combined with rolled eyes, needed no interpretation.

Phil was an enigma. More than bright, he liked to drink and enjoyed regular visits to the Atlantic City gaming tables. Divorced, he remarried and been widowed, like McGettigan. But, unlike most obvious things in life, the fabric of Spazutta was woven in intricate patterns, undetectable under the fluorescent lights of business or politics. Contradiction was Phil's stock in trade, truth teetering in artistic balance.

***

Casa Ruggiero was a few blocks from Journal Square in Jersey City—a storm of serenity where politics and money dominated conversation, and enough mob types ate lunch and dinner no mugger would come within a half mile. Johnny Ruggiero maintained an aristocratic bearing. No more than six inches over five feet, he carried a menu as if it was a jeweled crown on a satin pillow. His warm smile was genuine. Johnny remembered, despite the gap in time since I last enjoyed his veal picatta.

"Good afternoon, Signor McGettigan. It's wonderful to have you with us again." We exchanged a polite hug. "Are you joining someone?"

"I'm looking for Phil, Johnny." Spazutta wasn't in the dining room, so my question related to the single private room into which I'd never been invited.

Johnny chose a non-answer. "Let me get you a glass…the veal is truly special today." Guiding me to an inauspicious table, whether the veal or Phil's potential arrival hastened my compliance was uncertain even to me.

Phil Spazutta made no appearance. McGettigan was checking his phone, when a vision in a little black dress pulled up a chair. Smiling radiantly, acting as if I was her long lost lover man, she whispered, "Kiss me, Dr. McGettigan and take Phil's note from my right hand."

Women fit numerous categories of beautiful: Sexual and striking for selfish purposes was Ingrid; staged to appear unobtainable was the black-haired beauty offering me a new clue in the hunt to locate Phil.

I leaned forward, trying not to botch a simple kiss on the cheek.

Mata Hari pulled me close, locked lips and pushed her tongue halfway down my throat. Right hand open, I took the folded length of paper. After several moments, my brain wondered whether the Director had yelled *Cut*. Fingers lingered under my chin. Emerald irises contracted to emit a laser beam which cut my skull in two. Then her right eye winked and she walked away, illustrating to the patrons what they'd missed and what McGettigan might receive more of.

Nothing was written on the note. Two tickets to a fundraiser stared at me—scheduled for three nights hence and carrying a price tag of a thousand bucks a pop. The address was a wharf along the waterfront near a new hotel and two high-rise buildings under construction.

"You know, sir, where the crane fell off the building," the waiter said with polite attentiveness.

On my way out, Johnny granted me a knowing look: The kind saying he'd never seen a particular woman before today; the kind which should have troubled me. But, because I was a trifle embarrassed, and a little affected by a dramatic kiss, it didn't trouble a Fool.

***

Rivers Nest Towers wasn't going to win awards. When completed, it would fit in with other offerings near restaurants, PATH and light rail, as well as the Powerhouse Arts District and public parks. Needless to say it offered the single thing which made all the difference: Manhattan's skyline across the Hudson River. Tower 1 was nearing occupancy. On Tower 2, twisted steel glared down from the twenty-sixth floor at a scarred and streaked façade from a tower-crane caroming in a death spiral like a pinball machine gone mad. The crane operator died, as did two steelworkers and seven residents of the building next door.

Rand greeted me with a handshake better suited to strangers. As the elevator cage door clanged shut, my phone's light blinked incessantly. Modification of my cellphone to detect nearby transmitters hadn't come cheap.

Nothing about working at these heights made Rand uncomfortable. Walking me closer to the crane, he said, "Must be a relief, huh? Not getting indicted?"

I gave him back his own. "Aren't you worried about being in the same boat? How'd the crane wind up in the street?"

Rand's features contorted for less than an instant; endless practice made deceit conversational and guiltless. Wisps of blonde hair escaped his hard hat as he broke eye contact.

"Oversize loads…mishaps during assembly and rigging…reasons why cranes fall."

Rand's left eyebrow jangled in an insane modern dance.

"Jesus, Rand, I'm not a juror or a reporter. Tell me what happened. I've never been this close to a tower crane."

Deception, in my case, was a convenience. I'd never been *this* close to *this* crane. Not a true crane expert, McGettigan could operate one.

Rand's collapse occurred as riggers prepared to jump the crane, adding sections to make it taller. Jumps were the responsibility of Riggers from a local specialist, not Rand's employees. If Riggers were at fault, Rand should escape liability. He wasn't acting like a man escaping anything.

"Crilly Tatise is my Master Rigger."

Rand examined me to see whether the name meant anything.

"Reckless...what they were. Negligent rigging practices caused the collapse." He waited three or four beats before a clumsy addition. "At least there's an explanation for my problem. Not for you, though. How'd *you* rig it?"

Rand blundered-on, using Lincope's verbiage.

"You must have killed Hartnett...two of you alone, one comes out in a body bag?"

McGettigan showed signs of impatience, two men wearing wires for reasons of their own. At whose beckoning was Rand wearing his?

"So who's going to jail, Rand? Tatise?"

Beads of sweat popped from my Brother-in-Law's forehead; jail could make anyone question their decisions. Rand hesitated. Wanted to talk, so said his eyes, but couldn't, not when he was here to entrap James McGettigan. I gave Rand my best piercing look—reached out to pat where the tiny microphone was taped to his abdomen. Held up my cellphone as the reason.

"As long as I'm pressing this button, all transmissions in a twenty-five foot circle are scrambled. Who's pressuring you to chat me up about Hartnett's death?"

Hard-nosed in Rand's world would be jelly-soft in jail. Words spilled out from a fountain of unhinged anxiety.

"Feds and the County...they're a tag team. They say the crane fell because of improper supervision. Told me to take a deal...no prison, four years probation. They'll ask for ten to fifteen, if there's a trial. I can't go to prison, James. Bastard made it clear he wanted you, James." Incredulity caused Rand to shake his head in submission and disbelief. "Get McGettigan to admit the murder...you disappear from the front page...Tatise does the time. He gave me the wire I'm wearing."

Rand left out what mattered most. "It wasn't the DA, was it? Who?"

"Never said. They're waiting for me to deliver some admission from you. I'm sorry, James."

"What did he look like?"

"Slicked-back hair. Five nine or so...cheap clothes. Looked like a government lawyer should look."

"Has the DA approached Ingrid?"

Rand's reaction was immediate. "What for? Ingrid has nothing to do with my business. What could they gain?"

McGettigan valued family above all else, even if sometimes I didn't like it. So I told Rand about my little visit with Sheriff Donny Slater and US Attorney Bazel. I left out the part about Ingrid's willingness to testify against her husband and everything about Phil Spazutta. I released the button on the cell phone. We were back on the record, so I spoke for the benefit of whoever was listening.

"Sounds like the DA's way out on a limb, Rand. You hired Tatise Rigging. It was their responsibility, not yours. The DA has no basis to indict you. If he tries, tell the Grand Jury how it all works. Grand Jurors aren't robots. My jury refused to indict me, because they didn't believe I murdered anyone. And I didn't."

My soliloquy came out preachy.

Neither of us was quite convinced about the other's intentions. Suspicion and reluctance were colored by Ingrid's proven willingness to sell anything, family included, to arrange life to suit her selfish whims. In Rand's eyes there was skepticism. He wondered if James McGettigan had, indeed, shot Donald Hartnett. After all, everyone knew there were just two people in the room.

Was Timilty the Younger in cahoots with US Attorney Bazel? What tied the Jersey City DA to Bazel, Timilty or McGettigan?

Among details begging for attention was a list of companies on the massive sign advertising Rivers Nest Towers. In the largest type was a troika forming the development consortium. I began to write them down.

Begun high in the sky, the noise started as a vague intrusion. It ended as a long-winded scream before a whirling body impacted the sign, spraying bloody fluids like a lawn sprinkler in seizure. Head rotated fast enough to generate whiplash, I looked up to see where the body came from. Whom the dead man might have been was of little interest. Who threw him off the building was the critical question.

I tapped 911 on the cell.

Where was Rand Jellenek?

***

Jersey City's finest were finished with McGettigan hours after Michael Madson fell to his death. But for the 911 call and my pants, shirt and shoes spattered with blood and tissue, the ranking detective would have arrested me on general principle. In asking to return to the top of the building, I'd explained my professional interest in accidents involving heavy construction, and my family relationship to the owner of the crane. The detective suggested I return home. Those may not have been his exact words, but I'd translated his intent without causing a hernia.

Rand Jellenek's Mercedes sat forlorn in a parking lot. Deirdre's cell answered on the second ring.

"Hi there, are you calling to ask me out?" Light mockery trailed her words.

"I'm covered with bits and pieces of a nice man who fell from the top of a building in Jersey City." I waited a few seconds then added, "Graciously, the cops aren't arresting me."

"James, I'm sorry…"

Two tickets to the fundraiser rested in my pocket; I'd have to pay Phil Spazutta's ransom either way, so James interrupted Deirdre with a social lie.

"Put the jumper out of your mind, you're right…come to a cultural event here in a tiny metropolis across the Hudson River from New York."

"There's no culture in New Jersey." Deirdre said this with confidence born of her country club upbringing in the suburbs of Trenton.

"Friday night. Dinner at a wonderful place…with a diverse group of criminals and politicians."

"You want to take me to a fundraiser? Tell me you aren't serious."

"It's dressy…you get to wear something slinky." McGettigan was so out of practice, he couldn't be facetious without sounding like stone-age man.

"Where are we staying afterwards?"

I'd not thought past the invitation. But Deirdre was right; it would be way too late to get back to Boston. "How about the Peninsula…or the Pierre?"

My cell vibrated. "Deirdre…got another call. Grab a 4 pm flight to Newark, we'll work it out. Gotta go."

CHAPTER 8

"James, it's Martin. You need to be here tonight. Someone's been to see your friend, Robert."

Robert Linney had been the catalyst in McGettigan's war with Donald Hartnett. Early-Onset Alzheimer's assured the real Robert no longer existed, but he loved Cuba and was housed there courtesy of the Cardillo's influence—his care and feeding funded by McGettigan via Hartnett's money. Robert had steadily deteriorated since arriving on the Island.

Martin Cardillo was the freshly minted crown prince of Cardillo Crystals Corporation, a Florida sugar empire founded and operated by his great-grandfather, grandfather and his father, Harry. Until the transition, Harry had been dictator over vast fields of cane and a vast sphere of influence in the US and the *Island*, as either Cardillo would refer to Cuba. Martin held an MBA from Wharton and was the best catcher I ever taught. Alas, Martin couldn't hit the breaking ball and chose to become Captain of *Sugar Daddy*, his seventy-three foot sportfishing yacht. If Martin's sensibilities, and affection for his father, could have been discarded, anything would have been better than entering the family business.

Who breached Robert Linney's wall of privacy?

How could McGettigan fix what awaited in Florida or Cuba—and keep my date with Deirdre and Phil Spazutta less than three days from now?

***

Nearing midnight at Palm Beach International, Manuel didn't appear angelic although he was Martin's guardian angel. Wariness fronting bravado, fashion and grooming were a perfect mask. Macho in the truest sense, Manuel's presence assured Martin's highest concern for McGettigan.

Before reaching Australian Avenue, rotating lights and a quick siren burst caused us to stop. One Sheriff's cruiser pulled up behind, another in front. McGettigan's breathing got heavier fast. Manuel followed the lead Sheriff, made a left on Australian and settled in at the speed limit. When we turned onto Palm Beach Lakes, the Foolish stopped shaking and allowed understanding to dawn. In the mall's parking lot stood a sleek, sand colored jet helicopter, blades idling, door open.

Manuel and I occupied two reclining armchairs. The lone pilot, when she turned around, stunned me with her greeting.

"Welcome to Cardillo Air, Uncle James."

The voice's warmth was obvious underneath a flight suit and headgear. Dayami Machado was Luis Machado's little girl. I'd known Luis—de facto Captain of *Sugar Daddy*—and his family going on twenty-five years.

"Dayami...wonderful to see you...when did you leave the Navy?" Dayami flew F-16s from carriers during the latest Iraq war. Robert Linney flew F-4s from far different carriers during Vietnam. I crouched at her side for a quick hug.

Déjà vu all over again.

"Almost three months." She offered an apologetic expression. "Gotta get off this parking lot, okay?"

***

On the flying bridge Luis smiled as we remembered Dayami growing up—stories about their children were older men's favorite conversational fodder. Melancholy snuck up on me, invited by an overtired and overwrought Organism.

Whoever visited Robert Linney, they were connected to Donald Hartnett. Hartnett's Paladins killed without discrimination from the shadows.

Manuel and his two companions wouldn't over think any situation; they lived in close concert with Charlie Hamilton's rules. Would I remember, and act upon, those rules, if the need arose?

Manuel's smile was confident. He spoke Spanish. "What would you do without me, Señor James?"

The question wasn't complimentary.

Answering in his language was second nature. "How come you didn't bring them back?"

"We could have brought the woman…leaving no one to care for the man. Such a thing wasn't Señor Martin's wish."

Martin's wishes were commands to a large and invisible army.

"Where is Robert, Manuel?"

"He's safe. As is the one who cares for him."

"How long?"

"Before noon, Señor, if you walk fast enough. We won't have a vehicle and men like us…" He spread his hands to indicate our grubby clothes "…shouldn't possess a car."

***

Sugar Daddy glided towards an orange and black Cigarette boat which would transfer us to shore and return us to Sugar Daddy, when our business was concluded.

The first words McGettigan heard were a warning; the Cigarette boat would wait but a short time before abandoning us. Ten this evening would see our carriage turn into a pumpkin.

A rickety, hand built dock near Matanzas was miles from anywhere, even in Cuba. No ceremony accompanied us as we disembarked. Up a steep hill, feet already sore and sweat stinging my eyes, Manuel explained.

"They have Martin's cell phone number. How long they wait, if we're not on time, depends on how much Martin transfers to a bank of their convenience." Manuel walked faster and laughed out loud, seeming to be unafraid of police or army patrols.

McGettigan focused on the puzzle at hand. Who disturbed the peace of a man no longer in control of his faculties? For what purpose?

Attention reduced by a brand new blister, Manuel's hand gripped my arm in a viselike restraint. McGettigan followed his gaze along a gradual incline to the third house in what would never even be called a village. A uniformed guard was stationed by the red front door of a whitewashed bungalow adorned with flowering window boxes.

Two of Manuel's cadre disappeared into scrub vegetation.

Manuel instructed me. "Speak Spanish. Tell him you're willing to pay for the woman. Give him these as good faith. Kill him as a last resort." Manuel's expressive distaste lampooned the idea of McGettigan as a murderous desperado.

In my hand were three gold coins minted at the order of some long-dead Cuban dictator. McGettigan laughed without a sound escaping. It would be best, if Manuel gained no knowledge of my recent experience with killing.

Long strides gave the impression of lethargy, when in reality McGettigan covered half the distance before the guard took notice. I added a limp which was too real, halting to pick white flowers growing wild in the shade of an ancient tree. Manuel's two accomplices would, by now, have taken positions behind the small house.

McGettigan, in the here and now, was close enough to translate the guard's expression through a dense, spiky beard hiding an age ten years either side of fifty. A dirty, sweaty, Fool could be taken for ten years past sixty. I watched him relax; an old cripple was of no regard.

Our separation decreased to a familiar distance: one hundred twenty-seven feet from home plate to second base. I followed Manuel's direction, speaking loud enough not to be mistaken.

"I'm here to take the woman."

A guttural scream originated inside the house and was choked-off in an instant.

The guard's AK-47 began its swing from behind his back to a firing position. I pushed hard with my left leg, striding with my right in a motion repeated thousands of times in a previous life. From behind my left ear came a catcher's arm throwing a laser to second base. The rock spun hard, traveling in the vicinity of fifty miles an hour. Replanting my left leg, I watched the projectile cover the gap quicker than his rifle could be raised. Unable to move, a long moment passed before his knees buckled. When he crumpled, his left leg twitched in a violent seizure.

Manuel and his pistol stood over the guard. He damned my effort with faint praise. "It seems Martin is accurate when he raves about your baseball skills, Señor." He tipped an imaginary cap and dragged the guard into the house.

Upon examination, two dead guards and one injured belonged to Rodriquez, the buccaneer whose Cigarette boat put us ashore.

Manuel, switching to English, struggled to find a rational explanation for a complete fuckup. "Rodriquez has been dependable, if not honest. His loyalty to another would've been purchased yesterday or even today; Cardillo money had always trumped the competition before this fuck-up."

McGettigan assumed Rodriquez to be a Cardillo loyalist, prepared to kiss the ring of Harry the Patriarch. I considered what else might exist in my imagination, including Manuel's English, which improved with feelings of guilt.

My trip should have been simple: Arrive; converse with Marianna, Robert's caretaker; depart.

Not now.

Marianna stated the obvious.

"Señor Linney and I...we are no longer safe. There is sympathy for the sick American, but people are poor and won't help after you leave. The extra food I buy them is welcome, but Rodriquez is a bandit. You've killed his nephew. Vengeance will be swift."

Living out Robert's life in his beloved Cuba offered a chance to be away from the legal battle over his money and property, to live with dignity and die in safekeeping at the end of his terrible disease. No longer feasible, I addressed Manuel, who was responsible for getting us out of trouble.

"How do we get home?"

"Dayami cannot come."

As Manuel's easy charm evaporated, I waited and listened.

"A commercial flight from Havana or Varadera is no good."

Manuel turned to the window, eyes vacant for an instant.

"Jaime, bury the dead at the top of the hill. Take the other one with us...maybe we can trade him later."

Faculties regained, the guard I beaned rumbled a brave threat about Rodriquez dicing us into bait.

Manuel kicked him in the head.

"We'll give Luis a different rendezvous point. Somewhere he can bring *Sugar Daddy* in-shore. Luis will know. Luis was Rodriquez before Rodriquez could swim." Manuel concluded, "We'll go over the hills off the roads. Can Linney walk?"

This question was addressed to Marianna, who answered in a soft, sympathetic voice. "No, he cannot walk. He can do almost nothing for himself."

Manuel snorted, "Then we leave him."

McGettigan lost his temper, but not so anyone could tell. "I'd rather leave you, Manuel…and I like you. Give me the Sat Phone."

Hung around his neck, the phone with its stubby antenna connected after a small delay. "Luis, we need alternate GPS co-ordinates…and a car."

All the phone transmitted was static and hiss. Luis's voice returned, tight with worry.

"The resorts at Cabo Hicacos…Royal Hicacos has ski boats moored near the beach. Can you start the engine?"

Luis knew McGettigan had lived a lifetime around boats. He meant—*does McGettigan have the stones to steal a speedboat?*

"Yes, Luis." I debated what else to say. "Ask Martin to do what he can."

Luis seemed satisfied. "I can't come closer than the twelve mile limit, but will cruise there from midnight to dawn. A truck will come for you, driven by a very young girl. Pay her well…the truck means everything to her family."

***

Underneath a torn vinyl tarp, midday heat was relentless. Marianna stared straight ahead—angry this group of men wouldn't allow her a voice or a choice in her future.

"Marianna, I'm sorry all this turned into a mess. I'm very grateful for everything you've done. I sent Robert's mother the photograph of you two on *Sugar Daddy*, when you came to Cuba. Mrs. Linney wanted to…"

Out of the blue, James was struck dumb by what I thought couldn't be true. Had Gwyneth Linney used the photo, my sincere, sympathetic, gesture, to let Hartnett's goons find Robert and Marianna?

"Who came to see you, Marianna? What did they want? What did they look like?"

These were questions Martin Cardillo helped me enter Cuba to resolve. "Was it Rodriquez who came?"

In cerulean light she seemed to materialize from a renaissance painter's canvas: Each facial line endowed with character; eyes sparkled with intelligence above striking cheekbones. I noticed brushed hair and light pastel lipstick applied in the way women insist upon when going out, even to pilfer a boat. She could be thirty-five, or ten years older. Not demeaned by her care of Robert Linney, Marianna Salgado was not broken.

Whispers conveyed more than simple answers. "Rodriquez never came. Rodriquez is a man with big plans."

Eyes stared through me: Did this American understand?

"Two men. The older one spoke poorly, but was the leader. The younger, who talked too much, was tall but not as tall as you. Nothing about the tall man was memorable...thin mustache, dark hair and soft hands...mean eyes set too near his nose. The older one wore a bushy, straight mustache...losing hair on top. He wore two rings...one large, one a wedding ring. Heavier and shorter than the younger one...puffy cheeks and crooked front teeth. They had papers for Mr. Robert to sign. How can Mr. Robert sign papers without reading? I asked them to leave. The younger man pushed me into a chair. For a long time they asked and asked...not once did Mr. Robert speak or give a sign he knew them. Finally, they held his hand and made Mr. Robert sign."

Nothing struck a chord. The description given of Robert's visitors prompted no recognition. "The older one, the one who spoke poorly...which language did he speak?"

"He spoke English and Spanish, often stumbling over the words."

Nothing but a vast fortune would've brought vermin to feed on the dying.

***

Our plan was simplicity itself. Under the cover of a diversion, McGettigan would swim to one of the hotel's ski boats, start the engine and pick up five passengers from the beach. The ski-boat would then traverse twelve miles of open ocean to meet *Sugar Daddy*. McGettigan wasn't the plan's author, which proved immaterial when I failed to voice a stronger substitute.

Marta, the girl who delivered the truck, at no more than thirteen was an unexpected source of operational subterfuge. A wall of glass, surrounded by reflecting pools, formed Royal Hicacos' main entrance. Marta would, she promised with somber demeanor, crash the truck through the partition creating a giant commotion. Her auxiliary suggestion—destroy the night vision of pursuers by setting a line of thatched beach huts on fire—would provide cover as we departed. Thirteen going on forty, she was too good to be true for a group who needed what she offered. Paid for the truck and her assistance, the girl stashed gold coins and cash with a value around five thousand US Dollars

McGettigan and a Fool were skeptical, frightened, hungry, tired and in need of returning to Jersey City. Our plan's inventory of moving parts would douse the enthusiasm of a one-man band.

Varadero, a strip of land jutting into the ocean and lined with resorts, came to life after dark. A few lovebirds occupied neighboring huts; they paid Marianna and I no heed. Each with an arm around Robert, we reached our target hut without incident. The Organism's blood pressure rose, piqued by the sweeping hand of Marianna's watch. Marta was twenty minutes late.

McGettigan's fingers palpated the line of sutures holding front and back together. An intrusive Ghost judged it a long swim to where three ski boats were moored. On every stroke the Organism grabbed a breath, unsure how much time was passing. Freestyle gave way to a half-assed breaststroke designed to preserve a diminished puddle of physical capability. The ski boat floated a million miles away.

To exit the water I employed the weak, slithering action of an exhausted turtle. I looked back to shore to see what took place in the six hours expended to swim a quarter mile. Beach pitch black, the band played at ear-splitting decibels inside the resort. Marianna and Robert were invisible.

Alone on the ocean overtired fingers, connected to quivering arms, fumbled with ignition wires. Powered by a venerable inboard, the motor burst to life, then burbled a happy tune. At a crab's pace, unsure when a single propeller would hit bottom, McGettigan navigated inshore twice.

Two miles outside the reef, I heard a freight train. To triangulate the sound of racing engines became a matter of survival. If I chose the wrong moment to turn, Rodriquez would slice us to pieces—the ski boat couldn't accelerate into the waves, but could manage a turn parallel to them.

Rodriquez aimed a powerful spotlight, big waves at his stern like a rollercoaster going downhill. We six were blinded, but could hear him closing-in. Even Robert pricked his ears.

Someone fired an automatic weapon from the glare.

In Spanish McGettigan yelled, "Hang on. Right turn, then another."

One of my passengers could fall overboard in this maneuver. I jerked the wheel over hard—showing my tail to Rodriquez—making our boat a thinner target. I wouldn't look back; watching the waves was more important. Counting to five, I pushed the throttle to the wall and made a hard starboard turn. We passed no more than fifty feet apart at a closing speed approaching one hundred knots—Rodriquez at seventy, McGettigan climbing towards thirty.

Rodriquez entered a tight turn, headed back for another pass.

Zigzagging parallel to the waves, I hoped to avoid destruction.

Rodriquez would kill us by attrition; AK-47s firing in our direction would end this dance. On his third approach, Rodriquez flew past. Jaime screamed as bullets ripped through him, dropping overboard with less than a whimper.

Manuel returned feeble fire with his handgun.

Rodriquez would be undeterred.

High-speed maneuvers brought both boats another mile seaward; a pyrrhic victory left nine miles to the twelve-mile limit and International Waters. Turning north again, watching through sheets of spray, Rodriquez prepared another attempt to skewer us. He slowed, making his boat more nimble in rough water.

With no time to turn away, I pulled the throttle back. The ski boat settled in the water, tossed every which way on the next wave.

Rodriquez was in front and to our left, where his spotlight outlined a second target for less than a second. To his everlasting sorrow, Rodriquez came face-to-face with the USCG cutter *Thetis* from Key West. Headed at Rodriquez, the Cutter left him a single escape route. A pirate altered course for the Bay of Cardenas, gunfire pouring without effect in our direction. Threatened no longer, the ski boat settled on a northwest compass course in the wake of the hulking Cutter. Without a radio, we followed until *Sugar Daddy's* lights blazed their welcome.

Mug of tea cupped in two hands, sitting on the flying bridge in safety, one thing and one thing only mattered: Robert Linney signed documents for two visitors.

What would be the repercussions?

CHAPTER 9

With the exception of a single eyelid, the Organism remained asleep as sun reflected through a porthole.

"James, have you lost something off the fastball?"

Martin appreciated the cans of worms I'd opened: Rodriquez dared open rebellion against Cardillo supremacy; Manuel's use of poor judgment; and Martin ripping-up a get out of jail card with the Coast Guard to intervene in our escape. Martin Cardillo was too aware: An empire should never depend on luck.

Where was Robert? Marianna?

Martin anticipated the question.

"Mr. Linney, the pretty lady and Manuel are at my father's home, in one of the guest apartments. Manuel seems quite taken with Ms. Salgado."

Martin sat in the sunshine, face set in consternation.

"James, you know Meredith Lawrence well."

Martin had stated a fact, not asked a question.

"Meredith believes Astor should marry Jill Stoddard. She's determined to make it happen. Julian Rommery thinks they're a poor match."

Astor was Meredith's grandson, young-thirties and spoiled rotten. Jill Stoddard was the daughter of Wilson Stoddard, a big-time real estate developer suffering from recent and substantial setbacks. Wilson was a political creature. Jill was the epitome of a Lawrence wife. Julian Rommery exhibited the most common traits of a County

Commissioner: Self-absorption and arrogance. He wasn't altogether stupid or he'd be batting three for three.

Martin sighed, expelling breath in too dramatic a fashion.

"Julian wants *his* kid, Ryan, to marry Jill. For Meredith's money."

I raised my left eyebrow—maybe Julian *was* stupid. Everyone knew Stoddard's business was in the dumper. Ryan would have to earn his cash, not inherit it from Jill's father whom, last time I saw Wilson, was the picture of health.

Martin wasn't finished.

"We have mutual interests with the Lawrence family. The County sent emissaries to negotiate a buyout of Eco-Waste's big landfill. Eco-Waste covets Cardillo acreage. Astor, Ryan and Jill…a messy triangle could throw a wrench into the transaction. Speak to Meredith and Julian, please. Convince one or the other to cease and desist from a marital alliance with Jill Stoddard. Keep the peace, James."

Martin emulated Harry's understated speech, forcing a listener to extrapolate nuanced context. Did the County, and more to the point Julian Rommery, know Eco-Waste planned a new landfill on cane fields purchased from Martin? Who, among those with amoral tendencies, was aligned with whom?

McGettigan wouldn't smile. I said, "What's the second favor?"

Martin turned sheepish. This side of him was unlike Harry, who'd never been timorous about a business proposition.

"I've met a woman, James. She isn't Cuban. I'd like you to meet her."

Not being Cuban made this ill-defined woman an alien in Martin's world. It was a short leap to Martin's true request: He wanted to know if there were other impediments to a relationship, and couldn't use Cardillo resources to vet her.

"I'm not any good at romance, Martin."

"Please, James."

"She's special?"

"Her name is Ellen Harding, the daughter of Patrick's former boss, and an Assistant US Attorney in New York. I may be falling in love."

Dynamite exploded in the Organism's head.

Senator Warren Harding and McGettigan were oil and water. Our bad history came in two installments: He fired my son, and worse, I caught Harding ignoring, if not supporting, Donald Hartnett's international criminal proclivities. McGettigan's need for therapy derived from failing Patrick, and Martin was near enough to a second son. Then there was the ruinous third obstacle—the US Attorney's office, maybe even Martin's prospective lover, was involved in an attempted prosecution of Rand Jellinek and Phil Spazutta.

Three strikes—McGettigan was out.

And, if being struck-out wasn't enough, Meredith Lawrence was the owner of *Marvelous Lady M*. Putting the proverbial cherry on top, Martin was damned well aware Eco-Waste had been my client on one very short-lived, ugly, assignment.

So, no matter the obstacles for McGettigan, it was impossible to turn Martin down. McGettigan smiled a parental smile. "Anything for you, Martin."

***

Marsh Landing, Florida, where in the recent past I'd been Mayor, existed purely to allow its wealthy residents a tax advantage. Populated by two hundred and fifty families, a mere seven of us worked for a living. We were only just tolerated by the wealthy super-majority. My wife inherited the house from her father, Jan Solberg, when he died. I inherited it from her in the same way.

I'd run for office unopposed.

My constituents were accustomed to owning politicians, as they might own a valuable dog. They viewed McGettigan, prior to my resignation, as a public servant: Full emphasis on servant. During the Hartnett scandal, Meredith Lawrence, despite knowing my family for thirty years, phoned but once, disturbed about the diminution in Village services. Nothing in tone or content suggested she knew of, or cared about, murder charges lodged against me.

A fastidious maid of indeterminate age greeted me at Meredith's front door.

Because it was after lunchtime, but prior to thoughts of tonight's dinner engagement, Meredith was dressed in her definition of casual: an ice blue, button-up designer dress with a single strand of pearls. High heels remained her signature embellishment. Silver hair cut pixie short, face set in disapproval, civility demanded scant attention to James McGettigan, whose murderous presence would mix ingredients for high-toned gossip.

"You look lovely, Meredith. When do you head to the Hamptons?" Total drivel, she wouldn't talk should I fail to observe the niceties.

Narrowed eyelids expressing denunciation, she ruined the good intentions of the world's finest plastic surgeons. As if McGettigan could comprehend anything of her life, social schedule, or the Hamptons, where Meredith wouldn't dream of owning a residence. McGettigan, after all, was from some backwater on Cape Cod, itself no better than a cultural wasteland.

"You've led the Village to ruin, James. You had no business resigning. I want you to fix things…return to your responsibilities." She savored a Rosé from a William Yeoward wine glass.

"I hear there's a wedding in the offing…Astor and Jill Stoddard. Will the festivities be here at the club?"

She scowled. "Are you going to rebuild the shithole you called a home?"

Wealthy old women could use language frowned upon in polite society. Where the line of demarcation was drawn—having enough money to cuss with impunity—escaped me, but Meredith Lawrence lived on the curse-like-a-sailor side.

I attempted to placate her. "The children haven't decided."

"Julia and Patrick inherited their mother's money…I know the house is yours. Empty lot is an eyesore. Do the right thing. Build something lovely…if you can afford to…or sell to someone who will."

Meredith meant I should rebuild, if I wasn't in jail.

Focused on Martin's quest, I pushed a little. "Aren't you thrilled about Astor and Jill? I thought it was your dream match."

"Are you enjoying my humiliation, James? Shouldn't someone so soon adjudicated a common criminal empathize?" Mixing spite and sadness, did these words signal a truce?

We were fencing. Perhaps this time I'd catch her off-guard. "Will you be cruising on *M* this summer? I saw her in the Cape Cod Canal a few days ago."

Meredith's makeup was professional and perfect. One maverick tear scoured a track in its artistry. Furious, she spit at me. "You are mistaken. Astor and his friends are in the Med, the Greek Islands I believe."

She was lying. She knew I knew.

"Is Jill with him…an engagement trip?"

"Jill had a conflict…a land deal requiring attention. I'm meeting her at the club for dinner." Stuck in her throat, the lies wouldn't stop. "Jill's delightful, you know. All this talk about Ryan Rommery is just idle nonsense."

Meredith couldn't help herself; appearances were everything.

So now I knew: Astor was off the reservation; Jill was a free-agent; and who could tell where Ryan fit?

"So you think I should run for Mayor again?"

A movement of her hand dismissed me. "No one remembers you resigned." Meredith recovered the aplomb which marked decades of getting her way. "The office is empty. You're still Mayor…and still annoying. Do something with your damnable empty lot."

***

Hours passed in the Mayor's office.

The new Office Manager, Gayle something or other, was a stranger. Whatever happened to Marcia, whom I'd hired for the job several years earlier, and to whom I'd spoken less than a week ago?

Numerous calls, and the demagogic insistence of Julian Rommery, led to my attendance at the afternoon County Commission meeting. The Courthouse was an eleven-story edifice constructed with architectural presumption. I sat way in the rear of an auditorium holding several hundred, when blowsy, cheap-at-the-price Commissioner Suzy Wayland leaned over her microphone and screamed.

"McGettigan…we paying your ass? What the hell you here for?"

Suzy's vote, when McGettigan was first elected Mayor, could have been bought for two new tires on her pickup; I wasn't up to date on the current market price.

"First, because I was invited by Commissioner Rommery. Second, there's this odd concept called Government in the Sunshine, you might want to look up the definition."

I retreated to the hallway.

Five minutes elapsed before Julian Rommery could free himself. "What can you do about those landfill pricks threatening Jill?"

"Tell me about it, then I'll make suggestions if you'd like."

Astonishment covered his face. He was practicing for when he ascended to Governor of Florida, four steps above any office Julian was qualified to hold.

"They sent some thug...said Jill wouldn't look so good all scarred-up. Same guy pushed her around in a parking lot."

It was Julian who was frightened. Had he squeezed EcoWaste? Solicited a bribe, or worse? Julian was a churlish lout.

"Nothing for me to do, Julian. Jill should hire a lawyer."

"You'll need *my* help one day...you and your uppity Village."

Now he'd gone and exacerbated my mayoral anxieties. McGettigan's neighbors cared nothing about the rants of some County Commissioner, and even less about the views of their servant-Mayor.

"Jill is Wilson's kid, Julian, not yours."

Julian believed McGettigan was the same as a private cop. To keep the peace for Martin, I surrendered.

"Where's Jill? I'll need to hear about it from her."

Julian grunted. "At the Racquet Club with Ryan."

CHAPTER 10

The Racquet Club was the social epicenter for a broad range of shakers, movers and wannabees. Most of Marsh Landing belonged. Not McGettigan.

Jill and Ryan remained invisible until the Organism's still-functional peripheral vision caught their departure via a side courtyard. Disappeared around a high hedge, the parking lot would be their destination.

They headed west; if they crossed the Turnpike, the landfill was my bet. As their SUV crossed the bridge over the Turnpike, I made a hurried turn onto a service road, losing sight of their Land Rover, but gaining a perfect panorama of their destination.

Unexpected desperation made the landfill air more rancid. Ryan Rommery and Jill Stoddard were trespassers. They must've climbed the security fence, where James's field glasses proved Jill tore a ragged gash in her leg. Their ascent to the top of the landfill, terraced like a European vineyard, would have been strenuous and stressful.

Had they come to confront the parking lot thug?

An expensive camera bounced around Ryan's neck as he ran. Did they envision an exposé—photographic evidence of environmental damage made public?

McGettigan thought not.

Jill would have goaded Ryan's ego; a good game to play before a shower and drinks with friends back at the Club. Perhaps privileged backgrounds shielded them from plain reality: the landfill was a place of dirty and dangerous work performed by men with a reputation for ill-tempered brutality.

Frankie McShane was a textbook case—an angry, pitiful, drunk. Frankie was an extension of the landfill foreman's hand, in whose office CCTV would show Ryan clicking pictures with his fancy digital rig.

McGettigan synched his phone with the landfill's internal network.

"Run those idiots out of here, Frankie."

Raoul Dupree, the aforementioned foreman, must have chuckled—spitting a dark stream of chew out the window of his trailer.

I switched to the dozer's camera feed.

The sheepsfoot dozer roared, snorting diesel exhaust. Frankie heard Raoul's broadcast as a 007 agent's license-to-kill. Protruding steel feet compacted trash like studded snow tires on steroids. Ripped apart was what Frankie would have in mind for Ryan and Jill. Cheap vodka, fortified with grain alcohol, was Frankie's favored brew; it made a minor river down McShane's chin as vibration rocked the massive machine. Isolated from reality by soundproofed air conditioning, Ryan and Jill—little more than dark specks on CCTV—were pursued downhill by a bright orange predator.

I watched without emotion.

With each stride blood spread further on Jill's too expensive cotton pants. Her purpose was clear: Goad Frankie into a mistake and photograph the assault. The dozer's approach pushed her to run ever faster. Superiority, a presumed entitlement of the prosperous, was the first thing jettisoned when self-preservation took control.

Ryan should have abandoned the camera; he was being toyed with. Awareness made hot sweat stream over cold skin.

This playing field was, in the literal sense, tilted. For Jill, the first terrace passed with exhilaration. By the next, she arrived at a dark realization; this chase was a mistake and wouldn't end well. Lungs hurt and her legs burned. Darkness, though she ran towards it, would be too slow in saving her.

Frankie intended to silence voices in his head. With a single strike, he would provide illumination of his manhood, if not his humanity. He slowed the monster machine, extending the chase produced sexual excitement. Their upscale clothing would make for a massive victory in Frankie's chemically altered forebrain. The difference between Worth Avenue and Target contained the entirety of his hatred for South Florida's well heeled. No one but Raoul would bear witness, when he ended their lives. A long swig swallowed, the number of sprinting figures within Frankie's field of vision was reduced by one.

McGettigan saw why before McShane.

Methane gas vents were five feet in diameter concrete pipes driven deep into the landfill. In a hurdler's full stride, Jill lifted her left while pushing with her right leg. Unable to remain airborne, safety required her to grab the embedded steel handhold. Her face struck first, breaking bones, tearing muscles and dislocating a shoulder. Clinging to safety and life, instinct alerted by agony told her she would fall. She looked down and shivered. Shirt bloody and tattered, every moment she hung-on risked more than a blouse by *Pink*. Jill heard loud noises far away; loss of consciousness would be the end. Her brain instructed the left foot to push and it responded.

McShane swiveled his head to locate the missing woman. Saw nothing except Ryan darting left. Frankie toggled the dozer's lights, certain they would reveal the cute blonde.

McGettigan, eyes glued to binoculars in lieu of his phone's screen, yelled at the 911 operator. "Tell them to hurry."

Reaction in Frankie's pea brain an elemental fury, it was the blonde he most wanted to watch die. In the few seconds of searching for Jill, Frankie allowed the machine to wobble; its center of gravity shifted above the center of mass. Danger of rolling-over heightened, Frankie didn't give a shit. Search for the woman abandoned, he plunged after the man, who was closer than Frankie imagined to the fence line and escape. In a fractional moment to assess outcomes, Frankie grasped his miscalculation. He would catch the young man, but his machine would be upside down when it happened.

McGettigan heard sirens. Saw Jill Stoddard strive to focus with the orbital bone of her left eye sticking through her nose. Shock took hold of her. She half stumbled towards the bulldozer, rolling on its roof towards Ryan.

Frankie was too busy shitting his pants to realize the machine couldn't be controlled. Nor did he feel the glancing blow when a sheepsfoot struck Ryan, knocking him down and penetrating his right arm. The fence took the brunt of impact—torn to shreds by tons of orange machine.

Quiet interceded.

Four people would bear witness; two were conscious.

McGettigan sat in shock; disbelief acquiesced to what his phone's screen proved true.

Jill stared across a small gap to Ryan. Her thought was simple— *How could his arm still be attached?*

Frankie's neck was broken. In a haze of agony, he comprehended what a total absence of feeling meant.

EMT's arrived; Jill and Ryan were on the way to hospital.

Frankie was found protruding from the overturned dozer, face imprinted with the diamond pattern of the chain link fence.

McGettigan chose this moment to visit Raoul; shit scraped from shoes announced my presence.

Raoul's bulk belied a baby-face, all three chins vibrated when he faked a greeting.

"Don't get up Raoul. Turn the cameras back on."

"About to lock up, Mr. McGettigan. Dark out there."

Phony smile made dimples the size of canyons in his cheeks. In my shirt pocket the phone vibrated against my skin. It jolted me— our conversation was being transmitted. Did Raoul know his order to Frankie hadn't been private?

"You want me to get the disc? Deputies will be here soon…bet you didn't know about being on the radio, huh Raoul?"

His feet slid off the desk with a thump. Raoul wasn't stupid and knew McGettigan didn't bluff. He stomped on a massive cockroach, then replied.

"DVD's gone. New system sends wireless footage to the Regional Office." Smug and satisfied, McGettigan was foiled—Raoul was certain.

I held the cellphone so he could observe the red light blinking. "Countermeasures, Raoul. Never go anywhere without them. There's bandit audio right here inside your private little world. Someone heard you tell Frankie to hurt Jill Stoddard and Ryan Rommery. They're still listening. You, my friend, are fucked."

It was guesswork for certain, but Raoul's belief was transparent.

His expression lost color. Sweat stood out on his forehead. Raoul should have made a phone call—find out if I represented the big bosses like the other time.

"Take the fucking DVD. You know where it is."

Close enough so his body odor repelled me, I spoke in his ear. "Who paid, Raoul? Threatening Commissioner Rommery…pushing Jill Stoddard around a parking lot….attempted murder…poor, pathetic Frankie crushed, maybe dead? Who paid?" The question was rhetorical.

Letting me take the DVDs—Raoul's interests and mine might match. An admission, in any form, of who paid him? Not so much. Ghosts loosed in my imagination, the Foolish left him waiting for the cops.

***

Ryan was in surgery.

Jill would have been, but the on-call eye surgeon was finishing an earlier surgery.

Frankie, the worst of the three, was scheduled for a CT scan. It was Frankie McGettigan needed.

A man in a wrinkled suit, holding a spray of flowers, rounded the corner in front of me. Something about the hair, together with the way he walked, niggled at me. Speeding up, McGettigan slammed through double doors and collided with a boy in a wheelchair.

"Jeez, I'm sorry," was the best I could muster to a kid starting to cry.

The Organism continued moving, needing to see the face on top of the wrinkled-suit. I heard the orderly mutter *Pendejo*. Almost to radiology, the hallways in three directions were quiet.

McGettigan leaned against the wall; the last few days had taken its toll.

All four of me felt calmer because, halfway through the three to eleven shift, no one manned the desk. Through a glass door, Frankie McShane lay with his eyes closed, something stuck on each eyelid. McGettigan swiveled his head, hoping not to witness the arrival of Sheriff's Deputies or Shaggy the Fed.

A Fool urged me to demand Frankie's confession—who paid for Jill's intimidation?

McGettigan's Ghost clucked a cold warning, telling me Shaggy drove a government sedan on a sunny Cape Cod afternoon; a day which turned to shit in a hurry.

Vomit rose in the Organism's throat; Frankie didn't look too good. He looked dead.

With a pinky finger I dabbed at a line of oily fluid, tasted it and flicked two business cards off Frankie's dead eyes—James McGettigan's business cards. This particular olive oil, distinctive on my tongue, or in my imagination, was used in the Last Rites of the Catholic Church.

The hospital parking lot was the epitome of normalcy. Tan sedans with government markings made no attempt to run me down. Crazed ex-priests spouted no Latin curse or blessing. With legs weighing more than the Organism could lift, what was real and what conjured?

Wasn't fighting-off an accusation of murder enough?

Wasn't trying to help my wife's sister enough?

Was it loyalty to Robert Linney, a friend who no longer recognized me? A debt to Martin Cardillo? Guilt was ever a possibility. How much was manufactured, as Amanda insinuated? Or had McGettigan fallen down his own rabbit-hole to wallow and drown in mad delusions?

I tried to lift McGettigan from this church of dark angels populated by heretics and Jesuits.

Crank it up, James.

CHAPTER 11

McGettigan cracked a smile. Could a political fundraiser in New Jersey have more affinity with reality than a dead sociopath in Florida?

Rental of a tuxedo in Jersey City was the last sign of sanity's breach. The *Mellow Dude* equipped me with necessities and patent leather shoes. *My* bride always said a man looked his best in a tux. Perhaps Deirdre would agree, when she saw me greeting her flight from Boston.

When Deirdre entered the terminal at EWR, a shower, a drink and two hours to collect herself was her request. I checked us into two rooms at the Hyatt on the Waterfront, in Jersey City.

McGettigan planned an after-dinner stroll along the Hudson River Walkway as it wound through parks and open spaces until reaching our destination. Deirdre, as we stood in the Hyatt's lobby, glanced down at bejeweled pumps matching a gold sequined dress. Her puzzled expression appeared to ask: *Are you a complete idiot?*

***

Johnny Ruggiero's face remained placid: *Two visits, so close together; two women, so different. Who is this new James McGettigan?* A tad too loud, he spoke to Deirdre.

"A primo table for the loveliest woman in Jersey City tonight."

McGettigan concluded Johnny's compliment was genuine, if a tad arbitrary.

Deirdre draped a diaphanous headscarf around her neck, air-kissed his cheek and lowered herself with practiced grace at a table for two by the fountain in the center of the room.

"It's nice to get away, James, even if it's just one night. Thank you for thinking of me." As the waiter delivered her wine, she tossed an off-speed breaking-ball, "Did you have a nice chat with Julia?"

"When did you talk to Julie?" James cursed the error. "Julia," I corrected.

"She called from Africa. Yesterday. Wanted to know about the Grand Jury. Said you weren't answering your phone." Uplifted eyebrows enquired where McGettigan had been.

"How's Patrick? When's Julia coming home?" My face must have looked like an expectant puppy.

"She didn't say. Her father was the topic. Julia cross-examined me for fifteen minutes, James. Detail after detail. She loves you *so* much."

Derision stung and I felt my face redden.

Dinner passed with ease. Two adults bent on enjoying each other's company.

Deirdre excused herself to the ladies room. When she returned, glittery makeup repaired and headscarf in place, her entire aura was golden.

I puffed my chest, a bit like a jerk, as we departed.

Our cab stopped in a line of traffic near a huge white tent. Someone's campaign pulled-out all the stops to jazz up this affair. Under normal circumstances, in a crap hotel, lousy lighting would provide cover for envelopes of cash, glassine bags of drugs, keycards for sale, broken promises, prolific lies and disagreeable threats. Tonight, within the shelter of imported trees, conversation sounded cheerful as couples, and the occasional single, wound their way through a receiving line.

A formal receiving line in North Jersey—another sign of the apocalypse.

A pair of photographers worked the line. The woman was dressed in low-cut white and six-inch heels. Her male companion leapt out from the fashion pages: Tight abs, wavy hair, string tie with his dinner jacket and patent leather ballet slippers. He handed me his card.

"Special tonight is a fifty-shot montage of the evening, featuring you and your lady."

My job was to locate Phil Spazutta.

Deirdre whistled in appreciation—a hundred tables arranged in concentric circles, each set for eight and adorned with a gargantuan bowl of flowers. Outer circles were set in white—inner circles in Democratic blue. A band played at a subdued volume at the tent's epicenter.

"Are we white or blue?" Deirdre's eyes shone with intrigue. She pulled me closer to her. "How much?"

I held up a single finger—a thousand per ticket.

She pretended to brush imaginary lint off her backside, while giving me a seductive look. "A measly grand…how much should this tush be worth?"

I reminded myself about the job at hand.

We meandered towards one of four bars. A second wolf-whistle from my date accompanied what came into view on the tent's far side.

Gleaming stainless steel fixtures and waxed white fiberglass highlighted the yacht tied up against the pier. No armed guard stood on her bow, no rain sluiced off her decks. *Marvelous Lady M* wasn't hiding this summer-like night. A placard sat near the boarding ladder announcing a midnight cruise for *Admiral Level Donors*. McGettigan, temper spiked with recollection of *whoosh, whoosh, whoosh,* was no one's Admiral. Circumnavigation of the tent allowed me to scan the crowd for familiar faces. After an hour crisscrossing the room, it became harder to stay tense and ready, boredom being the plague of most investigations.

If Deirdre looked good at dinner, she looked better with each passing minute. We found a half-empty table and focused on nothing and everything; she was easy company. Half a dozen times I allowed myself to be dragged onto the dance floor.

For the zillionth time, helicopter blades vibrated the tent's walls. By now we understood: A thousand bucks bought us peasants a white tablecloth; five grand purchased blue; five on top of five and you flew around Manhattan under a full, translucent moon. Like most parties, the dancers were younger as the music got faster and louder.

McGettigan's attention riveted on the bar by *M's* bow, where a klatch of men gathered, drinks in hand, cigar smoke hovering around their faces. One face was out-of-place: I saw it in profile. Robert

Linney was sick with Alzheimer's. No trickery could have delivered him to Jersey City. By deduction the man in the corner was Henry, Robert's little brother.

Gwyneth's acknowledged favorite, Henry, from birth, believed himself entitled to whatever, whenever. At seventeen, McGettigan concluded nine-year-old Henry was a psychopath or sociopath, a distinction absent a difference back then. In the moment and with prolonged history on my side, I knew a sociopath was marked by antisocial behavior while a psychopath manifested aggressive, perverted, criminal or amoral behavior without empathy or remorse.

In simpler terms, Henry was an evil prick.

He used to work for Enron. After its implosion, I'd lost track until Donald Hartnett kidnapped Connie Durant—Robert and Henry's sister. Hartnett kidnapped Connie to ensure her husband Hub, short for Hubert, made no attempt to aid Robert or James. Hub was ex-Air America, maybe ex-CIA. Maybe not ex-anything.

I positioned myself where the other faces could be examined. When the music changed tempo to an old ballad, Deirdre was back in my arms. It took a moment before I realized—she needed the ladies room. Flat-footed without her, I stared at Henry then turned away.

Would this be a good time to sneak aboard? A Fool took three steps in the yacht's direction, when a hand touched my shoulder. Expectation anticipated Phil Spazutta. I found his messenger, the stunning, dark haired Mata Hari from Ruggiero's.

Demure in mockery, she suggested, "Let's dance, James."

I put my arm around her without a moment's hesitation; none of four of me issued a protest. Moving with the music, her hand rubbed my rear.

On the yacht's side of the band, I gathered myself. "Where's Phil? I need to speak with him."

She pursed her lips.

For a millisecond I saw her true role model: Ingrid, whose manipulative use of sex so disgusted me. In the next instant, Deirdre returned to my peripheral vision where a linebacker pushed her onto the dance floor. In the third increment, anger gaining control, I turned back to Mata Hari. Warm hand gone, something pointed and hard replaced it.

"Dance over to the gangway. Phil's nervous…he's sure the party's being videoed by the Feds."

"What's sticking in my butt?"

"My room key, if you have time after servicing your lady friend. Or instead of her, if you'd prefer." She stretched up to kiss me. I pulled away. This one was Ingrid—younger and prettier but Ingrid in every important way.

The Organism felt a bee sting where Mata Hari's hand had been. Stumbled. Strong hands and arms supported me two steps up to the yacht's main deck. I looked for Deirdre, but no golden dress or hair was in sight. A fog of darkness arrived on little cat's feet.

CHAPTER 12

I lay in a heap. Pain throbbed through shoulder, elbow and side as I was thrown about like a rag doll. A vague smell of flowers intruded, though my head felt stuffed with rags.

Could I stand?

It was out of the question. The crazy, random movement of my prison, and the residue of drugs injected into me, myself, the Ghost and I, wouldn't allow it.

What seemed foreign fingers began a tactile examination, then drew back in alarm; something gooey coated my right arm. Naked and cold, I'd been warm such a short while ago.

Who'd done this to me? Why? Questions appeared and disappeared. The who and why were for later. Where was I? How bad was I bleeding?

Time was slippery. When I startled awake, cold had turned to frozen. Position on the floor unchanged, I splayed my fingers against the wall and pushed. Twice I fell over. A wall switch was found to no avail. I listened to every sound, felt each motion and processed it all with the mental acuity of a seven-year-old boy. Incipient panic jolted me; James McGettigan was in the dark aboard *Marvelous Lady M*. M surfed the back of waves and my ears heard the wind's evil lullaby. Dry inside a captive space, my imagination witnessed spray sheet over *M's* bridge and green water sweep the deck as her bow bit downward, hull protesting the strain imposed upon its steel. M began to lift, building stresses as she twisted. Hesitation grew before the bow rose. Forces of buoyancy struggled to prevail.

New York Harbor sheltered vessels from summer's winds until Rikers Island, Laguardia Airport, the Whitestone Bridge and, finally, the Throg's Neck Bridge were cleared. Once Montauk and Block Island were left behind, the ocean's wrath would be unabated.

If half-assed estimates were accurate, the open ocean tossed me to the deck and ripped-out the IV inserted by my captors. Mind games kicked-started the Organism, pushing aside drug-induced anxiety. Mind games wouldn't green light the question which mattered: Did they plan to kill me?

Steadying myself against a mahogany berth, smooth, cool skin made me jump out of mine. Tentative examination confirmed: Yes, the skin was female. The Organism deployed its left hand to find her ragged breath. Naked as a jaybird, like the Organism, this wasn't Deirdre Collins. Finding the needle, I pressed down with one hand and withdrew it with the other.

Out of necessity, we two ought to be allies.

I pounded the door. Jiggled its handle like a maniac. Under the effect of some magic it opened. On the port side, I found *M's* galley. Refrigerator open, light ruined night vision and revealed enough food to feed a small army. Hurried, I re-closed the door, suspending hope my captors hadn't seen the spray of light.

Find a knife, James.

Thirty feet towards the stern, up a stairway, my captors steered *M* towards James's uncertain future. Three times the Organism could have stumbled; up the stairway to the salon and pilothouse was a job for hands and knees.

What must James McGettigan look like to a cosmic observer?

Plumbing dangling, blood smeared haphazardly on body parts, how could I have ended up like this?

Charge the wheelhouse.

McGettigan was accompanied by the labored thrum of diesel engines. Instinct sent me to the helm where destruction sapped resolve. GPS and radar screens were smashed. Engine indicators as well. Switches for bilge pumps, running lights, underwater lights, and who knew what else were damaged and inoperative. Whoever did this had been in a hurry; they left the autopilot, gears and throttles to maintain course and speed. A trivial guess suggested a chopper had landed on *M's* helipad and flown them away. They must have concluded lights and compass were of no consequence. Illuminated in a ruby glow, *M's* magnetic compass pointed north of due east.

Navigators had crossed oceans for centuries with no more than a compass, a timepiece and a crass estimate of speed. Tachometers were kaput, so I listened to two engines sing their song. As for a timepiece, the clock and barometer lay in pieces. I intended to look for my cell phone, when chores at the helm were complete.

What was impossible in below-decks darkness was now routine. Even the yacht's pitching and rolling was less frightening in the artificial light, although *M's* sluggish response weaseled its way on to the Organism's list of concerns. First things first: By turning to a due west compass heading, *M* would stumble onto land somewhere. Reducing speed and turning to port, the big yacht spun until waves impacted her hull at ten o'clock, and the compass read 270 degrees. Molded fiberglass steps led to the sun-bridge where a check of port and starboard showed operable red, green and white navigation lights—contemplation of a collision deepened the fear of drowning.

Drawers in a cabin marked *Captain* provided a towel, uniform pants, belt and a cotton sweater emblazoned with Meredith Lawrence's family crest. An embossed towel was left to drip in the Captain's shower after cleaning myself of blood. Boat shoes a half size too large were welcome; the engine room would be perilous without rubber tread.

No cell phone was found, despite a long search called to a halt in utter desolation. Physical stability, provided by *M's* stabilizers, was what McGettigan needed.

Before heading to the engine room, I returned to the cabin to examine the female whose life was intertwined with my own. Whore-shriek woman was younger than I remembered, petite, glassy-eyed and unaware of her circumstances.

I covered her with a blanket.

In bright light, my captors' plans for James were made clear; the IV bag was two thirds full. Bad weather rescued me from spending twenty-four hours through a looking glass at a mad Queen's tea party. After twenty-four additional hours of drugged stupor, *M* would have reached the North Atlantic Ocean. Hysteria bled into my soul at the thought.

A camera's black housing caught my eye. Wedged between mattress and curved hull, its purpose filled me with angst. The memory card was where it belonged. In living color, a full-figured Asian girl with the face of a child sat astride McGettigan in faux ecstasy. Another photo showed this girl stretched on top of me, tongue evident as she kissed me. A third involved her tongue in an altogether more private location.

McGettigan was certain the photographic proof had been downloaded.

I turned away.

You'd think a man who last had sex—with his wife, when she'd been alive, and before cancer warped our lives—might, just might, remember what these photographs depicted. My skin crawled. It was obvious what the future of these pictures would be. What would Julia think? And Patrick, would he consider these images credible? Would he ever look at me with affection again?

Oh sweet Jesus, Deirdre's reaction would be a revelation.

Check the engine room for the stabilizers, James. Dry land is a long way off.

Crank it up.

***

The yacht's engine room was cleaner than most hotel bathrooms. Meredith Lawrence had never seen an engine room, but this degree of cleanliness would have been her expectation.

Mammoth diesels shared space with a generator, freshwater converter and a ton of other equipment, wiring and instruments. Inside the doorway, where every surface was painted glossy white, nothing appeared out-of-place. Mounted next to engine gauges, a clock displayed 22:38. I'd been out of commission twenty-two hours.

Prior to leaving the helm, McGettigan reset twin diesels to seventy percent of wide-open throttle, near enough to twelve knots of hull speed. Before her drop in RPMs, sixteen knots would've been a close guess. If we left Jersey City twenty-two hours ago, spent four hours in the East River and the approaches to the Whitestone, and an additional six hours to reach Montauk, we'd traveled one hundred eighty miles on a east by northeast trajectory towards Georges Bank.

M shuddered.

The Organism's head banged into the ceiling, a trickle of blood from an inconsequential cut the limit of consequence.

Controls for the stabilizers were mounted on a panel located on the firewall forward of the big generator. As fins made of high-tech composite deployed from inside their external cavities and rotated into position, *M's* motion subsided.

Engineers could be anal about mechanical equipment, in particular when a huge swath of ocean lay between said engineer and safe harbor. On the assumption our captors sabotaged something unexpected or uniquely difficult to repair, I began an inch-by-inch inspection. In close proximity to the starboard engine, a large wave caught me in a precarious, off-balance position. I jerked away from a searing hot exhaust manifold. Halfway into an ugly fall, my ears picked-up the sound of sloshing water. Surprise was a poor portrayal of McGettigan's reaction when a thin layer of water sluiced along the deck, soaking my feet.

A moment of dormant brain activity presaged the Organism's soaring rise in blood pressure.

No, no, I pleaded with fate, please no—water on the engine room's deck meant the bilge must be close to full. Where was seawater entering? Would Astor Lawrence destroy his grandmother's treasured yacht? An incorrect question delivered an alternate verdict: Did Astor give a tinker's damn?

Two hatches led to the bilge. McGettigan opened the first to be reminded: *M's* bilges were dark caverns lit from above by engine room lighting. I went in search of a waterproof flashlight.

Bilge littered with half floating, half submerged laundry, McGettigan reached down, thinking the mass of clothes and bed linen suitable to seal whatever hole required repair. A pair of trousers was the easiest to grab. I pulled. Weighted by saltwater, the saturated fabric was too heavy. Second hand added to the effort, recognition was immediate; these pants held a leg. McGettigan dragged the body from the bilge. A dead Asian girl, no more than a teenager, caused the Organism's innards to convulse.

I leaned over to retrieve the next body, saving my life in the process. Whore-shriek filled the room, dwarfing the engines roar. A chef's knife whistled past my right ear, missed my shoulder and clanged off the engine, scarring its perfect paint.

To deter a second attempt, I whipped an elbow rearwards; a spray of blood covered me as she collapsed from a shattered nose.

M was sinking and she was obsessed with killing James McGettigan. Twice now, she'd tried. Who was she? Why was she here?

She spat a mass of phlegm and blood on the deck.

No time available to tend her face, McGettigan tossed her a clean rag. Faster than I could respond, she rushed for the door leaving a high-pitched wail in her wake.

I yelled after her. "We're sinking, you stupid cow. If you'd stabbed me, we'd both be dead."

Entering the water was inevitable, but the engine room door had no lock. Pouring into the aft bilge compartment ever faster, seawater would overpower bilge pumps. I dragged three more girls from the bilge, looking over my shoulder in constant concern. Seven to go— they floated away from the hatch like beach balls on a sunny afternoon. I'd never find the leak this way.

Underwater represented an unacceptable risk on every level. Ms. Whore-shriek might succeed in murdering me; hypothermia would, if I stayed too long, incapacitate or kill me; hitting my head was a constant, life-threatening hazard; claustrophobia would drive me crazy. All on a sinking yacht—a coffin for eleven and maybe thirteen before night surrendered to dawn.

McGettigan sometimes swam, on occasion floated, and in the most cramped areas duck-walked along the hull. One hand pushed bodies towards the hatch. The other sought obstacles utilizing the touch and feel method. At wit's end, four bloated obstacles remained; corpses of young women, they were no longer human. The Organism's legs stiffened, its feet were numb, and self-protection instincts issued a stern warning: Get out of the water. A robot without feel or feelings wrestled four corpses, yielding to tears when bloodshot eyes recognized the girl from McGettigan's posed sex photos.

I struggled, warning signs ignored, to focus on the hull—relying on the incoming rush of water to tell when I was close. *M* could sink five times over before I succeeded. Near the transom, lungs nearing explosion and fingers absent a glimmer of sensitivity, a bilge pump could be seen with it's wiring torn out. Two pumps should be in combat against the inflow; one wasn't enough. My captors made certain no repair would, or could be attempted.

It was true: *M* was sinking.

How fast was the bone of contention.

Regardless of the imperative to discover where *M* had been sabotaged—or to freeze my ass off and perish in a fruitless endeavor, McGettigan recognized the purest of folly. Without a period of recovery, a Fool's death was inevitable, and an accomplishment which would most satisfy my captors.

The Ghost, in a stunning change in nature, suggested a hot shower. Reinvigorated, capillaries in the brain opened, I needed a different plan. With my survey of the hull failed, where should I look next? What could they have damaged without a major effort? Look for a hammer, James, not a scalpel.

Had my captors known McGettigan would attend the fundraiser? No, pre-planning was too much of a stretch. *M's* injury had been on the spot; so where was it?

A rummage through *M's* storage lockers provided a wetsuit complete with head cover and gloves. Tied around my waist were a string of wooden bungs. Bang the bung—friction would hold it in-place. On my way to re-start the search, I canvassed the main salon and surrounding cabins. Opportunity not to be avoided, I yelled for a second time.

"We should work together. Whoever you are, I'm not your enemy. I didn't kill those girls. The boat's sinking. Help me."

No response.

The smell of death infused the engine room; it was not a place to improve one's mental health. Near an hour and a half of searching and I'd found nothing. Endless areas of the yacht's structure remained unexamined. With rising water, the yacht's performance was suffering. Over time she'd wallow in the waves. When seawater covered the engines, sinking would be irreversible.

Could I rig a second pump?

McGettigan's Ghost, fresh from reincarnation, or at least transmigration, decided McGettigan should prepare, should worry about the two who were alive. When everything contributing to survival was put in-order, I could attempt to postpone *M's* fate by wiring a jury-rigged bilge pump.

Four items were critical: Two survival suits; one multi-person raft; and one abandon-ship kit. The suits would defend against exposure, a sure killer even in summer. The kit would have an EPIRB, radio, flares, dye stain, lights, radar reflector, water, matches and other gear needed to stay alive on a raft. The raft, if it was expensive, which in Meredith-world was a sure thing, would be durable, enclosed, self-righting and low-drift. An EPIRB would broadcast our position to multiple satellites.

Sounded like a vacation.

McGettigan cursed the Foolish for disparaging our opposition's tenacity: Ragged knife cuts rendered the suits useless; the abandon ship kit was missing. Our last hope was the raft. McGettigan hoped those evil bastards hadn't tipped the self-inflating canister into a black ocean, where even now it floated in desolate expectation.

Sheets of spray lashed me as I maintained a death grip on *M*'s handholds. Splayed belly down on the teak like a man frightened to his core, McGettigan inched forward. An aluminum bracket held a functional canister.

Go rig a pump, James.

***

Admitting the time had come, she was no longer seaworthy.

On a pitching deck, McGettigan worried as he watched the life raft inflate in the pale, weak beginnings of a new day. If I'd waited too long for the woman's appearance, *M* would roll over. Three pillowcases full of blankets and food tossed-in, tucked into a ball and aiming my jump at the raft's tiny opening, McGettigan pushed forward. In mid-air the full meaning of *seaman* came into focus. My landing awkward but dry, in the full flight of regret, McGettigan thanked Poseidon for his tolerance.

Where was the damn woman? I screamed and begged for five useless, precious minutes. Why I cared was a mystery, except she knew things about people I couldn't identify.

Could she prefer drowning?

Rations, pouches of water, a medical kit, seasickness medicine, a signal mirror, signaling flares, fishing kit, a repair/patching kit and flashlight with spare batteries and bulb were the totality of my connection to normalcy.

A dim sun rose.

The hard, blustery wind lessened.

Yes it was a coincidence, but welcome nevertheless.

In the raft's accessway, paddle maintaining position, McGettigan visited a reverie of better memories.

Interrupted by a British accent, she yelled, "Pull the raft closer, I can't jump so far."

Barefoot, dressed in electric blue pants, a yellow summer weight sweater, matching hat and accessorized with diamond earrings and necklace, she wore bright pink lipstick and held a small bag. Her nose, broken and pouring blood when I'd last seen it, reflected an even, smooth complexion.

"So you can try to stab me again…show me your hands…pull up the sweater so I can see."

"Haven't you seen it all already?" Accompanied by a piquant expression, overt flirting seemed relaxed, unhurried, and unusual.

"Do it. Or stay where you are. You won't enjoy swimming, when *M* sinks."

With a stripper's insouciance, she complied.

I pulled the raft closer.

In a long-jumper's motion, she sprung over *M's* railing stretching her legs to complete an impressive entry. McGettigan's jump had mimicked a beer truck and so I refused to release a bad temper.

"I didn't kill those women. I wasn't a willing participant in the photos." Nonsensical was a litany ordered by an cataleptic mind. "Who the hell are you…where'd you get the clothes and makeup…and the jewels?"

"My name is Charanya." She arranged herself against the far side of the raft's canopy. "I'm an Inspector with the Royal Thai Police. And I don't believe you…about your sexual needs or your guilt in a mass murder."

Voice steady, she made continuous eye contact. Charanya was a serious person, unlike Ms. Whore-shriek. I asked my policewoman companion, "Do Thai Inspectors pilfer jewelry from crime scenes?"

An airy voice disagreed. "Everything is mine. They must have left it all in the bathroom, when your friends stripped me. The diamonds are necessary for my cover. I've been undercover over a year. My boss, Lt. Colonel Nantakarn, provided the diamonds before I left Bangkok. I've more jewelry and lots of clothes in my New York apartment. What's the white man's saying…catch more flies with honey?" She changed gears. "My government will ask for extradition. Your government will grant the request. Thai people…we understand the sex trade is about the white man's hang-ups and brown-skinned girls' need to support their families. What you do…selling children to be used and then disposed-of…no politician wants to be discovered turning a blind eye to such things."

Animus kidnapped her features, leaving the cool, British-educated mask in tatters. "They weren't animals in a zoo. What's wrong with you?"

Vigilance filled the void left by this fresh indictment. I could ask how she intended to take me into custody. Or why she told me her intentions, putting her life in jeopardy on a raft with a deranged slaughterer of guiltless girls.

Investigations of *bad people* doing *bad things*, McGettigan's lifelong occupation, left a single truth foremost in mind: Charanya's necklace belonged to Meredith Lawrence. I'd have known it anywhere. Among other attributes, it wasn't real—Meredith kept no pieces of her real treasure on the yacht.

Charanya wasn't an Inspector with the Royal Thai Police, or at least not an honest one.

***

Reluctant sea-gods gave-up their stranglehold. *M* died a short time ago, slipping under by the bow.

High in a May sky, heat from the sun drained strength and demanded more water than was available. Give or take a hundred miles the raft sat sixty to seventy miles East of Cape Cod's elbow. Those who abducted me had been ambivalent: If McGettigan turned up dead, fine; if he turned up alive, the sex video and Inspector Charanya's testimony would confirm him a mass murderer and all-American pervert. Prior doubts regarding my innocence in Hartnett's death would be swept away in a media driven feeding frenzy.

Had McGettigan been lured by Phil Spazutta? No. Phil would hit you in the mouth, but wasn't a man to lure anyone into anything. Lured by Mata Hari, she of the excellent kisses, was closer to accurate.

Henry Linney's presence had been the worst of anomalies.

Astor Lawrence? I hadn't seen him at the party.

Rand Jellinek? I didn't know what to think, but knew what thoughts to avoid.

Daniel Bazel? Was he on more than one payroll?

Timmy Timilty? Too complicated, although my situation smacked of his affection for irony.

There was the list of my investigation's status. At least one person on the list wore two faces.

***

A sou'west breeze withered at sunset. A half moon bathed the ocean in its glow.

McGettigan couldn't sleep.

Charanya sat motionless and awake.

Light penetrated our cocoon, blinding us. Two vessels approached, television lights from the first drenching the second in artificial daylight, revealing the ratty, creased Patriots caps of its crew. A lobster boat, her sheer-line's pinstripe ended in a caricature of a boiled lobster giving the middle finger to the world with its claw.

"You from *Marvelous Lady M*?"

McGettigan was on TV, a real life reality-show about catching lobster on Georges Bank. "*M* is gone. Sunk a day ago. Glad to see you."

The skipper, a well built guy with a wiry beard, said, "NOAA is broadcasting the *Notice to Mariners* every fifteen minutes. We all laughed…thought you rich-boys were still in the Bahamas."

I looked behind me, but Charanya's back was turned. She said, "I need a moment."

Stepping off the raft to a broad deck loaded with traps and lobster-buoys painted a garish green and gold, I said, "Thank you…glad to be aboard. There's one more…a young woman."

Whore-shriek filled the air. Lobstermen rushed to look. From inside the raft, she screamed in a heavy Thai accent.

"Don't let him hurt me any more. Please."

What had been a smiling TV moment, shifted like Grand Banks weather.

Skipper yelled, "Willy, help her out of there. Gerry, sit him down by the bait barrel." A carbine emerged from a rack by the wheel.

Pointed at me, it conveyed Skipper's message with less than total conviction.

Hiding behind Gerry, Charanya was again nude. Innocent arms wrapped around her breasts, her Brazilian looked vulnerable. She hissed and spit in my direction; it was effective with this audience. Makeup was what she'd sought on *M*—why she kept her back turned most of the time on the raft. Black and blue semicircles embellished raccoon eyes as she bled from the nose.

Two cameras captured the drama from different angles.

Willy swathed her in a jacket with *Malden Catholic* embroidered on the front. As a reward, she raised her voice for all to hear.

"He sank the yacht on purpose. To hide the bodies."

From the camera boat came a world-weary shout. "Do it again…turn her more towards me, I want the full-frontal."

Willy shouted, "You're a pig, Adam. Can't you see what a mess she is?"

Skipper said to his two boys, "Do it. She won't mind, will you Miss?"

A second-take of the rescue of Inspector Charanya Kasemsarn was filming. McGettigan sat next to week-old bait. Its stench wasn't why the Organism felt sick.

Klieg lights were extinguished, camera gear stowed in stainless steel cases.

Charanya was being catered-to down below, in a cabin without amenities intended for workingmen.

Hoping to establish some local connection, McGettigan told Skipper, "I'm from Monument Beach…you're a Highliner from Hyannis, right?"

A fat, rolled, blunt glowed orange red as Skipper drew on it. He turned to look at me. "I know you. Murder…they wanted to charge you with murder. Looks like they'll get another chance, shithead." A snorting laugh punctuated a self-satisfied expression.

"Billy Nichols is my closest friend. Bet you know Tom, too. Just got married out in Seattle. They don't believe I killed anyone."

Skipper made no response beyond adding throttle and radioing the camera-boat to do the same.

Willy interrupted, fevered excitation permeating his discovery. "Stevie, she's got a camera in her bag. Says there're pictures of Mr.

Slick sexin'up a bunch of girls. Showin'em dead. Let's beat the shit outta him…feed him to the fish.".

Stevie, Skipper's real-life name, would believe everything Charanya said, if photos made McGettigan look guilty-as-hell. A look of disgust came my way as he went below deck.

McGettigan doubted Charanya's charms made an impact on Skipper Stevie, although he might, in a fleeting moment of anticipation, picture himself getting laid. But a woman making accusations of murder on the high seas? It would make un-needed trouble for a man with two very different occupations.

When Stevie returned, his brow was wrinkled. Taking the rifle from Gerry, he leaned against a stanchion and observed me in some detail.

Trying not to inflame, I said, "There weren't any pictures. Did she tell you she's a cop in Thailand? Speaks perfect English, accent's as fake as she is."

McGettigan hadn't worried about pictures, because the memory card sat in one of two pillowcases resting beside the deflated raft. Sure, the raft would be confiscated by the cops; who got the pillowcases was a separate matter.

The fragrant cigarette's tip reddened to match his temper. "Wished I'd never seen your god-damned raft."

"Can I show you something, Skipper?" I crossed to the helm and showed Stevie the sutures running from armpit to below my ribs. "Happened when I rescued her from the Canal. She jumped off the yacht…they tried to run her down. I didn't know who she was, or what she was doing. Do yourself a favor…don't draw the easiest conclusions."

His rifle urged me back to my seat. Skipper passed the reefer to Gerry, who sucked hard.

Charanya fidgeted under the overbearing attention of Willy, whose desire was written plain in his lecher's grin.

"You'll be OK…face'll be clear on TV…get the credit for arrestin' this old girl-killin' freak show."

Charanya's voice quivered and was way more than a bit interested. "Do they use tape or P2?"

Willy screwed up his face. "Those computer things, ya'know?"

She smiled and tilted her head towards Willy's—co-conspirators in law enforcement.

Stainless steel cases and duffels sat waiting to be off-loaded. As did burlap bales in the cabin. Charanya wanted the video. McGettigan wanted the memory card. When the Kennedy Compound in Hyannisport fell behind, night terrors vanished. Buoys welcomed us. Kalmus Park Beach would pass less than fifty feet from our port side. Ten minutes would see the lobster boats berthed in downtown Hyannis.

Charanya moved towards me and near the video equipment bags. Screaming in Thai so she occupied the center of attention, Charanya lifted one of the hard cases; threw it overboard and dove after it.

Kalmus Beach. Timed to perfection.

"Fucking-A," yelled Skipper Stevie, perplexed and, in all likelihood, relieved.

Time to go was the sum and substance of my deliberations. The Organism hurled pillowcases overboard. After a poor imitation of a racing dive, I witnessed two boats continue on their way. Weighed down by saturated clothes, I followed in the direction of Charanya's splashes.

Charanya wouldn't be caught.

McGettigan was a classic case of a willing spirit burdened by a weak Organism. Having reached the street, surrender came with no further effort.

CHAPTER 13

Where was Charanya? Did I care?

Without phone, ID, wallet or money, a lost soul turned to St. Frances Xavier, the church where followers of John F. Kennedy's Camelot worshipped. A less than curious face opened the rectory door. Revealed in his eyes, James McGettigan was disheveled, wet and unshaven. Destitute? Drunk?

This priest wasn't young and pajamas expounded upon drooping eyelids. "Can I help you?" Not quite the Christian charity I'd hoped for, but better than a slammed door.

"A phone call, Father?"

"Wait here, my son," he said, as the door shut behind him.

McGettigan felt nothing like his son. Would he call the cops?

Again the door creaked open. "Put it inside the screen door when you finish. God bless." His cellphone appeared in the manner of a whole person shying from a leper. I dialed Amanda Nocito.

"Father Spencer, it's the middle of the night…are you okay?"

"Amanda, it's James. Can I come to the house?"

"Now?"

"Forty minutes."

"Trouble?" Pronounced with perfect clarity, Amanda woke with an abrupt sense of dread.

"Big trouble."

"I'll get dressed and make tea."

***

Under the air filter, in a sandwich bag encased in duct tape, was a spare key. My old warhorse transited Hyannis heading for Marstons Mills and a picture postcard Colonial where Amanda lived and maintained her office.

Amanda demanded, "What kind of trouble?"

"This chat count as doctor-patient privilege?"

"Have you killed someone this time?" Her look poked at me, like you'd antagonize a rattlesnake to piss it off.

"Eleven Asian girls...all killed on *Marvelous Lady M*...sunk out on Georges Bank. Maybe I'm been supposed to be dead as well. We were picked up by the TV lobster boats. She claims to be a Royal Thai Police Inspector...jumped off at Kalmus. Couldn't catch her."

Amanda's mouth hung open. "You're not making much sense."

Amanda was unfamiliar with rabbit-holes. McGettigan filled in the details.

Pensive, she started her enquiry with the personal. "Where's Deirdre? Were you two good together...before you were hijacked?"

Attention to detail was a focus of our therapy sessions—nothing too large or too small for examination. McGettigan, in a post-adrenaline funk, would've skipped over large blocks of a thorough analysis.

"You were my one call, but yes, I was enjoying her company very much."

"You were drugged and kidnapped. You killed no one. It sounds like you saved this Charanya's life by stopping the drugs and getting her onto the raft."

"Except no one can verify what I say...not if Charanya, or one of the kidnappers, says otherwise. Will M be salvaged? What could the wreckage prove? No, I didn't commit any crimes, but good old Sheriff Donny won't buy it. Not when Stevie the lobster boat's Skipper finishes telling his tale."

"What can I do, James?"

"Switch cars with me for a few days. Buy a throw-away cell...e-mail Julie the number."

Amanda grinned at my name regression.

***

Not much in an investigator's world happened without cash money. For years I kept a Harrods's tea can buried in the dark recesses of my cottage's crawl space. Today the can granted rainy day supplies—passport, duplicate driver's license, credit card, keys to car and boat as well as ten grand in twenties—all double wrapped and sealed in Ziploc bags.

I wouldn't be alone in a focus on money. Skipper would focus on his livelihood before anything else—his lobsters and bales of marijuana. Maybe he'd grab a few beers and a few hours sleep before calling Sheriff Donny; Skipper's self-interest would be a powerful motivation. Self-interest was always at the root of bad things.

***

Framingham was an hour and a half drive from Monument Beach.

Robert Linney and I were boys on this tree-lined street, unchanged with passed decades to my biased observation. Robert's house was unaltered; every detail of white paint, black shutters, single car garage, back and side yards surrounded by tall arborvitae, was the same.

It was James whom was altered.

Robert's old yellow VW beetle was gone, as was its owner. Gone where he couldn't be found. Gone where none of life's vagaries tore at the soul.

Foiled by hesitation, a boyhood of yesterdays worked against uncertainty. Despite our seamless affection through life's trials, Gwyneth traded my life for Henry and Connie's future. Today I expected Gwyneth's face would inform her thoughts while muzzle-loading those pistols. Was my survival an afterthought, or of critical importance to my second mom?

Could McGettigan's Ghost stomach the answer?

No longer a family member in this house, I crossed the driveway. Eyes darted in circles. McGettigan was an interloper, invading Gwyneth Linney's privacy. In the backyard, past the screened porch with its flat roof, a gray cat stood in defiance, spine arched in protection of the bird in its mouth. As I approached the kitchen window, the cat stopped its diffident retreat to keep watch. Stretched on tiptoes, I looked inside.

What I saw could have been a portrait of what made Gwyneth and James such special friends.

Maple wood kitchen table pushed against the wall, three chairs arranged just so, a white-on-white embroidered tablecloth was a simple embellishment. Framed photographs faced each other. Tall candles burned, held by elegant crystal. Two place settings of Gwyneth's everyday china were set with sterling silver. A single pink flower was centered in a bud vase. Within a silver tray, where milk and sugar bowls matched its design, sat an informal English teapot. Wearing a pale yellow shirtwaist, Gwyneth's head tilted upwards, in contemplation of an adjustment of the brass, swing-arm lamp. Together with half-burned candles, the lamp enhanced the room's mottled aura.

A dark cloud occluded the sun.

James grabbed the drainpipe and shinnied to where a leg could be thrown onto the roof. Sitting on his haunches, a single bloodstain testified to James's ignorance. Two windows overlooked the backyard. In the corner, a bedroom was little more than a cubicle with a closet. Wedged fingers under Henry's windowsill, McGettigan raised the eight over eight window. Henry slept; James reveled in the rage swelling inside. At the small boy's side, he sighed neither in hesitation nor regret. Forced around Henry's throat his hands squeezed. When frightened eyes begged for mercy, James closed the airway and waited for struggles to cease.

McGettigan's calves ached with the strain of looking.

I heard her heartbeat everywhere.

Within the screened porch, where a miniature Stars and Stripes flew on a pole held by a rusted bracket, the backdoor was a minor obstacle. The kitchen more resembled a chapel than a family gathering spot. An examination of Gwyneth provided nothing of how she died. Much like the Asian girls on *M*, bruises didn't enlighten the violence of her end. Still and all, McGettigan knew Henry Linney murdered his mother. Because Henry had been Gwyneth's bad seed. Because McGettigan wanted it to be Henry, so a Fool could exact revenge.

When had Gwyneth been killed? Ask the candles.

What was discordant would've been uncomplicated and offered satisfaction. What was orderly, and what wasn't, clambered for recognition. I allowed the entire milieu to seep into my storehouse of recollections: Gwyneth and James enjoyed tea at this table hundreds of times. Never with a tablecloth. Never with candles; she'd have thought candles preposterous. Never with ostentatious silver; flatware suited Gwyneth better. Leaning over the table to observe without touching, two photographs flanked the bud vase. One was familiar, fourteen boys and three adults from our last year in Little League. The opposing photo showed Henry's High School graduation, Stanley and Gwyneth beside Henry, Connie and her husband Hub, Robert and James. Everyone smiled in conjoined misery.

With care for minutia, the first floor rooms received a walk-through. No staged scenes were set for McGettigan, a visitor whose presence had been anticipated. Up the center staircase, I visited three bedrooms. Nothing like the old days, nothing like my violent fantasy, Henry wasn't in bed, asphyxiated.

A rabbit-hole beckoned.

The lunatic cat howled.

Taking stairs three at a time, I ran through the dining room back to the kitchen door, where I skidded into rigidity. The pitiful cat, skewered by the sharp end of the flagpole, its fake gold leaf contaminated with blood and fecal matter, hung from the bracket. A despoiled flag sagged in mourning. Gray-green irises glowered. Ever the stoic, its death rattle broke our shared silence.

I heard her heart beating everywhere.

She wouldn't want James to believe ill of Henry.

Hurrying back to the table, the picture of the baseball team was brought inches from my declining vision. There, in the corner of the back row, was Timmy, who never had tea with Gwyneth. At the top of my lungs, I projected the threat.

"You better come kill me, too, or start looking over your shoulder you rotten bastard." Through voluminous tears, my last words were transparent as well as false. "I'll make you pay, Timmy."

Seconds clicked off the grandfather clock in Stanley Linney's gunroom. I knew he was close; this was Timmy's idea of a dramatic interlude.

"You're allergic to cats. You hated the damned cat...and Boy-O, you're not paying adequate attention."

Time had been cut and pasted; James's childhood inserted in a present-day nightmare. Yes, McGettigan hated the cat; a serious allergy always irritated by its existence. But Gwyneth's cat was forty years dead. This cat, Gwyneth's last companion, was a stranger. As for not paying enough attention, Timothy Timilty raised a valid point. Upon more careful inspection, under the cat's tins of tuna, in a larder with more woozles than foodstuff, was an envelope with the return address of a lawyer, stamped to seal with light blue wax in which I read—*Gwyneth Frances Linney*.

Amanda cautioned me about misplacing details. Timmy told me to pay better attention.

Was it them who needed help, or McGettigan?

Would anyone other than a Fool ask such a question?

CHAPTER 14

There was nothing in the *Boston Globe* or *Cape Cod Times* about the sinking of *Marvelous Lady M*. No mention of a Royal Thai Police Inspector with a penchant for odd behavior. Not a syllable decrying well-known murder suspect, James McGettigan. Tempted to chat-up Sheriff Donny, instead I drove to Boston where Sixty State Street housed McQuilken, Collins and Strasburg.

Directed to Deirdre's office, I stood before her guardian-of-the-gate.

"Is Deirdre in?" The office door was closed, so my question was necessary and polite.

Balancing the phone on her shoulder, pen in hand, I gauged where my request stood in her mental queue. "What can I do for you, Dr. McGettigan?"

Deirdre's assistant hadn't laid eyes on me before today. "Is she in?"

"Sorry, she's on a conference call,"

"She get back from Jersey all right?"

Guardian's smile achieved a blend of tact and remonstration.

McGettigan was, to his total amazement, persona non grata.

"You'll tell her I came by, won't you?"

Her smile turned into something else. Down the hall another linebacker in a bad suit walked in my direction.

***

McGettigan was determined to pay better attention. Could there be a better starting point than an examination of players in a game devolved from a mental joust with ADA Lincope to a mélange of twists and turns populated with dead people. Including one death which mattered a great deal.

***

Two thousand five hundred dollars—the ransom required by Victor Stratton, official photographer at the fundraiser. In our original telephone chat, when he heard I wanted all the pictures, his price was more than twice what we negotiated. I'd assured him; *fucking with me*, in the Jersey City vernacular, wouldn't be in his best interest.

In a voice already spending my money, he said, "No need to be nasty. I'll e-mail them to you right after I close the shop."

McGettigan's concern with Mr. Stratton's sexual preferences was non-existent; when he would deliver the photographs mattered a great deal.

"E-mail them now, please. Now would be much, much better."

***

More than anything McGettigan needed a night in his own bed, the chance to lose myself in a shower and dry myself with towels smelling of *her*. Fly in the ointment, a small sedan was parked by my mailbox—off-duty sheriff's deputy, no doubt. Sent by Donny. Wheel yanked to the right, I pulled into a neighbor's driveway, executed a three-point turn and disappeared.

Billy Nichols, after shooting Hartnett's assassin and standing sentry while McGettigan and Hartnett killed each other, would've been entitled to deadbolt locks, hi-tech alarms and mad dogs in his decrepit, post Civil War kitchen. With steady disregard for life's uncertainties, his house key lay inside a pile of faux dog shit beside the steps. The fridge contained coffee, grapefruit and beer.

Steady purpose fueled my effort to reduce the number of Victor's digital images. Henry Linney I was certain of; he wore a persistent cat-ate-the-canary smirk. Had he known Gwyneth would be cold and stiff in less than a week? Had Henry ended her life with his large hands and dainty fingers? Astor Lawrence's face never made an appearance; neither had Mata Hari's. Disappointed, a Fool remained convinced Mata Hari threaded the needle into a vein and laughed at my trained-seal act with girls young enough to be *her* grandchildren.

***

US 1 & 9 dropped me onto Jersey City streets. Past *Victor's Professional Photography*, I cruised two circuits of the block, expanding the search outward from *Victor's* before I slid Amanda's gas/electric hybrid into a spot between an old Camaro and a dented Corolla.

A kid, who should have been in school, owned one corner where he peddled a morning high while muttering opinions about my appearance. Little shit's Yankee cap, flat brim twisted to the side, received a barely audible, "Yankees suck."

Pulling up his Rangers sweater, the hundred twenty dollar real thing, he pointed at the semi-automatic stuffed in his waistband. "Red Sox Glock." Little shit had the temerity to squeal with pleasure at his stand-up routine.

On *Victor's* street, an old man tended a pushcart from which I could select sunglasses, condoms, apples or wristwatches, all at the standard tourist discount.

Standing behind the counter, inside Victor's, was a man who would stop traffic in certain circles. Features carved from Carrera, he mimicked statues of Alexander the Great. Forty, wearing dark slacks and a fresh, ironed, white shirt, sporting shades from the blind man's cart and strawberry blond hair to die for, he wasn't the fashionista I'd taken him for at the fundraiser. This guy could be taken for a movie star inhaling the Jersey City gestalt for a new role.

"Good morning…" I offered "…any chance you're Victor?"

Head turned to expose a chiseled profile, James decided: Nope, he was *not* a movie star. He was the improved version.

"Who's asking?" Reaction good-natured, his mouth twisted at one corner imitating the toughness of a matinee idol.

His Bogart impression was on the button. "A good customer."

Just then a much shorter man, with implanted plugs of new hair, spread aside a curtain of glass beads threaded on thin strands of hemp.

"Mr. McGettigan, so nice to see you. Is there a problem with the files I sent?"

"Victor?"

With an affectionate touch of Bogie's arm, he pushed John Lennon glasses to the bridge of his nose.

"How can we help?" Seeing me hesitate, he answered with a knowing glance. "Your lady-friend called a day or two after the party...ordered copies of every shot Bruce or Mary took of a tall, well-proportioned, older man in a tuxedo."

I shot him my best look of accusation: Deirdre would never have described me in those words.

Victor hastened to add, "She did describe herself...and her dress. Made finding you a tiny bit easier." Both Victor and Bruce stared in a pleasant fashion.

"I'd like to see a list of all the people who placed orders from the fundraiser...and can you put names to faces?"

Bruce, the matinee idol, asked in an incisive tone. "Are you here in some official capacity?"

"I'm very much in need of your help." Asking in a pleasant way was always in fashion.

Bruce doodled in pencil on a sketchpad.

Victor played with a stapler, turning it over and over in his hands. "You know how you get the LL Bean catalog you never asked for?" Victor's reference bore no sign of greed; lists were a commodity like any other.

My response was tailored to Victor's question. "A Master-List would be perfect, if one is available. What's the going rate?"

"For what you need...names and addresses attached to an identifiable photo...let's say $150 each."

"Total?"

Settled on a high stool, Bruce gazed out a dirty, plate-glass window while his pencil slashed bold strokes.

I was invited to the backroom. Two hours later I possessed a stack of 5x7 prints on the backs of which I'd noted whatever information Victor dredged from his records. When he finished, we went through Henry Linney's group another time. Victor conveyed bits and pieces of hard data and suspect gossip until what he could offer was exhausted.

"The man on the far left is Juan Carlos Mosqueda. Big time lawyer. Very connected. Next in the circle, going clockwise, is Richie Tarrant, a contractor. The tallest man, next in line, I don't know him. Last of the four is Wiley Hoshall...another lawyer."

McGettigan didn't know anything of Mosqueda or Tarrant. Knew Hoshall by reputation. Victor hadn't recognized Henry Linney, which meant nothing if Henry was an invited guest like McGettigan. I pointed out another shot—showing Deirdre and the linebacker in the background.

"Anything on this guy?"

Victor's software searched without success.

Bruce joined us, sketchpad by his side.

Victor warned, "Don't Bruce. We can't go back, if you do this."

Bruce countered. "He's a nice man." As if being *nice* warranted what Bruce could tell.

As if I wasn't there, the two held each other's eyes for several beats of a silent musical score. After a final, slight hesitation, Bruce spoke.

"We've had others with interest. The woman you were with...gorgeous hair on her...wanted the originals of any shot where she appeared. Watched while those originals were deleted from our hard drive...after she paid a minor fortune."

"She sure looked great...gold hair, dress and shoes."

McGettigan, it seemed self-evident, was a Fool of mythic proportion. Flooded with inspiration, the sketchpad's Mata Hari was stunning in its detail. So many important questions came to mind.

"What's her name?"

Bruce was rueful. "Wouldn't say. Paid in cash. I'm truly sorry for you. Bewitched by lust...is a hard hole to climb out of."

An antique phrase was *bewitched by lust*. No wonder Deirdre wouldn't accept my calls. "Can you guys do one more thing?"

Bruce understood my pain on every level. "What could make your quest more productive?"

"E-mail the photographs to this address." I jotted down Martin's Gmail. "Text should read...*Marianna, are any of these the ones who came?*"

My roll of twenties diminished, Bruce walked me to the door. If Timilty's God sought to reassure me of support, Bruce was a more than adequate prophet.

***

Juan Carlos Mosqueda inhabited an office in the old Pan Am building, a McMansion in Spring Valley and a loft-condo on Garden St. in Hoboken.

The Pan Am Building, now the MetLife Building, was the largest commercial office building in the world when, on a sad day in 1975, a CEO jumped from the forty-fourth story on to Park Avenue pavement. McGettigan wanted Mosqueda to hunger for a similar fate.

McGettigan spent three days noting the Cuban transplant's comings and goings. Mornings Mosqueda took PATH from Hoboken, then a taxi to 200 Park. Lunch, delivered from a local deli, was eaten at his desk. Sometime after seven, the process was reversed. One night he made the hike to Spring Valley, where the wife and kids lived. Last night he stopped at a restaurant near Stevens Institute, a short after-dinner stroll from his Hoboken love nest.

They spoke in hushed, sweaty tones.

He replaced them like snow tires—the tender, placid and oh so young Asian girls he coveted.

***

While Julia's father was one of two Trustees of the Julia McGettigan Trust, and as Trustee held unlimited rights to invest or disburse its funds, James hadn't Julia's concurrence to carry a briefcase bearing two hundred fifty thousand dollars.

A lifetime spent investigating crooked contractors, architects and politicians didn't qualify McGettigan as a hard-man, but made him proficient with electronic devices which watched and listened. What germinated in my head wasn't so much simple as it was direct. Mosqueda exhibited the vices of a successful attorney: He enjoyed foot-long Vegas Robainas and, in a no-smoking world, slipped a maintenance man ten-bucks to gain access to the rooftop helipad. I explained my passion for a quiet smoke to Mosqueda's man with the key as we watched the sun set behind the Jersey Palisades. Five twenties and I'd been given his beeper number and a code.

McGettigan placed two wireless microphones where they would provide good coverage.

On Mosqueda's floor, the next-door suite was empty. Here, a hi-performance contact microphone would bring Mosqueda's stuttering baritone to sensitive earphones.

In an e-mail to Marianna, photographs showed two large rings prominent on Mosqueda's right hand. Come to New York, the email pleaded, to resolve Robert Linney's unfinished business. Asking her to take a considerable risk was selfish. Asking Charlie Hamilton might have proved simpler. Under Charlie's deft touch with a fourteen inch Bowie knife, Mosqueda would, it could be speculated, volunteer the name of his client and the identity of the younger man who accompanied him to Cuba.

A no-call to Charlie weighed heavily.

Charlie Hamilton walked close to insanity's cliff after two tours alone in Vietnam's jungles amidst debilitating heat, wet season rains and the demands of conscience. How Charlie came to grips with the reality of his death or another man's, no matter the color of one man's skin or the arrangement of his facial features, was not a topic of conversation between us.

Why was McGettigan, in the dark of his dreams, so close to an identical precipice, absent the peace Charlie made with madness so long ago?

***

Had I forgotten Manuel's infatuation with Marianna?

Had McGettigan bitten his tongue and performed the promised favor for Martin?

Had I taken AUSA Ellen Harding for a drink and made nice? Did she love a Cuban man or covet what could propel the right candidate to political Nirvana?

All these things ran a marathon in my head as Marianna and Manuel stepped into the terminal at Newark Liberty.

"Marianna, thank you for coming."

She offered a chaste half-hug.

When Marianna was again by Manuel's side, he offered a gesture expressing disapproval of McGettigan's request, Marianna's acceptance and, most of all, Manuel's abandonment of Martin, his meal-ticket.

Bruce's guidance provided an address in the vicinity of Columbus Circle, where a specialty shop catered to women who needed conservative clothes which appeared more expensive than their price tag. Mosqueda had invaded Robert and Marianna's cottage in Cuba; he wouldn't associate her peasant's wardrobe with a severe black business suit, light blue shirt and modest, but real gold, accessories.

Another of McGettigan's less than ethical skills was the art of forging documents. With Anton Petrovsky's authentic business card as the model, Marianna Salgado achieved the rank of Lt. Colonel in the Defense Intelligence Agency.

Lastly, I searched photos of female military officers and the manner in which they did their hair and makeup. Inside a high-end salon, a place where lines of gender were bruised by factors not part of a bodyguard's scope, Manuel disapproved of McGettigan's plan in its entirety. My instructions to Jeremy, the owner, were specific: Marianna must pass close inspection. It would be good I suggested, if she looked sexy while remaining understated and out-of-reach.

***

McGettigan listened through headphones, instructions whispered to an antsy Manuel hulking near the elevators.

Lt. Col. Salgado was on her own. No earpiece would tell her what to say, or how to say it. Jeremy's butterfly emerged, inches lost from long hair while subtle streaks of color highlighted piercing eyes. Titanium wrapped explosive was the effect. Mosqueda would delight in the hint of availability mixed with impenetrability.

"Good morning, Lt. Col. Salgado here for a ten o'clock with Mr. Mosqueda."

There was no camera woven into Marianna's hair. So McGettigan's mind's eye watched the Secretary examine her, wondering why an Army Colonel wore no uniform.

"Good morning Colonel," Mosqueda said, sucking in an ample belly and offering his soft hand. "Have a seat, please." Almost singsong, he added, "Something to drink?"

The idea he could charm her made McGettigan's morning.

In Spanish, as I'd emphasized to Marianna, Col. Salgado responded without breaking a neutral expression.

"Did you think nothing would come of it?"

McGettigan's script was honed to reflect Marianna's hostile feelings toward a man who invaded her home and done as he pleased with Robert, a man with no defense of his own.

Mosqueda said nothing, racking his brains for a connection.

"National security, Mr. Mosqueda, is something you cannot fuck with, when you're a shitball lawyer."

Had he placed her?

Mosqueda stammered more than normal. "Do you have some identification?"

Col. Salgado snorted a disdainful laugh: *Like dude, you think spies carry signs?* She slid a business card across the expanse of desk and said, "I work for General Petrovsky." *Like anyone would recognize the name.*

Mosqueda tried not to sound dense. "Who?"

"General Anton Petrovsky...Director of Field Operations, Defense Intelligence Agency."

Mosqueda went for simple and defensive. "What do you want?"

"I want you to call Petrovsky...explain what you wanted with Robert Linney, in Cuba, where you entered without the legal niceties. I want to know who you represented...and I want to offer you an incentive to value the benefits of patriotism."

He harrumphed, needing strong, acrid cigar smoke to deposit his drug of choice in the bloodstream. "What the fuck..."

She cut him off. "Call General Petrovsky, Mr. Mosqueda. Or calm down." She slid a second card across to his hand.

As if the card weighed a hundred pounds, McGettigan conjured him holding it in both hands. Say nothing Marianna. Let him decide. A sensitive microphone transmitted clear sound so McGettigan could decipher the numbers dialed.

In Petrovsky's office, an electronic voice insisted, "This is the U.S. Army Directorate of Intelligence, General Anton Petrovsky Commanding Officer. Press 7 for a list of extensions. Press 0 for an operator."

Three more selections would be made before a person answered; spies weren't easy to reach.

Maybe a minute passed before Mosqueda said, "Linney's a vegetable. National security, my ass."

"Mr. Linney is involved in treason against your adopted country, Mr. Mosqueda. Mr. Linney is an assassin, not a vegetable. His apparent condition is drug-aided. I would know, you see, because I cared for him…and watched you make him sign documents."

Mosqueda must have strangled on his tongue.

"You?"

"It's a simple choice, Mr. Mosqueda. Tell me whom you represent, tell me what Linney signed and I'll compensate you for your trouble."

McGettigan held his breath. Again he visualized her slide the heavy case and unlatch two leather flaps. Tidy and banded, the cash made its own statement. Get close to him, Marianna. Let him hear how much you want him to say no.

"Tell me, Mr. Mosqueda, or you'll never see your little Asian girlfriend again…because you'll be thrown off the roof after your next cigar."

Beady, rat-like pupils must have dilated. Perhaps he delved into the bag with his hands, seeking the depth of the pile. Even calculated whether he gave a flying fuck about his client. Felt flop sweat trickle from armpits to crotch, and his penis shrivel from engorged to flaccid.

His voice croaked. "How much is my fee?"

"Two hundred fifty thousand dollars. Decide."

"My former client is an attorney named Granville Proost, from San Francisco. The documents were a Durable Power of Attorney and a Codicil to Mr. Robert Linney's Last Will & Testament. All legal. Now will you, please, leave?"

McGettigan spoke into the headset. "Manuel, look like you'd be pleased to throw him off the roof."

In a final scene in my unobserved drama, Col. Salgado marched from the office. Mosqueda's hungry stare followed every sway beneath her skirt. Manuel would have entered by now, pointing a finger at Mosqueda in a universal message. Mosqueda would have shut the door to his office, uncertain whether to shit or go blind. He would've settled for a caress of the money.

Soon a cigar would be lit in the sunshine.

Marianna, once returned to the hotel's anonymity, washed her face seeking to rid herself of a dirty feeling. Then disappeared to nap.

Manuel went for a walk.

McGettigan had suffered a shock; recovery would encompass more than a shower, a nap or any walk could assist. Granville Proost was Donald Hartnett's attorney, the man who exchanged money for assurances Robert Linney's *List* would never enter the public domain. If Granville Proost broke our mutual deal with the devil, James McGettigan was, again, a dead man walking.

Three sat in a Towncar, bound for Newark Airport. From the front seat, the radio led with breaking news—*Mr. Juan Carlos Mosqueda, New York attorney and prominent Cuban activist, jumped to his death late this morning from the abandoned helipad atop the MetLife Building, formerly known as the Pan Am Building.*

Nothing besides McGettigan's eyes moved while Geppetto's wires were inserted to control the puppet. Similarities to another painted wooden creation ignored, the tear which escaped was real.

CHAPTER 15

Best guess: Manuel killed Mosqueda.

How could I have thought Marianna, if she and Manuel had grown close, hadn't confessed how Mosqueda's hands lingered, where no man's hands belonged, on the day the attorney visited Robert Linney? Manuel might have thanked me for my ruse—Col. Salgado threatening to watch Mosqueda fly—and appreciated the poetic justice of the real act. If a different motive applied, Mosqueda might have reached Cuba in the identical illicit transport Manuel and I employed. Which meant Mosqueda and Rodriquez exchanged money, loyalty, or both. An ally of Rodriquez was an enemy of the Cardillo family. Enough reason for Manuel to eliminate Mosqueda, the pig.

Next best guess: Mosqueda telephoned Proost to warn Hartnett's consigliore. To call the man you just informed on, seemed unlikely, but lawyers weren't often troubled by guilt.

Donald Hartnett was dead in his grave. Who still cared about his memory or legacy?

***

Martin Cardillo's scribbled handwriting led to 36th and 3rd Avenue, where Murray Hill offered carriage houses and brownstones sprinkled among ubiquitous shit-holes. Small businesses populated the ground floors of buildings which housed hundreds of walk-up apartments.

Pizza parlor, a liquor store, sporting goods, and Chinese laundry, Martin's specific address wasn't befitting an Assistant United States Attorney or the daughter of US Senator Warren Harding.

McGettigan wandered the streets, transposing numbers in the address until any possible mistake had been eliminated. All through lunchtime I loitered, drooling at the smell of eggplant and Baklava from a Turkish restaurant. A local market inflamed an empty belly.

Back where I'd started, counting windows at one apartment per floor added to six. Camera at the ready, there were hours left to sustain flagging attention. In the pizza joint, a lone staffer wore multi-day stubble and sucked the stub of an unfiltered cigarette. Offered a twenty to rent me the table by the window, he snatched the bill with a refugee's enthusiasm. Cell phone in hand, I supported my bad knee on a cheap plastic chair.

John Poncey was Robert Linney's attorney, and a true-blue baseball man. McGettigan and Poncey weren't what anyone would call besties. John approached me to teach Jackie, his oldest, when he hit high school. No use to anyone right after *she* died, I said no with too much emphasis. In the belief I hurt his son's college scholarship chances, he never held back talking me down. Acrimony lingered. John either knew what had happened with papers signed by Robert's empty shell, under Mosqueda's guiding hand, or he could find out.

I spit out the words. "John, got a minute for a matter involving Robert?"

"Robert's been missing more than a year. What could the Great McGettigan want...besides saving your fucking skin?"

"Not missing any longer. Two mooks found Robert...made him sign several documents. Made him sign under duress. Hoped you'd know what was up...you've heard Gwyneth passed away?"

"Attorney-client privilege, asshole. Hear me?"

"Are you still Robert's attorney, John? Because if you are, or if you've been removed without cause, Robert's money, house, boats...everything...is being re-routed to Henry and Connie's pockets without Robert's approval."

"Self serving dick...you're no friend of Robert's."

"I've been taking care of Robert, with Gwyneth's explicit knowledge and approval, since the Hartnett thing. Never heard two words from you, John. Seems odd, don't you think? Being you're the attorney looking after Robert's affairs."

"Where is he? Where's he been?"

"Nope, you first. What's going on?"

"What's going on? You're being replaced."

"Replaced at what and by whom? I've never had an official role in Robert's personal or corporate business."

This assertion applied, except when Robert sent me his *List,* and told Hartnett and his trained seals McGettigan possessed it; except when Robert had been hidden by his mother, during the infancy of his disease. I believed his life could be protected, and kept a promise to Gwyneth to see the job done.

James paid full price for saving Robert Linney.

John's vitriol had no expiration date. "But you've been prominent in Gwyneth's business…raising more than a few eyebrows. You, McGettigan, were appointed executor of Gwyneth's estate and, through Robert's Living Trust and Will, the manager of Robert's assets should he be incapacitated or declared dead. But, as I said, you're…being…replaced." John's pronunciation was crisp and words selected with precision, as would be the case in court with a stenographer.

"Has Robert been declared dead?"

"No."

"Has Robert been declared incapacitated?"

More pregnant silence.

"So I'll guess…Robert signed away my position as Gwyneth's executor, and manager of his affairs?"

No answer.

"So Henry can spend the money as he likes."

Almost to myself, I repeated my opinion of Robert's younger brother. "Henry is a prick. He's moved into the Cotuit house? Hub and Connie too?"

More dead air.

"Who gets what, when Robert dies."

John broke his silence. "I'm sure he'll live a long…"

Tired of the dance, I cut him off. "Stop it, John. He'll die sooner than later. Robert doesn't know me. Wouldn't know you. Can't feed himself. Can't dress himself. Who gets his money, when the time comes?"

A tiresome monologue took me nowhere.

"What's the chance the new documents can be challenged?"

"Preliminary hearing granted temporary rights. Final hearing's set for the middle of June."

"I could appear with my attorney…and with Robert's caretaker, who witnessed the forced signature. I'd have standing."

This time his silence smacked of self-satisfaction. Legal intonations abandoned, without a hint of regret, he dropped me with a fastball in the Organism's ear.

"Ms. Collins attended the prelim. Told the judge you couldn't challenge Robert's wishes…said James McGettigan was dead—lost at sea. Intimated you were involved in some sordid shit." John inserted a cynical laugh. "Love to see her act when she wants to hurt you."

All things considered, there wasn't much good news.

Deirdre Collins was what—a lawyer's lawyer, a charlatan or a woman who would do anything with the right incentive. What she'd left behind was a bit of a puzzle. McGettigan might've pursued a future with Deirdre, might've overcome the loss of *her*, but should've opened his eyes to see past the superficial. James's wrestling match with McGettigan must have amused Deirdre. *Stop feeling sorry for yourself, go back to work*—what McGettigan would have heard, in no uncertain terms, if *she* wasn't dead.

What good news there was, rested with John's failure to taunt me with my imminent arrest for the multiple murders of Asian girls, and dozens of charges associated with kidnap, assault and piracy. Bodies carried to a watery graveyard left Sheriff Donny, Attorney General Brendan Timilty, US Attorney Daniel Bazel, and who knew how many others, a dollar short in their pursuit.

Why hadn't Inspector Whore-shriek given the videos to the cops?

***

Weary and impatient, still bothered by an apartment building inconsistent with Ellen Harding's stature, McGettigan sauntered towards the target's vestibule. Listed by floor were intercom buzzers used to gain entrance. None suggested Ellen Harding was a resident. On the fourth floor, tiny type revealed an odd name: *Asian Flower.*

If you investigated crime and corruption in the construction trades, a whorehouse would be a common enough occurrence. A house-of-ill-repute which identified itself on the intercom must be well connected indeed. Would the brothel's proprietor shoot me? Worse, would they laugh after viewing my sex tape?

Mama-san, she called herself in a gravel voice greeting. Skin wrinkled and a half-smoked cigarette dangling, she giggled at the dumb ass soon to be separated from his salary.

Five minutes and each girl had been trotted out for examination: *Asian Flower* wasn't a haven for underage girls. With Mama's ridicule ringing in my ears, I stood adrift on the crowded sidewalk .

Stubble-dude at the pizza joint stood out, as he watched me exit. Cell in hand, his jaw moved furiously. McGettigan never saw it coming—an early warning system at the Pizza joint.

Crossing the street, my intentions must have been transparent.

Stubble's hand shook as his snub-nosed revolver pointed halfway between the floor and my belt buckle. False bluster clear enough, he snarled, "Gideon coming, man. Gimme tha' fuckin' camera…thas what you do now. Then you run like hell."

Whoever Gideon might be, would stand in the waiting line.

How hard to hit Stubble with the camera was my first priority, because I needed him conscious.

Right hand raised in a signal of surrender, still walking towards him, I pleaded. "Just wanted to get laid, man…got nervous…please, no cops."

Gun lowered as much as it ever would be, my right hand's movement took his gaze along for the ride. McGettigan measured the length of strap holding the Nikon with its telephoto lens. Stubble's right temple took the blow; his resulting muscle twitch fired the pistol into the floor. As he crumpled, the Organism's healthy knee impacted his solar plexus.

Concussed and unable to breathe, I inquired, "Who's Gideon?"

Stubble's eyes rounded up into his head, letting a puddle of drool mix with blood, bits of pepperoni and burned crust.

McGettigan tossed the snub-nose into a cold oven and flipped the door sign to *Closed*.

Gideon be damned, I couldn't leave the City without what I came for. Back across 3rd Avenue, the corner market again allowed me to amble its aisles while watching for Gideon's arrival.

Wearing a porkpie hat over coarse hair, a black leather jacket emerged from a dark sedan and scanned the pizza parlor before making his approach to the apartment with red doors. Moments later, in all likelihood reassured via phone by Mama-san, he re-emerged to fire a half-smoked stogie.

The dark sedan made an illegal U-turn and a door flung open. The driver's voice sounded unruffled. "Whassup?"

Porkpie shrugged; he was a cop making ends meet. Would he answer to Gideon?

No ambulance screamed down the Avenue, so Stubble was being left to arrange his own facial repairs.

A gymnastics studio above the pizza place was my best chance to photograph customers entering *Asian Flower*. Erstwhile Olympians, the petite blonde manager assured me, would be in danger from a strange man, if all he offered was fifty bucks. For two-fifty, I could be grandpa to the kiddies, with a swivel chair to rest my rear on.

The studio sold after-school appointments and a new tribe of aspirants traipsed in, trailing a parent behind. Focused outward, I alternated watching *Asian Flower's* entrance with scanning up and down 3rd for Ellen Harding's approach.

Enthusiasm waned as closing time approached.

As it pulled-up to the curb, a stretch-limo rewarded patience. Clicking fast I shot ten frames as Astor Lawrence exited. Both sides of the street examined once, and then again for good measure, Astor, a trainee criminal, shepherded six young girls into a protective cordon of no-necks. These first girls were similar to eleven others, ordered from an endless chain of supply. Out of view in moments, the future facing these innocents left me wanting to gag.

Briefcase and a half-eaten bag of walnuts in hand, I could've ignored the blonde in the Turkish restaurant's doorway. Despite annoyance and impending exhaustion, Ingrid's impersonation of McGettigan's bride was impossible to ignore. Dressed like *her*, James took photos of a white dress with patch pockets over perky breasts.

A bright blue pocketbook and matching stilettos broke the spell. Peach lip color re-applied, Ingrid did the hair thing.

Still dressed from work, Ellen Harding stood next to Ingrid. Mousey missed the mark; plain did Ellen a disservice. Side-by-side with Ingrid, any man picked my sister-in-law despite ten years more miles on Ingrid's motor.

Martin Cardillo was a charter boat Captain in Miami and heir to billions. Super-models competed for his attention wearing less than a little something. However I assessed the math, Ellen and Martin in love was similar to dividing any real number by zero—*ERROR*. Martin had something else in mind, when he imposed on James to inspect this address. Why the circuitous nonsense?

A powder blue Bentley idled to a stop.

I kept clicking.

As she turned away from Ingrid's disappearing Bentley, Ellen glanced up at the sixth floor. Face color blanched, the AUSA looked like she'd eaten bad köfte. McGettigan captured this evidence of her duplicitous nature in full color. Ellen Harding was up to her ass in something worse than alligators. Halfway up the block, Ellen bought antacids at a pharmacy.

Straight past a tall man with tired eyes, she strolled all the way to UN Plaza on 1st Avenue between 47th and 48th. From deep shadow a stocky figure emerged, navigating a line to intersect the Senator's kid. The shadow said something charming, I presumed, for Ellen waited for him and laughed at his joke. Grabbing his arm, she pulled him towards the lobby.

Like Astor Lawrence exiting the limo, Hub Durant, a man who spent his life in places darker than shadows, glanced around like a dog taking a dump on the Tabriz.

Months ago, Hub walked a tightrope of his own creation, counting on James to rescue Connie, his wife, from kidnappers. Hub had been conflicted, for Connie's kidnapper had been his mentor in the black arts of drugs, illegal flights, espionage, and assassination.

Hub's mentor perished.

In a high stakes game, where blind ambition could rise as far as a President determined, Ellen Harding offered Hub a ticket to the big dance, and the kind of absolution which pardoned sins with the white heat of ultimate power. Would Hub be able to hit the high fastball?

Would Hub remember he never could?

McGettigan felt old antagonism burn. Bit his lip, tasted blood and walked away.

***

Juan Carlos Mosqueda was gone, but his Hoboken love nest teemed with activity. Yellow crime scene tape caught the attention of the commuter crowd.

McGettigan sat at one of five outdoor café tables attended by a blowsy Jersey gal with electric orange hair. My earlier intention— talking to Mosqueda's Asian companion—was caput. I aimed the Nikon each time someone exited the condo's entrance.

Blowsy delivered a follow-on cup of tea with her left hand. A coffee pot occupied her right.

I asked, "Body gone yet?"

Never looking at me, she sighed, leaned over to scratch her ankle and selected a response. "I doe know. Yew goin' to duh siddy? Some kinda turst?"

"Visiting family."

Coffee swirled, a few drops escaping the full pot as she turned, expressive face puzzled. "Dawder? Whatcha doin' lettin' yew dawder livin Jurzee?" Pointing across the street with her chin, she finished. "Dewshbag's still there."

McGettigan sipped tea. With the briefcase open, laptop in place and earbuds plugged-in, detection of a small directional microphone was a remote probability. So far four uniformed cops, two detectives and the ambulance jockeys offered day-to-day chitchat.

Wrestling the gurney down steep steps, its body bag zipped tight, the rear attendant said, "I axe yew—whassup witch *Wiley*? Whakinda name issat? Wiley fukkin' Coyote?"

McGettigan leaned his chair back. Not Wiley fukkin' Coyote—no, I bet the deceased was Wiley fukkin' Hoshall, Phil Spazutta's junior partner. Hoshall was one of three wannabe bad-boys crowded around Henry Linney in Bruce's photos. Henry—Richie Tarrant— Juan Carlos Mosqueda—Wiley Hoshall: Two down, two to go.

Who's killing Henry's posse? Is the enemy of my enemy my friend? Calling Phil Spazutta was a knee-jerk reaction. Shocked I was, when Phil's dulcet tones stabbed my ears.

"Good fukkin' mornin', you murdering bastard. How'd they not indict your ass?"

A recent decline in my sense of humor caused McGettigan to ignore Phil's idea of semi-affectionate banter.

"Phil, I just watched them load your partner into a meat wagon."

Phil thought I was pulling his leg. "Good. More for me when the partners' share gets split."

"Wiley Hoshall, Phil. In Hoboken. In Juan Carlos Mosqueda's condo. Girlfriend's gone. You wanna talk? We both know some things, don't we?" My short-form conversation sympathized and accused, all in a single breath.

"Fukkyu." Phil's accent got thicker under stress. Then he caught on. "Wiley's dead? Really? How? Who's fukkin' Mosqueda?"

Phil's questions all seemed sincere; the way a mother-in-law seemed sincere when slathering passive aggressive mustard on the poor schmuck her daughter married.

"Phil, who's Richie Tarrant?"

"Developer. High-rises onda wadder." The jetstream of a Jurzee conversation was a threat to McGettigan's comprehension. "What was Hoshall doing with Tarrant?"

"Wiley's been hangin' around him." Jurzee accent vaporized, Phil set out to cover his ass. "Tarrant isn't now, and never has been a client of Spazutta & Randall. Good enough sound quality for your tape?"

Phil was speaking on his office phone. I was on a throwaway cell. So the tap, if it existed, would be on his end. It occurred to me: Phil hadn't used my name.

"Let's get together, Phil. Missed you at the big shindig. We can catch up?"

"My sailor-suit wasn't back from the cleaners." The line went dead.

Tarrant built high-rise buildings on the waterfront.

Phil's phones were tapped, nothing new there.

Wiley Hoshall had been acting on his own.

Sailor suit my ass, Phil knew I was taken for a ride on *M*. Has Phil picked a side against me?

***

One of the perks of Julia's recent elevation to partner was James's concurrent ascension from accused murderer to parent of a big boss. In a law firm, where pecking order reigned supreme, my indictment for Hartnett's murder might have derailed Julia's career.

Had Deirdre not understood why an indictment was anathema? Or was it the other way round?

When Julia's extension rung, I offered an engaging tone. "Good morning Jennifer. Any news from my girl?"

Jennifer, unlike everyone else at the firm, stood beside Julia during the Hartnett mess. "Just a short e-mail, Dr. McGettigan. Can I help?"

"Is Sid busy?"

Sid was a first-year associate whose future depended on Julia McGettigan, whose opinion would be influenced by Jennifer McMichael.

"He'll be glad to do an errand."

"Everything on the corporate structure of four entities: *Jellenek Construction Equipment, Tarrant Construction, TEKLOC Capital* and *Aerie Development. Jellenek* will be incorporated in Massachusetts. Or Florida. *Tarrant* is either New York or New Jersey. *TEKLOC*...maybe Delaware. *Aerie*...I've no idea."

Jennifer responded, "Where can I reach you?"

"I'll call tomorrow morning."

CHAPTER 16

Amanda's hatchback looked a mess. Sitting on blocks, tires and wheels were gone. Windows were broken, upholstery slit, the stink of urine baked in the heat. Part of me wished they'd burned it. A short message told Amanda to keep the GTO a little longer.

McGettigan plodded to the downtown office of a name brand rental-car company. Five hours and I'd be home.

Flashing lights sat on my tail. A Rhode Island State Trooper stared with open malevolence, jerking his thumb towards the side of I-195 close to the Massachusetts border. High leather boots strode towards me, strap securing his service weapon loosened.

Paranoia rampaged between the Organism's ears. To McGettigan, the Trooper positioned himself one step further to the rear than normal. I'd been stopped enough to know this wasn't a delusional aberration.

"License and registration, please. Be careful, please."

For certain this wasn't a routine stop for speeding; maybe I was a fugitive from multiple murder charges. Trying to not show the panic I felt, McGettigan handed-over the rental agreement and Florida driver's license with my left hand.

The Trooper retreated to his patrol car. Half expecting reinforcements to arrive, I watched him re-emerge.

"Mr. McGettigan, I've written you up at eighty. Clocked you closer to eighty-five. Maybe you aren't familiar with Providence, being from Florida?"

Troopers were straightforward: No bullshit, just a ticket. Wariness undiminished, mouth drier than Florida sunshine, I stuck to the truth. "My fault. I know the road. Let my mind wander, I guess. Sorry, officer."

Three steps closer, he handed over the citation.

"Confession and penance are what a failed Catholic needs, Mr. James McGettigan. Tonight at seven...at St. Francis Xavier. Find Father Quinn"

He returned to his vehicle and waited for me to pull into traffic. As Rhode Island faded into heavy traffic, his flashing lights remained the sole indication the encounter had been real.

Timmy Timilty was my first thought.

Whether a defrocked Jesuit's sense of the macabre would be overstretched by employing a State Trooper as messenger was a separate issue. For this particular defrocked priest, resident on the FBI's Most Wanted List, hubris knew no boundaries. Had this been Timmy's idea of a cruel practical joke? It would've been just as easy to shoot me dead.

AUSA Daniel Bazel could have sent this message.

Maybe Sheriff Donny Slater.

Both were law enforcement. Both must have friends who'd go to bat for them.

Granville Proost had far-reaching tentacles. Would he even bother with warning me?

If Hub Durant saw me watch his rendezvous with Ellen Harding, would he issue advanced warning of my demise to medicate a bad case of heartburn? Or was Hub the puppeteer whose ominous warning mocked a jester's parti-colored coat, ass's ears and bells?

***

Billy answered his cell before the voicemail message cut in. "James, I got home yesterday. Where are you?"

"Home in an hour, Billy. Could you wait by the bus station payphone at the bridge? I'll call again in ten minutes."

In the right-hand lane going sixty, the bare bones of a dubious plan formed in my head. If the message in Providence came from Timmy, it could just as easily have been accompanied by a bullet. The same applied to Proost. Or even Donny. I was still breathing, so confession was one way to learn more.

A fresh throwaway dialed the payphone. "Billy …it's not over."

Billy was direct. "What d'you want me to do?"

"I've been told to make my confession tonight at St. Francis-Xavier. Can you take Robert's Rigby…settle in the choir balcony by the organ?"

"On the way. Who'll cover the rear exits?" Billy thought like the Vietnam era Marine he was.

My silence was a sufficient lack of eloquence.

"Who else you calling, James?"

"Haven't got that far."

"Who do you think is coming?"

"Maybe Timilty."

"Timilty…the Jesuit hit-man?"

"We went to high school together, don't you remember?"

"I'll get a couple of guys. Get your vest, James."

***

Second pew from the front, in the east wing, was where President and Mrs. Kennedy sat when they attended Sunday Mass. A single worshipper knelt in this pew wearing a light colored business suit.

Members of the Secret Service, as well as other members of the Kennedy family, would sit in the first and third pews, empty this night with the exception of three teenage girls making half-hearted attempts to suppress giggles.

A senior couple worshipped at the shrine of St Joseph; one used a walker, her partner occupied a wheelchair.

Two middle-aged women made the Stations of the Cross. They didn't appear armed or dangerous as they maneuvered, rosaries in hand, to complete a penance assigned in the confessional.

A cluster of eight penitents knelt or sat adjacent to two confessionals created in elegant, carved wood. One appeared to be mother of those teenage girls; her glances of disapproval served as McGettigan's best evidence. Four men in work clothes were

Portuguese fishermen. A couple in their fifties, a brunette and her short-cropped blonde husband, were dressed for summer. A nervous woman in a waitress' uniform engaged in a relentless search for someone or something; her nerves made the Organism jumpy.

Inside the massive main doors, McGettigan wore ceramic body armor manufactured to look like ordinary clothing. Confession and penance was the Rhode Island Cop's suggestion, so I slid next to the nervous woman. I acknowledged her higher priority in the confessional's queue with a polite nod.

The girls' mother entered the confessional.

At the same time a large, well-muscled man in his thirties exited, making the sign of the cross twice in the process. Seconds passed while he stared at me. Then, with neither recognition nor commentary, but head bowed, he walked to the altar rail, knelt long enough to appear worshipful then hurried out the side door. After the door swung shut, I recognized one of Tom Nichols' Trooper friends.

Teenage girls made inappropriate noises as their impatience heightened.

McGettigan anticipated evil intent from churchgoers of every stripe.

Mom emerged. She and the girls disappeared.

On the left side of the nave, the elderly couple exited via the handicap ramp.

None of the Portuguese men moved towards the confessional box, though it was their turn. Looks of confusion were exchanged before first the pleasant brunette, and then her crew cut husband, entered, made their confession and departed.

The nervous woman stood, a raised gun extended towards the departing couple. She held the weapon with confidence born from experience. Yelled louder than necessary in a silent church.

"Promised you'd leave her, you lying creep." The gun's explosion shattered reverential solemnity.

Brunette's head snapped back as she crumpled in a heap. Gunsmoke smelled like a fateful mistake. Echoes bounced off columns fading to silence in the church's shadows. Crew cut's scream came a fraction late. Posture stiff in fabricated distress, he erupted in tears.

From the sacristy behind the altar, a young priest bolted into the nave in a tie-died shirt and jeans. "What's happened?" A stern voice reflected boredom.

There was no Father Quinn resident at St. Francis-Xavier.

Off the main altar, in shadows cast by the raised pulpit's prominence, a large caliber weapon fired. Between the nervous woman and McGettigan, the bullet's passage was felt at every level of sensation. Collapsed on the floor, I watched Nervous Woman direct her Glock towards the darkness. With no sightline, she was already dead if the unseen assailant chose.

Three rapid shots came from the pew where the man in a light colored suit prayed.

No shots came from the choir loft.

Silence descended; shoes pounded towards the injured woman. Portuguese men and the young priest crowded around the wounded brunette. Her husband pressed a cell phone to his ear. Nervous Woman ran to where the heavy caliber shot had been fired, eliminating uncertainty about her mental health. An older priest, not Timmy and not the man who'd lent the rectory phone to a drowned rat, left the confessional door open as he joined those waiting for an ambulance and the police.

None of these people seemed concerned with the second gunman.

Without moving from my knees, I rotated my head towards the choir loft. Billy stood, the Rigby's tripod propped on the railing, but without a target. Billy signaled the Kennedy pew. Light colored suit waved back, concentrating on the dark spaces not thirty feet in front of him behind two imposing columns.

The rabbit-hole, in which McGettigan took cover, was a scene from an unwatchable shoot-em-up.

McGettigan moved on all fours to the confessional. In its center cubicle, where a priest alternated among penitents via a sliding privacy screen, where moments ago the older priest redeemed souls, a micro-recorder sat on the floor. Head turned round, I took inventory of who remained.

The older priest had vanished.

When I reached down for the recording device, a gunshot impacted inches to the left of my spine. Fear drove me to the floor, where my head impacted the doorframe. Frantic return shots rung in my ears, or an overworked imagination.

From a mile away, I heard Billy demand, "Stay down, James."

From behind the pulpit, an automatic rifle could spray devastation. *Don't be any more stupid than you've been*—what Billy should've said, but would've meant. I crawled towards the maze of pews. A setting sun streaked through stained glass apostles; their images expressed disapproval.

"Billy?"

"Here James. You okay?"

"No, but yes." McGettigan snuck a quick look over the pews nearest the altar. Billy and I were alone, all the actors gone from the stage.

The actual pastor of St Francis-Xavier was livid, when Billy inspected the rear rooms of the church. Trussed-up in his own sacristy, bludgeoned vanity seemed the worst of his damage. Billy left without benefit of formal introduction.

No blood stained the stone floor.

Shell casings from the nervous woman's Glock had evaporated.

Just two real shots, the confessional worse for being in the line-of-fire.

In the night air, McGettigan found it hard to breathe. Either shell from the AK-47, identifiable by its characteristic sound, would've broken a rib despite the vest. With a glance back at St Francis-Xavier, Timmy's warning again regurgitated itself: *"This is some twisted shit, James. Think about who's offered you assistance…and who hasn't…and who may yet."* James was almost certain two real bullets, an aide memoire, were fired by a priest seeking redemption of his own making. Almost certain, when occupying a rabbit-hole, was a far cry from complete certainty.

*** *

There were still places on Cape Cod where none but locals ate a meal. Stuck in a shack near a rundown marina in Wareham, on the mainland side of the Bourne Bridge, we were safe and our conversation of no interest to other diners. From the micro-recorder, an unidentifiable woman's voice spoke in a nasal twang. *"Ignore New Jersey. Focus on the milk-maid tending many teats."* For seconds we expected something more, when the recording played an odd combination of background sounds ending in unsatisfactory hiss.

Billy chewed and talked. "Sound like your Jesuit?"

"Elaborate, paranoid drama suits him. He spent like a sailor on actors to perform...for the sole purpose of sending a cryptic message. Maybe Timmy learned more tonight than we did."

Billy stared into space. "So you think the shooter with the AK was separate from the other bullshit? Why would it be that way?"

I explained the last several days and, in the end, nominated Ellen Harding as my best guess of a *milkmaid tending many teats*.

Billy whistled in bewilderment. "I can't make heads or tails of most of it, never mind guessing about milkmaids and teats. What if it's all one big stage? What if the message was the diversion...and you *were* Timilty's target? Or someone else's target?"

Had McGettigan seen what he expected, not concrete reality?

CHAPTER 17

In a recent Board of Directors election, Gillian Orenstein became CEO of *BGFH*.

Donald Hartnett's lone child from three marriages, she held an engineering degree from Stanford plus an MBA from Tuck. An Olympic sailor, she was known as a fierce competitor. Donald Hartnett and now Gillian Hartnett Orenstein—long live the Queen.

Was the Queen seeking vengeance for the King's execution?

Were a Queen's ways the same wanton, violent methods of the fallen King?

***

Last night we dropped my rental and returned to Billy's house.

After hours of talk, I walked four miles home on a two-lane road. No vehicle passed in either direction. Each room examined for signs of unwanted visitors, I secured the Nikon in a closet and its memory card in the crawl space, where spiders were the governing body. Spiders and McGettigan operated under an unwritten treaty: Arachnids lived nowhere but in the crawl space. Spiders weren't trustworthy and shattered this hard won truce as a routine matter—something a Fool should keep in mind.

Residue from bacon and eggs stained a plate. Tea was hot in a mug adorned with a photo of *her* hugging Patrick on his tenth birthday. McGettigan watched the clock tick towards eleven; Granville Proost lived on west coast time.

McGettigan believed the direct approach was best. "Good morning, is Mr. Proost available?"

Without a response, regret pierced an engineer's strategy. What could I offer Granville Proost to alter orders from a monarch? Mercy wouldn't be granted by the Hartnett clan, but there would be a good reason why Proost no longer feared King Donald's exposure as a sociopathic criminal.

"Mr. Proost is traveling. Would you like his voicemail?" Her voice gave off a taint of loyal lie.

McGettigan guessed Proost was listening in his airplane.

"Granville…even spiders break a truce with caution. You sent Mosqueda to retrieve Robert's Power of Attorney. Your henchman strangled Gwyneth Linney in her kitchen. What else do you have in mind, I wonder. And why is Gillian no longer wedded to the preservation of Donald's place in history…or worried about reprisals from those sullied by crimes committed for Donald Hartnett and *BGFH*."

I'd never heard Granville Proost speak. Nevertheless, his wasn't the female voice which replied.

"Time is a great healer, Dr. McGettigan. Time allows preparation. Preparation is everything. Scream your accusations. Release the content from your website. He whom you accuse is dead and buried…not so much as yesterday's news. As to others shown on Mr. Linney's stolen videos, they've also had time to prepare. But you, Dr. McGettigan, have you prepared? Failure to prepare is preparing to fail."

Icy calm was Gillian's hallmark, so it seemed, even though she twisted the meaning of one inspirational quote. McGettigan felt a lump rise in his throat.

"You have no allies, Dr. McGettigan, no one of even small import to our game. I appreciate your athletic background, though baseball is too slow for my tastes. People like you think there will always be another time at bat. Cherish the myth."

One of a Fool's prominent flaws was poking tigers with a stick. In this case, the stick was another of Coach John Wooden's life lessons.

"Gillian…be more concerned with your character than your reputation, because your character is what you truly are, while a nasty bitch is what others think you are."

It was more than a little interesting—and curious—both Timothy Timilty and Gillian Hartnett Orenstein were concerned with my level of attention.

***

The phone rang in Julia's office.

"Good morning Dr. McGettigan, I've got your data…let me grab my notes."

"Jennifer, can you ask Sid to join us?"

Music played until a male voice said, "Good morning, sir. Nice to speak with you again." Sid was frightened his research would be inadequate.

"Let's hear what you found."

McGettigan had generated guesses, which were far worse than assumptions. Assumptions wouldn't replace preparedness, not in a battle with Gillian and Granville.

"*Jellenek* is a Delaware Corporation owned by Kristian Solberg and his sister, Ingrid Solberg Jellenek. Rand Jellenek is President and minority shareholder."

Sid waited for a non-existent comment, then continued.

"*Tarrant* is a New Jersey corporation owned by Richard Tarrant. Tarrant is President."

Another few beats of silence.

"*TEKLOC* is incorporated in Delaware…its majority owner is Astor Lawrence. *Lawrence Foods* is a minor shareholder, as are other members of the Lawrence family. Astor Lawrence is President.

Aerie is a Florida corporation owned by Jill Stoddard. Ms. Stoddard is President."

McGettigan filed away the first expected fact: Rand Jellenek told lies. Rand said Ingrid wasn't involved in his business—as if owning the damned company wasn't an involvement. Sid's tremulous delivery had been full of restrained excitement, and Lawrence was an iconic name in the business world. My money bet the Lawrence's reputation juiced the young lawyer.

"Anything unusual about the companies?"

"Well…I checked the relationship of these companies to each other and to other corporations. *TEKLOC*, *Aerie* and *Tarrant* together own *Rivers Nest Towers*…where the crane accident happened. *Jellenek* owns the crane. There's speculation in the *Wall Street Journal* of Mr. Jellenek being exposed to criminal charges."

Bored with the obvious, I asked, "Anything else, Sid?"

"Rivers Nest is out of money. Subcontractors have filed liens and lawsuits. *TEKLOC* has missed their last two contributions of cash. Gossip columns in Palm Beach say Mr. Astor Lawrence has been cutoff by his mother. Whole thing's a mess."

Meredith cutoff Astor? Astor remained a trust-fund boy, forced to live on a stipend's leash in the twilight of his thirties. If Astor didn't control mammoth wealth, well, everything I knew required more thought.

"Is that everything?"

I sensed beads of sweat falling on expensive carpet. Sid gulped, then spit it out.

"A very small shareholder in *Jellenek* is a shell company thrice removed from *BGFH*, but listed among dozens and dozens of *BGFH* subsidiaries."

Gillian Hartnett had forged a formal alliance with Ingrid and Kristian Solberg. I shouldn't believe it, but couldn't doubt it. What were my wife's siblings, these idle rich dilettantes, playing at? Ill temper replaced reason.

I heard Gwyneth's heart beating everywhere.

A sickened feeling crept over the Organism, which, like a hound baying at the moon, screamed muted accusations: Gwyneth died to satisfy petulance and gluttonous whimsy.

A Fool seethed at his errors.

Not unlike the last go-round with a Hartnett, my children were again exposed. To prepare meant first to protect those I cherished. To make preparations required the assistance of Charlie Hamilton.

I heard the high-pitched whine of a metal lathe, when Charlie answered. "What you working on, old friend?" My faux-Tennessee drawl was unworthy of comment.

"Jus' nice to be workin' Boss. Standin'on my feet not feelin' like to keel over."

Charlie had both hips replaced in prior months: One surgery performed before he saved my children's lives last November, and another soon after the New Year.

"Ever seen Africa, Charlie?" Charlie and my kids were close. He wouldn't like this sentence.

"How many there be?"

Did he mean friend or foe? "Just Julia and Patrick. Could they visit with you and your bride for a while…like before?"

"Where and when?" Charlie wouldn't mince words.

"I'll send a plane to *Island Home* this afternoon. Or would *McGhee* be better?"

"DKX be fine, it's quiet these days. I'll take five with me. Regular rates, Boss?"

Regular rates were five hundred a day per man, although I wasn't purchasing mercenaries. Money wasn't sufficient for Charlie to protect my kids, but it was necessary.

"Fine. I'll have Sat phones on board for you. Call Julie, when you're two hours from landing. Thanks, Charlie."

Four hours passed before final arrangements were concluded: One charter capable of non-stop travel to Harare, Zimbabwe where Julie said she and Patrick were staying; a second would fly me from Hyannis to Palm Beach. The cost, at over a quarter million, required conference calls with suspicious bankers as well as wire transfers to guarantee the flights.

***

Hyannis dropped below on a cloudless day. As the jet crossed between Nantucket and Martha's Vineyard on its climb-out, then went feet-dry above New York City, the Organism was transfixed by a feeling of déjà vu.

Trepidation, doubt and panic had been the first emotions during the early days of my test of wills with Donald Hartnett—in fact before I knew Donald Hartnett was my adversary. Hopeless, sad and determined followed like soldiers marching in rank. Sadness morphed to despair. Hopeless turned to bloodlust. Determination to save my children emerged as a false god to be worshipped and a series of retributions to be indulged. Though they deserved their fate, McGettigan reveled in the deaths of Hartnett's profligate trio of hired hands: Dragon Lady, Pipe-man and Spy-dude. I gave them nicknames to make killing them easier to stomach. When the situation in a hard rock tunnel ripened to kill or die, the Organism felt the thrill of executing an executioner. McGettigan's devolution to the level of madmen, whose humanity melted in a mist of blood-coated currency—gold, elections, or entire countries without distinction—defiled my own short-lived death.

Nausea returned.

My rabbit-hole closed in.

Gillian's concern shouldn't be McGettigan's lack of preparation, though her accusation was valid. She was a new Queen, as I'd been a neophyte crushed under her father's stone wheel. The Organism's failings and contradictions might be unattractive, but I'd learned through punishing experience: Events controlled Queens more than Queens controlled events.

***

Ryan must have tossed the camera from around his neck? Where was it now? What would its memory card reveal, if I could find or steal it?

If McGettigan had not been conscripted aboard *M* and her crew of murdered young women, things would be different, and I'd still possess the DVDs taken from Raoul Dupree. Which was why my inspired conclusion—Ryan's Canon was important and Jill Stoddard wasn't innocent—could prove critical. Jill wasn't a struggling young businesswoman or a nice person. Jill Stoddard never went to the landfill for a futile joust with an environmental black-knight. Her purpose had been darker.

I found Julian Rommery at home, his monologue describing the accident's aftermath of no interest. By his account, surgery restored Jill to a satisfactory level of attractiveness—*satisfactory* being Julian's word—and Ryan seemed clear of amputation.

Nothing McGettigan witnessed would support Frankie McShane's death as suspicious. "Julian, have they determined cause of death for the dozer operator?"

"Wish I could have killed the bastard myself." Julian suffered politician's disease—no governor between brain and mouth.

"Where's Ryan, Julian? I'd love to stop by and give him my best."

"Why didn't you stop them, McGettigan? Just kids with no business on the landfill. You took too long to call 911."

Julian Rommery shrunk to the size of an insect. In lime colored pants drawn too tight by a white belt overrun by forty pounds of hard earned suet, his reputation as a dickhead was well deserved .

I reached the door before turning back. "Jill's not interested in Ryan. Never was."

Ryan had been too injured to retrieve the camera, if it went missing during the lad's mismatch with a bulldozer. The same could be said for Jill, though she wasn't transported in the same ambulance. Maybe EMTs collected the Canon. Maybe it was lying by the fence, or recovered when the dozer turned right side up. In which case Raoul Dupree—*Jabba the Hut* of the landfill set—possessed its memory card.

Golden Rhino was a high-end flesh pit where steaks and bare titties were both served medium rare. Approaching *Rhino* I was reminded— a year ago Manuel fixed-it so the thug who buried me alive took two .44 slugs to the chest in *Rhino's* parking lot. So McGettigan held no illusions: The moral high ground would be empty, when this mess was brought to a conclusion.

Like a beached whale, Raoul sat at a back table wearing-out a Porterhouse, two baked potatoes and a gallon of creamed spinach. His waitress, a brassy Latina, wore black lederhosen whose suspenders covered naked, plastic boobs. Redheaded with jet-black roots, she dawdled by his left side in a bent-over position. He lifted his left hand, which lingered to touch the skin of her right breast. Between his first and second fingers were three glassine baggies.

McGettigan snagged the dope and lowered himself into a chair.

Face rearranged into pissed-off, she demanded in husky Spanish, "Give it here, motherfucker."

This high-class retort illustrated the difficulty hiring good people at a place like *Golden Rhino*. "Tell her to go away, Raoul."

Dupree grunted, trying to re-arrange his mental processes. "Later, Chiquita, we'll take ice cream home."

Chiquita muttered something uncomplimentary; hoisted a tray of dirty dishes.

Raoul smiled, a sneer encrusted with sincerity. "Wanna eat?"

"More than blank DVDs are what I want." I speared a chunk of Raoul's garlic bread, my accusation blind conjecture. "You still got the kid's Canon? Sold it? What?" Half a cow was headed towards Dupree's mouth, when a Fool added, "You interested in being public-spirited...or should Manuel's Sheriff buddies shoot you in the nose?"

Everyone who skirted the law in Palm Beach knew Manuel, who sat atop the food chain of men with guns. Raoul Dupree knew McGettigan was close with Martin Cardillo, for whom Manuel worked under an exclusive arrangement.

"Don't matter what you do, man." His jaw masticated beef while admitting another shovelful of spinach. "Get nothin' from me." Raoul raised his hand to signal Chiquita, who straightened her spine and bounced away on stilettos with blinking lights along the heels.

So the DVDs were blank.

And Ryan's Canon held, or had held, something more frightening than Manuel's violent nature.

What would push my corpulent tablemate to be more definitive— or make me believe him?

"So who got buried, Raoul? I can excavate the site. Either your bosses will do it to get out front of a huge scandal, and sell you down the river as a scum-sucking shitbag…or Commissioner Rommery will send a hundred Deputies armed with shovels. Their real job will be setting your appointment with a lethal injection. Sure as shit you'll die…or you tell me, then run very far away."

A long swallow of red wine gyrated his Adam's Apple and set multiple chins vibrating. Words escaped a corner of his mouth, like a mob movie. "I need cash…full immunity. Running's expensive."

Raoul was disingenuous; buying time was the go-to plan for the intellectually challenged. Raoul would make a simple choice: Die today for sure; or be put to death for murder seventeen years from now.

***

Tonight, in part because of my work for Eco-waste LLC, the main gate would be a formidable hurdle. So a bolt cutter became the tool of the moment. Razor tipped, the fence was neither electrified nor in range of CCTV. I cut a two-foot by two-foot section and wiggled underneath. Night-vision goggles and a directional listening device would serve my needs.

Forty-five minutes searching produced no result.

Steps retraced, wire ties attached to reinstall the piece of fence, at least my intrusion should go un-noticed until I left town. Next stop would represent a higher degree of difficulty.

B&E wasn't one of my strengths.

Catching frauds and exposing corruption rarely required burglar's tools—and the Organism was allergic to jails. On the plus side, petty crime in Palm Beach was rampant and went more or less went unpunished. Raoul's place on the first floor, one flight up from garages which underpinned every unit, caused a disturbing thought to flash like strobe lights—what if the camera isn't here?

Red and blue. Blue and white. Multiple colors made for a carnival atmosphere. Cruisers arrived with screeching brakes as McGettigan reached Raoul's open door. No way down, not without being stopped, questioned and accused, I climbed to the third floor where three apartments were uninhabited and police radios were less about McGettigan and more concerned with Raoul Dupree.

Two deputies pounded up the stairs. One yelled, "Door's open."

Prone on the concrete walkway above, I watched two additional deputies and two plainclothes cops aim their weapons.

A resident in his pajamas called out. "Heard someone rousting the place, but you fellas are too late."

From Raoul's apartment a Deputy yelled. "Place's a wreck. Gonna take a while."

From behind me, a muffled tap-tap-tap on the window intruded. A cherubic face pressed against window glass through sheer curtains. Maybe ten or eleven, her world-weary warrior's stare came from huge lavender eyes. If she opened the door and screamed, McGettigan would be inconvenienced, if not screwed. Holding an index finger to my lips, open wallet extended towards her, she fixated on the gold badge.

Risking another look down, the suit nearest the unmarked sedan was in full profile. A shaggy coiffure draped his face, when he spoke to an unseen occupant of the back seat. Directional microphone still attached, I heard Shaggy say, "Not like it's some random burglary, Manuel. Who besides McGettigan is looking for this turd?"

"Knock down doors. It's what you do best." An ironic chuckle punctuated Manuel's instruction.

Moment's later I heard a first strident demand: "Federal officers. Open the door." A quick glance showed Shaggy and his accomplice conducting a door-to-door search.

Turning to Lavender Eyes, I pointed to myself—then pointed to her door. Dour expression unaltered, she left the window and cracked the door. McGettigan slithered through the opening. Extended arms cradled a girl who needed a hug. Rocking back and forth, I smoothed her hair. Murmured a children's poem in Spanish.

The cops were gone.

Shaggy went through the motions—banging on doors, not knocking them down. No one opened their door at the insistence of closed fists and raised voices. These apartment blocks housed young people with no cultural imperative to love law enforcement. When they got to our door, we held each other tight underneath her mother's clothes in the bedroom closet. Her body trembled, but she made no sound. Footsteps retreated as soon as they finished beating the door like a Reggae drummer.

I pressed my finger to her lips. "I need to make sure they're gone."

Fingernails dug into my forearms.

On my return, I turned on the bedroom light to find her where I'd left her, head turned to the closet wall in a pitiable sort of acceptance. I knew the feeling—if you didn't look, maybe nothing bad would happen. Or it wouldn't hurt as much, if you didn't see it coming.

I insisted she call me James.

She whispered, "Pilar is my name. Like my gramma."

McGettigan needed no degree in Child Psychology to gauge her trauma. "What's wrong, sweetheart?"

In the bathroom a body lay contorted, head against the rim of the tub. A black vinyl kit's contents strewn on tile streaked with vomit, a filthy needle protruded from a vein. A pulse was evident, but weak.

"Pilar, is this your grandmother?" The unconscious woman in the hooker's camisole and short-shorts was fifty going on ninety based on thirty years of track marks.

Pilar wept without speaking.

"Have you called 911?"

Pilar shook her head. "I called momma after George left, like I'm s'posed to do."

"Who's George?"

"Gramma's boss." Pilar understood George's real relationship to her gramma.

"Is mommy coming home?"

"No." Tears flooded her cheeks.

"Where's mommy's number?"

Temporary refuge from Shaggy the Fed was what I needed, when this episode began. Shaggy, who may have been Frankie McShane's executioner, was a hound dog with McGettigan's scent in his nose.

Now there was a child to protect.

My gold shield was realistic, but not real. I was stuck sorting gramma's trip to detox or a grave. Already McGettigan wanted to backhand mommy for leaving a kid in a position like this.

The living room held cardboard boxes full of cell phones, laptops, iPods, iPads, cameras, briefcases, pocketbooks and wallets—enough to run a high-end yard sale or a part time fencing operation.

"Where does mommy work?"

Pilar showed me phone numbers affixed to the fridge, written in large print with a red marker. "She works at Avis during the day...a waitress at night."

Pilar ran to an end table not stacked with stolen stuff. Returned with an 8x10 glossy of mommy standing next to Raoul Dupree. Mommy was Chiquita. I called 911 and gave Chiquita's address and a description of the circumstances. Called Chiquita, got her voicemail.

"Chiquita, your mother overdosed. Ambulance on the way. Get home ASAP."

Chiquita's electronic stash wouldn't go un-noticed.

"Pilar is coming with me. County will take her, if I leave her here. Tell Raoul...James McGettigan says hello."

McGettigan shouldn't be such a predictable do-gooder. Pilar would be safe with Children's Services, but I was a bit sensitive about disappointing a kid.

One box held more than fifty cameras—four Canons. One was scratched, like it bounced around a dump. Battery still charged, the memory card had been removed. McGettigan theory: This memory card held photos of dead Asian girls, the ones I'd seen on a New York sidewalk outside a Turkish restaurant and Mama-san's cathouse.

Raoul must have ignored the listening device in his office; his tactical error brought Shaggy the Fed and Manuel, my new question-mark, to his apartment. Raoul could thank his survival instincts—having hidden the Canon amidst Chiquita's stolen booty may keep him alive and out of police custody. Or not.

Gathering clothes for Pilar, we left the door open.

Avery Reynolds' house smelled unoccupied. Near enough to June, my friend and next-door neighbor departed Marsh Landing for summer in Oregon.

McGettigan's empty lot awaited a decision to rebuild.

Carried on the breeze, and McGettigan's imagination, were the odors of loss and the stink of a King's whimsy. A different aroma resided in the bedspread where Gus the St. Bernard, my frequent winter walking partner, slept. Avery and James loved Gus. We loved our wives and shared the difficulty of forging a future without them.

Pilar begged me to sleep on Gus' side, beside her. When her breathing indicated sleep, I moved to the living room couch with Avery's 30-06 close to hand.

CHAPTER 18

Light hadn't touched the morning sky as I pondered Ryan's camera and the evidence contained on its memory card. Burgers and fries, washed down by a milkshake, had been Pilar's late night snack of choice. Twelve ounces of grease tormented me as I walked-off abdominal discontent.

If Asian women were buried in the landfill, and Ryan's pictures proved it so, had an FBI agent eliminated Frankie in a cover-up? Could McGettigan intuit Ryan and Jill were next to perish, or were they on the side of Frankie's killer?

If next in line to die, why weren't they dead?

McGettigan's stomach rumbled. Was this a protest by the grease or the Organism staking a claim for more healthy sustenance?

Less than a quarter-mile and the Village office was visible in the shadow of large trees and the Marsh Landing clubhouse. Windows lit, a blue Volvo was parked where it could be missed. The car belonged to Marcia Whooten; the same Marcia I'd been told no longer worked for the Village; the same Marcia I'd hired, mentored and who never called to say goodbye.

She looked up in astonishment at her former boss. Uncertain how to react, she babbled and sniffled, hands searching for a tissue.

"Dr. Mac...oh God what must you think of me. They told me I couldn't call you, couldn't tell you anything."

By this time I'd crossed the small room, reversed a chair and sat waiting for her emotions to find a level of equanimity.

"Who are *they*? What's going on I can't know about?"

Marcia made short work of calculating loyalty. "I was called to Mr. Bagby's office in the clubhouse." Marcia frowned for a moment. "Do you know Mr. Bagby's the new club Chairman?"

Sterrit Bagby was Meredith Lawrence's personal lawyer.

"Mr. Bagby was there with Agent Swain of the FBI. Mr. Bagby said the Village would be cooperating with the Bureau in an investigation I could know nothing about. He instructed me to come into the office at four in the morning…and be gone by seven. *Pay the bills, Marcia, handle the critical stuff…*that's what he told me. I'm on sick leave. Agent Swain is my temporary replacement. I don't have a clue what she's doing here."

"Do our security people know she's FBI?"

"I'm sorry…nobody says anything to me."

"Does Swain spend time at Meredith's house?"

Marcia shook her head—the body part she buried in the sand. Who could blame her?

"Keep doing what you're told, Marcia. No more, no less. It'll work itself out."

"But…"

"No buts. No questions. No answers. Don't believe everything you'll hear."

***

The phone rung once. Like Chiquita was holding it at the ready.

"Chiquita…you there? How's your mother? Pilar will want to know."

Spanish flowed like boiling oil. "Name's not Chiquita, you prick. Bring my baby-girl home."

McGettigan didn't like her tone. It reflected a person at the edge, looking down and thinking it wasn't so far to fall.

"How's you mother?"

"Momma died."

"What'd she die from?"

A new voice switched to English. George-the-Pimp explained with dramatic emphasis added.

"Huge fuckin' overdose…thas what the docs say. I say you did her…like you did the billionaire dude. Momma didn' have nuff dope killa cockroach."

"You didn't give her enough dope to kill a cockroach?" Silence greeted the obvious truth. "Why am I talking to you, George?"

"You bring the cunt's whelp and two grand...pay me for my trouble. Get what you want, huh?"

"Not yours to give. Belongs to Raoul."

George near to shouted, "Raoul just as dead as gramma after last night. Maybe you bring three grand...or else."

McGettigan was a newcomer to a violent world, where human life was spent with the abandon of hyper-inflating third-world currencies. But I'd been lied to by the very best. Raoul wasn't dead; he was standing next to a pimp with an outsized sense of himself.

"The Publix at PGA and A1A. Three this afternoon. I'll be there with the cash. You bring the camera's memory card."

In rough Spanish the 911 operator heard McGettigan say, "A guy gonna rob Publix PGA 'roun tree. Be with a fine lookin' redhead."

McGettigan's Jamaican accent was piss-poor.

***

Like acid dripping on skin, secrets burned deeper the longer they sat un-neutralized. A big enough secret could burn bone.

Meredith Lawrence's home wasn't the largest in Marsh Landing, but it contained twenty thousand square feet of living space within attractive architecture. No one would ever accuse Meredith of bad taste. Constructed of stucco and acres of rough-cut stone, accented by a slate and copper roof, the building was proportioned to disguise its size. Elaborate gardens were a precious link to her past. It was in the garden I'd find Meredith, even this early, if she was in Florida at all.

No walls or gates permitted to front, or surround, homes in Marsh Landing, McGettigan's unobstructed view of two well-dressed security guards, standing by a stretch limo, demanded a re-think. Two others lingered at each end of the multi-car garage. Attached to the front door with super-glue, an additional twosome's professional stature put me off.

Six armed security types—how many more roamed the house and garden?

No weapons were visible. No faces were identifiable.

Meredith would protect her secrets.

McGettigan abandoned his plan to confront her, turning instead to the golf course where I would release the Organism's mind while returning to Pilar.

***

For enough time to realize its absurdity, I considered asking Marianna to watch over Pilar. Then made sure small fry was showered and neat-as-a-pin. My newest friend was happy to describe her family—an Auntie in Delray and half a dozen relatives scattered south to Lauderdale.

Auntie was already familiar with Pilar's plight, when I explained its exigent circumstances.

Pilar wasn't shocked to be dropped at Auntie's home near the beach, by James with the gold badge. She told bleached blond Auntie about sleeping in James's big bed. Auntie, dressed and carrying herself with a marked bearing, whisked the girl into another room. I waited while Auntie conducted a thorough examination; suspicion was a permanent state-of-mind for anyone who read the newspaper. With another of Pilar's hugs and a guarded smile from Auntie, McGettigan drove away.

Auntie hadn't been allowed to inspect the gold badge.

***

Who was being guarded at Meredith's manse?

For a man struggling to pay better attention, it was a critical question.

Marsh Landing Security wouldn't be a foolproof source. Owner's vehicles were fitted with barcodes; people not so much. If Meredith, or any resident with a chauffeur, elected to come and go without being identified, the bar code guaranteed admission. It made operating a security force difficult, because the very wealthy possessed odd ideas about which benefits they were entitled to.

I called the guard shack anyway. The woman officer told me Lawrence vehicles made several round-trips today, but were now safe and sound within the Village.

"No, Dr. McGettigan," she said, when asked whether specific ID of Lawrence family members was confirmed.

Village Security wasn't convinced an ex-Mayor should request such information. Marsh Landing's Resident Directory, a classified document, listed Meredith's private phones and e-mail. I began with the house in Bermuda, which was bottom rung on her ladder of personal priorities: a servant answered. Bar Harbor was next: a pleasant voice was identifiable as Meredith's confidential secretary. Where LuAnne was, Meredith would be. I hung up.

Process of elimination complete, whoever came in the limo was here to meet Astor.

Who traveled with so many linebackers?

Who would arrive so early in the morning?

Nothing of the happenings at Meredith's estate comported with the way things were done in Marsh Landing.

***

Publix was less than four miles up the road. More than a half-hour would pass before George the Pimp should pull into the lot. Slumped behind the rental's wheel, sunglasses and Red Sox hat covering my face, McGettigan composed an exit plan should things go wrong. Ex-Reverend Timilty would be proud.

Six minutes till three: no cops. no Pimp.

On the dot, the lot filled with ear-splitting bass. A '77 Monte Carlo in gold paint and flames bounced up and down in front of a '63 Impala SS Convertible doing the low-rider bob and weave. The convertible driver's bling blotted out the sun. Surrounded by the orthodontic perfection of five *Low-rider Girls*, straight from the magazine's glossy pages, leather bras matched bikini-shorts fronted by three-inch chrome belt buckles. Three muscled men in baggy shorts and wife-beaters, tats everywhere, exited the Monte Carlo and strolled to the convertible pushing a reluctant fourth. Raoul Dupree, dressed all in black, oozed uncontrollable flop sweat generated by mindless dread.

George and the babes on stilettos headed inside.

The remaining entourage, with the exception of Raoul, made no attempt to conceal their weapons. Besides no cops and no sign of George carrying a felonious .45 auto, the Foolish was at ease. Minutes stretched to a half-hour. Imagination fired-up every possible combination of events, but not the re-emergence of the six carrying hoagies and three plastic bags of groceries. Music blared. The two-car motorcade moved with the addition of undercarriage lights synched to the music. Turned north on A1A. Left on Juno Isles dropped the covering traffic and McGettigan was forced to hang back. Right on Ellison Wilson suggested they would cross the Donald Ross Bridge. Regretting the distance between us, the light at Donald Ross would catch me. I accelerated, needing to maintain a visual ID on Prosperity, Old Dixie, or Military. When this produced no Impala or tricked-out Monte Carlo, a sane man would conclude they jumped onto I-95.

A sane man would've gone home.

A less than sane man headed for Auntie's crib. In a miraculous fit of wisdom, McGettigan stopped for hot tea and a doughnut; the hot tea's temperature a bit cooler than my temper.

***

Earlier it seemed logical. To cover-up the wholesale slaughter of Asian sex slaves required the elimination of Jill Stoddard and Ryan Rommery.

Assumptions being rife with potential flaws, I decided to subject the Jill and Ryan premise to a step-by-step re-examination. To begin, Frankie knew bodies were buried in the landfill; he was now dead. Raoul walked around with identical knowledge; he'd departed to meet Frankie in hell. Elemental progression suggested Jill and Ryan couldn't deny their identical knowledge of the women's fate; ergo they would soon be keeping Frankie and Raoul company.

At Rommery's door in late day heat, a rumble of thunder followed a burst of lightning five miles distant. Curtains over sidelights pulled aside, Ryan blinked, trying to wake up.

"Whaddya want?"

"Ryan, I'm James McGettigan. Your father asked me to look into what happened at the landfill. Just before the dozer came after you, did you throw the camera away?"

Ryan looked puzzled, as if his answer involved astrophysics.

"Come on, Ryan. What happened to your camera? Will you testify about what you saw?"

Long steel pins stuck-out of the plaster cast covering Ryan's upper body. He remembered what it felt like to be hunted, what it felt like to empty his bladder in fear, and pray in a way he'd never prayed before. What were his exact thoughts as he lay convinced of approaching death?

Flimsy lace curtains released from his fingers, a gap of inches was a canyon never to be crossed.

McGettigan could explain the process of recovery to Ryan Rommery. Could tell him a year would be inadequate and a lifetime insufficient. Could suggest therapy. Could argue hitting back would guarantee satisfaction. Could insist revenge was a dish best served cold. I could do all those things, but Ryan wouldn't listen. So I stuck to basics.

"They're gonna kill you, Ryan. You're worth nothing to them. Jill doesn't care…she used you."

Jill may have cared, but it seemed less a likelihood with each passing moment. Ryan Rommery was alone without allies, an innocent, if pathetic, sitting duck.

Jill Stoddard didn't answer her home or cell phone. Her office occupied the third floor of a six-story building in Golden Bear Plaza. *Aerie Development* wasn't listed in the directory. *Stoddard Development* was. A Fool rang the bell. Wilson Stoddard appeared, scowling as he saw me.

"Can I help you, James?"

"Looking for Jill, Wilson."

I'd not selected Stoddard Development as the architect for the Marsh Landing clubhouse renovation. Wilson and Jill had thought Meredith would fix their selection. Hard feelings were close to the surface.

Wilson's face screwed itself into a twisted pose. Part pained. Part ironical. Part inscrutable. He turned without uttering a word.

McGettigan concluded with finality: Jill didn't care about Ryan, so maybe I shouldn't care about her.

***

Who cared about any of them, when the Jupiter Hammerheads were taking on the Clearwater Threshers? A cold beer and hot dog sweetened my mood. Six hundred fellow baseball nuts cheered these kids, the vast majority of whom would never play in a major league stadium.

Sitting a single row below the press box, I scanned for Martin Cardillo. Going to the Cardillo estate would have been more productive, but doubts about Martin lingered. McGettigan lectured the other parts of me: Friendship should trump infantile suspicion. Sounds good they responded, but why had Martin misled me about a romance with Ellen Harding?

I'd have preferred to drink my beer in the company of Robert Linney, even if he wouldn't know me. With Robert, I'd have been able to conjure memories of better times. Better times could wrap me in *her* arms. I encouraged my mind to drift away.

A long home run jolted me. The Threshers scored five runs in the top of the sixth. Light had abandoned a starlit sky. Thunderclouds hurled lightning bolts a few miles west. Indigestion made me uncomfortable. Time for an old man to beat the storms home, except there was no home to go to.

CHAPTER 19

From A1A, taking the left turn towards Marsh Landing's guard shack was a robotic result of repetition. Genuine comfort was derived from the shack's overhead spotlights, when my car tripped the pressure switch.

The female guard offered a limp salute.

McGettigan's heightened attention to detail noticed new Village uniforms. This new, forest green, garb reminded me too much of fatigues. The blonde's hair, tied back in a bun under an ordinary ball-cap, made her look like a paratrooper. The pleated blouson, with no buttons but an open half-zipper, accentuated heavy breasts. Altogether too strident, too military. Even the semi-automatic pistol…Jesus Q Christmas. At fifteen feet, the uniform disappeared. I saw Chiquita's arms outstretched, experienced hands affixed to a gun.

McGettigan's Ghost made a noise like a squirrel dying.

All my conscious parts fixated on a line drawn from my eyes to Chiquita's 9mm. The suppressor's length narrowed the distance between us to nothing.

Muted flame erupted.

The sloped windshield fractured, but failed to shatter. Behind the suppressor her face registered disbelief and she fired again. A hole appeared inches above my head while bullet and glass fragments recoiled through the backseat.

A panicked Organism slammed the accelerator; yanked the steering wheel left. Impact tossed a rag doll into and through the shack's doorway. No part of the Organism's reflexes were able to brake the car to a halt. Plowing a second time into her mangled body, the shack's roof collapsed on the hood. Silence broken by steam hissing from the radiator—back up, James—was the instruction received from another planet, from another place and time, not from a man riveted on how two bullets could have impacted the Organism's face, yet McGettigan was unscathed.

Adrenaline pumped full throttle.

A finger palpated Chiquita's carotid for an imperceptible pulse. Words formed without sound on her colorless lips. Questions rattled in my skull like Chiquita's second bullet pinballed through the back seat.

Where were the real Marsh Landing guards?

Where was Raoul?

Or George the Pimp and his muscle-bound posse?

Survival was the collective priority for all four of us.

Taking her weapon was an admission from the old McGettigan, and a practical certainty for my newer self. I pointed it at her nose, semi-automatic vibrating with uncertainty. What did Jesuits say about taking a life? How did Timmy do it? Thunder rolled over Marsh Landing and the sky opened; the devil's response made eloquent feedback.

George the Pimp was with Astor; it made some sense, when good sense was nowhere to be found.

Astor Lawrence wasn't his mother's son.

A Fool laughed, telling me to quit unproductive speculation and plan for the opposition's arrival before rain soaked McGettigan to the skin. Perhaps an ambulance for Chiquita, was McGettigan's pithy retort.

Would one ambulance be adequate by night's end?

Twenty seconds into the storm I was in danger of electrocution. As I reached the Club's office a transformer sprayed fireworks a hundred feet in every direction. Parking lot lights winked and faded from useful to irrelevant. Two Village guards were propped-up, cheek by jowl, in chairs—sleeves rolled up, needles inserted. Pulses steady, the scene was too familiar.

This wasn't the signature of George the Pimp.

Needles withdrawn, I stood transfixed as rainwater puddled on hardwood. If the drug was the one used on James and Charanya, an hour would bring them to full consciousness. Their calls for help would be useless to James McGettigan, whose need was more immediate. A quick check of office computers found Marsh Landing's extensive CCTV network offline.

Rain sluiced off my hair as I crossed the parking lot towards the cellar entrance. A series of kicks gained no advantage against a new steel door. Drenched and bedraggled, my next best option was Avery's house, where the kitchen door was unlocked, swinging back and forth in a gusty wind. In a catcher's crouch, protested by the Organism's orthopedic maladies, lightning lit the kitchen brighter than Fenway Park. Chased by the smell of singed trees, the deluge drummed harder on the roof. A party of one was seated at the kitchen table, profile facing the door as if anticipating my examination. I recognized him from somewhere, but couldn't force recollection into a name.

Chiquita's automatic pointed, I demanded, "Stay put."

Sweat mingled with rainwater and dripped off my nose. If there was one intruder, why not two or four others? Panning the gun back and forth I moved one cautious step at a time in rhythm with darkness swallowing the room in each lightning bolt's aftermath. At the sink, I stopped to pull on garish yellow gloves. A broom handle protruded from the rear of his suit jacket beneath two small holes in his skull. A nondescript watch told time its owner no longer possessed.

What about this linebacker's job had been worth dying for?

Why prop-up this pawn? This seemed important to understand, because McGettigan held a similar rank. Ears strained, but located no sound close to human.

A short hallway took forever. McGettigan's nerves made movement emulate paralysis. I swung the gun into the laundry room, prepared to fire upon one false move by the dryer. The den was paneled in rich, dark wood. The smell of stale cigar was a legacy of my absent neighbor, not my opposition.

Down a second hallway the dining room was undisturbed. Not the Master Bedroom. Straddled on the exercise bike was the great bulk of Raoul Dupree, lashed in-place with electrician's wire-ties arranged in the manner of professionals. Most of his face was gone. Bowels empty, the hardwood floor installed months ago by Avery and McGettigan over a pleasant weekend, was covered in an ungodly soup. I couldn't reach the body. To step in this abomination would be wrong on many levels, including the one where self-incrimination resided. Avery's dead bride would haunt the Ghost for layering aquamarine bath towels to bridge mayhem's aftermath.

Raoul's wallet was of no interest. His hands sported three diamond rings. Around his neck a rectangular black stone hung on rawhide—some kind of Haitian talisman—Raoul's killer must have thought it unwise to pilfer a religious artifact. McGettigan recognized its alternative purpose and slipped it off Raoul's head. Chicken shears removed the other item I would need.

Meredith's home—where critical action occurred while I lollygagged with dead men—would have to await a complete search.

Impossible to avoid, the living room filled me with dread along its trail of drying blood. Several sets of footprints imprinted the thick rug alongside drag marks. Paused outside the first bedroom, I gulped air in preparation. A pink top sheet was stained deep red in the rough outline of a torso. Sheet peeled back by gloved fingers, McGettigan's involuntary scream caromed off walls until stored breath was expended.

I stared at the beheaded man.

One part of me, perhaps the Fool, wanted to know whether he'd been dead before the blade severed his neck. McGettigan was left to look for identifying marks. Irritated by something dripping on my head, eyes rotated upwards. I tried not to believe Manuel's head rested on the post above his body, mouth stuffed with his testicles.

Dry heaves continued until all McGettigan's several parts were exhausted.

Disemboweled and mutilated while alive, then beheaded, then festooned with the symbols of his manhood, like a bad LSD trip images from a staccato slideshow were hurled at me: Manuel's head; Chiquita's bullets in transit through my skull; Juan Carlos Mosqueda falling through air; Michael Madson's brains staining my shoes; a sharp blade carving my side; a cluster of young Asian women demanding to know why they perished; and a parade of black-robed Jesuits holding tapered candles in the darkness.

One priest smiled: Granville Proost.

Another glowered under his monastic hood with the eyes of Hub Durant, CIA survivor extraordinaire.

A third cleric sat at a ballgame drinking free beer. At first he appeared to be Timmy, but no, it was Martin.

McGettigan tried to barf, like a sick cur; failure allowed anger to show its teeth.

One of Avery's duck-hunting jackets, replete with knife, penlight and energy bars, provided meager protection from the storm. Two large treetops peered into a large bunker by the 7th green. Drizzle masked the outline of a helicopter in the clubhouse parking lot. There could be no doubt: Dayami and Martin were on the premises. Following the fence line, clogged with decades of dense vegetation, was the fastest and most secure way to enter Meredith Lawrence's rear garden. In my head McGettigan re-examined the architect's drawings of her beloved labyrinth. At the first intersection an Organism running on adrenaline squatted near a life size statuary of *Legatus Legionis*. Imbued with Whitford Lawrence's features, the old soldier pondered long settled battles.

Knowing the lay of the land offered a home court advantage.

Offshore the thunderstorm performed Son et Lumière.

From McGettigan's point of view, the house was two hundred feet of right-angled and curved garden paths in the starlit distance. Filled with trepidation while following hand-cut pavers, my home court felt like a shooting range tailor-made for the opposition. Hunched-over at a second statue, its intersection brought the expansive rear staircase into stark relief. Oceans of flowering plants separated the maze from the rear courtyard. None would obstruct my view of guards who, if professionals were involved, would be posted like good *Sesquipilarii*. Behind second story windows where the library was located, a warm glow of lamps threatened night vision—I looked away.

Emergency generators kicked-in within seconds after the transformer blew-up. High capacity A/C units hummed behind privacy walls covered with climbing vegetation.

Everything about Meredith's home was excessive.

Though invisible from the Organism's vantage point, twin chandeliers lit the grand foyer and staircase. Behind French doors at the top of curving stone steps was the massive family-room/ballroom. On the most direct path, no more than a minute would be required to enter the library.

Who would I find?

Astor Lawrence and Martin Cardillo must be participants.

George the Pimp didn't fit with Martin. Why had George hauled Raoul all the way to Marsh Landing to shoot him dead? The landfill would've been a simpler body dump; so would a dozen other locations. George fit with James, but not because I kept Pilar from Chiquita, her mother. I guessed George knew, or guessed, about Chiquita's car accident. Were his muscle-boys and high-heeled girls here in Meredith's house?

A car engine revved around front.

Multiple automatic weapons shattered the peace. A man crashed through stained glass, screaming. Trying to raise his weapon, a shadow inside the house spit flame.

I heard, "Three down. Get upstairs…kill everyone." The voice belonged to George the Pimp.

If Astor Lawrence calculated the odds against survival, he and Martin would run down a well-concealed stairway used by servants. Secreted out of the ordinary flow of foot traffic, it led to the kitchen, butler's pantry, freezers and food storage.

My goal, after plotting a path through the maze, was a service entrance into the multi-purpose butler's pantry. As McGettigan reached the final corner, automatic weapons filled the house with cries of pain. Flattened against hand-hewn stone, I watched Dayami Machado half-pull, half-carry Martin Cardillo, whose vacant eyes and limp body made him appear catatonic. Driven by instinct, she swung her off-hand in an attempt to smash my head with her gun.

Inhibited as she was by Martin's dead weight, I managed to catch her wrist. "Dayami, it's James."

Her face reflected changed circumstances; tonight's firefight lacked the detachment of a fighter jet's cockpit. Retreat and defeat writ plain, those features showed strained desolation.

"Dayami…at the biggest statue turn ninety degrees right until you reach the tallest hedge. Go left to the property line…then left at the fence to your chopper."

She looked at me, hearing the words but uncertain whether to trust. Her eyes asked why McGettigan was in this horrible place at her moment of need.

"Twice as fast my way. Go."

Martin gathered himself. I saw tears. "My father ran at them like a lion…to let us reach the stairs. He's gone, James."

Dayami dragged Martin towards safety as his words faded.

McGettigan entered the butler's pantry, headed for two walk-in freezers which held the possibility of feeding the crew of an aircraft carrier. The kitchen held sinks, stoves and ovens galore. Refrigerators, cold drawers and dishwashers were placed in strategic positions. Meredith hosted glamorous parties for glitterati, including Kings and Presidents. Three hundred revelers could be served a formal sit-down dinner from these facilities.

For the first time an engineer's tools would apply—not weapons, not clever lawyer's words, but tools nevertheless. Secreted in the rear of one freezer, a false wall beckoned. Security touchpad torn to shreds by gunfire, plastic parts and wiring hung shattered and useless.

McGettigan chuckled: Someone went away disappointed, because the obvious keypad was a decoy. Thirteen tiles to the right of the fake keypad, a specific tile glowed orange, when touched. It read my palm print and, on a whisper of compressed air, slid the steel door aside. Eighteen by ten feet, the command center was constructed to exceed the specifications of the Secret Service, who, like McGettigan the engineer-Mayor, consulted during its design. Among so many things differentiating colossal wealth from pretenders, this room was a prime example.

Dual terminals allowed me to touch a map of the house to hear and see normal as well as thermal images. Pin-spots, installed to dramatize Meredith's extensive art collection, provided a rapid scan exposing George and his posse roaming second floor halls, armed with AK-47s. Paused at the double doors to the library, they anticipated resistance. Behind them in the hallway leading to the main staircase, a small man in a tailored suit lay curled in the fetal position: Harry Cardillo hadn't hesitated, saving his boy child with the ultimate sacrifice.

Three men climbed the stairway to the third floor: one well dressed and armed with a pistol; two in black combat gear carried high-tech automatic rifles with long, evil looking suppressors. The last man's face became visible.

Was Hub Durant here in an official capacity?

Or was this another case of a rich man's Rent-a-Spook.

A simple touch of the screen drenched the hallway from fire-suppression sprinklers recessed in plaster ceilings. George looked up, distracted and uncertain whether the building was burning. Zoomed-in, McGettigan studied the Pimp's face in high-definition. A collage of features were examined and re-arranged to form a hierarchical image. The Organism allowed those images to settle and clarify. Conviction formed a fresh rubric, shattering what had passed for uncompromised history.

A second touch lowered interlocking hurricane shutters over every window and door. Ceramic and bullet-proof, customized shutters served a dual purpose: Neither George nor Hub could shoot at Dayami and Martin while they escaped; nor was there a way in or out of Meredith's killing ground without McGettigan's blessing.

A third touch jammed cell phone transmissions. Hub and George could kill each other at their leisure. There was a particular and satisfactory symmetry to such an outcome.

Oxygen consumed at a high rate to feed the Organism's adrenaline rush, I located Astor Lawrence—looking ever so pleased with himself alongside my brother-in-law, Kristian, in Meredith's panic room. Equipped with toilet, shower, food for a week and a modest selection of art on the walls, sophisticated high frequency communications exempted them from jamming. An independent system supplied fresh air. Nothing short of a small nuclear device would open the door. An extensive weapons case offered self-defense capability.

Kristian adopted his bored, puissant façade, a veneer to cover powerful apprehension. Adrenaline junky since his father's death, the difference between bought-and-paid-for adventures and this real life killing spree may have blurred. Fit, with enough money for ten lifetimes, he may believe himself able to outrun a bullet or bribe its shooter. Still, what the devil was he doing here?

I turned up the audio.

Kristian was first to be heard, though I missed part of an ongoing discussion. "How long will the goddamn Jesuit keep us in here? I have to get back to New York sooner than later." He made a mocking face and added, laughing, "She misses me so much…such a pig."

Astor shared Kristian's impatience. "As soon as both Cardillos are dead, we move on. I'm so damned tired of waiting for my mother to kick-off. This will wake her up…make her see who's got real stones."

Mean-spirited drivel, it was almost enough to make me use the dedicated and secure line to the County Sheriff. Let law enforcement sort out the dead from the living—and the most guilty from the indecently so. Guilt, in the real world, was a messy concept.

McGettigan could be sucked into guilt's vortex; the *whoosh, whoosh, whoosh* of M's propellers resounded in my head. Phone halfway to my ear, activation of the wall-panel's air-suspension was more than a surprise. My gun swung around.

Defiant, Timmy stood hands on hips. Face filled with comic rapture, he made the sign of the cross.

"Mr. McGettigan. You are the standard bearer of ignorance in the western world." Monsignor Everett's infamous lampoon of James McGettigan lessened the tension. I couldn't resist a short-lived smile. Timmy was unarmed.

He told me, "Put the foolish weapon down, Boy-O. You'll hurt someone."

McGettigan suggested the Organism keep the gun steady. "Your behavior doesn't seem like a man seeking salvation. You're more of a lying sack of shit."

I said this for the obvious reason, though accusing a professional killer in this way could be ill conceived. McGettigan wasn't confident of much, except this: Timothy Timilty had need of James McGettigan. Needed me like flowers need rain. Like I needed him.

Timilty's face intimated nothing of anger or annoyance. He was serious and focused when he said, "*I will follow like a puppy dog, if I can find a way to salvation.* Do you know the entire quotation, James?"

"Where will salvation come from, when you serve Astor Lawrence…a colossal shit if there ever was one…who's waiting for his mother to die."

Timmy leaned against the wall, settled-in for a protracted discussion of the state of our affairs.

"You're an educated man, James, a man with experience in this old world. I told you by your hospital bedside…I serve myself in this twisted affair. By what calculus do you compute me a liar?"

Answering was pointless, when evidence was all around us in plain sight. Nevertheless McGettigan stated his position.

"Harry Cardillo was my friend. Martin's a wreck…knowing his father sacrificed his life to save his son. Manuel's head sits on a bedpost. George the Pimp is a low-rent assassin; he succeeded in damaging the Cardillo Empire, but there's no escape route. Hub Durant is outnumbered and barricaded on the third floor. What's a serving CIA officer doing here, Timmy? Do you know? Astor sits fat, dumb and happy waiting for the *Jesuit* to clean his dirty laundry. I plan to watch everyone annihilate themselves...right on these screens...with a video record for posterity. Or I could call the cops. Which would you prefer, Father Timilty? Either way your client and my brother-in-law can get on with their self-absorbed lives."

At ease, Timmy shifted his mass into a more comfortable stance. Scratched the skin under his Roman collar, tilted his chin upward and squeezed out a minor soliloquy.

"The Society of Jesus has always been a cultural and political weather vane, a way to understand the intellectual trends and fashions of a time and place. Jesuits have been attacked as plotters, assassins, as men too clever by half...as often from within the Church as from Protestants and atheists. Jesuits believe salvation can come from mystical experiences. Jesuits are informed on how to master the soul to manipulate the body. I told you weeks ago...this is a twisted affair. My weather vane points in the direction of a moral quagmire. Jesuits have often been misunderstood reformers. Reform is what I seek. Through you, Old Son. Open the shutters, James. Let sewage seek its own level. Go home to your children. Open your mind. Wet your finger to the wind. For the mighty must fall for their sins."

Timmy knew the right buttons. My fear level skyrocketed. "What about my children, Timmy?" I raised the tip of the suppressor higher, false threat though it was.

"Charlie couldn't keep them in Tennessee. They're at home, waiting for daddy."

Breath controlled with my best effort, I lowered the automatic.

"You're not a Jesuit anymore. Moral quagmire my ass. You're conscripting me for your personal, private army. Give me some help. Tell me who's doing what to whom."

"Don't assume I know, James. Knowing is for God. As for my help, you've had it all along. So don't be coy, Jimmy Catch Corn. You have to do this job alone, uncontaminated by advice of the wicked. Keep your temper. Keep going. Pay attention. Deception is everywhere. Loyalty is adrift on the waters of mortal weakness."

Timmy wasn't Shakespeare.

I pressed the computer screen where it said *Restore Defaults* and ejected the DVD. On the walk past Timmy, an epiphany found words. "You had no idea this would happen, did you? All these bodies...you're making it up on the run, just like me."

"Ad maiorem Dei gloriam."

Confirmation of my guess was unsettling. There was no point in asking Timmy about the different methods used to kill Raoul and Manuel. Or the drugging of the security staff with controlled IV drips. Because he didn't know the answers. Because he was afraid. Just like me.

As I passed into the freezer, Timmy made his most disquieting statement. "Crank it up, James. Crank it up."

CHAPTER 20

McGettigan unscrewed the suppressor, stuck the gun inside my pant's waistband and exited with a to-do list which began with Chiquita and my car. My night was just beginning.

Near the Village office, the transformer enclosure was surrounded by FPL repair trucks. Seen through a window, the male guard held an ice pack to his head, the woman a phone to her ear. Minutes from now the Village would be a major crime scene and national news. McGettigan pushed on towards the immediate goal.

A dark blue panel van screeched around the corner, blasted through the semaphore and braked hard. Hidden by the identical trees utilized earlier, I watched George leap out of the van to examine Chiquita. Moments later, at the wheel again, his opinion was conveyed by a high-pitched cackle.

"Messed up bad. Won't be fuckin' no more pretty boys like Manuel."

***

Ten minutes at a self-wash removed any surface signs of Chiquita and the guardhouse. At this time of night a blasé response from a third-shift airport crew, interested in whether I'd purchased the collision damage waiver, sent McGettigan walking towards Congress Avenue to call a cab.

***

A different high priest tended the dead, when the taxi returned me to Marsh Landing's gatehouse. Detective Joe Potts wore his disdain for everything Marsh Landing on the sleeve of a pale pink designer knockoff.

Timmy was long gone, as was the limousine Astor and Kristian departed in. Hub Durant hadn't lingered to exchange points-of-law with local Gendarmerie. Marsh Landing's security duo was on the way to Jupiter Medical, where a first ambulance took Chiquita. Though worse for wear, McGettigan walked the scene at the gatehouse and Village office with authority, righteousness and the privilege of apparent wealth on my side.

Potts's attitude was nothing new, but the Lone Ranger wasn't aware of the shit-pile he'd fallen into. Headed in the direction of those FPL trucks, McGettigan felt Detective Potts's contempt press against my spine. Away from the klieg lights of the electric company's repairs, darkness spread its protection and accepted my return to Meredith's abandoned mansion. Front doors splintered by George's gang, I was greeted by the cuprous odor of multiple blood pools. The Organism stepped around and over two thugs, whose tattoos were chewed away by a hail of bullets. Rivulets of red drooled in a congealing mass down the staircase's graceful curve. On this same staircase three black-clad men were ripped apart by return fire. Removed by Hub and his surviving team members, their outlines testified to the futility of a tragicomic opera.

McGettigan cared about none of this human detritus.

To lift and carry Harry's stiffening body was a Fool's errand. I reminded myself with each step; this gesture of respect, preventing Harry's corpse from becoming a topic of conjecture and ridicule, could exact a high price. Questioning my friendship with Martin was inevitable as his father's dead weight caused my legs to tremble and cramp across the fairway to Avery's home. I lowered the eight hundred-thread count shroud, which protected Harry on the short journey, into a bright red SUV. Avery's front door, left open to incite law enforcement's interest, was visible as the big V-8 hurled me towards the gatehouse.

McGettigan leaned out the window; suggested Detective Clouseau check the homes of Mrs. Meredith Lawrence and Mr. Avery Reynolds. In my most privileged tone, I informed the sneering

Detective the front doors of both residences were ajar.

Potts curled his lips at *ajar*. With luck and Potts's indifference, it would be another hour before tonight's massacre was discovered.

***

Luis Machado wasn't answering his cell.

Nearing the wharf where Sugar Daddy floated on a post-midnight breeze, McGettigan pulled the red SUV to the side of the road. Massive diesels rumbled and a glowing-red running light indicated someone planned to move the boat. An odd shape on the aft deck filled the space regularly occupied by a fighting chair. With no wharf lights lit, Sugar Daddy sat in the water like the flame at the end of a long candela.

So many reasons plausible, one stuck in my throat: Luis was concerned with his safety. Or waited on a valuable passenger. Or expected to be attacked by George. Or all the above.

If the lights were off because George could deploy snipers, how would McGettigan get Harry's body aboard the boat?

How safe was I half a mile up the street? Eight hundred eighty yards—Charlie Hamilton considered a thousand yards difficult, but not an unusual shot for a professional. McGettigan would feel so much better with Charlie here to reassure me.

I dialed, hoping Luis would answer the landline. "Luis, it's James. Is it safe to come aboard?"

Whispered words chilled my spine.

"I do not know, Senór. They may be anywhere. Or nowhere. I'm waiting for you, since speaking with my child, never knowing if you would come."

McGettigan said nothing, but my mind couldn't help but wonder: *Which child?* "I'll come by water, Luis. Half an hour."

More like an hour saw the inflatable I borrowed bump the bow of Sugar Daddy. Inched hand over hand towards the stern, Luis heard me murmur and manhandled Harry's mummified remains onto the teak deck. Hidden beneath the gunwale as we were, no headlights were visible on the street.

"Luis, put Harry in the fish box."

Not meant to debase the dead, the fish box was refrigerated; Harry could be kept in obscurity and safety until the Cardillo family decided on a course of action. Pictures of a billionaire sugar baron shot to pieces would echo through cane fields, Washington's halls of power and across the Straits of Florida to Cuba. Who could say whether US relations with Cuba would be affected?

McGettigan installed Harry with reverence.

Luis's strong hand squeezed my own. His normal three-day growth shaved tight, fishing shorts and stained t-shirt replaced by pressed white trousers and a crisp, powder blue, button-down embroidered with *Cardillo Crystals*, Luis spoke to me with authority.

"Martin's at the community hospital. The wound's serious, but he is stable. Dayami has flown to Miami for a specialist surgeon. I'll use the waterway to the summer house."

McGettigan plumbed the depths of Luis's coal black eyes, all the while examining refined cheekbones, the shape of a nose, set of a jaw and a high forehead. Details hidden from attention at other times, I'd noted their presence on three others in the very recent past. This newer Luis was much younger, perhaps no older than a Fool who'd been oblivious. Without this remade Luis, the similarities would've been lost. Manuel said *Luis was Rodriquez before Rodriquez could swim.*

Manuel had been third in command in the closely held Cardillo structure. But Manuel's dead. Harry's dead. Martin's in the hospital. Luis understood the negative consequences of a vacuum at the top; so now he issued orders to the Cardillo establishment. Was he trying to stem a revolt, or prepare for something more terrible? McGettigan's priorities differed from Luis's. I pulled him close.

"Tonight has seen enough sacrifice, Luis. You can't do this awful thing. There is some other way, my friend. There are things I can do."

Luis's loyalty to the Cardillo family was singular. He deserved a better explanation of my intent, but his weak assent left talk to another day. Luis Machado didn't believe James McGettigan could appreciate his dilemma, or cure heartsick despair. He tried to pull away. Tried to look away. I held him tight: James was Luis's lifeline.

"Run Sugar Daddy into the mangroves…give me an hour…pick up your cell when it rings. Please, Luis. Don't dock at the summer house before you talk to me."

Committed to what must seem a singular decision, he choked back tears.

"Promise me, Luis. An hour is a small thing after all our years as companions. You may not think I can help, but Harry trusted me with Martin's life. Bet on a man like yourself...a man who knows secrets."

Luis's forehead creased with worry. Like McGettigan, Luis believed a man must rely on himself, must sacrifice what he must sacrifice for his family. Luis was wrong as McGettigan had been wrong. Slipping over the side, I pushed the dinghy under the wharf and held on tight to one of its cross-braces.

Luis entered the main salon where a secondary helm was located. Raised from his crouch, he pushed the throttles forward. Not the proscribed method for leaving a dock, the hull lifted and within seconds eighty tons of sportfishing yacht roared towards the Lake Worth inlet and Peanut Island at thirty-five knots. No shots ripped the air in pursuit. No one ran towards the wharf.

I'd missed Martin's injury, chalked up his incoherence to grief and the overwhelming nature of events. Now I was curious; Luis had said *wound*.

What type of wound?

Gathered in the recesses of my mind was a disturbing reality: Timmy, Hub and George hadn't been the only killers loose in Marsh Landing last night.

***

Patience was a depleted resource as the SUV started and I aimed for Chiquita's apartment. The order of my actions was a quagmire of indecision.

Was McGettigan embroiled in unalterable events?

Should I abandon Luis and Martin? Had they abandoned McGettigan?

Raoul's talisman in hand, I parked without regard to personal safety; Chiquita's apartment wasn't anyone's target, not any longer. No signs of further disturbance marred the living room. A heavy cardboard box held laptops. McGettigan pulled the box to the sofa and began. High-end Macs disregarded, I segregated remaining machines into cheap, mid-range and more expensive; Raoul had an ego, so the most expensive would be examined first. McGettigan booted one laptop after another, inserting the Obsidian-like talisman into a USB port, waiting for recognition and pressing Raoul's amputated finger onto the cool surface. Seven machines sat stone silent, refusing to acknowledge either the device or Raoul's gruesome digit; an eighth whirred to life. What I sought would be in photo and video files; photos because Ryan's camera took single frames and video because Raoul, a scumbag with a black heart, downloaded the landfill's security video before destroying it.

Bingo.

On the trip south I took stock. Nothing close to what a Fool surmised, what I found was better. The meeting of Harry and Martin Cardillo, with Astor Lawrence, was pre-planned. The Cardillo/Lawrence meeting lured Hub Durant and Timothy Timilty to Florida, like flies to ripe dogshit. George was the interloper. Neither Timmy nor Hub took precautions related to George or his arrival. Which left a puzzle: How had George known of Harry's presence at Meredith's? McGettigan placed a wager on Manuel, who fell under the spell of Marianna, and as a result decided to grab for the brass ring.

Every contradictory priority screamed for attention, yet McGettigan dialed Marianna's pay as you go cell.

"Are you both safe?"

Awkward described a growing silence, then, with a labored voice, she said one word in English, then switched to Spanish. "Yes. We are safe."

"Where are you, Marianna?"

"I'm a fool." She sucked air into her lungs and added, "I let myself dream."

Harsh though it was, I demanded, "Where are you?"

"When Manuel left yesterday, I was frightened. I called a taxi. We're at the Wellington Roadside Inn, near the mall." Silence grew from its own seed. Then she stated a fact, not a forecast of future events. "There's been trouble."

"Don't go out. No calls. I'll be there in less than twenty minutes. Listen, Marianna…Manuel is dead…Harry Cardillo as well. Martin is wounded. We're all in danger, but I'm coming."

***

Despite the weight of shame, Marianna was the picture of grace under duress. Inside the low rent motel room, Robert Linney was washed, shaven and dressed in clean, ironed, clothes. Marianna clutched McGettigan's hand as I led them to the SUV.

For a second time, I'd been the bearer of unbearable news. She allowed herself to fall in love with Manuel. She'd wanted to fall in love. I'd seen it in New York. I could have, should have, done something to prevent this result. But what? Was love, even the unexpected, dangerous variety, something to be gamed? McGettigan tried to be gentle, telling her what she guessed, when spiriting Robert away from the Cardillo compound.

"Manuel got tired hanging around the fringes of Cardillo wealth…never sharing in the fruits of his labors. He was too close…watched the family enjoy the things his strength and cunning delivered to their front door. Never invited inside, the hurt stuck in Manuel's throat. Happens all the time, but it didn't happen to you, Marianna. You listened to Manuel and didn't like what you heard."

McGettigan forced her chin up with his non-driving hand.

"You kept your word. Because you're a good and loyal person."

"Where will Mr. Robert and I go now?"

"In a few hours, we'll leave Florida for my home in Massachusetts, where Mr. Robert also owns a home. Where he belongs. You're welcome to come and care for him. Or you can stay in Florida. If you decide to stay behind, I'll send money until you choose where to live. Either way I'll be forever in your debt."

For the first time suspicion infiltrated her eyes. She'd lost her self-esteem to an outlaw who used her. Now she calculated what McGettigan might take, no longer accepting me at face value.

"I'm frightened. I'd like to go back to Cuba."

Cuba was a million miles distant while Rodriquez was at war with the Cardillo family. Pushed well past every speed limit, I'd asked Luis for an hour because any longer would've been rejected out-of-hand. An hour was too little; a lifetime wouldn't be enough.

***

The doorbell was a complex melody played by harps. I pushed the button repeatedly—Auntie was asleep.

Auntie my ass.

Heavy feet, accompanied by the clatter of bling, suggested I stand aside. As the door opened the sentry grabbed his thigh, when my bullet entered too close to his groin. He'd live, but, writhing on the floor in nothing but a wife-beater and tighty-whities, his colorful tats, in particular the hawk with orange talons above a yellow songbird, seemed subdued.

In the living room Auntie reached for the telephone.

"Don't do it, Angeline. Get Pilar dressed in something pretty. All you need is a bathrobe."

I gripped the sentry's collar and dragged him across the tile floor. Unrestrained by pants, the blood trail was substantial. Trussed with one of Auntie's drapery cords, he couldn't walk. A second cord, sliced into a shorter length, was a functional tourniquet.

"Great ink, man. All your lady friends…they love a man who speaking Arabic thinks of women as a meal?"

Spitting arrows with his eyes, he muttered, "Fix ya ass, what I'll do. Can't shoot through a fucking wooden door."

Charlie would be proud of McGettigan, more than I was of myself. More than ever I subscribed to the old saying: *Intelligence leaves the room, when you pick up a gun.*

Our merry band numbered five: A child, a childlike man, a Madonna, a Witch and the ever-present Fool. Robert sat in the third row alone. Pilar drowsed on Marianna's shoulder, not cognizant of her destination. Angeline Machado sat next to McGettigan, spine ramrod straight in a pair of dark pants and tan shirt. Without makeup, she looked every inch as old as her husband, Luis, though she was ten years his junior. Legend, repeated over and over through the years, told McGettigan precious Angeline, and her oldest child, Jorge, perished in a Cuban ravine on Dayami Machado's tenth birthday.

Not true.

Pilar shared Luis's facial bones. Blessed by her gene pool, she acquired Angeline's eyes. Luis and Angeline had fallen out of love, and out of their marital partnership in the piracy and smuggling business. Maybe Luis wanted better than a life of banditry for his son. Angeline committed adultery, like Chiquita, with Manuel. Whatever else happened, Jorge took his mother's side. Hated the Cardillos for more reasons than he could fathom, beginning with Harry splitting the family by luring Luis away. Dayami chose her father.

Tonight Luis hurried to an unhurried death. Clouded by grief and emotion, he believed an accommodation could be negotiated.

Believed his life could be forfeit to Rodriquez, the nom-de-guerre assumed by father and son in an involuntary succession. Believed, when his life was forfeit to Angeline's loathing, the younger, newer, Rodriquez would, in the dénouement of a perfect fantasy, spare Martin Cardillo's life.

Normal, thoughtful, loving, people could experience temporary insanity, if the strain of treachery proved too much. Luis would gain nothing for laying his life on Angeline's altar of seething resentment. Angeline wouldn't bargain unless McGettigan made her weak. Being Auntie to Pilar gave Angeline freedom to play other roles, to create deceptions meeting her needs. Could a grandmother ask Pilar to watch as her father executed her grandfather?

McGettigan planned to gamble one Pilar against all the accumulated Machado angst and vitriol.

***

On a stretch of inland waterway from Palm Beach to Fort Lauderdale, hidden from street side observation, mansion after more impressive mansion snuggled against the water, docks adorned with impressive yachts. Houses—structures which defied humdrum description—showed-off walls of glass, turrets, mock lighthouses, helicopter landing pads, Chinese gardens, car collections, paintings, sculpture or any item qualified as collectible and priceless.

The Cardillo summerhouse was an elegant misnomer. In a moment of delusion after his wife's burial, Harry allowed Wilson Stoddard to build a monumental glass box. Featured in architectural magazines like the emperor's new suit, bad taste was naked in its display. Sited on a point of land at the intersection of the waterway and a large canal, constructed of steel and glass, clear glass walls transformed to opaque white at the touch of a button.

Any former Mayor would report armed men roaming unchecked in a residential neighborhood. McGettigan provided the address to a 911 operator, then, in a more personal gesture of goodwill, I phoned Detective Joe Potts.

"Detective Potts, this is James McGettigan. I'm in South County, near the waterway, to visit a friend." A Fool allowed *friend* to inherit salacious indignity. "There are men with automatic weapons at the house next door. Maybe there's a connection to Marsh

Landing…home invasions or something?"

An all-knowing snort filled my ear. Potts wouldn't be able to deny my call later, but he could discount it now.

Luis was next. "How far away are you, Luis?"

"A mile, maybe less. I'm mid-channel. Waiting." Luis's voice was full of revulsion; he wanted to finish this long-running drama.

"Be at the dock in ten minutes. I expect to be on the big lawn by the patio. If you don't see me, do whatever you wish. If I'm there, look for Jorge's boat. Sink it, if you can."

Nonsense filled this description, for the *lawn* was the size of Fenway Park's outfield and *Jorge's boat* nothing more than distraction, something to keep Luis from coming ashore to wreck an ill conceived gamble.

"Cripple his boat, Luis. Or Harry's killer gets away. SWAT will be here in minutes."

Luis was no fool: He heard me use Jorge's name. In anything approaching a normal emotional state, he would laugh at my diversion.

"I'll sink the devil-boy, or chase him to hell." Haunted, Luis wanted one of life's elusive do-overs.

On a semi-circular drive constructed of crushed pink stone, McGettigan pulled past the front door. Handed Marianna the semi-automatic without its suppressor.

"Move to the driver's seat after we go. Shoot anyone who comes close. If you hear shots fired on the lawn, drive away and call Dayami. Find a way to call my children. Tell them you have Mr. Robert. Ask them to help you return to Cuba. Tell them I loved them. Tell them I'm sorry."

Scant warmth resided in Marianna's expression.

Angeline struggled, but she, Pilar and James marched arm in arm to a lawn backlit by the yellow-green glow of house lights diffused through thick glass. Without night vision, we could see nothing. Headed for a tight arrangement of wicker furniture, I spoke at the top of the Organism's penetrating voice.

"Jorge, SWAT is coming. Spend your time worrying about the video of Harry Cardillo's execution, about photos of your hawk-shouldered buddy delivering a body to Raoul Dupree and Frankie McShane…both of whom you murdered. I've got two DVDs in my pocket: One came from the security system at the Lawrence mansion…another from Raoul's laptop. He hid it in Chiquita's living room. Raoul never slept with her, like Manuel did. Real clear pictures, Jorge. Too many murders…you get caught tonight, they give you the needle. Pilar…she doesn't want her daddy executed. Your mother, Pilar's grandmother, is drowning in her own bile. Run away, Jorge. Pilar doesn't know she has a grandfather, does she? Run away, Jorge. Shoot Luis…let him bleed to death in his granddaughter's arms…not worth it, Jorge. Those who fight and run away live to see their child grow to a woman."

McGettigan had bastardized Tacitus and left off the coda…*but he who is in battle slain, will never rise to fight again.*

A little girl pointed an upturned face in my direction, troubled by what she'd heard her new friend, James, bellow into the darkness. In a spontaneous reaction, she yelled, "Daddy, I'm scared. Come get Auntie and me. Please."

The SUV's engine roared: Marianna had abandoned me.

Jorge's words floated across soft morning air accompanied by a psychotic ego.

"I can do both; kill you and my so-called father. Harry's death makes me head of the Cardillo household." Jorge tried again, his best effort too maudlin. "I'm heir to the Cardillo Empire, not the Ivy League pansy who ran away. George went to college…studied agriculture and farm economics. George is an American citizen, not some pimp. Martin is the pimp."

Voice raised for a final effort, he screamed.

"Mama. Pilar. Be very still while this house-fly is smashed on the wall."

The Organism listened and triangulated, assessing Jorge to be in the southern red cedar and magnolia trees on the lawn's northwest boundary. McGettigan gathered the woman and the little girl close.

"High risk, Jorge. Don't kill Pilar by mistake. Run away. Run away and I'll bring Pilar to Cuba. Like I brought Robert Linney to live his final days in peace." I taunted him, while sweat leaked down my back and the Organism's capacity for bravery faded. "You aren't Harry's son. Angeline told you fairy tales to feed her obsession. She cheated on your father…maybe with Harry. People make mistakes, but mirrors don't lie. You, Dayami, Luis, Angeline and Pilar…all the same genes Jorge. You'll never own the sugar fields."

Out of the pitch black waterway came the sound of a pile driver slamming steel. Wham. Wham. Wham. Wham. Luis fired the evil looking .50 caliber machine gun mounted where the fighting chair would have been. The first shells, fired in random design, shattered trees and maybe arms, legs or chests. Each impact felt like the end of the world. It terrorized the three of us: We fell to the ground. I pulled Pilar to where my body almost covered hers. Second thoughts were my first thoughts. Wham. Wham. These last two shells penetrated fiberglass and engine blocks. Escape for Jorge's crew became an unattainable mirage.

In response were the sounds of AKs. Tracer rounds flew like angry wasps in the direction where Sugar Daddy was a platform of death. Luis fired now on automatic. The reverberation was deafening.

Sirens wailed to the west.

Then no sound at all. Never had silence been so welcome. I shook with fear.

Why this lull? Was Luis wounded? Or had he relented?

A figure sprinted across the lawn, bent over in a crouch.

The Organism's eyes experienced all this in slow motion as Jorge came, fists pumping, one hand holding an AK. Jorge's speech was labored with physical exertion.

"Give me Pilar. Give me the discs."

As I fantasized, he must have realized the DVDs were copies. His first priority was his daughter—Jorge had too little time. Caught between sirens and the inevitability of the machine gun, he clutched Pilar. With Pilar in Jorge's right arm, his left hand was free to receive the DVDs. I pushed them into outstretched fingers as his rifle targeted my chest. Time again slowed to a pathetic pace as certainty plunged towards McGettigan, who shoved Angeline at Jorge.

Under Pilar's weight Jorge stumbled. His time had expired. Face exposed in an ocean of regret, no refuge from his parents' marital warfare could be found in this place. He pushed to his feet. Glanced towards the parade of strobe lights. Lumbered towards the waterway, where wreckage of his fast-boat was a smoking ruin.

Jorge was the perfect target for the original Rodriquez to exact a final reprisal.

Pilar was Jorge's guardian angel. No grandfather could harm a grandchild.

Angeline lay on damp grass, muttering something unintelligible. Warped dreams tasted of acid, when they went poof in a humid nightmare.

This ugliness, where all were seen at their worst, was the bargain McGettigan made with the fates, cloaked in the uncertainty of playing God with real lives.

There was nothing left except to disappear.

McGettigan began to dogtrot in Sugar Daddy's direction. Bathed in light, the yacht was a beacon coming alongside the Cardillo wharf. Luis and I should be roaring north by the time SWAT unloaded its officers. Mesmerized by our similar intent to escape, McGettigan watched Jorge crossing a hundred yards of forever as I renewed my effort to find safety.

Jorge and Pilar fell to the ground.

My hands grabbed my head in shock, having heard no shots, no sound at all.

Pilar keened, foretelling the last chapter of Jorge Machado's legend as Rodriquez.

McGettigan realized—I'd been rooting for him, for them both to get away. I shook my head, failing to comprehend these emotions.

Luis was a blur. Running past me towards the small girl, he said, "Hurry or you'll have to swim. My life is Pilar."

Sugar Daddy drifted with no one to tend her. Just like at the Cape Cod Canal, without hesitation I dove. Killing all her lights, I made the big diesels snarl. Minutes later, mind functioning once again, I used the boat's telephone to call the pilot of my chartered jet. *Wheels up ASAP* was the short message.

***

General aviation occupied the south side of Palm Beach Int'l, across the tarmac from the airline terminals. When I exited the cab, Avery Reynolds' SUV was parked in deep gloom, Marianna standing by the passenger door. Her intentions clear, she held Raoul's laptop.

"You'll need this." This short sentence held no animosity. Just grief.

McGettigan assisted his oldest friend from the SUV. Robert shied away, then asked in an almost inaudible whisper, "When can I go to bed?"

Turning to Marianna, I repeated my earlier pledge. "I'll get you to Cuba when I can. Go to Dayami...explain her father isn't hurt...her niece is with Luis. Dayami will provide for you until I can."

Without a response, she turned back to the SUV.

Minutes later Robert Linney and his childhood friend, James, lifted off into a different day. James was worried. Robert serene.

CHAPTER 21

Left over from a shit-storm, McGettigan passed time on a chartered jet sifting through the wreckage for tidbits to guide future lines of investigation.

Ryan's landfill photos showed no bodies of Thai women. Pursuit of Astor, aiming to find him responsible for dead girls at a Palm Beach landfill, proved fruitless. The decomposed carcass, buried amidst tons of trash, turned out to be male. Last seen alive when he exited a New York pizza joint, Gideon was a cop, and an enforcer, but not a Jesuit. Nevertheless, how to square Gideon's alliance with Mama-san, into whose care young Thai women were delivered, was a concern.

Timothy Timilty worked for Astor Lawrence; denial of the obvious may have seemed endearing to my delinquent Jesuit, but obvious won-out over insipid posing. Timmy wasn't a businessman, an extortionist or a priest; he was a skilled and inventive killer for hire. Astor was impatient and imprudent. By weight of evidence and deduction, Timmy's ultimate assignment was Meredith Lawrence's passage to the afterlife.

Kristian Solberg was, in the kindest light, a putz. A bit too harsh? The Fool suggested Kristian was equal in guilt to Astor. A Ghost pleaded with the Fool for a recitation of evidence against either man—the kind of evidence which elicited indictments—and giggled with ghoulish delight at our silence.

Luis Machado would never be the same. Whether a good or a bad thing was unknowable. I would root for him like I cheered for Jorge. Hope was not such a terrible thing.

Martin Cardillo aged a hundred years last night. Why did he meet with Astor? What had been so damned important?

Why did our combined ruminations refuse to yield a coherent picture?

More important than all the above, and contrary to her father's request, Julia convinced Charlie to deliver my offspring to Cape Cod, instead of rural Tennessee. Maybe Julia channeled her mother and divined her father needed all the help he could get.

***

Hancock County Airport, in Trenton, Maine, was a short drive from Bar Harbor. McGettigan dismissed the jet and grabbed another rental. Bar Harbor Road crossed Mount Desert Narrows and turned into Eden Road before entering town.

A simple fact: Timmy reveled in the ease of tracking James McGettigan.

Here in rural Maine, where Crooked Road was a seldom-traveled country lane, following would demand real effort. Any electronic trackers were drowned by my swim in the Intracoastal Waterway, alongside McGettigan's last prepaid cell. Any human assigned to follow would, in the end, drive down Crooked Road's cracked and uneven pavement to continue my pursuit. Under the protection of towering pines, Robert and I waited half an hour for such an appearance.

Tall Pines Village agreed to provide temporary care and lodging for Mr. Robert Linney, who suffered from Alzheimer's disease. Paperwork and payment formalities occupied more than an hour. Three months in advance was steep, but Gwyneth would expect nothing less than Robert's complete safety and well-being. Robert looked past me as I left him, a nurse's aide delivering ice cream as a cool breeze blew off the Atlantic.

The calendar in reception declared the date to be June the first.

***

Meredith Lawrence was too young to remember the *Gilded Age,* when Bar Harbor rivaled Newport for extravagance. She'd been regaled with stories of garden parties at the Pot & Kettle Club, horse drawn carriage rides up Cadillac Mountain and horseracing at Robin Hood-Morrell Park. Bar Harbor, once upon a jaded time, was synonymous with elitism and wealth. Meredith, I wouldn't doubt, could remember the 1947 wildfire. Sparks at a cranberry bog ignited a blaze which consumed half the eastern side of Mount Desert— including the Lawrence mansion among sixty-six other palatial summerhouses on Millionaires Row. Meredith, when her inheritance ripened, was among the few who rebuilt. As she constructed Lawrence Foods into its present colossus, her Bar Harbor presence expanded.

Dressed in a long-sleeved, blue and white checked shirt, a pair of tan trousers and bare feet in boat shoes, all purchased on Cottage Street for the occasion, McGettigan lifted the brass knocker and let it fall. Hinges protested as the massive door spread its invitation. A head of strawberry-blonde, ringlet curls greeted me without letting go of the door.

"Dr. McGettigan, what a nice surprise. Do come in."

Search initiated to match voice and face, McGettigan couldn't remember the woman standing close enough for her lilac body lotion to permeate my brain. Focused harder, Marcia's description of her interim replacement in the Old Marsh office resided in a category titled mousey and unimpressive: Dark hair, not today's strawberries and cream; no makeup versus flawless skin. Swain, if I remembered Marcia's recitation of events, showed up out of the blue, her presence validated by Sterrit Bagby, Meredith's eunuch escort on the Palm Beach social circuit.

My disbelief must have been obvious. "Gayle Swain, isn't it? Marcia mentioned you. Who's taking care of my poor little Village?"

Undeterred by derision, she gave as good in return. "Oh, Marcia's back at her desk. She misses you being Mayor. Maybe you should stand for election again."

Among things which made Swain a surprise was her ensemble: Long peasant dress in bright yellow, cork espadrilles trimmed in matching leather and a startling necklace of orange-pink stones. She managed to hit the Bar Harbor *look* on the sweet spot, and, because Ingrid was my point of comparison for all social-climbing women, I gave her high grades. But how was the *look* affordable on a Federal employee's salary? McGettigan saw a wolf in sheep's clothing.

"What can I do for you Dr. McGettigan?"

I thought my purpose might have been obvious. Focused on the orange-pink necklace, anger rose and receded. Snappish reply pushed away, I told her, "I'd like to visit with Meredith. Is she in?"

"She has a small group coming for lunch. I'll ask her whether there's time...or what time might be better. Okay?"

"I'll join you...save you wear and tear on your nice new shoes."

Smiling from ear to ear, she retorted. "You too...right off the pages of *What the Man with No Style is Wearing This Summer.*"

Too bad McGettigan the widower was immune to derogation of his wardrobe.

A wide, tall porch reminded me—only if farsighted or deranged, could this massive house, hard by the ocean, have taken its theme from tumbledown shelters of an earlier epoch. Despite the best work of Meredith's legion of public relations pros, shingle-style homes never were humble dwellings of Bar Harbor's fishing folk. Meredith wouldn't be caught dead fishing.

While scurrying might well apply to other busy hostesses, Meredith glided like a dancer among caterer's staff, edicts issued under the guise of suggestion. Four tables of four were set in a china pattern McGettigan couldn't in a million years identify.

With a tad too much volume, I said, "Is this the Spode, Meredith? Don't the blues clash with the awning?"

She pivoted. With less than an instant's delay, the Lawrence charm, for which Meredith was famous, shone on me as it had when *she* preceded her husband into some endless, mindless, charity luncheon.

"James, my dear, come and sit. By some miracle we have a few minutes before my guests arrive."

No biting sarcasm, her sincerity blended seamlessly with contrived affection. Meredith by now, without question, had skinned some Vice President of Lawrence Security alive, but in doing so obtained stiff facts which failed to enhance the smell, sound and brutality of last evening's events at her Marsh Landing home. Right this instant she wondered whether her favorite ex-mayor could provide broader insight. As water materialized in my hand, a puff pastry filled with fresh salmon mousse was offered by a waiter turned-out just so. McGettigan was glad for the drink.

"You've heard, Meredith. Who was your source for the news?"

Too thin legs crossed in the act of a much younger woman, one emerald leather pump slipped off as its foot danced to an unheard rhythm. Seconds ticked away with no suggestion she understood my question.

I waited. If Meredith wanted a pound of flesh, McGettigan would not invite its removal.

In an act of dismissal, she used her hands to smooth a lime green skirt and fixed me with a penetrating laser. "Is Harry dead?"

We were playing games. For whose benefit, I wondered?

"Harry who? A female security officer was hit by a car at the guard shack. Unconscious I heard, when the ambulance took her to Jupiter Medical. On the critical list this morning."

McGettigan was satisfied; he'd given a satisfactory performance for Miss FBI. Meredith knew better.

"Did the accident happen while the power was out?"

I lied. "FPL was gone by the time I arrived. They replaced a transformer." This was information Meredith had no use for.

She wore a half smile, its meaning a mystery. We were fencing to no positive effect. McGettigan would have preferred Agent Swain leave us alone.

A firm grip on the desired outcome, Meredith enquired, "Can you stay for lunch, James?"

She rattled off the names of politicians, celebrities and Captains of Industry who would attend.

"Isn't Astor here? I'd love to see him. And Jill?" My thin impression of a happy smile was smarmy. "No Jill?"

Meredith fiddled with a long strand of pearls, her facial color and respiration undisturbed. The slightest wrinkle defied Botox and set itself in place above her left eyebrow. Normally this was a sign I'd be dismissed in short order.

Meredith turned to Miss FBI as she told me, "Gayle needs an escort to lunch. Doesn't she look lovely?" Nostalgia contrived, Meredith added, "I'd give several billion dollars to be your age again, my sweet girl. With hair like strawberries." A pause for effect kept McGettigan in suspense. "The necklace is perfect on you. Diamonds and pearls are for old ladies like me. What do you say, James?"

No Lawrence would give several billion of their own, not for anything short of immortality. Give away other peoples' money, yes, because charity made the best shield for a corporate raider. Absent an obvious reason, Meredith was focused on this banal exchange. I played my part and returned an insipid volley.

"Have you always been fond of Citrines, Ms. Swain?"

To her credit, Gayle Swain bestowed a winning grin upon a beaten opponent. Then offered what might well have been a lie.

"I *am* a November child, Dr. McGettigan…my mother as well. Mother left it to me when she passed."

Cheeky indifference on display she fingered the necklace, turning it round and round her neck while doing so.

Examined at close range, McGettigan couldn't fathom whether expensive clothes fit her upbringing as well as her body. Fit, she might have been, inhabiting the taut, over-trained body of a distance runner. Well educated. Pretty enough, but unhappy.

To parry the thrusts of Meredith Lawrence, who disliked Miss FBI, was a constant challenge. The necklace we discussed was a perfect example, because Agent Swain couldn't know its provenance. With a clasp in the shape of a sea horse, the piece was unique. It wasn't set with Citrines, but with Padparadscha Sapphires the size of small boulders.

Swain was caught-out. It was Meredith's way of sending James a signal: *Tread with care.*

How Swain came to wear the necklace was a separate matter. Gifts from their mother, Anna, when each sister graduated college, two necklaces were almost indistinguishable. Ingrid's sea horse clasp had an emerald eye; her older sister's held a diamond. Ingrid felt slighted by their relative value. After their father's funeral, Ingrid's jeweler implanted a larger stone; the innocent sea creature had grown malevolent and well suited to Ingrid's narcissistic nature.

This outsized green eye winked at McGettigan. I choked back growing impatience with this charade.

"I'd love to stay for lunch, but I'm underdressed."

For the first time, Meredith approved of McGettigan's tactic.

"Go upstairs, James. Astor's boyhood room is on the left. Next door is the boys' bunkroom. Something in the closet will be appropriate."

Turned to the catering manager, she instructed, "We'll need a place-card for James McGettigan, Ph.D. Oh, and Walter, tell Mr. Bagby he's developed a nasty headache."

Bunkroom lacked something as a description: No bunk beds littered scarred floors; odiferous boys' sweatshirts didn't decorate cheap iron bed frames; tennis shoes weren't strewn in every corner. On the contrary, bunkroom described a large space suitable for unmarried male occupancy during visits to Meredith's summer camp. The closet held a varied selection; I chose a white sport coat over a blue dress shirt and black trousers. No tie. Black loafers too tight. In a fit of social insurrection the Organism went barefoot.

In the far corner of the room, a mirrored door opened and Meredith appeared from a private elevator. Next to a bank of four windows, she leaned against the glass as if speaking to the ocean. Her words were crisp, tone no longer cheery.

"Why are you here?"

How to inform an old woman her son intended to do-her-in? Did the old woman's net worth, north of many countries' GNP, soften the impact or make a whit of difference?

"Astor's hired a contract killer. You're the target, Meredith."

"Nonsense."

Her hands moved behind her back, producing a look of vulnerability and helplessness, neither of which were characteristics of Meredith Lawrence.

"Astor's a good boy."

Defiant, she tilted her chin in my direction, daring McGettigan to tender a contradiction.

"I've guests to see to, James. Are you *quite* finished?" She knew I wasn't.

"Astor's real estate venture in Jersey City...out of cash. Don't the accountants keep you up to date? It's your money, after all. Did Astor tell you *M* sunk. I was aboard at the time, drugged to the teeth. There were young Thai girls in the bilges. Dead. Murdered. Astor's in the sex-slave trade, in business with Kristian Solberg of all people. They've hired Timothy Timilty, a Boston mob guy in the killing business. Astor hates you for not making him CEO. I have a video of him droning-on about wasting his life waiting for mother to die. You wouldn't want to see it. Astor isn't a good boy gone wrong. He's well over the age of consent and what he's doing can't end well."

God, I sounded like a B-movie actor spouting from an hysterical script.

"Would you recommend the police, James? The proper authorities in Thailand and Ms. Swain, perhaps…working together to save the world from male sexual perversion? Or should I phone Anna Solberg and commiserate with her about our misanthropic progeny?"

Meredith had survived two small heart attacks. At this moment, her body was motionless as eternity. McGettigan watched fingers fidget, longing for the cigarette she'd been known to beggar from house staff. Almost an afterthought, she inquired in a conspiratorial tone.

"James, do you think Astor negotiated to purchase Harry Cardillo's land and sugar mills…or the entire kit and caboodle?" A concerned mother no longer, an opportunistic businesswoman usurped her place.

I tried to throw her off stride. "Maybe Astor was a seller…planning to sell a majority of shares in Lawrence Foods to Martin Cardillo, after you're out of the way."

She produced an impression—pondering universal fate. While taking the few steps back towards the elevator, she let me know where she stood.

"They made a great, grunting mess of the house. Damnable hooligans. I'm told Harry Cardillo bled to death on my second floor parquet. Perhaps we elders *are* dispensable."

While the elevator's tarnished and grimy brass grill rattled shut, she spoke again, seeming to be without a care.

"Are you keeping score, James? Don't those wretched baseball managers cross out the names of players who've left the game? Really, who is left to continue? Dear James, I don't think you know."

Four of me assessed her reaction. On a vote of three to one, we concluded she wasn't overwhelmed. Possibly Meredith was satisfied to hear about Astor's initiative.

Not an iota of this was good news.

***

Hearing Meredith toss off the names on her guest list, and seeing those luminaries gathered on her porch, were very different things. After all, it wasn't July or even August, when Bar Harbor would be a sought after interlude for power brokers of all stripes. On June 1st, this was fund-raising business by the look and sound of it. Each introduction began and ended with one topic: Whom would I support and how much would I commit to a specific bundler of contributions.

Vacuous on purpose, a mid-western congressman asked whether, by any chance, I was related to Patrick McGettigan, former Chief of Staff to Senator Warren Harding. Before I could respond, he grabbed my arm and swung me to face the event photographer. Phony smile in place, the flash commemorated our little talk. Pompous schmuck shook my hand, wondering in a sardonic tone whether my son would ever work in politics again.

I resisted giving him a piece of my mind, in large part because I needed all of them.

Agent Swain and I were seated at a table with New York State Senator Blanche Santee, a tall, matronly woman running for the House of Representatives. Wearing a black and white checked suit and sensible shoes, her appearance projected competence. Simon Cantrell, a man of indeterminate age, who described himself as a collector of fine art, sat to my right looking like a dark-eyed vulture. Blackish-purple bags hung below a very poor hairpiece and a sharp beak heightened his small stature and curved spine.

After small talk was dispensed with, Senator Santee seemed perplexed. How could a Fool be unfamiliar with her stance on the economy? What bothered the Senator more than the budget or deficit, was her inability to dredge my name from a mental directory of six-figure contributors.

Cantrell's wariness persisted. Uncomfortable for no obvious reason—as if his relaxing day in Bar Harbor was doomed to end in disappointment—he was unnerved. I picked at a magpie's outer layer of feathers.

"Simon, do you and Meredith share similar tastes in art?"

Head shifted towards me, away from a study of clouds, he responded in a refined accent from nowhere in particular, but perhaps the stage.

"No, not really. Poor Meredith experienced a significant loss at her Florida home. She asked me to come up today to discuss restitution...I mean restoration."

A flicker of bruised ego, caused by an unfortunate selection of words, crossed the man's face. In one inflamed moment he appeared aged, fragile and ill. Downstream of several deep breaths, Cantrell hit his stride with a discourse on works of art damaged by the Iraqi wars.

Before long McGettigan drifted; Cantrell's words washed over me with but occasional impact. Upon delivery of the soup course, I concentrated on my spoon until startled by Senator Santee's questioning of Miss FBI.

"Gayle, who at the Department of Justice was nice enough to send you to Meredith's home for little wanderers?" Senator Santee's impish question was a bon-bon dipped in chocolate with innards of seagull droppings. "Are you just a country mouse? Or were sexual favors exchanged for this wondrous privilege?"

McGettigan translated to himself: *Who's your rabbi, Agent Swain? How far up the food chain did Meredith reach to get an FBI Agent assigned for personal protection?*

Miss FBI gurgled. Tried-on a winsome smile. Then fumbled and mumbled.

Santee set a sea anchor and shortened sail. "Come on sweet pea. Was it our beloved Senator Charlfont? He likes blowjobs from young women and money from old biddies. Or was it your boss, the good and wise US Attorney Ellen Harding? Or her daddy? Senator Harding would lick any Lawrence's rosy red arse. Tell Cousin Blanche who did you so nicely?"

"Truly, Senator, I'm not evading your question...I just don't know. I'm not a very senior Agent. I work investigations with AUSA Bazel, in New York City. Mr. Bazel informed me of this assignment."

McGettigan's antennae grew extensions; Daniel Bazel's name shouldn't have anything to do with Meredith or Astor Lawrence. Bazel was an insect with a hair across his ass for Phil Spazutta. Rand Jellenek's crane accident served as Bazel's ticket up the ladder. Bazel wouldn't talk to Ellen Harding twice a month.

In my right ear, the one closest to the art dealer, I heard soft-spoken words. "Parva scintilla saepe magnam flamam excitat."

Latin was unusual luncheon fare.

James resisted the nonsensical conclusion—could the angular little man once have been a Jesuit? Impossible to ignore—*a large flame growing from a small spark* was a decent, on the spot translation—and Agent Swain hadn't been sent to Meredith by accident. She worked for Bazel on the Jellenek case. Been in Ingrid's home with a search warrant in-hand, and stolen Ingrid's necklace.

Had she been found out? Or suspected? And if so, by whom?

There was no dispute about one outcome; Swain was banished to a nothing job watching an old lady get older. Who Meredith called to demand protection didn't matter. Daniel Bazel sent Swain to the wilds of Maine as the perfect solution to a nosy complication. Bazel no doubt found amusement in the BoGo he achieved; Meredith's protection was more flimsy veil than solid wall.

Could Cantrell be Timmy's stand-in assassin?

McGettigan drained his champagne in one swallow, watched the room spin in the after-buzz and munched salad. Bread slathered in butter soaked up bubbly, but not overactive flights of fancy.

Around our table the air sparked with silent electricity.

Swain scanned the room for a workable escape hatch.

Her Senatorial inquisitor sat with arms crossed. No arterial blood had been drawn.

Cantrell's cough spewed droplets of unknown biologic composition; red in the face he'd succumbed to inner demons or an unspecified ailment. Turned away to capture sputum in a polite, surreptitious stroke of his napkin, Cantrell spoke with concentrated intensity.

"Beatus, qui prodest, quibus potest."

It was McGettigan's turn to look away.

Attention of the waiter gained, I signaled for a fresh napkin. Without an opportunity to digest what I heard, Monsignor Everett's hold over me was re-established: Six years of Latin; two years of classical Greek; no advanced math; no chemistry or physics. How had a hodgepodge of secondary education produced a Ph.D. in engineering? How deep had Everett drilled into my brain so an interminable drumbeat produced two alternate translations: *He is lucky who helps everyone he can*—or very different *He is lucky who gains advantage from those over which he has power.*

Satire clear, a Jesuit would revel in the contradictions.

The second translation suggested McGettigan had been hasty: No assassination was planned for today. A related corollary alleged an alternative theory of Swain's actions. Like the proverbial bad penny, Timmy's admonition returned: *Think about who's offered you assistance...and who hasn't...and who may yet.*

Simon Cantrell and Meredith Lawrence would be the strangest of bedfellows—McGettigan believed they both offered assistance today. In an odd parallel, ignoring apparent contradiction was too risky. If Cantrell was Timmy's alter-ego, who better to act a killer's part than a Jesuit's caricature spouting proverbs in a dead language.

Blessed for my patience, the luncheon broke up. Invitees drifted from the porch to lawns, interior rooms and varied modes of transport.

McGettigan watched Cantrell the Vulture like a hawk, seeking to deny him an opportunity alone with his hostess. Although he seemed a better candidate for the emergency room, each time Simon Cantrell shifted his weight, or re-arranged his scrawny frame on the ocean blue satin divan, a Fool expected him to abuse Meredith's hospitality. Minutes before two o'clock, the doorbell rung. Meredith's senior housekeeper entered the slumbering Summer Room to announce the arrival of a taxi. In an exercise of doggedness, Cantrell rose to limp at the servant's heel. Upon reaching the double doors, he turned to offer James McGettigan a formal bow. A final Latin phrase erupted from a murmur.

"Amicus certus in re incerta cernitur."

McGettigan might not have agreed, but could not dispute how this chunk of wisdom fit Timmy the altar boy: *A true friend is discerned during an uncertain matter.*

***

In my Cape Cod cottage during better times, the kitchen was the hub of family activity, a place to linger over conversation and dreams. In Meredith's Bar Harbor kitchen, frenetic caterers dominated the long rectangular island where Gayle Swain, intent upon ignoring me, gulped from a tumbler of ice and clear fluid.

McGettigan swung a Thomas Moser stool into position beside her.

"Not the world's most glamorous job...Senator Santee should give it a try sometime. Why does Meredith need FBI protection?"

Expert at the task, she dragged a cigarette from a pack, flared a lighter and exhaled a stream of smoke in the direction of a folk-art sign prohibiting tobacco use where food was prepared. Butt dangling in an unattractive pose, right eye squinting in smoky irritation, was it Gayle or the vodka who replied?

"Why would I give a shit? Doing what I'm told like a good little girl."

"Aren't you a little old to describe yourself as a new Agent...or were you just messing with the good Senator?"

No acknowledgment on-deck, she showed exasperation. "Whaddayouwan?"

"Thought I'd ask...what's Ingrid Jellenek gonna get for violating Title 18-201?"

Agent Swain ground the cigarette into the butcher-block surface. Darting from floor to windows to the twisted butt, her eyes belied boiling emotions. Her fingers shouted *guilty*, for Agent Swain worked over the one-eyed sea horse like a string of worry beads. Was it a do-over she wished for? If she could do it again, would she reject the bribe?

I moved to familiar ground. "You know what they say, Gayle. Citrines or Sapphires don't define who you are...they're the price tag."

In response Miss FBI hiked her ankle-length skirt over a knee, revealing a small semi-automatic holstered on her leg. This act could, McGettigan speculated, be intended to threaten. Or in a long-shot alternative might be an offer of dangerous sex. In truth it was neither, so James laughed at her.

No one enjoyed being ridiculed. Swain yanked the gun free, wracked its slide and pointed it at my nose.

In an attempt to avoid the trite discussion of whom held the gun and who was in-charge, I told her, "Bazel sent you to interview Ingrid. Ingrid's go-to move is seduction. You gay?"

She lowered her eyebrows as if deciding on a reply.

Before she could choose, I added, "Either way, you accepted the necklace. You gonna say it was a gift from a new lover? Have any idea it's worth sixty grand? Bazel know about it? He'll want a share of the money...or a share of you."

"You a perv? You want a turn screwing the FBI girl?"

"Not a girl any more, Gayle. Dozens of photographs show you wearing the necklace today. It's one of a kind...you should know. Identifiable by a close friend of mine, the jeweler who made it."

Miss FBI's brow crinkled and her face sagged; she knew there was an offer on its way.

"I want to know whether Bazel's invented evidence will stick to Rand Jellenek. Tell me where Bazel's going…how to stop Jellenek's prosecution."

There was more McGettigan wanted to know, but pushing too hard could get me shot.

Smug blossomed into elation. Sadness stirred-in, this newest facial manipulation announced the guillotine's imminent fall. Not triumphant, but not merciful either, her half-sneer severed the Organism's neck before words altered my perceptions.

"Maybe you can screw me over, maybe not. Rand Jellenek's gonna get what he deserves. Bastard rigged the crane to fall. Pushed Madson off the roof." Seeing my mouth drop open, she supplemented her statement with more bad news. "Madson was gonna testify against Jellenek before he proved unable to fly."

A moment passed as she seemed to appreciate the events under discussion.

"Why would Jellenek murder Madson, you ask? Murdering one witness does no good…there's a second and a third waiting in line. Bazel has Jellenek by the balls." Swain examined the highball glass as she might the body of a naked lover. Spilled some on the butcher-block. "What's all this got to do with you…a small time ex-Mayor?"

Swain was getting comfortable, not the outcome McGettigan wanted.

"Accepting a bribe is one thing I could help you with. Murder might be another. Where'd you work before the FBI?" Tendons in her gun hand twitched in response to increased tension. To my chagrin, the chance she'd shoot me went up. "Hub Durant won't understand."

Halfway to the necklace, her hand stopped. Shaking from the booze, she glanced at me and saw reality; McGettigan hadn't plucked *Hub* from thin air.

Blunt, she asked, "Whom do *you* work for?"

"It was you, Gayle. Hub and his team needed quiet access to Marsh Landing…shooting their way in would've been counterproductive. So he worked out a way to have you assigned to Meredith. You drugged the security guards. Blew the transformer. Welcomed Hub's SUV at the gate. Then Gayle Swain disappeared.

You weren't present when a billionaire sugar baron was shot to death, or when two teams of hard-men slaughtered each other in Meredith's home. No one but Hub took his dead with him. For Hub, it's a leftover from Nam…no Marine left behind. He flew a Medevac, you know. Used to be a good person. Not any more. He'll cut your throat when he hears his pathetic, off-the-wagon gofer talked to James McGettigan."

I tossed a villainous grin at her. Without a governor to prevent a serious mistake, McGettigan told Miss FBI the unvarnished truth. "We hate each other. I'll see him in prison or a grave. Makes no difference."

Realization set in then—like spray from an icy winter fire hose it took my breath away. Reliance on Gayle Swain's statement, even if I got it from her, would convince few and influence none. Would McGettigan tear apart his wife's family? There seemed no next best strategy.

"I can't help you…" said a Fool, sounding like a cop show from thirty years ago "…unless you give me the name of the second witness?" Daniel Bazel told me Ingrid would testify against Rand. I haven't believed she would. I still didn't.

"Leave me alone." Gayle Swain's entire body shook. "Hub Durant's raising a hundred million for the election. He'll be a kingmaker. If he hates you, you'd be better off drinking yourself to death."

Raising her glass in mock salute, she finished, "Cause I agree, you sure as hell can't help me." Unsteady, she walked away, gun-hand pointed at the floor

McGettigan ran his finger through the puddle from her drink. Tasted it and made a face. The allure of an easy way out drained of possibility, McGettigan fell for it hook, line and sinker. Hadn't Cantrell's Latin seemed full of gravitas—use Swain's corruption to gain power over her. Turn the threat of her changing sides to McGettigan's advantage. Simple and elegant as a concept, it lay on the floor disproved and discarded.

CHAPTER 22

Crossing the Bourne Bridge over the Cape Cod Canal, I was minutes from the cottage.

McGettigan had satisfied a self-imposed requirement to alert Meredith Lawrence. How to defeat or eradicate the threat posed by Astor's rampant entitlement was above my pay grade. Or so I told the other three.

Through the looking glass and down a rabbit-hole, McGettigan alone was in complete control of his faculties. Characters in my drama lived on the fringe of societal norms, if not in a nether world beyond them. A Queen promised to rain on my parade. A priest assured me I alone could deliver salvation. The Emperor of Sugar lay in cold storage, adorned by the Minister of Death. Cheshire cats exaggerated their stories or told outright lies. The Empress of Frozen Food existed on a higher plane, where pieces were moved on the chessboard by invisible hands. Usurpers and pretenders abounded, their true form hidden under costumes taken from the dead.

What did they want from a visitor to their tea party? Who would tell me? Would I recognize the truth, if it appeared in a distorted vision carrying an electric guitar?

Snatched from the loony bin—how it felt to be in the cottage's kitchen, in the bosom of friends and children. Since we were last together, Patrick packed outdoor work muscle on a heretofore medium frame. His eyes, brighter than when he left, were a sign of promise. Julia was tired from worry, from being in-charge of her brother and father, from being away from her own life in service to the family, from being afraid of things which went bump in the night. My daughter would brook no nonsense from Dad. If there were things, or people, to be faced and beaten, Julia was ready.

Charlie Hamilton was tranquil on the surface. Lighter after twin hip replacements, the square set of jaw more noticeable, forearms rippled like cords of twisted wire. In an inner space, where he stored the remnants of a soldier who learned the worst of everything too early, Charlie looked outward with discretion and doubt. Like a good engineer, he measured forces allied against him and calculated methods to resist. Four of Charlie's regulars were stationed in and around the cottage. On the counter above the dishwasher was his homemade machine gun. Black and lethal, its optical sight stared like an unfocused eye. Fitted with a sophisticated suppressor it made almost no sound and emitted almost no flash. Its presence would've frightened McGettigan a year ago, but I could bear witness to Charlie's use of this weapon to positive purpose.

Still and all, killing may not be needed in a subterranean fantasy.

Billy Nichols made life simple. He was my friend. He loved me. And I loved him. Billy was eager to hear of progress or setbacks. So I told them all, with edits to protect me from disappointment and contempt. Fast and furious came their questions, each helpful on one level, none helpful on another.

Julia frowned. "Where's Gillian Hartnett right now?" Julia left off *Orenstein*. "D'you think her husband knows about the family vendetta?"

Patrick followed. "How bad are Martin Cardillo's injuries?"

McGettigan shook his head. I didn't know the answer. Hadn't called Dayami Machado, who I hoped was in charge of Martin's health, and who, in a different but certain scenario, could be in charge of Cardillo Crystals.

Charlie understood the real starting point. "Maybe we should have a longer chat with the priest?"

James could see how intimidation and prejudice worked to subjugate McGettigan's needs to Timmy's interests.

"Timilty is hard to find, Charlie. I don't go to him; he comes to me."

"Wrong man lookin', Boss."

Billy sat with his laptop, sporting a contemplative look. "You say the yacht sunk offshore, somewhere on Georges Bank?"

Something in Billy's question assured me worse news was on the way.

Pointing at the laptop's screen, Billy continued. "Just hit the news. Divers with a salvage outfit from New Bedford found *M*. Called the State Police sayin' a bunch of bodies are inside her hull. Whole damned yacht's a crime scene."

All eyes focused on McGettigan. My description of Thai girls in the bilge had been clinical, absent gory details. Among other reasons, I never wanted to remember what the dead girls looked like or how their deaths would impact fathers and mothers ten thousand miles across the world.

Billy tried to maintain a neutral tone. "Story says James McGettigan, of Monument Beach, is a *person of interest*."

Julia said what they were all thinking. "Bullshit. There's no evidence Dad knew those women. He didn't know those women. You woke up drugged with the Thai Inspector...she'll corroborate your story."

No parent could possess a sex life. The very idea of sex was TMI for sons and daughters. Mothers and fathers procreated, kissed in the kitchen and were in love. But sex?

I locked eyes with Julia. "Charanya will not confirm my story. Lie to assure my conviction is more like it."

Eye contact involved physical pain. When they heard the whole truth and nothing but the truth, my two children would see their father's feet of clay; would understand their father lied to save himself humiliation.

"I hoped *M* would never be found."

Breathing labored, confession to these loved-ones was harder than to a priest.

"I hoped you and Patrick might never see the photographs."

By now all I could do was gulp air and speak until the truth was told.

"One of the dead girls...performed oral sex while I was drugged. Awful photographs. Charanya accused me of murdering those young women. Tried to take the video with her, when she swam to the beach."

Watching these few who cared about James McGettigan, shame morphed first into annoyance and then something else entirely.

Charlie Hamilton shook his head in mock astonishment. "You tellin' us you cain't remember cause of the drugs? Holy cow, Boss, don' think you gettin' another chance." A laughing fit made Charlie spit his wad of tobacco into a handkerchief.

Billy snickered.

Patrick pretended to look away; he'd have joined the men's enjoyment of dad's mortification, but was afraid of his sister.

Julia folded her arms.

I exploded. "Don't you understand? These pictures, they'll…"

Julia grabbed my arm. "It'll be okay, Daddy. You're upset. No one thinks you cheated on Mom. Honest, we don't." She cupped my chin like when she was four. "Gotta pick yourself up off the floor, like Mom always said."

Patrick nodded at me. The more emotional of the two kids, if disapproval lurked behind empathy it would have shown through with clarity.

Billy offered, "Why not hold a news conference. Tell your side of the story before the pictures hit the front page and the evening news."

Melted under juvenile humor, uneasy feelings began to subside. Obviously, James needed a moment. So I listened.

Billy combined a practical thought with caustic teasing. "Might be able to create sympathy, if we got the right venue. Not as stupid as it sounds."

Charlie asked the obvious. "Did'ya see Charanya again? She tryin' blackmail?"

Patrick added, "Have you spoken to anyone in Thailand, Dad? I could call-in a favor…find out about her Thai Colonel."

Julia added, "Why not check with Colonel Petrovsky…he'd know about Colonel Nantakarn…and he'd be interested in Hub Durant's off-book activities."

Hours and a massive take-out order later, Billy Nichols, executive in charge of McGettigan's exoneration, summarized our collective duties.

"Patrick…focus on the Thailand connection. See if we can locate Charanya and Nantakarn. Julia…you and Charlie go up to Boston…figure out what's happened to Deirdre…why she showed up at the preliminary hearing on Linney's estate without James's authorization. Charlie's guys stay here at the cottage. I read about some regatta for Olympic sailors in Marblehead. Maybe Gillian is headed there. James, we all understand…you're certain Gideon's murder is the key to breaking-up the white slavery ring…but none of us want you going to New York alone. So…?"

Charlie followed me through the back porch and backyard to the edge of Buzzards Bay. Among long days in my life, this ranked in the top five. I picked up a stone and skipped it in the direction of the Merchant Marine Academy, where high wharf lights streaked saltwater like a starburst. Stooped to locate a better stone, a hand grabbed my shoulder. Lessons from Charlie were worthy of all the respect McGettigan could muster, so I waited in silence.

"Not foolin' me, Boss. Don' guess you give a damn 'bout the lawyer woman in Boston. Guess maybe you a little hurt is all. Sendin' Julia as if it's a big deal? Give'em kids credit. Came allaway from Africa to help Daddy. Keep'em in bubble-wrap won' do no good. Just as dead if this thing's a mess. Just as dead as you and me. And you goin' off alone? Gonna screw-up, like gettin shot-at in church with Billy. Why you still alive? Folks keepin' you livin' for some reason. Gotta bring'em to you…to your ground, where they the ones 'fraid alla time."

Charlie could be a therapist, except therapists were paid by the hour. Charlie would go broke dispensing wisdom in two-minute chunks. Having been hit on my head with a hammer, I was left to cobble together a dignified lie. He'd know—Charlie'd been lied to by the best the military had to offer. And he'd understand.

"I need Julia to figure out a strategy for this hearing about Robert's estate. Can't let Henry Linney get his hands on Robert's money, or all this shit means nothing. It's important."

"Listen up, you hear. You prolaby not good nuf to fix this an stay livin'. Stubborn as a pig…thas you, James."

"Keep her safe, Charlie. Keep Patrick safe."

Charlie shook his head in dismay. "Best I can, Boss."

A minute or two passed among close friends. Neither of us had more to say on the wisdom of a stubborn Fool's options. But I saw there were details a man like Charlie wanted to discuss. We began our detailed review in the backyard of Harry Cardillo's summerhouse close to twenty-four hours ago.

"So, you were runnin' towards Cardillo's boat. SWAT not there yet. This Jorge guy carryin' his little girl towards *his* boat. Right?"

Charlie stopped to absorb the scene, picturing everyone's position.

"Luis firin' the .50 Cal inna woods? Jorge's crew return' fire for a while."

Charlie rubbed his eyes with both hands to fight off fatigue.

"Then Jorge fall dead... halfway crossa lawn. Not hit by the 50 Cal?"

"No. Luis was at the wharf by then."

"You sure SWAT didn' take him out?"

"Positive."

I let the mental movie feed through the mind's projector. In this newsreel, Jorge is down. Pilar is screaming. SWAT arrives with no job to do. Luis runs towards Pilar. McGettigan is paralyzed until he sees **Sugar Daddy** drifting away.

"Absolutely positive, Charlie."

"Figure who pulla trigger on Jorge. Wasn' on the lawn, wharf or neara house. Long gun from far away."

Charlie left the rest to speculation.

"Who shot Jorge, Boss? Your priest? Some Cardillo gunsel? Durant, the CIA fixer? Whoever shot Jorge, he saw you. Might make you a *person of interest* to him. Might mean you got more to worry 'bout than what you awready worried 'bout."

"So?"

"So...maybe Julia goes to Boston with my boys, Rick and Toller. Jimbo and Sammy stay with Patrick. And I go with you. You turn up dead, Julia gonna take my head off."

Charlie was a master of understatement.

James countered with a smirk. "Julia turns up dead, her momma coming back from the dead for you."

We smiled. Charlie released my shoulder from his viselike grip.

"One more thing Boss. Don' believe anythin' lessn' some story taste good in your mouth. People get crazy for money."

McGettigan thought Charlie would find Timmy interesting. Latin jumped out of my mouth, "Is fecit, cui prodest."

"Fetch what?"

"Latin, Charlie, a language favored by Father Timilty and his ilk...means *done by the one who profits from it.*"

Charlie's face showed complete agreement.

***

Another nondescript rental took a circuitous route to New Jersey. Though it was not yet seven, I rung Amanda's prepaid cell.

"Good morning James. How you feeling?" Amanda sounded cheery, but distracted.

Checking the time I saw why; her first appointment would be antsy in the waiting area. "Did a friend of mine come to see you?"

Her voice wasn't troubled, more like fascinated.

"Father Timilty, the paid killer, you mean. He's quite the comedian, James, not at all who I would have expected. You never said...how many of us have a confessor we went to high school with?"

I wouldn't tell her Timmy was a flame and Amanda the moth. What had Timmy wanted with her?

"Timmy is fond of microbrew and practical jokes. Assuming he didn't bring beer, he must have wanted your help with a prank. Give it up."

"You're too suspicious, as usual. Father Timilty is concerned for you. Talked about all the stress you're under. Asked what your friends could do to help."

Father Timilty? Timmy spun his web. "And you suggested...?"

"I told him what I always tell you...you need to fight through the bad times."

"Crank it up...my motto of the month."

"Good for you, James. Father Timilty likes pointed advice. Said he'd use it in a homily one day."

"Amanda...he was excommunicated. It's certain to be a prank...he told you something else. Can you remember? It could be very important."

"Small talk mostly. He did ask for suggestions for your birthday. Wants to do something special." I heard her rifling through a box of memories. "Said he'd been thinking of taking you and the other altar boy to a Sox game. What was his name?"

McGettigan broke out in a sweat: There'd never been a third altar boy.

Triumph filled the phone. "Yes...it was biblical...Gideon Wainright. I'm pretty sure."

"Good old Gideon. Timmy say anything about his health?"

"Just about the Sox game. He's quite charming, you know. Maybe he's misunderstood."

Yup, exactly what I'd expect a therapist to say. "Hey Amanda…thanks. GTO running all right? I'll get your car back soon. Keep the cell phone close, will you?"

From Newark Airport's rental car return, a cab took me to the PATH station in Jersey City. For a fleeting moment, I wondered what was on the menu at Ruggiero's—and tasted Mata Hari's kiss again.

Herald Square was where McGettigan found tea and a gooey pastry. Bad for the waistline, good for the spirit. As carbohydrates boosted blood sugar, *Gideon v. Wainwright* came back to me. The 1965 Supreme Court ruling was infamous, holding a criminal defendant had the right to an attorney, even if the defendant couldn't afford one. Timmy knew my children were attorneys, knew Deirdre was my criminal representative, knew a free lawyer wasn't one of my needs; so what was the message? In need of a laptop, McGettigan walked a few blocks to a nearby hotel where laptops sprouted from every corner of the lobby. Glad to be dressed in a business suit, I targeted the lady in stout walking shoes holding an iPad.

"Ma'am, could I ask a favor?"

Guarded examination of McGettigan completed, she replied, "What can I do for you?"

"Could you search *Gideon v. Wainwright*, please? I've run out of battery."

"Are you in town for a trial?"

Trial had seven alternate dictionary definitions; I was in town for one of them.

"Yes, Ma'am."

Holding out the screen to me, the third listing was gold. *Gideon's Trumpet* was a TV movie, play on words using the famous defendant's last name and the biblical story of Gideon ordering his small force to attack a much larger enemy camp. Noise and light tricked Gideon's enemies into thinking a much larger army was attacking. McGettigan as Gideon could win no battle with trickery. What noise and light could I still generate?

Expressing thanks, McGettigan left the nice lady with her device.

On a low humidity June day, a second cup of tea was welcome. Face covered by the *Post*, I stood in the market where McGettigan had hidden to avoid Gideon's arrival. Nothing had changed; McGettigan wanted to know more about Gideon—and Stubble proved uncooperative during our first encounter.

Perhaps this time would be different.

I crossed the street to where a small *Closed* sign hung on the pizza parlor's door. No twirling rounds of dough, no pepperoni and melted cheese, no Stubble. Did a closed pizza joint mean a closed brothel? The thought made me turn to look. As if on cue, Mama-san and a linebacker exited, carrying a bulging laundry bag.

Briefcase swinging in step, McGettigan sauntered uptown and held position outside a sporting goods emporium. The old woman in a plain Kimono and the no-neck in dark slacks and sport-jacket entered the Chinese laundry.

Shit. The transfer wouldn't be here on 3rd; it would always have been set for the back alley.

Inside the sports shop, McGettigan noticed a rear door window covered with bars. A pretty young woman in shorts and a trendy soccer shirt asked, "Can I help you?"

"Baseball bat. Catcher's mask. Please."

"Aluminum?"

"Little-League, yes." McGettigan was an anxious granddad.

The bat's heft felt good. Pitchers were never dangerous hitters. This could be my day to belt one. The lightweight mask fit with ease. A hundred and a half later, with a hurried smile, I said, "Can I go out the back?"

Puke, urine and less sanitary items marked my cautious passage to the laundry. With a quick glance inside, I opened the briefcase and removed blue latex gloves. In a catcher's crouch, mask in place, coiled shoulders were the required mechanism to generate power. The Organism awaited its first time at bat in decades.

The door opened.

Preparation shredded with the appearance of a dainty black shoe and white stockings, I adjusted on the fly, connecting with Mama-san full in the belly. Falling backward, her torso tangled with the no-neck security guard, and, while she moaned from broken ribs and lack of breath, the bat recoiled. Linebacker tried to free his arms. As he shoved her forward, the bat began its inexorable forward arc.

McGettigan bats right-handed, so linebacker's left temple produced a solid impact. Not enough power for a double or triple, but enough so spittle flew at my face. He dropped on top of Mama-san, unconscious. Neither moved in the moment it took to snag the laundry bag and his gun. A small Chinese man threw his hands above his head and disappeared behind the counter.

Taking the money would attract someone's attention—McGettigan's version of *Gideon's Trumpet*.

Outside, a throaty engine could be heard pulling into the far end of the alley. Armored trucks didn't stop at Chinese laundries or closed pizza joints, so I stepped past the prone forms of Mama-san and her escort to identify the oncoming vehicle.

Mama San coughed. Head turned, I watched her struggle to point a tiny gun at me. The Organism's eyes got big in a hurry.

Bam.

It sounded like a toy.

Bam.

Glass broke. The Chinese counter-man screamed in pain.

The gun wavered, always seeking McGettigan. Without remorse, McGettigan pointed Linebacker's weapon and pulled the trigger. When I tossed the gun, it landed next to its original owner. Out the front door went a Fool of gigantic proportion, a man guilty of armed robbery, assault with a deadly weapon, assault with intent and, in the worst circumstance, manslaughter. Gloves ripped off, gait smoothed-out to balance briefcase and laundry bag, the hounds of hell crawled up the Organism's back. Upright and uninjured I reached East 36th and walked towards 2nd Ave. Sirens audible in several directions, no one gave the well-dressed man carrying a briefcase and dirty underwear a second look. A store selling china and glassware beckoned on my left. I browsed. Ten minutes of restless observation expired, the rear exit was accessible. I turned north.

Labor problems pervaded all organizations, even criminal ones. Had the armored truck stopped at the laundry? Found linebacker out cold? Found Mama-san gut shot in need of immediate medical attention? Perhaps the men in the armored truck elected to call an ambulance before giving chase.

Further east on 37th, I ducked into a medical office building. In an empty men's room, trembling hands examined my loot. Neat, banded bundles totaled twenty-eight grand. Credit card receipts tripled the cash amount. The brothel's business, noted in an unexpected ledger, was identified as *Therapy for the Ages LLC*. In fine print Mama-san recorded a summary of her business with CIA, represented by Reginald Tucker. This tongue-in-cheek misdirection must have given Astor and Kristian a month's amusement.

The ledger provided McGettigan a blurred picture of how Thai girls were kidnapped, sold and buried.

Matrices offered month over month comparative analyses. What first resembled a jumble of nonsensical entries, an engineer's interpolation exposed as rudimentary code. Layers of shareholders, management, subcontractors and employees became an organization chart. Revenue and expenses became a basic profit and loss statement.

Subcontractors lured girls from Thailand's countryside with offers of jobs in America. Transporters took possession to trans-ship human cargo, via intermediate points, to Florida. Hub Durant's storm troopers, the seamier underbelly of National Security, took over for the journey to New York. Girls were delivered to customers on a pre-paid basis. Six figures to low seven figures were common enough; young, inexperienced Thai girls were a rare and expensive hobby. Trash was collected and disposed via the Raouls and Frankies of this world.

Mama-san's largest client, and a principal investor in the scheme, was Astor Lawrence, although the ledger contained no actual names.

No analysis would end the criminal enterprise or keep young women alive, because among a forest of information were too many trees. Yesterday McGettigan expected EcoWaste's landfill to contain girls, not Gideon. Now I believed, with access and a backhoe, the remains of both would be excavated.

Astor's customers were wealthy *and* murderous perverts?

The Organism's adrenal gland pumped despite McGettigan's override command. Two hours passed and still McGettigan knew nothing of Gideon, my trumpet blower. Under severe stress, an altered view of the world could produce flashes of brilliance, or great blunders. McGettigan had batted from both sides of this equation in the past.

Again I tapped 911.

"I have information about Gideon's disappearance. Tell his partner to call 969-222-4721."

Analysis of the 911 tapes would show the call originated on a burner phone purchased this morning. I hadn't lied; McGettigan held information about Detective Gideon Kusneski, but wouldn't share with Gideon's partner without a quid pro quo.

Ledger and cash transferred to the briefcase, laundry bag full of credit card receipts close to my side, I took the elevator down. On Broome Street where the taxi would enter the Holland Tunnel, I dialed *Victor's Professional Photography*.

"Victor's Photography, Bruce speaking, how may I assist you?"

"Bruce…James McGettigan. Do you have a few minutes?"

"Certainly, James. When?"

"Fifteen minutes depending on traffic."

CHAPTER 23

A warm smile rested easily on Bruce's face. Victor, on the other hand, was angst ridden. McGettigan addressed Victor.

"Looks like you've kept up with the news."

Victor was apoplectic. "We don't want trouble, Mr. McGettigan."

Bruce remained relaxed, unperturbed in the presence of a *Person of Interest* in multiple murders.

I turned to Bruce. "There's not much to tell. I'm a professional investigator...engineering disasters are my specialty. Collapsed buildings. Yachts which sink, but shouldn't have. This tragic event generated particular suspicions...the yacht's owner retained me. Law enforcement wants the evidence I've gathered. Hence the designation as a *Person of Interest.*"

Bruce clapped Victor on the back. "I told you Mr. McGettigan is a good person. I know these things."

Victor eased away from the counter, body language betraying a strong case of disbelief, or at best ambivalence.

"What can we do for you...something we haven't done already?"

Julia's business card and Mama-san's ledger presented on the counter's glass surface, I showed them page after page of neat, handwritten numbers.

"Three things I need: First, an exact duplicate...with the original delivered to my daughter address. Second, I need a brilliant forger."

Victor's face expressed pure incredulity. I glanced at my phone to check the time.

"Last, I'd like Bruce's impression of a New York cop, who'll show up here sometime this afternoon."

Victor was indignant. "Now see here…"

Bruce interrupted in a most gentle fashion. "Vic, maybe you could copy the ledger, while Mr. McGettigan expands on his needs." Watching Victor's retreat, he said without lowering his voice, "Victor's a wonderful man with too many good qualities to list. I love him very much." Grin widened, he turned to business. "*Brilliant forger*…was very kind of you. What do I add or subtract from the ledger?"

A yellow legal pad contained copious notes made in the men's room stall. Product of a fertile imagination, when enhanced by Bruce's artistry the names of real people and corporations would blend with stark, uninformative numbers in Mama-san's original. James handed Bruce an exact replica of a common ledger, purchased at a stationary store in Journal Square. I wouldn't insult an artiste by insisting on an ink match and the original's weight of hand.

Bruce shouted to the rear of the shop, "Vic, how many pages?"

 "Half full…maybe forty or fifty."

Businesslike, Bruce considered the costs and risks. "Not a problem. Copies of the newer ledger?"

"Three."

"Now…to your third item. Who's the cop? What are your prejudices? What do you think he's done wrong? Is he dangerous?"

"Just guesses. Could be a man or a woman. I think he, or she, is the partner of a missing cop. I assume he, or she, is frantic with worry and boiling with anger at whoever's responsible for abducting their partner. As for dangerous…it should ooze from his or her pores, if he, or she, is one of the bad guys."

"Would you like a portrait?"

"Two likenesses, if you will. What does he or she look like on the outside, and what you intuit about his or her insides."

Bruce's more ethereal skills must frequently be taken for granted. Our shared formality continued. "Why is he, or she, coming here to the shop?"

"So you can be my gatekeeper. If he, or she, pass your sniff test, send them to this address." I scribbled and ripped off another sheet from the pad. "If not, plead ignorance. Suggest the entire thing must be a prank. Whatever it takes to get him, or her, out your door."

Bruce's tone became serious and sincere. "I'm complimented by your confidence. I'll finish the second ledger and the copies by, say, seven this evening. Hand delivery would be best, don't you think?"

"Brown wrapping paper tied with white string. Don't deliver it yourself. Pay one of the local kids to leave it with Johnny Ruggiero. Just make sure the kid tells Johnny it's mine."

Bruce turned-on his Cary Grant the Spy expression. "Cash will be best."

McGettigan assumed Mama-san's cash was unmarked. Ten grand on the counter, I shook Bruce's hand and yelled to Victor. "One copy of the ledger, Victor. Temptation is the devil's work."

Hours to kill until meeting Gideon's partner, and a late dinner scheduled at Casa Ruggiero, I stuffed a FedEx box with Mama-san's credit card slips, and addressed it to Julia. On the walk back to Journal Square, the phone's muffled sound intruded. I answered without speaking.

"Dad, it's Patrick." Like I wouldn't know. Wait—his voice sounded wrong.

"Who's listening, son?"

Patrick was rattled. "I was in a coffee shop near the Capitol…with a buddy whose boss sits on the Foreign Affairs Committee. I asked him about Nantakarn, the Thai policeman. He made a couple of calls…now I'm sharing a table with two women who claim to work for General Petrovsky. They want you to join us."

"Ask one of them: *Where in Poland was Anton born?*"

A new voice, one I'd not heard before said in a breezy, unprofessional, and possibly threatening tone of voice, "We'll keep Patrick with us, Dr. McGettigan…too ensure we get everyone's perspective."

It sounded like Patrick's first trip to the orthodontist; nothing to worry about, we're going to straighten those teeth in a jiffy. On the other hand, the disembodied voice in no way proclaimed Anton to be a son of Wisconsin. The woman's blow struck at my soul; McGettigan summoned rage to disguise weakness.

"Listen very carefully," a deep breath aided supposition. "Call Hub Durant, your employer…tell Hub he missed the control room in the walk-in freezer…tell him I've got video from Astor Lawrence's fundraiser in Palm Beach…tell him Astor's a weak link. Tell him I've got photos of Gideon's final resting place. Tell him I'll meet him at the crane on Rivers Nest Towers...tonight at eleven. Hub should remember...there are people he cherishes and what goes around *will* come around. Then ask Hub whether Patrick should stay with you ladies."

Bathed in nervous sweat, the engineer comprehended: NSA's vast listening capabilities were programmed for certain key words: *Nantakarn* was one. McGettigan hoped Hub Durant, Astor Lawrence and Gideon were also flagged.

If Hub intended to leverage McGettigan with Patrick's safety, I'd accept help from any source, no matter the cost. Should Hub make an error in judgment, and Patrick be harmed, the Organism set aside a corner of its brain to devise its worst, to imitate practitioners of persecution glorified by storytellers. Terrified of harm done to *her* beautiful boy, a Fool peered over the edge of insanity, while McGettigan held on tight.

Monsignor Everett held a viselike grip on my throat. Useless as studying Latin seemed at the time, it poured from me like sacramental wine, when the phone rang a second time. *"Quos Deus vult perdere, prius dementat."*

"Excuse me, Dr. McGettigan," the disembodied voice said. "I didn't catch what you said." She'd tell Hub I spoke in tongues. Or if a Latin scholar, she'd recognize: *Those whom God wills to destroy, he first deprives of their senses.* "Your son left the café, Dr. McGettigan, alone and safe. Tonight we'll meet as you propose, but not at your preferred location. Please suggest an alternate...where we all might feel comfortable."

"How about the Oak Room around eight?" Jerking Hub's chain was a guilty pleasure. He wasn't comfortable surrounded by wealth; yet wealth was his madness. Since the entire idea of a face to face was a farce, since I'd be crazier than a Fool to show up, a Red Sox fan could have suggested the pitcher's mound at Yankee Stadium.

Hub's spokeswoman ended our little heart to heart. "Sounds good. See you there."

***

Patrick's phone went to voicemail. Needing a plain vanilla location to collect my thoughts, the Jersey City Museum on Montgomery was a twenty-minute hike. Alone in an air-conditioned gallery, logic could be derived from chaos. McGettigan raised the phone to call again, when like a prophet of the future it rang. Once again I answered without a word.

"You jerkin' my chain...or what? Whaddya know about Gideon? Nothin'...cause you're a jerkoff." Someone from Gideon's precinct was out of sorts.

"Have Gideon's partner call in an hour." I read the number from the screen of a fresh out of the box burner.

A cruising cabby had no interest in a four-dollar fare; folded twenties changed his mind. I gave him the address of the Yankee kid's street corner. When we pulled up to the blind man, I passed the cabbie another twenty. "Wait here, I'll be less than five minutes."

Ear tilted towards the idling taxi, the peddler anticipated a drug sale with a smarmy look of satisfaction and increased prices.

"Where's the kid with the Yankees hat?" McGettigan had little patience for protracted conversation.

"Certain to be in school, my brother. Can I help you get through the day?"

"Kid had a Glock. I'd got seven hundred reasons you should sell it."

"Need two Gs, Bro."

Fifty of Mama-san's twenties made a convincing argument. The semi-automatic emerged from the skirt of his cart along with a lollipop. "Ease your pain, Bro, before you shoot youseff in the ass." High-pitched cackling laughter followed me into the taxi.

Montgomery ended at Exchange Place, a block from the Hyatt. I grabbed a table, needing something bland to neutralize an acid stomach. A group of men across the room laughed in unison—Phil Spazutta returned my gaze.

Crumbs of bread and bits of cheddar were left, when Phil plunked himself down in a chair. Relaxed and tan, he was dressed for summer in seersucker and a bow tie. Hair slicked back, what bothered him was the no-smoking rule. "Let's get oudda here, James, I need a smoke."

Under an umbrella, near a pool with no swimmers, Phil sucked on his second cigarette.

"Phil, is Bazel still trying to make something stick?"

Spazutta's expression lightened, a wry smile leaking through a dark cloud. "Little prick capitulated." Phil inhaled, let smoke curl out with a sigh. "Sent me a formal letter...*the FBI and the US Attorney have determined Phillip Spazutta, Esq. is no longer the target of any open investigation.* They're done with me." With a wider grin of anticipation, he added, "Course this'll last till a week from now, when Bazel hasn't taken a shit for days."

The waitress brought scotch and a diet soda. Phil drained the whiskey and made a face at my glass. "Honey," he whistled at the busy blonde. Another drink appeared. Sipping this time, Phil said, "I'm not suspicious, mind you, but why you wanna know?"

Answering a question with a question was rude, but so what. "Was there an understanding among men of good will?"

"Good will your ass." Mocking laughter was genuine. "No trade. No nothin. Bazel's got other fish to fry...what he said onna phone. Come on, this some kinda big deal on Cape Cod?"

"You got anything on him, Phil? Something I could borrow."

"How'd you get to be a *Person of Interest?* Dead girls, the news said. Not like the Dr. Straight-laced I know."

"Rivers Nest Towers...the Crane was owned by my brother-in-law. Bazel offered a trade...brother-in-law for Spazutta. Now you're off the hook...you win the lottery? What's Bazel thinking?"

"Rivers Nest...is this the thing Richie Tarrant's involved in...was involved in...with Wiley Hoshall?" Phil made the sign of the cross with overblown ceremony in remembrance of his now interred law partner.

Phil didn't give a shit about Wiley, and wasn't much bereaved.

"Close. There're three partners in Rivers Nest: Richie Tarrant, Astor Lawrence of the Lawrence empire and Lawrence's on and off girlfriend, Jill Stoddard. Rivers Nest is broke. Astor Lawrence is involved in a very unpleasant attempt to raise capital."

Phil looked at me cross-eyed.

I answered his unasked question. "How could a Lawrence have money problems? Exactly what's confusing me. Astor's mother won't let him off the leash. Trust fund children, you know."

Phil gave me the finger. Having never established trust funds for his kids, Phil didn't know Julia and Patrick were different products of the system which produced Astor.

"You remember the fundraiser, when you couldn't get your sailor-suit from the cleaners? Tarrant was hanging around Lawrence, Hoshall, Mosqueda and a guy named Henry Linney. Hoshall and

Mosqueda have been murdered. An attempt has been made on Lawrence. Richie Tarrant should be very careful."

"You want me to warn Tarrant?"

"Someone's executing Lawrence's friends, Phil...I'm the one being set-up. I was on the yacht with eleven dead girls. Never laid eyes on even one of them, before the damn thing started to sink. Same yacht hosted the fundraiser a block from where we're sitting. It all started with Bazel twisting my arm about Phil Spazutta."

Phil wiped beads of perspiration from his forehead. "If this horseshit story is gonna be your defense, you need a better lawyer." Scratching a match he lit a new one while the old one smoldered in an ashtray. "Look, James. I wanna help. Maybe there's a thing might do you some good...Richie bailed outta the fuckin' building. Sale closed couple days ago."

"You know this how?"

Phil flicked a long ash without looking up. "Cause my son handled the closing."

"For which side?"

"For Richie."

"Who you swore up and down your firm *didn't* represent the day Wiley got himself murdered. Who'd Richie sell to?"

Phil shrugged his shoulders. Patted me on the head and walked off. One of the reasons I liked Phil—he wouldn't lie to a friend unless it was crucial. In his version of honesty, he told me enough.

The Fool was like a squirrel with winter approaching, gathering acorns to fend off starvation, gathering them one by one because I was too dumb to buy a basket.

Daniel Bazel was no longer pursuing Phil.

Richie Tarrant sold his stake in *Rivers Nest*.

How many acorns would be enough?

***

Reaching-out for Julia took patience. Not on her cell or in the office, I tried Charlie's phone and got voice-mail. Deirdre's office wouldn't put me through, but told me Attorney McGettigan left over an hour ago.

Minutes expanded to hours.

Less than an hour equaled a year; her phone answered.

"Julia?"

"Hi Dad. You okay?"

"I'm good, kiddo. What's the story with Deirdre?"

"Claims the guard is her idea. Says she was pretty damned upset, when you disappeared on Mrs. Lawrence's yacht. Doesn't consider herself your lawyer...sent you a final invoice. Wouldn't talk about anything to do with the Linney family. I told her she'd no basis to speak as your representative at the preliminary hearing. She cringed a little, but not enough to help us. She's out of sorts, Dad. Not afraid, exactly. Shaken. Not interested in you...not socially anyway."

Julia was all business, so I followed her lead.

"Jennifer and Sid did some research for me. A man named Richie Tarrant just closed the sale of his interest in a high rise called Rivers Nest Towers. Sid's got the details. Find out who the buyer was. It won't be a simple transaction, so do whatever you need to. Can you put Charlie on?"

"I'm catching a bite to eat. We'll get on it this afternoon."

"Charlie? Please."

"Indisposed."

"Tell him to crap on his own time. Have you spoken to Patrick?" My voice failed to conceal a parent's deepest fears.

"Yes, he said things were interesting for a while. Said one of the women who intercepted him is a babe. Patrick isn't going to break in half, Dad...he's way tougher than you think. We both are."

A familiar sound, a reverberating *boom*, rolled through the receiver drowning out Julia's next words. "Where *are* you, Julia?"

"On the road...they're blasting rock or something."

Not the right sound for blasting, but what could an engineer know? "Listen Julia, d'you remember the woman from *Boston Live*, the one who hounded me for months about an interview?"

"Blake the Barracuda?"

Taken aback by my daughter's commentary on a bad idea, a Fool wasn't deterred from idiocy. "Call her, please. Negotiate the terms of an exclusive interview. Get something in writing."

"Billy was joking, Dad. None of us thought we should invite the barracuda into the kitchen. She'll never agree to a pre-approved list of questions. She won't."

"No restrictions on questions, Julia. I want a five-minute opening statement. No other guests. We do the whole half hour on James

McGettigan's criminal activities."

My kid believed me certifiable. "Dad, you've always said no one wins against the Press. What makes you think…"

"Don't want to win. Irritating sharks is the goal. A Barracuda should be the perfect tool."

***

Liberty Landing Marina was an oasis. Both Liberty State Park, which the marina bordered, and Liberty National Golf Club, its contiguous neighbor, had once upon a time been hazardous waste sites. Today two hundred slips were home to every type of sail and powerboat. Among smaller craft was a versatile little sloop used by the local sailing school. Tie and dress shirt removed, McGettigan sat waiting, the Yankee kid's Glock pressed against his spine. Pants rolled up to the knee, bare feet dangled in the water, a red and white mainsail luffed in a zephyr. A New York cop was my missing link.

A tan sedan provided a first inkling.

When boyish, streaked hair emerged, I was certain. Sedan-man from the Cape Cod Canal, and Shaggy from Raoul's apartment complex, were one and the same—here to solicit information about Gideon's disappearance with Bruce's blessing. Uncomfortable in slippery leather-soled shoes, he was out of his jurisdiction. By the time he loomed over me, hands on hips, an accusation was his highest priority and a tenuous bluff.

"Planning to spend your vacation at Rikers?"

"Take your shoes off and climb aboard."

"Get out the boat. Get in the car, we'll head back to the City."

Head back to the City? Or somewhere quiet where he'd beat the crap out of McGettigan? The probability of me reaching the Glock, before he could aim and pull his trigger, was too small to calculate.

I asked, "You got a gold shield?"

Surroundings swept with an animal's darting eyes, he opened his suit jacket to show me.

"Think you'll keep it, when my video of you impersonating a Fed…burgling Raoul Dupree's place…is seen by your bosses? Take a load off, Detective." Putting my hands in the air, I lied. "No weapon. We'll go for a little sail…and talk about how Gideon got himself killed."

"You ain't got bupkus."

He wasn't sure enough to try and arrest me. Not sure enough to shoot me, either. Tentative, he stepped on the gunwale, rocking the boat under his weight. Clumsy, he slid onto the seat. Not a sailor.

"Easier in bare feet." McGettigan pulled in the mainsheet. The racing sloop heeled to port and jackrabbited in the direction of the George Washington Bridge. My passenger was already sorry he came.

After a while, when his nerves subsided a smidge, he said, "Isaac's my name."

"Well Detective Isaac, what were you doing at the Cape Cod Canal a few weeks ago?"

He examined me, squinted hard at the sail, and then gazed back towards dry land. Reached for his sunglasses, wanting nothing more than to suggest I fuck-off. One, right between the eyes, was his fondest wish.

"Chasing the yacht."

"Not following me from the Court House?"

"Nah. Found out after your little accident."

"Wasn't an accident, Detective Isaac." I showed him crusted and scabby staples.

"Shoulda had those out by now."

"Who did Gideon identify in the white-slavery ring?" Isaac frowned at the mention of Gideon's investigative ability. Somewhere in his lost soul was the residue of remorse. Poor bastard.

"Old babe who runs the cat-house…one of the mob families. We had some good leads, but they're none of your business. What do you know about Gideon? Said you had information."

"Did you suspect there were girls on board the yacht?"

My new friend struggled to remain patient. Not because of any fealty to Gideon but because this exercise was a waste of his time— Gideon being over his head in shit and this dickwad having put him there.

"Gideon said no. He wanted me to follow the yacht to each stop. See when and where the girls were loaded."

Loaded wasn't the term I'd expected. *Loaded* was a word best applied to corpses.

"Any chance the girl who jumped is feeding you information?"

"Nah. Gideon never had anyone inside. The chink…just pussy. Didn't like being for sale, I guess."

Detective Shaggy needed help with his memory. I watched him try to figure a way out, to walk away with the one piece of information he cared about: Would Gideon's corpse, buried in a Palm Beach landfill, send him away for twenty to life? Shaggy couldn't care less about his paymaster, or those who ended the lives of children after feeding their sexual urges.

"You think Gideon's alive, Detective?"

"We're praying for him."

Timmy's opinion: Prayer in Shaggy's position would be melodramatic overkill.

Easing the sail, I handed him a photograph from my briefcase.

He tried to act unprepared—his partner's mostly buried remains a true and sorrowful shock. Imitation tears and trembling were third-rate theater.

Course changed towards the Jersey shoreline, near enough to touch a group of old, rotting pilings, we tacked away seconds before becoming a wreck ourselves.

"Where was this taken? You got co-ordinates? I need to recover Gideon's body."

Now we were on ground Shaggy cared about.

"Landfill where Raoul worked. No co-ordinates. You'll have to dig by hand and use search dogs."

Relief flooded his face for less than a heartbeat before he wiped it away. Raoul and Frankie were out of the way. No Coroner was interested in Gideon's body. Science wouldn't expose this crooked New York cop.

"How did he die? Who did it?" Isaac hadn't asked who took the photograph.

"First things first. Raoul Dupree had the photograph in his possession, despite you and Manuel not finding it. Raoul was shot later…shot in the head. Manuel the shooter?"

Yes, this was a trick question. Still, he was too eager to deny involvement. "How the fuck would I know?"

"You were with Manuel."

"How would you…?"

"I was watching. From above. With my video gear."

"When Manuel couldn't get me the photos, I dumped him. Went back to the hotel."

"Let's try again. Who gutted Manuel?"

"Manuel's dead?"

"Yes, Detective Isaac."

In a short time this circle jerk would advance past necessary and beyond tiring.

"The same Manuel who burgled Raoul's apartment in your esteemed company. The same Manuel who shot Raoul in the face four or five times. Manuel was opened like they do a shark...to examine the contents of its belly. Manuel brought the girls from Cuba, right?"

Detective Isaac knew about Manuel's bad end. He stared at the horizon. McGettigan kept a foot on his neck.

"How about Frankie McShane? In the hospital?"

Still no disclosure. Time to see if I could shake it out of him.

"You notice a pattern, Detective? Anyone involved with kidnapping Thai girls turns up deceased. Was Gideon involved...or looking to stop it? Were you protecting Ellen Harding? If so, *you* are on a short-list to be dead."

I worked the little boat back into the wind. This Detective and I, we were going nowhere. McGettigan's accusations resulted in no evidence of his involvement. Shaggy was certain I wasn't alone, and his decision not to shoot me was sixty/forty in McGettigan's favor. Neither of us would say more until the sail came down and momentum eased us to the dock.

As he put on his shoes, I tried again.

"Keep the picture of Gideon. Souvenir. Did you know Mama-san kept a book of accounts? Names and amounts paid. Mama-san got robbed...got shot. Ledger with the accounts is gone. Be careful Detective Isaac, bodies by the dozen piling up."

This time McGettigan's smug superiority tempted the cop. His right hand trembled with how much he wanted to shut McGettigan's mouth. A curtain descended as a big breath rescued him from a bigger mistake.

"Isaac's my first name, McGettigan." He handed me a card from his breast pocket.

McGettigan began to reciprocate.

"I got your business card." He held it up to show me.

With the sun behind him, the stain from holy oils resembled a Rorschach Blot. Frankie McShane's executioner removed himself from the boat, looking like he stepped barefoot in a nest of fire ants.

"You need to be cautious, Detective. Mama-san's employers will want their ledger back. Maybe they'll be suspicious of a two-faced cop. And worse, there's a dedicated executioner out there, hunting each of you for what you've done to those girls."

Make my opponents afraid—was Charlie's advice.

Well the other team would never fear McGettigan, so I hyped the New York mob and an unknown, all-seeing boogieman. Isaac hustled along the dock, halfway to dry land, as McGettigan muttered, "*Through this holy anointing with oil may the Lord in his love and mercy help you with the grace of the Holy Spirit and may the Lord who frees you from sin save you and raise you up.*"

Those were the words Timmy used to anoint Frankie McShane, not murder him as I initially believed. Detective Isaac took care of Frankie. I bet he eliminated Gideon as well. And Manuel. A regular Mr. Clean.

In any postgame analysis, Bruce was scored a psychic. McGettigan's early innings strategy was half-right. I asked Bruce to screen the cop who showed-up strictly for innocence—which limited Bruce's to half a chance to help. Bruce's insight—Shaggy's obvious guilt—resulted in a guilty as sin Detective delivered into McGettigan's hands. Whether one particular outcome occurred to Bruce—McGettigan shot dead, carcass floating in the river—didn't merit speculation after the fact.

McGettigan's extra inning gamble turned on a purely physical observation—Shaggy couldn't swim. Most cops would've tried to save Charanya from drowning. Not the Shag-man. Once under sail, fear messed with Detective Isaac's instincts, which contributed to keeping the Organism alive.

***

"Daniel Bazel, please."

"Whom may I say is calling?"

"James McGettigan." I drummed four fingers on the sloop's gunwale.

Bazel wasn't polite. "Whaddya want?"

"You know Ruggiero's. Come at ten tonight...wait outside the door. I'll present you with a trade you'll love."

"Don't need you any more."

"Not about Phil Spazutta. What I'm offering is a career guarantee. Promotion and glory. All the things you've dreamed of."

"I'll give you five minutes."

My next call was trickier. "Hi Rand, it's James." Before he could speak, I drained a bucket of bait into the water. "I've negotiated a deal. No jail. Suspended sentence. Big fine. Dinner at Ruggiero's tonight at nine-thirty. Bring your girlfriend…no deal without her presence."

"What girlfriend?"

No one cared about Rand's affairs or denials. Jail or no jail should've been Rand Jellenek's single-minded concern. Rand didn't know it was Hub Durant who impersonated the District Attorney's representative. Couldn't know Hub demanded James's admission of guilt in the Hartnett mishmash. Didn't know his girlfriend wasn't his girlfriend, although sex was sex despite its concealed agenda.

"The gorgeous woman fifteen years younger than Ingrid, Rand."

The woman whose kiss McGettigan remembered too often.

"Can't we meet alone?"

"I want to hear you tell her it's over. I'll explain what happens, if she testifies against you; eighteen months in the Hudson County Jail should keep her mouth shut. If she's greedy enough, I'll pay her blood money. For God's sake, this deal won't come again."

Rand Jellenek's funds were low. Let Rand wallow in every murderer's dream—certainty he'd gotten away with murder.

"Can't thank you enough, James?"

"Anything for the family, Rand."

On my third successive call, McGettigan listened to an electronic voice catalog my options. Selecting non-emergency personnel got me a disinterested male who said, "Jersey City Police…tip line."

"Gang's gonna burn down Victor's Photography tonight."

Despite precautions, I was tailed. If it were Timmy, he wouldn't hold a grudge at this defensive ploy. If the wrong group saw me in Victor's, they could destroy what I left behind, or break-in to retrieve what frightened them. Maybe Jersey City cops would take the tip at face value.

CHAPTER 24

The Plaza Hotel was a major New York City landmark. In the Oak Room, one could conjure legends of Hollywood, Broadway and politics enjoying a tête a tête. Scanning for Hub Durant, or for two women dressed like his female clones, McGettigan came up dry.

With one scan of the room complete, it turned out General Anton Petrovsky was my host. I asked the Organism to rewind my rant at the woman detaining Patrick. Much of what I told her was unfit for ears other than Hub's.

Approaching the table, the second man rose to be introduced. Petrovsky's giant paw squeezed till my eyes watered.

"Colonel Sanun Nantakarn…let me introduce Dr. James McGettigan, a professional investigator of sorts. James…meet Colonel Nantakarn of the Royal Thai Police."

Twins fit as a first impression. Both bald and barrel-chested, either could hold his own in a bar fight. Both examined me with separate purposes in mind. Neither would grant quarter to an enemy. Nantakarn drank Vodka. Petrovsky coffee. McGettigan ordered a beer.

Nantakarn offered a toast, "Choc-tee, my new friends."

Petrovsky frowned. "Imagine my surprise, James, to find a younger McGettigan searching for Colonel Nantakarn. And to discover Patrick is *your* son." Anton swiveled to the Thai and told him, "James turned down a Presidential medal for service to his country. Crazy thing to do, does it make him modest, or guilty?"

Nantakarn laughed at an apparent joke.

Attention fixed on McGettigan, Petrovsky's lecture allowed my brain to leap ahead.

"Colonel Nantakarn is responsible for aiding young Americans, who find themselves accused of crimes while vacationing in Thailand. The Colonel's wisdom and understanding have been critical to avoiding international misunderstandings. The government of the United States is grateful to the Royal Thai Police for everything it does to assist our servicemen and women."

Official lecture on the record, McGettigan had been warned: Petrovsky wouldn't allow this bird's feathers to be ruffled. To give Nantakarn his due, blank green eyes never broke from their assessment of McGettigan. I'd watched alligators examine me with less obvious hunger.

Petrovsky spoke with brimming annoyance. "One of Colonel Nantakarn's staff investigators has been cooperating with American law enforcement. He and I have wondered whether, in any of your investigations, you've come in contact with such an officer?"

Diplomatic double-speak didn't suit Petrovsky. Army Rangers, ordered to blow up a tunnel into Baghdad Int'l Airport, had been more his style and mission directive. He was a military spy whose satellites could watch McGettigan brush his teeth in high definition. Anton was here to keep the Thai Colonel feeling warm and fuzzy, and engage McGettigan in a discussion about Hub Durant's involvement.

"How would you define *come in contact?*" It wasn't just the Jesuits who were too smart by half.

Nantakarn's lips drained of color. Left hand lifted in gesture of disdain, the Colonel said, "Assuredly, Dr. McGettigan, our information is incomplete. It's possible Inspector Kasemsarn is out of touch with good reason. But, if I may speak in confidence, we are concerned for the Inspector's safety."

McGettigan doubted the sincerity of such horseshit misgivings. "So your Inspector is missing. For how long? Where was she, when contact was lost?"

My use of the female pronoun would move this show along. How desperate was Nantakarn? How much rope would Petrovsky give me?

Scrubbed of harsh emotion, Nantakarn's statement morphed into a lyrical Apologia of sorts.

"Walking the byways of Bangkok's red-light district, throngs of humanity move like a giant caterpillar…filing past bars and energetic brown girls. These men are every man: Arab, Asian, American and European. Black, white and brown. You hear Russian, Spanish, Arabic, English, Dutch, Afrikaans, Greek, Italian, Japanese and Korean."

Built like a bowling ball, the Thai Colonel froze me with a look asking why McGettigan was unsympathetic to his plight.

"The experience isn't without a religious component. It's possible to partake in uninhibited sexual delight across the street from an age-old place of worship. Quite interesting, one sees male and female couples moving along the streets of Patpong or Soi Cowboy, holding hands as though shopping at the mall or engaging in secretive foreplay. We Thai do not judge. Even when a Farang emerges with alarm bells ringing, angry at what seemed a female sex worker turned out, in fact, a man. We Thai are calm and collected. Live and let live covers a multitude of situations and what other cultures might see as a multitude of sins. I've visited Amsterdam…prostitutes stand in windows with eyes directed inward, seeing nothing. These women look as though a hoarder had stolen their souls and flown to another world. Things are so different in Thailand."

I shot a glance at Petrovsky. Nantakarn's differentiation of the Thai sex trade from all others had caught the DIA spy unprepared. Nantakarn and McGettigan were, in the moment, on a private planet while Petrovsky struggled to catch-up.

"Thai people understand…the sex trade is about the white man's hang-ups and brown-skinned girls' need to support their families. You are an experienced investigator, Dr. McGettigan. And yet, alas, you have a proclivity for awkward situations…like this unfortunate business with the sunken yacht. What advice would you have for me?"

"Your investigator's assignment is…?"

Nantakarn wouldn't bite. "My officer is present in the United States to assist in educating American military personnel about the wonders of Thailand."

"Then this missing Inspector should be by your side."

The Colonel was tired of fencing. Napkin dabbing his lips, he said, "Perhaps you shouldn't have been on board a yacht with young, innocent Thai women. Perhaps in the near future, we will request you be delivered to the Royal Thai Police to answer our questions on the record…and off the record."

Petrovsky's official interest was keeping Nantakarn happy. Murdered prostitutes wouldn't warrant Anton's presence. Young girls kidnapped, used as sex toys and murdered—maybe. Either way, Charanya's point of view had been correct: Petrovsky would hand me over in a New York minute. Accrued to McGettigan's good health, Anton Petrovsky wasn't drunk on power or seeking to overthrow civilian authority. To avoid bumps in the road, he needed certainty and concurrence from a civilian court—unless I'd slept through Senator Harding's hoped-for ascent to the White House—and Hub Durant's meat wagon adding space for James McGettigan's actual Ghost.

Anton proceeded with a direct approach. "Were you on the yacht, James?"

"General, you don't want to trample my civil rights in front of the Colonel. Why don't we excuse ourselves?"

A starlit night was diminished by New York's multi-million artificial lights, even in Central Park across the street from the Plaza. McGettigan squeezed a button on his modified cellphone. No vibration was felt and no red light flashed.

"For the record, General, are we being monitored or recorded, in any way, by any agency of the United States?"

Anton rolled his eyes. Why be such a jerk, he beseeched, without uttering a sound?

"Humor me, General."

He used the two-way feature of his cell. "I'm okay here. Go dark."

Anton would be displeased to discover my recording equipment. "What do you know, General?"

"I've heard the tape of your phone conversation with my people. Observed with interest the poker game between you and Fatso in the Oak Room. Corruption is pretty acceptable over there. But all things equal, they don't like girls being hauled overseas into white slavery…though the homegrown variety is fine as long as the right people profit. I'm not *officially* interested in murdered girls…or your part in murdering them, if you played any part at all. My job is limited to placating Nantakarn. He can put our military kids in jail…televise messy trials when things get out of hand. Whatever else I'm responsible for, eliminating any chance of American kids, stuck in Thai jails, is job number one. Good enough?"

"How about Hub Durant?"

"Been around a long time…which says something in his favor. We're not colleagues or pals. Why would a CIA professional hurt your son?"

Anton and James had met in one of life's unorthodox intersections. Together we saved lives, soldier and civilian alike, but whatever we accomplished was old news. *Not colleagues or pals* would be an apt description of our current relationship.

"Your Colonel's Inspector occupies the intersection of murders, kidnappings, white-slavery, election fraud, governmental corruption, and bribery. Nantakarn believes she's off the reservation. I believe she has eliminated, or hopes to eliminate, some of those implicated in a high priced scheme where Thai girls are supplied, used sexually by the customer, then killed. Disposal is part of the service. You and Colonel Fatso want harmony; Nantakarn believes in harmonious cash flow. He'd like to send his Inspector home before her shit sprays on him. Hub Durant is on her list."

"Could be, or definitely is?"

McGettigan shrugged.

"And the Lawrence family is mixed up in all this?"

Another noncommittal gesture from the Organism.

"And where do you fit James? Are you looking for this Inspector, or is it the other way round?"

If only Timmy could have heard my rejoinder to a moral swamp of a question.

"My sister-in-law got herself in over her selfish little head. Her husband's a target of the US Attorney for the Southern District. I'm trying to keep my family together." Petrovsky wouldn't tolerate a pictorial of the alligators inhabiting James's swamp.

"Would I recognize the folks who commit these heinous crimes?" Anton's face wore a smart-ass smirk as he unwrapped a long cigar from an aluminum tube.

We'd reached Détente. "General, if I ran your operation, I'd keep close watch on anyone who could jeopardize your relationship with the Royal Thai Police."

"Goodnight, Dr. McGettigan. Stay safe."

I watched Petrovsky on the sidewalk, when four figures, two of each gender, joined him. Counting on assistance from DIA would be unwise. McGettigan flagged a cab, returning to his role of a businessman in possession of cash stolen from organized crime, miniature electronics of several varieties and a semi-automatic bought on a street corner from a drug dealer.

How could Charlie think me incapable of muddling through this morass of dishonesty?

I observed the ever-symbolic government SUV lurking in the cab's exhaust. Inside, a driver and the two women agents who intercepted Patrick, yawned in anticipation of a long night. Unseen, there could have been others in this procession to Ruggiero's.

Timmy would enjoy Johnny's Osso Bucco.

Having little interest in fine food, Hub would order steak and McGettigan's Ghost, well charred.

Astor was a fish sort of fellow; he smelled like week old mackerel.

Ingrid would order her husband grilled on a spit.

Kristian would favor cuisine nouveau, its promising aroma emanating from the tiniest of substance.

Gillian, despite Proost's advice to the contrary, and the benefit of history's teachings, would select revenge served chilled on a bed of shaved ice.

Ellen Harding would be too busy killing puppies.

Henry Linney, who'd been remarkable for his absence, would sip hemlock consommé, featuring a flavoring of animus, from a faux silver spoon.

***

Limos lined the street. Chauffeurs stood in tight groups, armed with their weapon of choice. By the front door the valet was attentive, when I asked him to bring Johnny outside. Johnny strode first to a massive sideboard ornamented with Venetian lamps and fresh flowers. McGettigan saw him clutch a package wrapped in brown paper tied with white butcher's twine. Bowing as he passed important customers, he waited for the kid to hold the door.

"Signor McGettigan, I have your package. And your guests have arrived."

Bruce's work product carried a professional heft; I felt the ribbed spine of a bound ledger. Nothing seemed amiss.

"Thank you, Johnny. I'll stay outside a few moments…could you join me again when you next see me alone?"

"Certainly, Dr. McGettigan. I'll have your guests' wine refreshed." With a salacious twinkle he added, "She's beautiful, this one…a bit like Anthurium." He retreated to his duties as host, chuckling at a witty analogy.

My cell showed 21:54, when the diminutive figure of Daniel Bazel approached through a gauntlet of chauffeurs, some of whom he sent to prison. Uncomfortable, Bazel opened with an insult.

"Reached your comfort level, huh? Dinner with the upper crust of the criminal world…you're a social climber after all."

"Why lie to me Bazel? There was never a deal on offer for Rand Jellenek."

"Jellenek's going to prison. But of course you're correct… prosecutors lie. You still could give me Spazutta. Spazutta deserves prison more than Jellenek."

Was Bazel an honest prosecutor, who parenthetically was a grating pain-in-the-ass? It would seem so, his misjudgment of Phil not to the contrary. I thought he told me the truth back at the cottage; truth filtered by perceptions, or whatever truth consisted of these days. Withdrawn from the briefcase, I handed over an unbound copy of the forged ledger. Centered in a floodlight's brilliance, McGettigan and Bazel were there for the picking. Ideal for reading, the light was. Ideal as well for a sniper.

To Bazel I explained, "It's a proffer. Take your time."

Bazel looked like a trapped rat choosing between hunger and freedom, wondering whether the cheese was poisonous. A waiter brought two glasses of wine. Bazel refused with a look of disgust. McGettigan sipped in silence for a long ten minutes.

"Whose handwriting is this…who kept this journal?"

"Woman who manages the whorehouse on the west side of 3rd Avenue north of 36th Street."

"What's her name?"

"No idea. She was robbed and shot this morning. Ledger was stolen. Right about now she's not popular with her employers."

"Who did the robbery?" It was fascinating how Bazel phrased the question, asking whom I'd hired to do the dirty work. Would the ledger's provenance bite him on his dick? was a more useful translation.

McGettigan displayed his patented shrug. "Maybe you got it from an informant. Maybe from a true-blue, crime fighting cop...one Detective Isaac."

"Is it real...the names and transactions?"

"Yes sir." It got easier, this lying business. When everyone lied, everyone expected lies.

Bazel weighed risk versus reward in personal terms. "When this blows up, if this blows up...I could go with it."

"Yes sir, you could lose everything...including your life. Or be the biggest hero in recent law enforcement history...Daniel Bazel, savior of democracy and the American way of life."

He probed for mockery in a sentence delivered with sincerity. "How much money are we talking about...for Harding's campaign?"

"I've been told by a source...over a hundred million."

Bazel whistled involuntarily, then reality got the better of suspicion. "What do you want in return for the original? Do you even have it?"

"I want a number of things, all non-negotiable. Let's start with a gesture of good faith: Who's the woman sitting with Rand Jellenek?" I pointed to assist his identification.

Bazel jumped three feet off the ground. Shrunk in a moment of exposed terror. Recovered with the application of serious effort. "You want a Federal prosecutor to go into Ruggiero's alone...and talk to Jellenek?"

"Nope. I want you to ID the woman."

Like a Pit-bull he turned towards the door. Returned inside a minute. "She's an FBI agent assigned to Ellen Harding. Don't know her name."

McGettigan's credibility had increased by an infinitesimal degree—I could see it. "Would this FBI agent who works for Ellen Harding know about your hard-on for Spazutta?"

Taken aback, he admitted, "Not exactly a secret on either side of the river. I can be zealous."

No shiite, Sherlock.

Mata-Hari's single task—invite McGettigan to the fundraiser where he could be shanghaied aboard *M*. Even now I could summon the taste of her kiss. Even knowing its purpose.

"With Michael Madson dead, who's the government's witness against Jellenek?"

Bazel and McGettigan were teammates all of a sudden.

"I told you weeks ago…Ingrid Jellenek, his wife."

So Ingrid couldn't tolerate being thrown over for a younger, more ravishing woman. Yes, it fit the Ingrid McGettigan knew. But hatred for Rand didn't explain dinner at the Turkish restaurant with Ellen Harding. It couldn't have been a coincidence.

"Ingrid gets blanket immunity for everything and anything associated with the ledger. Agreed?"

Bazel didn't know how to quit when he was ahead. "Ingrid Jellenek's name doesn't appear in the journal. Is she your source?"

"Yes sir. She had it stolen by a professional. The wealthy buy what they need."

"But her brother's in the journal. And she doesn't like you. How does it all mesh?"

"I'd be guessing about Kristian…your job, not mine, to fit all the puzzle pieces together. As for me, I don't like Ingrid either."

"When do I get the original? Nothing moves forward without it."

"Soon. You should protect the whorehouse madam. Consider immunity in return for authentication."

Perplexed was a good description of Bazel's face, when he realized our meeting was closed. He walked towards Journal Square with a bounce to his steps. As it winked off, the floodlight made a buzzing electrical noise similar to a backyard mosquito control device. Within seconds Johnny was at my side wearing an expectant, almost anticipatory expression.

I handed him the briefcase. "Please alert any special customers…conversations will be taped for the next hour or so.

Could you position my bag so the upper right corner points at my table?"

"Will yours be the only active device?" Johnny was nobody's fool. He enjoyed satisfying the needs of his clientele, and managing the risks of being a restaurateur in Jersey City.

"At least three. Maybe four."

McGettigan finished the Merlot and felt its warmth spread.

Hesitation rested on Johnny's lips before he told me, "Signor Spazutta phoned me. Requested *every* courtesy be extended for your pleasure and safety. Signor Spazutta is a wonderful man, don't you think?"

Handing the glass to Johnny, I said with good cheer, "The condemned man ate a hearty meal."

We each chuckled for altogether different reasons.

***

In candlelight, the milieu resonated with decades of Ruggiero's history. Tuxedos present, though not dominant, women dressed with refinement were, for the greatest part, wives of their dinner partners. McGettigan stood-out not by being tall, or even sixty-ish, but for the Glen Plaid suit in need of being cleaned and pressed. I counted three tables with meals interrupted by Johnny's calm advisory in regards to listening devices.

Johnny's appearance remained serene; not his first rodeo.

James's table occupied the center of the room. Rand waited, impatient at the delay. Mata Hari sat to his right. A couple appeared deep in conversation behind her, against the wall. In back of Rand, three ladies in their seventh decade gestured at a stack of grandchildren's photos. To Rand's left, six men admired a waiter, who poured snifters of Brandy. Since Mata Hari would've brought reinforcements, my money rested on the middle-aged couple; they were in good position to sweep the room and couldn't be approached from the rear.

Rand Jellenek, in contrast to a Fool, arrived out of the pages of GQ, though he appeared to have swallowed something distasteful. Mata Hari was transformed. Tonight she was white-blonde in a whiter than white sheath. Wearing no adornment other than diamond studs, it was fire engine red lipstick which completed the Hollywood glamour. Halfway across the room, her aura enveloped me. Maybe Rand could be forgiven his lapse in judgment. Maybe Rand had some deranged plan to keep her. Did he never think this unwinnable game through to the last out in the 9th inning?

Mata Hari's hopeful uncertainty turned into a flight reflex as I approached. Not limited to discomfort, she was apoplectic as those gems of eyes ransacked the room for a suitable escape route. I read her thoughts: *What's happening? This dinner should be fluff, keeping poor Rand on the hook.*

The man at the adjoining table witnessed her distress. Rising in unison, his female companion attempted to block my path. A collision was avoided by tilting to the side—the Organism rotated so my right hand gripped Mata Hari's wrist, pinning it to her chair. In the same motion, I brushed my lips against her cheek and whispered. "Be still. You'll want to hear this." When McGettigan half fell on top of her, she missed the cynicism.

Mata Hari issued a threat loud enough to be heard at nearby tables. "They'll shoot you." She meant the twin FBI agents in the early stages of embarrassment.

In my head a sweep second hand moved at a glacial pace.

At one-thousand-one, James turned to the twosome behind me. The female's hand reached for the gun in her purse. The male agent began a similar motion. Eye contact with the male maintained, McGettigan clamped Mata Hari's wrist tight enough to bruise. Rand wore saucers where his eyes should have been.

At one-thousand-two, the five of us stopped in our tracks. A targeting laser drew a mesmerizing red line; its spot danced in a frenzied circle on the female agent's forehead. Before any one of us grasped the totality of the situation, a primitive reaction began. Pillars of salt fearing God's wrath, each of us was possessed of a single thought: To who's weapon is the laser attached?

Lasting an immeasurable fraction of time, the man's momentum continued to seek his weapon.

At one thousand-three, two things happened: A green laser, brighter than its red cousin, ended on Mata Hari's linen dress above her ample left breast, and our waiter materialized with a Champagne bottle wrapped in a white towel.

McGettigan's countdown went no further.

The couple who would have shot me, a little flustered and truly mortified, returned to their table.

The Organism needed two tries before it released Mata Hari's wrist. McGettigan sat before the Organism fell. Appearing confident was a necessary task, because Mata Hari and her escorts were convinced both lasers belonged to McGettigan.

The ominous green light vanished.

Mata Hari recovered in an instant. Smiled at the waiter, who poured golden liquid into three tulip shaped flutes. Sweating like a longshoreman, Rand would have given anything to have never met Ingrid Solberg. Shocked silence in the dining room ebbed. Diners told themselves nothing of importance happened.

There was something worth remembering about a green gun-sight laser, but the Organism's memory was in failure mode. I was left to conclude Johnny was more than a wizard with veal, and my balance of debt to Phil had swung yet again.

Leaned close to Rand I told him, "Notice they didn't scream *Federal officers, nobody move*?"

Still rattled, Rand peered through glazed corneas. "What?"

"She's a fraud…an FBI Agent working a second job as paid enchantress."

A blank expression greeted sardonic humor.

"She set you up, Rand. You didn't seduce her. You were targeted so they could play on Ingrid's monumental insecurity."

Rand's blank face turned incredulous.

"Ingrid will testify against you. Your prosecution and imprisonment is Ingrid's payoff from US Attorney Ellen Harding…both for Ingrid's testimony and a very large contribution to Senator Harding's campaign war chest. You're going to jail for a long, long time, my friend. Ask your sweetie-pie whether she'll rescue you."

There was nothing like the prospect of life in prison to sober a man. Rand's attention was instant and complete. Pointing an accusing finger, he said, "Really, Vicky? You're screwing me over?"

Vicky, the two-timing Fed, let a satisfied look escape at Rand's unintended double-entendre. Reached for her Champagne, preparing a strategic withdrawal.

I looked at her. "Her name isn't Vicky."

McGettigan spread Bruce's rolled-up pencil portrait on the tablecloth, admiring a gift of artistic genius.

"Think it through Agent Massey. This house of cards could transform Ellen Harding into Humpty Dumpty. What happens to you then?"

McGettigan placed a second copy of the forged ledger on the tablecloth in front of her.

"Will Ellen protect the foot soldiers, like you or Isaac? Are these two…" I jerked my thumb at the other table "…here to protect you, or to assure you stay on-script? You, Lauren Massey, work for Ellen. Those two work for Hub Durant."

Half a quizzical look escaped before it became clear—FBI Agent Lauren Massey didn't know Hub Durant…and *Need to Know* still applied.

"Hub's a CIA man with side interests, a Mr. Fix-it if you will. Hires out to solve problems for the very wealthy. Hub won't weep at Lauren's funeral…all those dead Thai girls weigh him down. You pretended to be a messenger from Spazutta, passing tickets to the fundraiser, intimating we could be lovers, sticking me with the needle…all very skilled, but over. You've been written out of the script."

Lauren began to gather herself. "You've got so much wrong…"

McGettigan interrupted her, having not implanted adequate doubt.

"I almost forgot. The Royal Thai Police are on the scene, working with the State Department…they brought an assassin with them. The ledger you haven't touched…" Vicky placed her hand on the ledger, but didn't pick it up. "…makes you a key player in kidnapping and killing those girls."

Like the pages were electrified, her hand jumped off. "But I didn't…" Biting her tongue, McGettigan watched an otherwise intelligent woman estimate probabilities.

"But you did…you put McGettigan on the yacht where eleven Thai girls were killed. Lauren Massey got paid…the ledger says so. McGettigan's name doesn't appear anywhere on any page. So when Thailand seeks extradition, you'll be on the list. I'd find somebody to tell my troubles to…if I were you."

James flipped Anton's business card the way kids used to flip baseball cards. Left a neat pile of Mama-san's cash. "To cover the bubbly…I've lost my appetite. Keep the sketch, I've lost interest in you."

Passing Johnny, I offered a handshake and my thanks. "Your service is impeccable, as always. I'll think of the veal I missed all the way home."

Gunsight laser in hand, Johnny showed me there'd been no pistol attached. As he slid it into a drawer, a question was asked between men who'd bluffed and won.

"Would your outside man have taken the shot?"

How could Rand or Lauren have reached a different conclusion?

The green laser protected James McGettigan.

I supposed it made sense, though morbid curiosity and niggling doubt remained. The eerie green light entered Ruggiero's through the fixed windows above the front door. A mild downward angle allowed it to shine on Lauren's heart. No doubt, a second story window across the street housed the rifle. And yes, there was a building across the street, fronted by a massive tree occluding each and every window. Foreknowledge implied, I lifted my left eyebrow. Johnny could make of this reaction what he would. He'd shit his pants, if he knew the truth.

CHAPTER 25

Upside down, head stuck in the sand, McGettigan struggled to regain his bearings. Entangled in an unrelenting grip, the Organism heard a grumpy Charlie say, "Gotcha tea Boss. Get offa yer ass."

Mug in hand, I mumbled, "Nice way to disturb a man's beauty sleep." An examination of Charlie left no room for doubt; bags under his eyes were doubled since I saw him last. "You didn't sleep much either, huh?"

Legs folded underneath him, Charlie joined me on the warm sand. "Seen the news?"

"Why?"

"Inrestin' clip bout yer fren Gillian."

If the sun still rose in the East, and pre-dawn rays filtered through trees as they were doing now, it was five in the morning.

"When did you go to bed?" A more pertinent question became, "How long you been up?"

Charlie stood, extending his hand to lift an old fart. Streaks of sunshine turned the clouds red and pink: *Red sky in the morning sailor take warning.* McGettigan shivered.

Bacon sizzled while we awaited the news. The kitchen's ship-clock struck three bells of the morning watch: 05:30. Charlie's four Tennessee buddies slouched in chairs, noisily slurping coffee. No wisecracks passed between men with similar backstories; it was evident they'd screwed the pooch. What pooch was the lingering question?

The early-morning news anchor updated national stories.

McGettigan watched Charlie drain bacon fat and break a dozen eggs into a cast iron skillet.

Local news began with film of a small fleet of catamarans leaving Corinthian Yacht Club's dock in Marblehead. In the next video, they appeared like wraiths from a fog bank. Three leading boats, crew garbed in colorful foul weather gear, rounded a large yellow marker in somber procession and, sterns to the camera boat, tacked away. A dripping camera lens panned back to the main group and caught a faint rainbow as sunshine penetrated before being swallowed in mist.

The reporter's voice-over restrained, her excitement bled through as intended.

"Yesterday, as patchy fog threatened to cancel races off Marblehead, a horrible accident may have taken the life of Preston Orenstein, son of Gillian Hartnett Orenstein and grandson of Donald Hartnett, former CEO of *BGFH* Contractors, whose death a year ago on Cape Cod remains an open case and an intransigent mystery."

File photos of Preston, his mother and his late grandfather filled the screen.

Salt and pepper hair added gravitas, when the station's oldest veteran picked-up the thread.

"While details of the incident appear conflicted, Marblehead Police and the Coast Guard confirm a collision between a lobster boat and two becalmed catamarans. Four sailors found themselves in cold water. Three have been rescued at this hour."

A separate clip showed a wall of fog and, seconds later, viewers heard, but couldn't see, the crunching of fiberglass and aluminum, multiple screams, then one final cry of *Help* before the video ended.

"Marblehead Harbor and its vicinity are home to thousands of boats during the summer season. Onlookers say dozens of pleasure craft and working boats intruded on the racecourse yesterday. This tragedy, if Preston Orenstein has been lost, will re-ignite the debate over the need to license boat operators."

Thrown back to the woman, Preston's photo filled the screen. In a hushed voice, the female anchor continued.

"Preston Orenstein is the college student heir to his mother's vast fortune, inherited from Preston's grandfather upon his death. Mrs. Orenstein was unavailable for comment after being rescued by a spectator boat and transferred to a Coast Guard vessel. The lobster boat, which failed to stop after the collision, hasn't been identified. A massive search continued through the night and is ongoing this morning. When asked by our on-site reporter whether the incident was being treated as a crime, officials told us they were gathering facts."

The screen filled with photographs of Donald Hartnett's body and McGettigan's booking at County jail. Hartnett looked dead. I looked like a man who'd seen death up close. One of us looked like a criminal.

With the male voice presenting, the segment concluded.

"James McGettigan, of Monument Beach on Cape Cod, was the central figure in the death of Donald Hartnett. District Attorney Brendan Timilty sought an indictment of McGettigan for murder in the first degree. A Grand Jury disagreed with Timilty, who admits the case is a difficult one to prosecute. James McGettigan has agreed to appear on this station in a no-holds-barred interview. McGettigan, no stranger to high seas hijinks, is a *Person of Interest* in the sinking of a yacht where eleven Thai girls are thought to have died. Our Blake Burke will interview McGettigan and, no doubt, inquire about McGettigan's possible involvement in Preston Orenstein's disappearance in the mean, cold waters of the Atlantic Ocean."

Charlie bit a strip of bacon. "Betcha'd lik'ta re'range little prick's nose."

On the contrary, footage previously unseen allowed identification of the sound transmitted through Julia's phone—a small cannon's starting-signal for a sailboat race. With recognition came the identity of the pooch who got screwed.

"Where's Julia, Charlie? Where's Patrick?"

"With Billy."

"On his boat?"

Charlie scanned his four stooges. Imitated McGettigan's best shrug, performing it better than I ever could. Without the aid of words, his advice was crystal clear: Don't cry over spilled milk, mop it up.

Billy wouldn't tell me. Julia would stonewall. I dialed Patrick.

"Dad, we had nothing to do with whatever happened. We were safe in the spectator fleet...expected the race to be cancelled. No wind. Visibility was all over the place, sometimes half a mile, sometimes zero."

"Where are you now?"

"Gloucester. With a friend of Billy's."

"Your sister all right?"

"She took the commuter train back to Boston."

McGettigan swore under his breath. "Has Julia lost her mind?"

"She had research to do, Dad. Julia will meet you at the TV studio. You know what she's like."

Dad knew Julia's strengths and weaknesses: Keen insight from Mom, mule-headedness from her father. But, in this moment, Gillian might be ordering a contract killer to eradicate the McGettigans. No risk to Julia or Patrick was acceptable.

Charlie held eye contact, agreement with James's unspoken intentions in plain view.

***

Bryan Owens was a man for all seasons, who operated a sightseeing business using a floatplane from Cuttyhunk. Bryan's daredevil streak and hardcore rejection of overbearing law enforcement caused him to accept jobs which skirted regulations and, now and then, good sense.

"James, saw you on TV. Didn't look your best. What can I do you for?"

"Pick up four behind the cottage. Two to Logan. Two to Gloucester."

"When?"

"How long, Bryan? No slack in this line."

"Fifteen minutes. Row'em out to your boat. Gotta be quick. Someone will remember my tail numbers."

"Which numbers you referring to?"

***

"What the hell happened, Charlie?"

His guys had flown away with Bryan, under strict orders.

Paranoia squeezed reason into the smallest closet in my brain. Reason was less than useless at a time like this. Gimme Charlie's machine gun screamed the Organism. Kill Gillian before she kills my own was a Fool's mantra.

"Were'nt here, Boss. Inna tree keepin' silly old fool alive."

Of course.

My savior hadn't been Timmy. Hadn't been one of Anton's lady spooks. Hadn't been a specialized photographer from Victor's. Charlie's homemade machinegun was one-of-a-kind, made from nothing but the best parts. It was Charlie who told me about green lasers.

McGettigan allowed himself to look abashed.

Charlie's voice was belligerent.

"I'll tella kids 'bout your shenanigans. Almost shot the guy at the marina. Hadda stroke when ya bought the bat and mask...near nuff got run over keeping armored truck in the alley. Didn' see me gettin' grub at the Plaza. Then gotta get in the buildin' and onna tree wif those girl spies hangin' round doin' nothin' t'speak of. Tollya before. Hard keepin you livin'."

None of my escapades evolved quite like I perceived them. I had the finest kind of assistance.

A car stopped on crushed shells. Harsh sounds from the cottage phone reminded McGettigan: Rome was burning while Charlie and I fiddled.

Charlie was at the front door. He mouthed, *Sheriff*, and closed the front door behind him.

Phone in hand, the caller could be any of two dozen people whose interests swirled around me in indecipherable patterns. I'd regained control, or so I thought, but Preston Orenstein's death made no sense.

"Dr. McGettigan, this is Granville Proost. I wonder whether we could meet?"

Voice civilized, assured and steady, my mental picture was prejudiced by images of earlier encounters with BGFH's courtiers. I saw a round, curious, elder face wearing horn-rimmed glasses. Tweed would be his fabric, even in these pleasant days of June. His notes were constructed with a fountain pen—no ink dared stain his hands. Granville was fastidious in all things. This imaginary Proost derived from the anonymous men who dismantled civilizations to remake them in the British image of an Empire.

Proost would assume his voice was being recorded.

"Is there good news, Mr. Proost? I've been in New York, but watched the news minutes ago."

"No, sadly." His ultimate purpose was clear as mud.

"When and where?"

"You plan to be in Boston for a television appearance, I believe. Could we have lunch at the Algonquin Club?"

"I wouldn't expect us to have much in common, Mr. Proost."

"The pursuit of peace, Dr. McGettigan…a worthy endeavor, as my long dead father always assured me."

***

"Tell me again who you might be, Mr. Charlie Hamilton from Tennessee? Why you living in McGettigan's house?" Donny's tone suggested disbelief and something stronger; our intrepid Sheriff was intimidated.

"Like I tollya…jus a fren' visitin' James anna kids."

"Tell me again where McGettigan's gone to?"

"Spect you been watchin'…he's up Boston for th'interview."

"Who did the plane pick up?"

"Dropped off fishin' gear made special down Cuttyhunk."

Donny took a step towards the front door.

Charlie didn't move, but raised his voice a notch. "Awready said got no warrant. Open the door, you like as not fall offa stoop…maybe breaka leg."

Sheriff Slater put his hand on his holstered service weapon.

Charlie remained by the patrol car, calm as could be.

"Breaka leg *and* losea job. Be a fine mornin's work for uppincomin' man like you. You not the fuckin' Gestapo. Or are you?"

Charlie's question may have been short and vague, but it struck a chord somewhere in Donny Slater. When he backed down and returned to his cruiser, it wasn't Charlie's intimation of physical violence which changed his intent; Donny's body language told a more significant story. Last time, Donny had been in the company of Daniel Bazel. Today Donny was a creature with money in his pocket and apprehension in his loins. He came to arrest McGettigan, warrant or not.

Like Judas' betrayal, Donny suffered mixed emotions, though not for loathful McGettigan. Who could force Donny to his knees, to take a payoff while pissing his creased, pinstriped Sheriff's trousers?

Charlie stood aside to avoid the hail of debris kicked-up from Donny's tires. Looked toward the cottage and shook his head. "Man's a tool," he said to no one in particular.

Back in the kitchen I asked, "Did he know about the plane when he got here?"

"Nope. Toll him, so we had sumpin talk bout wasn' James McGettigan."

"So who sent him? Why today?"

No answer from Charlie. We'd reached a well-travelled point in our relationship; it was time for James to make decisions.

Push a single rock down a slope, and, like pinball, one rock would soon be two. There were mathematical equations to predict the random destructive behavior which ensued. I'd pushed one rock. I intended to push more. Was it fair to think one of the guilty should be spared to carve away James's culpability.

"Let's go be on TV."

"Offense or defense, Boss?"

"Just like Jersey City. Reckless, offensive and in need of a green laser."

Charlie went to collect his tools.

***

The Algonquin Club's gray stone edifice occupied prime real estate along Boston's Commonwealth Avenue. Between Fairfield and Exeter Streets, five blocks from the Public Garden and its Swan Boats, the club was either refined or stuffy dependent on one's point of view. McGettigan was escorted under the massive chandelier to a window table hidden beside a paneled wooden arch sixteen feet high. Hush dominated an almost empty room. An older waiter placed water and a silver cradle holding rolls wrapped in white linen. My dry throat was glad for the liquid.

Nervous perspiration wiped off my hands, McGettigan rose for the social niceties.

"Dr. McGettigan. You arrived early."

Tempted to explain the length of time it took to break-in to a Brownstone, where an unimpeded laser line to this particular window and table would be available, a Fool bit down on his tongue.

Proost began without fanfare.

"I'd prefer our lunch to focus on what might be possible, but, to clear the air, I know of no instructions to harm your family or yourself. Can you make a similar statement about Mrs. Orenstein's son?"

"I can and do. You took notice of the body count during the deceased Mr. Hartnett's violent splurge against my family. I, Mr. Proost, was the one who died on our side. Mrs. Orenstein and BGFH lost her father and several useful, though replaceable executives, subcontractors and allies. Never were Mr. Hartnett's family members threatened or harmed. Whatever happened to Preston Orenstein, I am unaware and uninvolved."

"Thank you, sir. Your sincerity in these matters has always carried the ring of truth. Our Donald could be indulgent, when challenged. Mr. Linney's behavior was a taunting betrayal...Donald wouldn't suffer such offense in peace. But past is past, and no longer our concern. I'm here representing the BGFH Board of Directors as their General Counsel...as well as Gillian as a family friend. I don't consider either position to be a conflict. Do you?"

A nest of wrinkles appeared around his eyes; Granville Proost made a joke and was pleased with it.

Proost was my host through reciprocity with a club in San Francisco. He requested the Sole Meuniere. McGettigan tried to remember when he last ate a meal in this room, not knowing when the opportunity might come again. Filet Mignon with mashed potatoes and green beans was my selection, just like dozens of winter evenings when my mother and her young son enjoyed each other's company in this room.

Lifting my water glass, I saluted him.

"Are you suggesting my abduction aboard *Marvelous Lady M* occurred without the involvement of Mrs. Hartnett?"

"It's not my intention to insult your intelligence. Seeing you humiliated, seeing you indicted, reading about your demise...any or all those events would have, without question or doubt, pleased Mrs. Hartnett. Although in truth, what Mrs. Hartnett Orenstein desires may not any longer comport with the policies of the Board."

"*May* being the operative word?"

"Correct."

It would have been offensive to inquire whether the entirety of BGFH's execrable business philosophy was up for reexamination.

"What, may I ask, is the impetus for this mid-course correction?"

McGettigan was, for the moment, quite enjoying a discussion where words mattered and bullets didn't.

"I would prefer to focus our talk on ways in which BGFH, including *all* its executives and Board members, might convince you, Dr. McGettigan, and *all* your friends and allies to withdraw from confrontation."

Proost was the perfect ambassador of diplomacy; a nephew offering a helping hand to an older uncle who'd fallen and lost his cane.

Time to change direction. "Is Preston lost?" *Lost* didn't sound as final as dead. *Lost* was so much more ambassadorial.

"His family is frustrated with the official search. BGFH reached out to augment the search process…and still there's neither a body or a live young man."

McGettigan needed no super powers to see we were coming to the crux of this matter.

"BGFH must have all the resources it could need."

If it suited BGFH, their influence could task satellites, infrared cameras on drones and towed-arrays behind nuclear submarines. Not one of which would help, if Preston wasn't in the water and wasn't free to communicate.

"Do you believe I could assist with the search's outcome?"

"Can you?"

"As we sit enjoying a wonderful lunch, I don't know what I think I might know. Which can't offer you much comfort."

A hand extended a crisp, white business card embossed with the corporate logo and a phone number. No name. No e-mail. No address.

"For when you do know."

A business card printed in digits made an under-embossed engineer wonder: Would a modern Minister to the Crown plot to overthrow the Monarch? Treachery, adultery and murder were the ingredients of a simmering stew of such events. McGettigan indulged his curiosity.

"How is Preston's father holding up?"

"Mr. and Mrs. Orenstein are estranged." His facial muscles made every effort to achieve a good-natured exterior, although the question was out-of-bounds.

So Gillian's having an affair. Proost wouldn't give a good damn, if bad behavior belonged to the husband. Because there was no 'O' in BGFH. Was Gillian's indiscretion discovered by Paparazzi? Or was treachery more widespread? Either way, there must be photos. McGettigan understood photos.

"Will Gillian be staying for the Lawrence wedding?"

McGettigan the Foolish sent the Organism's fingers on a search for a handhold—a sheer cliff belied a fatal drop.

Proost's pained expression was an open wound. For a man who could announce the imminent end of the world with stylish aplomb, this was tantamount to a screaming admission: BGFH's Minister of State had lost control of the Monarch.

Gillian Hartnett had been seduced by Henry Linney. Henry must have approached her with a strategy to exact revenge on McGettigan, advertising himself as the ideal Trojan Horse.

Proost gathered himself, perhaps in response to my introduction of personal matters into a meeting about Statecraft.

"Are you anxious about this afternoon's encounter with the Media?"

I wondered how much Granville knew from internal BFGH espionage—or had been told or shown?

"Are you familiar with *Blind Man's Bluff*?"

Greeted with Proost's smile bordering on outright laughter, McGettigan waited for the punch line.

"Back in my father's day, when innocence was a childhood norm, backyard games were the best amusement. He regaled me with stories of watching blindfolded friends whirl around trying to tag other players."

"Tune in Mr. Proost, we'll see who can still play."

Worried whether our truce lay in tatters, next to vanilla ice cream smothered in the Algonquin Club's homemade chocolate sauce, he asked in a too polite tone.

"Is BGFH liable to be tagged?"

"I wouldn't think so, Mr. Proost. But then alliances have a habit of shifting on soft sand. A blindfold puts me at a distinct disadvantage and may cause discomfort where none is intended."

"You sound like a Jesuit, Dr. McGettigan. With your parochial education, you remember how, eight years before the attempted Spanish Armada invasion of 1588, Jesuits plotted the overthrow of the English government. Using disguises, aliases and secret codes to slip in and out of England, Jesuits organized and led a mission of sedition. When the invasion failed, these provocateurs turned to another scheme. Thirteen Catholic noblemen and five Jesuits conspired to explode gunpowder in the cellar of the House of Lords...all to kill King James and members of the House of Commons. Sad for the Jesuits, the explosives were discovered. Five Jesuits were involved; two escaped, one died in prison and another two were executed. Being a Jesuit is dangerous business."

Proost was satisfied with his warning. Whether Granville Proost employed the services of Timothy Timilty, or was frightened of being their victim, remained unknown.

"I'm a lapsed Catholic, Mr. Proost. My grade school teachers were Carmelite Nuns. Several of my high school's faculty belonged to the Society of Jesus. You and I need to remember...above all things Jesuits are confessors. Their services to royalty were urged upon them as they heard the confessions of emperors, kings, queens, princes, princesses, royal mistresses...and as those at every level of government revealed their secret plans, intimate sins and inner-most thoughts, those lives became an open book. Jesuits worked their way into Offices of State, climbed to be counselors of Kings. But it was hearing the confessions of penitents, and being wise religious guides, which keyed their successes. Jesuits made sure it was they who filled royal needs, instead of other orders of priests, by providing an attractive policy of leniency as enticement for their penitents."

"Just so, Dr. McGettigan. Just so. We all should show penitence. We all seek leniency from God and man. I pray you and I may exhibit the first and find the second."

CHAPTER 26

Charlie confirmed the sound quality was acceptable. What he wanted to know was, "Whas alla mumbo jumbo bout Boss? Jesuits, pen'tence, leenency…loada hooey. Wha'd he rilly want?"

"Granville Proost is orchestrating a power grab. Gillian Orenstein will be shitcanned from her position as CEO…embarrassed by revelations of an affair with Henry Linney, who approached her with a scheme to exact revenge for her father's murder."

"Weren' no murder, was there?"

"Doesn't matter, Charlie. You know people who dream of payback?"

"Whas Proos' power grab gotta do wif us?"

"Might've been Proost who arranged Preston Orenstein's disappearance. As long as the boy stays lost, his mother will behave. Proost has some reason to think we've figured all this out. Wants us to know the war between the Hartnetts and the McGettigans will be over, when Gillian's claws have been extracted. Wants us to wait and see."

"Wait'n see what? For how long?"

"See what Proost does, before we find a way to kill Gillian and Preston. More than anything else, he's worried we'll find a way to kill Proost himself. He remembers what happened last time."

"So?"

"So we poke a stick in as many eyes as possible. See who cries crocodile tears, see who runs away, who wants to make a trade, who goes to the cops."

"Gotta big'nuff stick, Boss?"

"Believable lies, Charlie, are what we'll use. Because truth doesn't make a good sound bite."

***

Having makeup applied was a new experience.

I'd resisted at first, then relented when the makeup artist befriended me.

"Don't give the bitch an edge. She's gonna sandbag you with a surprise guest. If he looks tanned and healthy…and you look like shit? Game over, you lose."

Twenty minutes later, I opened my briefcase to find white and blue dress shirts and four ties. Julia told me to look at the show's set and dress accordingly. McGettigan wasn't certain what *accordingly* meant, so took advantage of the nice lady who, in a last effort to spiff me up, trimmed overgrown eyebrows.

"Which one do you recommend?"

"Got a smart wife, huh?"

"Smart daughter. Wife died."

"Sorry…wear the blue shirt and red tie. You'll look better than the fricking DA."

***

Somewhere beyond the startling lights was an audience.

Julia was backstage throwing a breach of contract fit evidenced by DA Brendan Timilty appearing as a second guest.

Charlie Hamilton roamed the rear of the small theater watching for anyone wishing us harm.

McGettigan hadn't yet seen Brendan. Relaxed in one of three chairs facing forward in a cozy arc, Blake Burke would occupy the center chair so she could be shown in profile as she grilled her two guests. According to the makeup gal, Blake insisted on profile shots.

Tuxedo style blouse, tight skirt and high-heeled pumps, Blake Burke was past her network prime. She did the New England show's introduction standing. Before the audience got comfortable, she made a first strident demand.

"Did you kidnap, or in any way harm Preston Orenstein?"

McGettigan found the camera's red light and spoke to it, not Blake.

"I've just come from lunch with Mrs. Orenstein's attorney. Given past history between the Hartnetts and McGettigans, we're determined to focus on Preston's needs in this difficult time. No accusations have been lodged against me, nor should they be. I've never met Preston Orenstein or his mother."

"Most residents of Massachusetts, according to polls taken at the time, believe you shot and killed Donald Hartnett, Preston's grandfather. Why should we believe your denial?"

"Because Donald Hartnett shot me. Because when I lost consciousness, he stood on the opposite side of a table holding a smoking pistol...very much alive. And when I died on the operating table, he was, for a short time, guilty of murder. *Hartnett* was guilty. Not McGettigan."

Blake showed a hint of indecision. "You can't prove even one of those things."

"The Commonwealth's Grand Jury decided the weight of truth was too large a burden for the prosecution. No indictment was returned. I suppose we'll hear Brendan Timilty's thoughts on the subject, when you shock me with his appearance."

"You mean *District Attorney* Timilty? A man with your lousy reputation should show respect for the legal system you manipulate."

"No Blake, I wasn't referring to Brendan Timilty the District Attorney, but Brendan Timilty who was a year behind my class at St. Coletta's in Waltham, and who hung around with his brother Timmy and I...when we let him. Timmy Timilty, Brendan's older brother, is, as your audience knows, the well known hit-man for hire."

"Are you accusing District Attorney Timilty of being connected to his brother's crimes?"

Blake Burke didn't care who got wrecked on her show, provided it wasn't her. She also didn't realize how correct her accusation was; McGettigan *was* accusing Brendan of assisting Timmy.

"In seeking an indictment against me, Brendan pursued justice in the way he thought best. He was wrong then. He's wrong today. Now he needs a better explanation of how Hartnett died." Here I spoke to the audience and suggested with enthusiasm, "Bring Brendan out here. I intend to expose a massive criminal conspiracy...I'll name names, provide independent proof and illustrate how corruption infiltrates the highest levels of government and law enforcement. Brendan can help you ask the right questions."

Under an obligation to be perky for the folks in TV land, she introduced the District Attorney. When she turned to me, venom dripped from perfect white teeth.

Brendan strode onstage with the look of a proven performer, waving to the audience with a professional politician's polish.

McGettigan stood to shake hands with an old schoolmate.

Brendan approached me like a poisonous snake. I took him by the forearm, pulling him close enough to say, "Timmy doesn't want you doing what you're doing for him." Since I still wasn't sure what Brendan *was* doing, I tried, "You made a deal with Deirdre to allow my indictment. You're playing footsy with Ellen Harding. Ellen's gonna fall hard, Brendan. There's not much time to save yourself, let alone Timmy."

We both smiled for the camera.

Blake figured sincerity would go over best. I saw her calculating the odds; heads she won, tails McGettigan lost.

"So *Mr. I'm Not a Murderer*, wow us with your big news."

"Teenage girls shouldn't be prostitutes. Teenage girls should never be kidnapped and sold to sick bastards as sex slaves. Being a sex slave seems the worst thing any mom and dad could imagine happening to any daughter. But it isn't. Never knowing who took your baby away, who paid for the opportunity to repeatedly defile your pride and joy, who murdered your child after keeping her prisoner...never having this monster pay for his crime because the monster is wealthy, protected and near the seat of political power in this nation...never knowing why she died, or where she's buried...those things are the worst. This nightmare starts in Thailand where recruiters entice country girls with promises of jobs and safety in the USA.

"Hub Durant is a senior CIA operative who moonlights in the white slavery business. Hub pays the recruiters. Ships the girls to Cuba via Jorge Machado, a pirate and human trafficker sought by the Cuban and American governments. Brought by boat to the Florida coast, the girls are delivered to rich, perverted men along the entire East coast, but with a particular, strong market in metro New York.

When the girls arrive in New York, they're primped for delivery at a whorehouse operated by organized crime.

"Organized crime is an enabler…a sub-contractor. They collect the money; deliver the girls to customers and pick-up the corpses for disposal.

"A special Thai Task Force, working with Detective Gideon Kusneski of the NYPD, was trying to stop these terrible crimes. Gideon was murdered by his partner, Detective Isaac Franklin, to protect himself from discovery as the insider working with these criminals. Isaac Franklin is paid by Hub Durant to betray fellow cops. Durant pays others as well: FBI Agent Lauren Massey, who, while assigned to US Attorney Ellen Harding's office, made certain law enforcement came nowhere near disrupting the multi-million dollar purchase of human lives; and the tandem of Raoul Dupree and Frankie McShane, who buried the bodies in a private Florida landfill before they, too, were murdered to protect the men making the largest profit.

"The creator of this abomination is Henry Linney, who provided start-up money, found the monsters who wanted sex and death from these girls, recruited Durant and made his bed with the mob.

"One of these investors-in-death is my brother-in-law, Kristian Solberg, himself a man of great wealth. Kristian Solberg is the lynchpin of Linney's scheme, because Solberg understood Ellen Harding wouldn't be corrupted by bribes, but would sell her soul to elect her father President. Solberg's role was to solicit massive illegal contributions for Senator Warren Harding's planned run for President of the United States. So far Kristian has commitments of over a hundred million dollars.

"Kristian's sister Ingrid will testify to Ellen Harding's, and Kristian's involvement.

"As to other participants, there's a ledger detailing names, places and payments for everyone I'm accusing, and others I've not named. Tonight I'm passing this ledger to District Attorney Brendan Timilty here on this stage. He'll do the right thing. Working with the Royal Thai police, whose officers are relentless in the pursuit of sexual offenders, and US law enforcement, Brendan can stop these horrific crimes. To make them stop is why I came here tonight."

With righteous ceremony, I opened the briefcase and handed Brendan the embellished ledger. Brendan looked ready to revisit his lunch, but didn't drop the inexpensive book with its mottled black cover and red binding.

Blake Burke wasn't to be trifled with. Consulting notes, she became the inquisitor again. "Those are sensational, and perhaps irrational claims. Isn't it true *you've* been designated a *person of interest* in the drowning deaths of numerous Thai women?"

"I was drugged and taken aboard a large yacht by Lauren Massey, on Hub Durant's orders. Far offshore, in rough seas, I rescued a member of the Royal Thai Police. Working together we found eleven bodies in the ship's bilges. The yacht had been sabotaged and it sunk. After a substantial time in a raft, we were rescued. As a licensed investigator, I've been involved since our rescue."

Blake rotated her profile to the alternate camera, turned on the sunshine and announced, "Ladies and gentlemen, I'm getting a desperate signal to break for commercial. We'll be right back."

An assistant jumped to light Blake's cigarette. Sucking in a lungful, she yelled at the world, "I will not have my fucking show hijacked."

Next up, Blake would do an audience segment where guests were peppered with inane questions. The segment represented too big a risk for McGettigan, whose semi-fictional accounts of events were designed to create tension among the guilty, not satisfy the prurient appetites of reality junkies. Time to abandon ship, when I departed my chair the Producer raised his voice.

"Where the hell are you going? You've got an agreement for the entire half hour."

Julia answered him from off-stage. "Don't push your luck, dickhead. Same contract said he'd be the sole guest."

Brendan and James removed their microphones and, in a quiet corner, he asked, "Are you insane, James? How much of your diatribe is true?"

"Don't be cute, Brendan. Lawrence Foods. Eco-Waste. Cardillo Crystals. BGFH. The Defense Intelligence Agency is all over the Thailand part of this. Selling girls to fund an election for President; Ellen Harding will go to prison, if she lives long enough, which I doubt. Does she have video of your deal? Audio? What?"

"Nothing so formal. She approached me through a third party. Her offer was a pardon for Timmy, if Warren Harding gets elected. In return my office indicts you and puts you on trial for murdering

Donald Hartnett." He hung his head. "Wanted a chance to save big brother."

All politicians were disingenuous. I changed the subject, ignoring the emotional puffery about big brother. "Did Ellen tell you why?"

"Of course not."

"So you figured it was about Hartnett's death?"

"Two and two still equals four."

More like a feisty District Attorney, Brendan was making headway. "Tell me the third party wasn't Deirdre."

"It wasn't Deirdre. But you're right about the trade I made with her...although she was too willing. Does Timmy know all this?"

"He's at the very center of it, Brendan. I'm helping *him*...not the other way round. He doesn't want a pardon or anything else from little brother. He wants you safe and sound...and out of the way. So get yourself to high ground and stay there." Brendan's face was full of worse news. "Or are you already drowning?"

Brendan was everything to Timmy. *This* moment—*this exact moment* was why Timmy contacted James McGettigan. Not to save the integrity of the electoral process. Not to save teenage girls. Just to save Brendan, when Timmy could not.

Brendan swallowed hard. He'd need something to trade, when the Feds came knocking on his door. Something to explain what he'd done. Something to mitigate in his favor.

"Henry Linney's the third party?" His face filled with the threat of tears.

"Come on, Brendan...? Little late for remorse, huh? How do you know Henry?"

"Out of the blue, he brought a bunch of money to my campaign last year."

"Jesus, Brendan. Henry was priming your pump. The money was from Gillian Orenstein, Kristian and Ingrid Solberg and Astor Lawrence...right?"

"And some others. I don't remember all the names on the checks. I'll have to resign, if Linney goes public."

Politicians and their endless groveling for money; there was no end to it. So what if you lost an election? Life wouldn't be over. Poor stupid James. Money, power and lust ruled the world.

I grabbed Brendan's arm. "Give me your private number. I'll try to find you a life preserver."

***

Two SUVs pulled to the curb. Billy drove the first. Patrick's face leaned out the passenger's window with a look of anticipation. We all piled in, signaling Charlie's foursome in the second car to follow. Minutes down the road Billy slammed the brakes, rousing me from a stupor. Looking around, Julia's face was drawn tight. Charlie focused on traffic. Patrick's left knee vibrated like a tuning fork.

McGettigan stated the obvious. "Something wrong, Billy?"

"Patrick knows what happened to Preston Orenstein." Billy's declaration, in its most attractive light, needed elaboration.

Dad put his hand on Patty's shoulder. "What's the story?"

"You figured out why we went to Marblehead. It was stupid. Believe me, the idea of shooting Gillian Hartnett didn't last long. We were pissed-off...so we found a tuna boat with a full tower. Hired it for the day. What a confused mess, Dad. Boats everywhere. No wind. Couldn't see at all...visibility would get better...then wind up worse. The racers appeared and vanished like ghosts. In a tiny break from the fog, the lead boats caught a gust, rounded the marker...and seconds later a lobster boat roared into view on the same course as the racers. It crossed the clearing in seconds. The sky closed in. It got dark and began to drizzle. Next thing we heard was the crunching sound of the collision. The lobsterman's engine sounds diminished; maybe the crew threw the boat into neutral. Another minute and it roared off at full throttle. We didn't get much of a gauge on their heading...guessed due East out to sea."

"You followed?"

"Never occurred to us...people were screaming, boats buzzing around like angry wasps. A few rammed each other. We used the radar to thread our way through the craziness. Should have monitored the screen for the lobsterman, but we wanted to get out of there."

"So how do you know where Preston is?"

"Remember your description of the Hyannis based lobsterman? You know...the one that rescued you and the Thai cop?"

Patty was serious about a loony-tunes hypothesis: McGettigan had been rescued and Preston taken hostage by the same boat. Which meant Charanya's rescue-at-sea had been planned in advance by her or her Colonel. Which suggested Charanya's presence on *M* had been planned with Mata Hari and Hub Durant. My headache exploded trying to fit irregular shapes into a patterned mosaic.

Why couldn't our rescue have been random luck? Was everything a plot? Or, as Amanda said on occasion, maybe what was—was.

I needed to be sure Patty remembered correctly. "Fifty feet. Pretty sheer-line. Name's *Home Cookin*. Lobster caricature on the side-hull just in front of the transom—bright red lobster peeking out of the pot, claw sticking up like a middle finger."

Patty did some fact checking of his own. "What's her hull color?"

McGettigan checked his memory. "Off-white."

"Transom color?"

"Battleship Gray with red lettering. Same boat?"

"What I saw from the tower was a white hull, and a gray transom with no name...gray wrapped around onto the white, like it might've looked if you painted over the obscene lobster."

Billy's sardonic chuckle punctuated our discussion. "I should be embarrassed. What kind of professional fisherman am I? Never noticed the paint job."

"Her home port is Hyannis, Dad. Why would they take Preston anywhere else?"

For about a million reasons, I thought, taking pains not to express such a hard-nosed opinion. With a glance towards Charlie, I rewound the conversation with Proost. Charlie's return expression suggested full agreement: Proost voiced a veiled suspicion of McGettigan's involvement.

Had Patrick been spotted in Marblehead? More spilled milk. Mop's going to be saturated real soon at this rate.

Our group debated what to do, or whether to do anything: Call Gillian, Proost, Petrovsky, and/or the Gloucester cops—or call Amanda, who could be counted on to recommend voluntary commitment. McGettigan made a mental list of those who knew details of my rescue by *Home Cookin*. Added others who might have been told in its aftermath. Stevie the skipper and his crew were obvious: Gerry and his carbine; Willy and his drool; Adam the Producer; the unnamed camera-guy; and the second boat's captain. Stevie intended to report the rescue to Coast Guard Hyannis and to Sheriff Donny Slater. Charanya was obvious; she must have told

Colonel Nantakarn. I'd told Amanda. Had Amanda told Timmy? I shared my tentative list.

"Who else knows about *Home Cookin?*"

Charlie hadn't said much, but cut the discussion short with, "Sumpin' bout six degrees sep'ration, right? Wha'd Sheriff Donny say to some third guy…and so on. Same fer ev'body who knew."

Billy agreed. "Lemme call Tom. He could send a cruiser to see if the boat's back in her slip."

Julia stated a fact. "You don't have any way to contact Timmy."

Patrick. "Would there be a reason to kill Preston?"

Charlie answered. "Don' needa reason. Shoulda lern'd awready." A father grimaced at the hurt to his boy, and waited for a reaction.

When it came, Patrick's response was matter of fact. "Guess what I meant…who gains the most by killing Preston? Or holding him…threatening Gillian with losing her son."

Julia offered a striking analysis. "Charlie's on target, Patrick. We may never understand the connections among these people. Gillian could have staged this whole deal to have something else to accuse Dad with. Tonight Dad stirred the pot. Maybe hit a nerve. So we find a way to deceive these bastards."

Frustration claimed her attempt to choose the right words.

"I don't know…maybe tell each suspect Preston will be at a certain place at a specific time. See who shows up. See who doesn't. Who *doesn't* might tell us more than who *does*."

These bastards—paint applied with too broad a brush, but a perfect color. McGettigan preferred hoisting opponents by their own petards. Julia wanted deception. I was thinking along the lines of unadulterated deceit.

CHAPTER 26

Tom Nichols confirmed—*Home Cookin* was in port tied up next to a pier off Pleasant Street. No lights, no movement, there were no signs of habitation or preparation.

Tom's research also produced results. Stevie the Skipper was home in Yarmouth with his wife and children. Gerry was on Georges Bank, crewmember on a different boat. Adam the Producer lived in New York; he answered the landline, when Tom called. The cameraman lived in Boston, where he was a stringer for anyone who paid a daily wage. Willy, who would freak out forever on wet dreams about Charanya, was in the wind.

McGettigan's crew were tired and bad-tempered.

Tom shook his Facetime finger at Billy as a way of demanding to know: *What are you gonna screw up now?*

"I'm not dumb enough to miss the connection, Billy. You think Stevie rammed those two sailboats and plucked the missing kid out of the water. You think it's so easy? Get real, Billy, whoever did it coulda killed all four of them."

Billy was the older brother and wouldn't enjoy Tom acting like their mother.

"Someone did that very thing…with Stevie's boat. Saw it with my own eyes." Billy's affirmation stuck up for Patrick.

Silenced by his brother's insistence, Tom's two dimensional on-screen image conveyed a stunned State Police Lieutenant. Attitude adjusted, ready to listen, he posed a question to no one in particular.

"Where would Preston Orenstein be, if he's being held for ransom?"

I was half listening, but perked my ears when Billy answered. "All we've thought about…could be anywhere. Where would you stash him, Tom?"

Cops were cynics. "Never would've brought him home to Hyannis. Woulda dumped him."

Julia joined the fray. "Dumped? You'd have killed him, Tom?"

Tom Nichols hadn't seen Julia in a bunch of years. He looked at her, through the phone's screen, with a faraway stare. Wore a forced grin on a sad cop's face. "Yuh, I would."

Julia wasn't satisfied. "Would a billionaire pay a ransom without proof of life?"

An obvious parallel flooded McGettigan: Donald Hartnett had taken Patrick. With Patrick as bait, McGettigan had been sucked into a vortex of despair. Until Charlie lifted Patrick from a casket rolling towards a crematorium's inferno. Murder by surrogate, by an undertaker run amuck, had been Hartnett's intent—and two sisters perished in the ghastly bargain. Yes, they'd been greedy, guilty and stupid in turn, but issuing a death sentence had never been Hartnett's dominion. McGettigan couldn't escape the phone call to their father. His moan, alternated with wailing, remained an intolerable weight on McGettigan's overburdened soul. Still there was hope; my child survived what Gillian's child now suffered. Try as I might, justified as I felt, McGettigan couldn't wish this ill upon Preston Orenstein.

Our collective moment of silence splintered by the ring-tone of Julia's cell. We listened, when her head turned to the wall. Paralyzed by what she heard, Julia turned to me.

"Dad, remember you wanted to know who bought Richie Tarrant's interest in Rivers Nest Towers? You said Phil Spazutta represented Tarrant, but wouldn't give you the buyer's name?"

"And the winner is…"

"A BGFH shell company owns a chunk of *Jellenek Construction Equipment*…a shell BGFH took a lot of trouble to hide."

Granville Proost provided one key to a double lock. Julia's information completed the set. With despair for how some humans treat each other, I stated my intention, but hid its intent.

"Tomorrow morning I'm gonna go see Ingrid. Tom, thanks for the input. Billy, I'll call you around lunch. Charlie...want to meet my malicious sister-in-law?"

***

Anna Solberg's manse overlooked East Bay and Nantucket Sound from Ship's Chandlery Lane. Wings housing bedrooms and baths sprouted from other wings until anyone would wonder how many rooms a widowed woman needed for ten weeks of summer.

Ingrid dropped in occasionally, like now, and occupied one of the guest apartments on the second floor of the attached garage/barn.

Kristian didn't enjoy Cape Cod, but visited mummy one weekend each month to protect and preserve his cash flow.

Reggie lived in the caretaker's bungalow, a twenty-five hundred square foot, three-bedroom home furnished in the same Delft Blues as the main house.

"Sum kinda place." Understatement was one of Charlie's strengths.

Charlie rapped the door with his knuckles, eschewing the brass knocker in the shape of a diving Osprey. Reggie's reaction, given his recent introduction to a nail gun, was easy enough to predict. A minute passed. Finally, Charlie looked at me and said what we were both thinking.

"Oughta find Ingrid."

Reggie's bungalow sat at an angle to the garage/barn. I pointed. "Try down there, Charlie. Reggie's big, blonde and stupid. Don't hurt him too badly."

Charlie threw a half-assed salute and started to walk.

In the rear of the main house the door to a glass enclosed garden room was open. Passing it by, I hugged red cedar shingles until the expanse of lawn and a dock came into view. Behind a fair weather cloud, the sun's retreat sent a spasm of chill down my spine. Without warning, a deep growl threatened from behind an overturned wheelbarrow by the potting shed.

"Lucifer... here boy."

Emerged in a hesitant crawl from the sanctity of his hideout, the Irish Wolfhound was generous and affectionate. Bleeding at the shoulder, Anna's favorite male—whether man or dog—wasn't the finest watchdog even under ordinary circumstances. Given Lucifer's loyalty to Anna, Ingrid and Kristian was unconditional, I hurried to where he lay, flopped in the grass, unwilling or unable to move. More than a foot long, the jagged slash was reminiscent of my own. Bandage fashioned from my fishing shirt, I tied it tight; comforted him for too short a time.

Lucifer's tongue hung on his paw. Hose dragged ten feet, opening the bib to a continuous dribble was better than nothing.

"Stay big boy. Stay." An excellent dog's leery eyes told his story.

McGettigan gained the patio and its entrance to a three-season porch. Curled in the fetal position on one of half a dozen upholstered chaise lounges, Ingrid sniffled under the huge pillow covering her head.

A cloud of unfiltered cigarette smoke encircled Reverend Father Timothy Timilty.

Unarmed, I sat, pulled the pillow aside and simulated genuine sympathy. "Did he hurt you? It's his specialty." Without looking at Timmy, I hurled a verbal bullet. "Why the dog, Timmy? You make it all so damn hard."

"You know dogs frighten me, James, in particular a dog bigger than a house. If you'd figured out who was doing whom a little sooner, the devil's creature would be slobbering on his mistress' lap."

A good sign for Ingrid was the enthusiasm with which she hurled herself into my arms. Melodramatic, her whisper told me, "He's a fiend. Came out of nowhere with a knife dripping blood." Pointing at the blood trail, she feigned falling faint.

"Sit up Ingrid." McGettigan pushed her away. "You're not hurt. You're not innocent. And to think I figured you might not be aware of Kristian's favorite avocation...selling young women. Or Rand's affairs. Or what happened to Preston Orenstein."

Ingrid convulsed, an act refined through years of practice.

"Oh, I get it, the wayward Parish Priest told your future...or asked questions even a self-centered train wreck could figure out."

She sputtered each word like it might be her last. "Said...Reggie's...dead. Said...a Jesuit...is a warrior for Jesus. Said...I need to make my final confession."

Timmy blew smoke rings towards stagnant ceiling fans. His affectation was blatantly intended to annoy.

Too early in the day by a wide margin, Ingrid needed reinforcement from the large pitcher of Martinis I found making a wet ring on a priceless antique table.

"Give it a rest, Ingrid. Lucifer has a gripe, not you. If this Jesuit wanted you drinking gin with the Antichrist, you sure wouldn't be here sucking gin."

Ingrid did the hair-tossing thing out of habit. She spoke in a slack, slurred voice. "So…is Reg dead?"

From nowhere and without a sound, Charlie appeared in the doorway.

"Sorry, Ms. Ingrid, priest meant Reggie be dead real soon. Like maybe Reggie go and take too much steroids. Or shoot hisseff inna head. Or slice his own gizzard. No Ms. Ingrid, Reggie not dead now, but he be inna care'o Our Lord real soon."

Charlie Hamilton was a spiritual man, but not one to express opinions about where we go afterwards. *What it gonna hurt, Boss*—his face said to a friend who'd seen no sign of *Our Lord,* when I'd gone where Reggie would soon be. If I'd been where Reggie would be going.

Charlie's lethal green laser had, all this time, not left Timmy's nose.

Timmy crushed out the cigarette. Remained motionless. Timmy wouldn't mistake Charlie, a fellow tried-and-true killer, for James McGettigan.

McGettigan's sympathy was exhausted. Mean was how I felt. Mean was what I delivered to Ingrid.

"I met Rand's latest sex partner. Wow, you're chopped liver, Ingrid…even though Ellen Harding paid her to screw your husband. Your buddy AUSA Bazel joined us. Looks like he'll keep the bargain you made…Ingrid testifies against Rand and makes a huge contribution to Senator Harding. Rand gets life in prison. Ingrid dances at the inaugural ball with Kristian and Astor."

Admittedly, Ingrid wasn't at her best, what with Lucifer being knifed, her downing half a pitcher of Martinis and hearing Reggie would soon be deceased. Wearing a drunk's version of a puzzled expression, her mouth ran ahead of her brain.

"Fuck Rand. Fuck Astor. Fuck you, Father Shithead. Fuck you too, Saint James. Money goes to Ellen, not Bazel. Thai witch can't hurt Kristian—he's gettin' married in the White House. Gonna rule the world." She laughed until hysteria turned into depression. "Astor's *not* gonna be married inna White House. Gettin' married at fucking Henry Linney's house. Linney fucks her—Rand fucks her—now she's really and truly fucked."

Head buried in her hands, Ingrid burst into tears, then stopped, covering her mouth with a hand as revelations ceased.

James kept focus. "Ingrid, where's Preston?" No response.

Charlie held the landline up high: *Who did I want him to call?*

McGettigan intended to leave Ingrid to the ministrations of Reverend Father Timilty, the phony. But not before hustling to the garage/barn, where Lucifer's bed and the estate's tractor resided. I'd be damned if Anna's best friend would be left in a puddle of blood.

***

"You think about shooting Timmy back there?"

Charlie shot me a strange look. "Nope."

"Why not?"

"Know who's runnin this show t'day. Mebbe t'morrow be diff'rent. Mebbe he get me. Mebbe not."

Charlie had an abnormal knack for staying still. What he thought, or if he thought as he sat unblinking and undisturbing of the air we breathed, was inscrutable. I'd endured these abstract absences before, but this one ended with a barrage of examination.

"Didn bring Ingrid? Figger she don know?"

"Ingrid doesn't think too far ahead. She's not stupid, mind you...just self-centered, pampered and not quite of this world."

"Ingrid know this gonna end poorly?"

"Maybe. Thinks a white knight will fall in love and rescue her."

"Dumb."

"Worked all these years."

"Reggie gonna kill the kid?"

"Not if he can sell him back to momma."

"Reggie smart'nuf t'deal wif Hartnett?"

"He'll have help."

"We shouldn' hurta kid, Boss. No mind his middle name Hartnett."

"If the kid's alive, he'll stay alive. Best I can do Charlie."

"Thas good, Boss." For the first time in the exchange, Charlie looked at me. "Why'd priest stay behind?"

"To save her soul."

"Don' mess wif me, Boss."

"Timmy is complex. He's been hired to assassinate Meredith Lawrence by her son Astor. His little brother Brendan's in the shitter for making a deal with Ellen Harding. Timmy won't move on Meredith till I figure out how to save Brendan's ass. I've got to save Brendan without anything but peripheral help from Timmy, who knows way more than he's told me. If I don't save Brendan, Timmy will kill me, regardless of whether I'm put on trial for the murder of Hartnett or eleven Thai girls…and regardless of whether I'm found guilty or not. Timmy may have been excommunicated by the Pope, but he remains every inch a Jesuit."

"Where'sa kid?"

"On our way to find out."

CHAPTER 27

We parked on South Main, in Centerville, at Four Seas Ice Cream where Donny's shiny cop car sat with the motor running. Four Seas was mobbed with a crowd, many of whom recognized him.

Donny would have preferred to be elsewhere.

Charlie's large Strawberry cone disappeared in his left-handed grip. Hanging around folding tables strewn with logo t-shirts, his presence made Donny's nerve endings jump.

McGettigan, who held a medium of the same flavor, inquired as to the Sheriff's favorite and received a glare full of daggers in return.

I heard Donny say, "So, you're telling me the Orenstein kid is alive. You'll get life for taking him. You think I'll help you? Anyone ever let it slip…you're an arrogant shit."

"This is the final second-chance you get, Donny. Ingrid confessed. You ought to analyze your permutations and probabilities." Word selection admired, I watched our lazy-boy Sheriff squirm. I was enjoying the hitch in his giddy-up, because Donny's vocabulary evaporated after a second syllable.

He reached for the cuffs.

Rear-end rested on the cop car's hood, waving Charlie off any overreaction, I added to Donny's thought process.

"Arrest me, you'll miss out on Reggie's accusation of Sheriff Donald Lawrence Slater as mastermind of Preston Orenstein's kidnap and murder."

"You haven't found Reggie or the kid."

Open mouth, remove shoe, insert foot—Donny couldn't get even a short sequence in correct order. I should have told him: Speak into the shirt button. Or explained his options in a more direct manner.

"Don't have to. Ingrid promised Reggie her undying love and access to her checking account. Reggie's been dipping into the steroid jar for too long; he went straight to his old chum Donny. You, Donny, took Stevie Curran's statement the night he rescued McGettigan. Stevie gave you the rescue's GPS coordinates…you sold the information to Hub Durant, or Henry Linney, for future considerations…that's like a player-to-be-named-later. Then you sent Reggie to Stevie, who used the steel hand in velvet glove approach…run down the sailboats and kidnap the kid. Stevie agreed because you impounded the poor schmuck's bales of marijuana. You and Stevie are, maybe, unaware weed is sold legally in Massachusetts."

Donny's sigh did me a world of good.

"How much did Reggie give *you*? Ingrid gave *him* a hundred grand."

Doing math made Donny blink faster.

"Nice touch reserving Wing's Neck Lighthouse for the week in my name. Hub Durant suggest it? Or Linney? Leave my DNA somewhere prominent, huh Donny? Then, when the kid never turns up, you arrest me…like you started to do a second ago."

McGettigan counted to ten, giving Donny a chance to catch up.

"You remember the police training course on surveillance? Charlie's listening. Tom Nichols is recording what we say. Reggie will roll before he hears what the offer is, but there's an alternative…if you've got the stones."

Donny was a delicate creature at heart, like most bullies. Slumped in his cruiser's passenger seat, he wanted to hear about a way to heaven. Believed asking would make him look worse on the tape recording.

"Where…is…the…Orenstein kid?"

Donny framed words for his listening audience. "I don't know Reggie Tucker too well. But he's been talkin' about buying Stover's Shellfish over on Child's River. Old shack with bad saltwater plumbing. Maybe he'd be there, *if* he took the kid."

"Was your hypothetical a mirror on reality, Donny? Here's another one. What if Donny Slater made an anonymous call to the kid's mom? Give her the address where the kid might be. Suggest she come get him…maybe with her private security folks. Tell her Reggie is off his head on drugs and armed to the teeth. Tell her everyone be better off, if Reggie winds up dead. She'll understand your message."

A glimmer of hope sparked and subsided. "Stevie would still know. And Linney…he's smart. He'd figure it out. And *you*." Donny hadn't reacted to Hub Durant's name.

Up by the t-shirt table, Charlie tossed the rest of his cone in a trash bucket. Dialed his cell.

Donny's ignorance was terminal. I gave him Last Rites. "Stevie needs your permission to breathe…or he does five years in County, if he's lucky. Linney…he's having an affair with the kid's mother. As long as the kid's healthy, Linney will forget your venial sins."

What I said about Stevie was true. As for Henry Linney, *forgetting* couldn't be further from the truth.

"As for McGettigan…I'll own you forever. It's the way things work in the big leagues, Donny. You wanna call Gillian?"

Concentrating on sounding anonymous and cool, it never dawned on Donny; McGettigan's directional microphone/transmitter was still functional and Gillian Hartnett's expensive associates would employ voice recognition. Donny wasn't much of a cop, a criminal, or a human.

Gillian needed time to prepare.

Gillian needed time to travel from Gloucester to East Falmouth.

Preparation was also needed by McGettigan, the State Troopers and Granville Proost, whom, I was willing to bet, appreciated Charlie's call to his super-secret phone number.

***

Seapit Road bordered Childs River more or less halfway between my cottage and Anna Solberg's mansion. Across a sliver of salt-water river, Washburn Island was an uninhabited part of the Waquoit Bay National Estuarine Reserve, where McGettigan's boat was beached. I hiked across tick-infested scrub carrying an investigator's bag of tricks. Charlie's personal tools were slung over his shoulder in a waterproof carryall. Soon the gloaming would linger over this long June day. Our field of vision was unobstructed behind five yards of sandy beach. Run-down, abandoned dinghies were overturned in haphazard fashion. Torn-up pavement sloped to the water where it became a slime-covered boat-ramp. To the right of the pavement was the shellfish shack where we assumed Willy and Reggie held Preston Orenstein. Tidy summer homes and cottages surrounded the shellfish shack in stark contrast to its neglect. Several homes showed glowing lights of summer's anticipation.

For the moment, Tom ordered no civilian evacuation; this was a bad place to exchange gunfire. Our biggest variable was who, and how many men occupied the shack. Stiff resolve demanded no risk be taken with Preston's life in order to arrest his mother—Tom forced McGettigan's agreement against self-interest.

Charlie sprawled on the ground, bipod supporting his weapon next to the tripod supporting the video gear. Officially, neither of us was here. Whatever would happen, this was a State Police operation.

Night sounds began a preview of coming attractions as a small outboard motor intruded. A decrepit wooden dory, it scraped to a stop on broken macadam. No electronic enhancement was necessary, when Billy called across to where the shack squatted without signs of life, or the living.

"Willy Côté, Billy Nichols here. Bet you're tired of babysitting the kid…just a fuckin' college boy, Willy. Momma's richer'n shit. She'll pay a nice reward. More than Reggie ever give'ya."

Our plan was simplicity itself.

Donny's reaction, when told about Reggie's imaginary hundred grand, was to whine. Donny's share was way less than half. Stevie's share even less than Donny's. Willy's share would've amounted to a pittance—trickle-down economics lesson for Cape Cod lowlifes. Willy might be slow, but knew for sure he was holding the fort and a bag full of dog shit.

If Willy wanted out, Billy's offer left everyone in one piece.

If Preston was recovered unharmed, Tom and the Troopers would stay put long enough to observe what would happen, if Gillian showed with her storm troopers.

If we heard Reggie's voice inside the shack, the backup option would be put in motion without delay.

"Kinda bored in here, Billy. Whatcha been doin'?"

"Caught some schoolies…dug a bucket of quahogs. Bout to be headin' home. Thought I'd buy you a beer. Maybe smoke some of Stevie's weed."

"No weed left. Just stale doughnuts."

"Where's Reggie?"

"Gone to pick up the ransom."

Willy might escape prosecution by claiming brain injury. None of us would look this gift-horse in the mouth.

"Come on outta there, Willy. Be a hero. Betcha get ten grand reward from his mom. Walkin' round money for a rich bitch." Billy climbed out of the dory.

Not part of our plan, Tom cursed his brother through his earpiece. Holding his arms up to demonstrate he was no threat, Billy advanced to the ramshackle door. Pulled it opened. Remained motionless, hand glued to the doorknob. Charlie moved his rifle left to right in small increments, seeking a target, seeking an option to keep Billy safe.

A flashlight shone on Billy's face from the interior. Ice in his veins Charlie said, "Clean shot, Billy." Willy's flashlight was better than a laser.

Billy sounded like an afternoon watching the Sox on TV. "Come on, buddy. Beer's gettin' warmer by the minute." The flashlight switched off, leaving its residue to wreck everyone's night vision.

Real casual, Billy walked inside.

Tom cursed a blue streak.

McGettigan bargained with the fates, with nothing valuable left to barter.

Preston Orenstein emerged, body language describing the terror he felt. Willy followed, looking resigned. Billy, relaxed and smiling, opened the cooler in the dory and gave each man a cold can.

Meek as could be, Willy sat in the bow.

Preston was guided, rigid and tense, to the mid-ships seat.

Billy waded to the stern, whistling some ditty. Pushed off and hopped in like he was eighteen again. One pull on the starter and the dory burbled towards a small boatyard bordering Route 28, where Troopers waited. At worst, Willy would abandon ship and swim for his life. No one would give him a second thought.

Charlie made a simple request of James. "Don't drown."

McGettigan must have been a sight, dressed in an odd combination of water sandals, bathing suit and body armor. In saltwater not yet warm, an extended arm held a canvas bag above the water with considerable effort. Fifty yards across the Childs River seemed to take forever. I slipped in the shallows, when an attempt to hurry became futile. Communications gear re-attached, I checked-in with Tom. If Gillian arrived before I was ready, swimming for my life would gain a fresh meaning.

Tom issued a one-word reply. "Negative."

Sheet-steel tanks once held processing water, the combination of salt and fresh needed to make oysters, clams and mussels suitable for human consumption. On one knee inside the largest tank, the sawzall ripped through the tank's bottom vibrating like the world was ending. Saw extended down through the hole, rotten floorboards took no time to cut away. Underneath the floor, it took several minutes to arrange myself in a prone position, head pointed at the door.

McGettigan felt the rally cry of spiders, as nests emptied to forage upon the intruder.

Without leverage, the saw bucked as it cut through the floor from the tank to the doorsill. Covered in moldy soil, spider shit and goose bumps, McGettigan tested how much of his exposed body could be protected by body armor; the news wasn't encouraging.

Before tonight, there'd been many times Donald Hartnett made me afraid. His daughter was imbued with no such power.

Days from now James McGettigan planned to celebrate his birthday, in the company of friend and foe alike, at the wedding of Astor Lawrence and Jill Stoddard. If tonight deprived me of this dubious pleasure, I'd be sure to search for *her*. Memories of *her* calmed me. With time suspended, Charlie's call of *Saddle-up* dragged me back to full attention.

Inside the shack, inside a steel tank, McGettigan was a bit player, little more than an irritating voice, a crippled animal hung in front of a hungry hunter.

Tom's voice spoke to his State Police team, who were unaware Charlie, Billy and I were listening on their operational frequency and communicating on a separate channel.

"Two vehicles on Seapit…half mile out. Lead…driver and two. Second…driver and one."

BGFH could have sent a brigade of well-trained private soldiers to our soiree. If outnumbered or outgunned, Tom would've met them on the road to inform Gillian of her son's rescue.

Gillian must have forgotten three critical elements of royal success: A Queen must be vigilant; ambition didn't belong to royalty alone; and when the chips were down, an army's loyalties were more to its stomach than its monarch. This Queen had failed to absorb the lessons of her father, the dead King, who prepared his own battle plan, hand selected soldiers who would shed blood, stood by the wounded and cared-for the families of the dead. This Queen delegated, leaving her to call on mercenaries, who were the definition of Hub Durant's diminished band of villains.

McGettigan wagered Hub was elsewhere, delivering a ransom and a bullet to addled Reggie Tucker. Hub would be sorry to have missed the opportunity to send James McGettigan to Hell.

The shack's walls were tissue thin; I heard engine sounds fade to quiet.

"Lead vehicle…one female, two males, all with pistols. Second vehicle…two males with MP-7s. Armor piercing rounds."

Charlie warned. "Don be innat tank too long, Boss." *Armor piercing* frightened Charlie.

"One MP-7 by the water. One pistol between the shack and the closest civilian house. Three behind vehicle doors." This status update was McGettigan's cue.

Yelling, while conveying nuance, was harder than it sounded. "You weren't prepared, Gillian, were you? How'd poor Preston wind up in this shithole without his mommy?"

"One pistol moving uphill."

Sticking to a script was too antiseptic for the antipathy between Gillian and James.

"Does Preston know you fuck anything wearing pants…anyone who isn't his dad? Does he know you wouldn't pay the ransom…instead you sent Hub to shoot Reggie? You couldn't care less about your son."

Charlie warned, "Thirty seconds 'fore they comin' at ya. Do sumpin diff'rent."

Tom instructed his Troopers. "Lights and sirens at the first shot."

Enraged as hoped for, Gillian spoke in a squeaky voice. "Preston's not here, is he?"

Shrill and venomous was what I aimed for. "Rescued an hour ago by State Troopers. I'm here to give you a chance to end this. You're nothing like your father. No dueling pistols for Gillian. Run home to California, like a good little girl." My laughter sounded insane even to me.

Charlie whispered. "Two comin' Boss. Get down."

No pedantic novelist's description of automatic weapons fire did the real thing justice. In a millisecond the door and wall were shredded. Inside the shack, beneath the floor, explosions ripped through everything, fragmenting my ability to keep a coherent thought.

Then it was still.

Charlie, cool and collected, demanded, "Changin' magazines. Do sumpin diff'rent."

McGettigan wriggled on his back. The Organism injected enough adrenaline to push a Fool faster *towards* the doorway above. Head slammed into a rickety column, chest heaving, breath came in rasping desperation. A burst from her assault rifle was a cataclysm of sound and fury. When certain James McGettigan was destroyed, Gillian Hartnett would lower the MP-7 and come inside to gloat.

A loudspeaker squawked: "Cease firing...Massachusetts State Police...put down your weapons or we *will* fire on you."

Gillian hadn't tasted McGettigan's blood. Non-compliant with Tom's demand, while firing on automatic, her second step sent her foot and leg through the sawn floor. Gillian's arms may have held the weapon, but her brain's electrodes directed arms and hands to break her fall. Gillian's organism was in self-preservation mode. The MP-7 continued to fire as both her arms stretched-out to save herself.

McGettigan would soon be a shattered, bleeding husk.

I thrust the sole available weapon at Gillian's ankle.

Her scream covered three octaves. Agony forced every muscle fiber to twitch upward, but escape was a futile ambition. A severed Achilles tendon wouldn't permit motion and her hands lost their grip on the machine gun before her head hit floorboards.

McGettigan's legs burned from a thousand red-hot pokers.

We both lay moaning.

Gillian vomited.

A platoon of spiders crawled along my jaw.

In minutes, Tom joined me under the shack to retrieve my tools. Unsympathetic, his hands herded me into a dinghy.

"Don't matter about your legs. Wood shrapnel's all it is. No one can identify you, if you're not here."

Charlie and I were living ghosts, when we abandoned the dinghy, loaded its outboard motor aboard my fish-boat and merged with the outgoing tide into Nantucket Sound.

Amid the private war between Gillian and James, Billy would be a deserved hero—the fisherman who rescued Preston Orenstein. Preston would be the chief celebrant of Billy's achievement. Gillian would be hospitalized under arrest for the attempted murder of Billy Nichols and her assault on police officers. Her defense could be hampered by the Board of Directors decision to dismiss her based on a morals clause. Of Hub's mercenaries, little would be mentioned by the media. One who held an assault rifle would be found floating dead on an ebb tide. A second would recover from a chest wound. The third and fourth sat handcuffed and silent in Tom's Blue & Gray.

***

Needle nosed pliers boiled, Charlie removed dozens of chunks and splinters from both the Organism's legs. Those resistant to pliers were excised with a sharpened boning knife. Storied bullshit about slugging whiskey to douse pain was proven to be heartless fiction.

My son pushed his sister away. Patty's gesture, by itself, made my day.

Slathered in anti-bacterial gel and bandages, the news got worse quick: The lurid video of James McGettigan's drugged to the gills blowjob was online in vivid color. Nothing I'd thought or imagined could have prepared me.

Julia told me the video wasn't yet viral; wishful thinking was cold comfort. Mentioned on Boston's local news, she admitted the now disconnected phone had rung constantly.

Patrick sat by my bed, holding my hand.

McGettigan retreated to sleep.

Crank it up, James.

CHAPTER 28

A recluse was what I'd been. No interviews. No statement of explanation about my sexual habits or the events surrounding Gillian Hartnett's arrest.

Reggie Tucker remained at-large with the five hundred thousand dollar reward Hub Durant claimed to have delivered. Appropriated was more like it, if there ever was a duffel full of cash. State Police released Durant after a lengthy interview.

The Board of BGFH removed Gillian. In her public statement, flanked by Preston, she vowed to regain her position (Gillian owned seventeen percent of outstanding shares) after disposing of charges filed by District Attorney Brendan Timilty. Gillian maintained Preston's statement to State Troopers was the result of coercion.

Billy Nichols granted no interviews after his interview with State Police.

Willy Côté wouldn't shut up: Willy never kidnapped anyone; Willy had been duped; Willy'd been too stoned to form *intent*. As a strategy, Willy was more likable than the ham sandwich. Julia thought he might get off.

***

Robert Linney sat in the backseat, leaving Tall Pines Village for Cape Cod. Patrick sat beside Robert, begging him to corroborate Dad's tall tales of days-gone-by. On occasion Robert answered unasked or unrelated questions. Patrick wouldn't give up. It made me smile, despite myself.

There was time to listen to my son. Africa had been a rebirth and a catalyst; Patrick would spurn his mother's gift of wealth. Together with his sister they would start a Foundation to improve education for underprivileged kids on Cape Cod. McGettigan's first reaction negative, blessedly I stayed silent. Out of the corner of an eye, I saw *her* nodding approval of bite marks on my bleeding tongue.

I phoned Martin Cardillo in hope he would intercede to obtain Marianna's testimony at Robert Linney's final hearing. Something wasn't right with Martin, though losing his father was a ready explanation. Marianna, he told me, wasn't interested in providing testimony.

Julia would represent her father at the hearing.

Robert would sleep this night in my cottage, on the third floor where all visiting children bunked. Robert would sleep next to his friend James, who was guilty of much, but nothing as tragic as abandoning a friend. A Fool promised not to cry too often, too hard or too loud.

***

Patrick bought me a new suit; I wore it with pride as the McGettigan clan, plus one, entered Barnstable Superior Court.

Julia made her way to one of three tables used by opposing attorneys.

McGettigan guided Robert and Patrick to the last row on the left.

Deirdre Collins, accompanied by a linebacker, sat beside John Poncey.

Connie Linney Durant and her husband Hub were situated one row behind Henry Linney, who, with his attorney, occupied the table adjacent to Julia.

Duncan Talbot, the attorney to whom the wax-sealed letter from Gwyneth had been addressed, was eager to complete his service. He whispered something to the Court Clerk, then made his way across the room to Julia. Two attorneys spoke until the gavel slammed.

Blake Burke and a cameraman prowled the miniscule space allotted them.

Brendan Timilty was the morning's surprise. In a far corner, he joined in hushed conversation with Stephen Lincope.

Today was bittersweet; Robert and I should be somewhere else, enjoying life. My friend's clothes hung like the skeleton of his body and mind.

Henry's attorney requested the judge rule on briefs filed previously. Julia objected, as did Duncan Talbot. After hearing arguments, the judge agreed additional testimony and evidence was appropriate.

"Julia McGettigan representing Dr. James McGettigan, your Honor. At this time, I'll simply state Dr. McGettigan is alive and present in the court, contrary to sworn statements made in an earlier hearing by Attorney Collins. With your permission, I reserve the right to call witnesses at a later time."

Robert's diaper needed urgent attention. Darkened when we returned, the courtroom watched a video recorded by Attorney Talbot at the wishes of Mr. Robert Linney and Mrs. Gwyneth Linney, Robert's natural mother.

"I, Robert Linney, being at this precise moment in time of sound mind and body, but having received a diagnosis of Early Onset Alzheimer's…"

McGettigan teared-up at the vibrancy on the screen, while decay and sorrow sat by my side.

Robert spoke the date which matched the video's date/time stamp. His statement was simple, but rocked the room.

"Any and all Trusts, Wills, Power of Attorneys or documents of any kind affecting either my future care or the disposition of my assets during my life, or after my death, from the date of this video forward, are revoked and of no affect. Appointed as Replacement Trustee and sole heir is Gwyneth Linney, my natural mother."

The video showed Talbot and Robert executing documents.

Talbot introduced Robert's physician, who certified the diagnosis and his expert opinion: As of the video's date, Robert Linney was in complete control of his faculties.

With Talbot's preliminaries completed, Gwyneth's on-screen persona wore a face I'd seen a thousand times. Gwyneth spoke in private to James, for all the world to hear.

"I, Gwyneth Linney, recant all earlier statements to the contrary and confess to the premeditated murder of Donald Hartnett. I loaded two pistols and shot Donald Hartnett after he fired on James McGettigan. I shot Donald Hartnett because he threatened to kill my children and tried to kill James McGettigan, who might as well have been my own child."

Blake Burke gasped. Speechless, she pointed at Robert and I, instructing her cameraman to rotate for our reaction. The judge chastened her.

Henry's attorney objected. The judge over-ruled.

Brendan Timilty and Stephen Lincope tiptoed from the room.

Gwyneth's recorded message played another few minutes, revoking any Will ever made and replaced any such Will with a declaration which appointed James McGettigan her sole heir and Successor Trustee.

When the lights brightened, the judge questioned Attorney Duncan Talbot for an extensive period; Talbot never waivered.

Henry was a madman.

Called to the stand on Henry's behalf, John Poncey testified the video was improper: Talbot wasn't Robert Linney's legal counsel; McGettigan was unfit to be the guardian of an Alzheimer's patient. Poncey referred numerous times to the Internet video of McGettigan's sexual antics. His testimony claimed Robert Linney would be at-risk in my care.

The judge inquired whether Mr. Poncey had evidence which invalidated Gwyneth's video statement. When John repeated his earlier harangue, the judge discharged him with an admonition about his obligations under the rules of the State Bar. A ruling in my favor followed.

Julia had been prepared to question Henry about a number of subjects, including the murder of his mother.

Deirdre exited without a glance in my direction.

The room emptied quickly. Connie Linney slid in next to her brother. "Hello, Robert."

She made me sick. "It's not an act, Connie. He doesn't know you."

"He could speak, if he wanted to. I'm his sister." Her tears were real enough, but, like McGettigan's guilt, too little too late.

"Connie, make certain you remove everything you and Hub brought to Robert's house...but not one thing belonging to Robert. Day after the wedding be out...not a day longer or your shit goes to the dump."

"You're so cold-blooded, James."

"Where were you, Connie, when Henry put Gwyneth down like an old cat?" Her vacant expression *was* cold-blooded. In the stillness of an empty courtroom, one guilty verdict was returned by a jury of me, myself, a Fool and I.

***

Astor's wedding day dawned bright and clear. Why was *his* wedding being held in *this* place? McGettigan had no better answer today than months ago, when Ingrid first mentioned a way to avoid the ceremony. Like a curtain call, my actors were scheduled to bow and receive plaudits from a worshipping throng.

Donny Slater suggested off-duty deputies be paid for traffic and security at Robert's Cotuit estate. Gracious to a fault, I referred him to the wedding planner working for Meredith. Six valets in white shirts and navy-blue shorts whittled away at their to-do list.

Robert's gunroom, secreted behind exquisite paneling, made for a primal recollection. Charlie stood staring at a collection like few others. One by one, we checked the antique pistols. I showed him the pair which killed Hartnett and McGettigan.

"Amazin' Boss. Don' think I believe it yet. Woman her age loadin' those guns…shootin' Hartnett tweena eyes."

Uncomfortable in the tuxedo Julia rented for him, Charlie's tools were stored on the padlocked Widow's Walk, safe from inquisitive eyes.

Of four hundred guests, members of the wedding alone would park within the estate. Standing on the driveway, watching guests arrive in shuttle buses, allowed McGettigan to become a fly on the wall.

Anna Solberg arrived towing Kristian and Ingrid in her wake. Was Ingrid headed for prison and Kristian not far behind? My mother-in-law oozed a smile from a numb, plastic face.

Kristian would be Astor's Best-Man.

Among those who qualified as a mild surprise were: Ellen Harding, who suffered under a fading cloud of suspicion generated by my televised accusation; Julian and Ryan Rommery, who wouldn't be happy losers in the competition for Jill's affection; Connie and Hub Durant, who couldn't be pleased at twelve different agencies looking into his sideline; and Marianna Salgado on the arm of Martin Cardillo, who appeared in the pink of health.

In the shocking category was Gillian Hartnett on crutches, escorted by her son, Preston, who'd appeared on every television program in the universe since his rescue.

General Anton Petrovsky and Colonel Sanun Nantakarn wore a chest full of medals and ribbons. Petrovsky waved at me. Seated among the groom's invitees, Petrovsky's presence with the Thai Colonel was a deliberate provocation.

Meredith's entrance was extravagance and simplicity, when a massive Mercedes limo rolled to a stop by my feet. Where her face could be seen through a window's slit, Gayle Swain was bright-eyed and chipper.

"Lauren tells me your dancing needs work. Come to the party later, after the lucky couple takes off."

Meredith and Astor entered the tent to the strains of *Ave Maria*.

Jill Stoddard arrived on the bluestone drive by helicopter. Without a glance in my direction, a golf cart whisked the bride and her father to the rear of the tent.

Almost immediately, the tenor began *The Wedding Prayer* and when finished, at 10am on the dot, the organist transitioned to *Here Comes the Bride*.

***

The happy couple departed while the band played-on. McGettigan sat at an empty reception table where I watched Robert and his nurse on the rear deck of what was, once more, his home.

"Never gonna work again, no sir." Julian Rommery was in his cups and looking for someone to piss on.

"Probably right, Julian. Worked for enough assholes. Get's old. How're Ryan's injuries?"

"Things gonna be better than fine." What an odd thing to say? Ryan was lucky to keep his arm.

McGettigan headed for Gayle Swain, who was dancing by herself. "May I cut in?"

"Whashusay?" Her's was an effective slur, played for laughs.

"You drink water, Gayle. But you do a nice imitation of a skanky drunk."

"Your imitation of an investigator isn't all bad, either."

"Why do I think your temp-work isn't a big worry anymore, Colonel Swain?"

Swain was decked-out in expensive duds accessorized by Ingrid's necklace, unworried by consequences. "I feel bad, James…may I call you James?"

McGettigan watched her decide what else to reveal.

"Be glad the Hartnett murder isn't your *Sword of Damocles* any longer."

"Have I been playing Dionysius or Damocles?" By her puzzled expression, a Fool deduced she didn't read Latin.

Swain ignored me. "With BGFH's new CEO, I can't imagine you'll be troubled…won't have to be looking over your kids' shoulders, slugging assassins with your cane." I must have looked dumbfounded. "Haven't heard?" She pointed at the bar. "Right over there. My boss until a few days ago."

Anton Petrovsky pointed a cigar in my direction with a million dollar grin. Petrovsky was still in uniform, so I played straight-man, "And *your* new boss…?"

"Great looking gal in the gray and blue Chanel." Meredith was deep in conversation with Martin Cardillo.

"What's your new job?"

"Acquisitions." With a Cheshire Cat grin, she added, "Maybe Mayor of Marsh Landing, if you sell me your lot."

Letting go of tension felt nice. I asked, "Shall we compare notes?"

"Let's dance…we can exchange a little gossip."

"So…Lauren's a buddy?"

"No…she got caught up in the idea of Harding being President. Did what the Harding crowd wanted and got screwed" Swain winced, when I stepped on her foot. Took a turn in who-did-what-to-whom quiz, "Who was the sniper on Jorge Machado? Hard shot."

McGettigan's mysterious smile substituted for an honest answer. "Too bad you left DIA…you could get the skinny from Petrovsky before he retires."

Seeing Martin's return to health clarified the bloody evening at Meredith's. Martin wasn't wounded; he was ashamed. But Dayami, detached to Petrovsky's unit of spies, surely must have known the identity of her target. Must have seen her mother, father and niece on the Cardillo's lawn. Was there any question a career as *Rodriquez* awaited Dayami?

There *was* something McGettigan didn't know. "Who killed the eleven girls? Who left me to die?"

"You're cheating…two questions is unfair." Swain didn't know. She countered two questions with one. "Who threw Mosqueda off the roof?"

We stopped dancing. Curious, I tossed a grapefruit towards her bat. "How many people did Petrovsky have working this thing? How far would he go to shelter Nantakarn?"

"Classified. More than once we thought you'd give up and go away. Eventually we got paranoid, wondering if you had a source inside DIA. I'd love to know who he, or she, is? Do you work for your source, or vice versa?"

This fresh minefield proved something was amiss, lingering like rotten eggs in Meredith's, now Swain's, expansive world. "When you tell me…who strangled Gwyneth?"

No longer swaying to the music, or my charms, she reached in her clutch for a cigarette and walked three steps before turning back to examine me with a deep frown. What was left of professional pride told me Timothy Timilty, a man whose purpose was inexorable in its finality, remained unseen in this drama. Smart-ass syndrome interfered, when I offered Swain free advice. "Ulula cum lupis, cum quibus esse cupis."

An approach to Marianna and Martin was necessary, but more than difficult: Martin used me; I used Marianna. Whether Martin or James acted with malice was debatable.

When Marianna excused herself, it was time to clear the air. "Are we friends, Martin?"

"Best friends, James. If you forgive this bump in the road."

"Are you buying Lawrence Foods or selling Cardillo Crystals?"

"Please, James, give me a little more time?"

"You sent me to Cuba with Manuel. By then you and Harry must have gathered chapter and verse on his plans for a coup. Sent me to a New York whorehouse to see Ellen Harding. Both times you sent me to a graveyard with nothing but a shovel. Why?"

"Sort of indirectly, we learned about Jorge transporting women to Florida."

McGettigan surmised *indirectly* meant Manuel.

"Next we were solicited for a large contribution to Senator Harding's campaign."

The solicitation came from Astor Lawrence, without a doubt.

"Indirectly, we were advised to defer linking a contribution to other negotiations."

Interpreting this use of *indirectly* wasn't straightforward; first choice was Dayami, who would've grasped the wider conspiracy from Petrovsky. Either way, Petrovsky issued the order which dispatched the Coast Guard cutter to save McGettigan's ass.

"Sending you to Cuba with Manuel had two purposes…one selfish, one obviously not. When we heard of the visit to Linney by an American and a Cuban American, you had to be told…your friend was at risk. Sending Manuel was the selfish part. Harry and I expected him to show his true colors…it didn't work out well. Asking you to visit Ellen Harding was intended to be transparent. Harry insisted we be discreet…told me to have faith in you. His exact words were, 'James will smell the *raton*. The smell will lead to the Hartnett woman.' Harry thought very highly of you."

Insisting on discretion was consistent with the Harry Cardillo I knew, as long as discretion benefited Harry's empire. Either Cardillo could have told me what they knew—and relied upon my discretion, not their own. McGettigan extended his hand in friendship.

"My therapist tells me life will be easier, if I can be more accepting of others. Call when the big fish are biting."

***

Hyannis's social scene was jumping as Robert and James attempted to capture summer's lost essence. Robert's condition reached a plateau—a way for doctors to describe a hopeless situation. I held his left wrist to add balance to a shuffling gait. At the intersection of Main St. and Bassett Lane, a swimsuit store, where Julia in another life sold bikinis, bustled with customers. The owner rapped on the window, waving to me. I waved back.

Robert struggled to lift his left arm; McGettigan's eye-line went along for the ride. Twisting as Charanya shoved it at my right side, the blade had a life of its own. In a single motion, McGettigan shoved Robert onto a bench and stepped backwards. The bee-sting rattled the Organism's resources. A trickle of blood stained my shirt.

Charanya radiated cold calm. She retreated, banging into people who appeared not to notice. Halfway up Bassett Lane north of Main, the crowd dissipated.

Darkness enveloped her, but I hurled the words anyway. "I didn't hurt those girls. Maybe you did. Who else, if not you? It's just a process of elimination."

McGettigan was a fixture in Charanya's litany of the unpunished. Behind stores fronting Main Street was an expansive parking lot; it's where Charanya would be headed. I dialed the cottage.

"Hey Dad."

"Patrick, get the gun Charlie left for you. Anyone but me, Charlie or Billy comes in the house, shoot'em. Promise me."

"What…"

"Promise me, damn it."

"Yuh but…"

At the entrance to an alley which led back to Main, I waited, desperate to stay in contact. Did Charanya have a gun? If she did, our game of hide or die would come to a premature end.

There she was, at the entrance to the alley, looking in every direction before moving.

Hidden in shadow I sought to provoke her. "Bet you've checked-out the town's layout. I've lived here all my life. Good luck losing me."

At Pearl St., a negative thought arrived with a deflating thud: Is bald-headed Colonel Nantakarn hiding in the bushes? I dialed 911.

"There's an Thai woman with a knife on South Street"

Charanya pushed hard, increasing the distance between us to fifty yards. McGettigan caught a glimpse of the American flag flying above the entrance to Aselton Memorial Park, where stragglers from a *Concert in the Park* would be enjoying panoramic views of Hyannis Harbor.

When I made the turn and came into view, she hesitated, uncertain for the first time. McGettigan yelled over the crowd noise.

"I won't go easy. You could've gone back to Thailand with nothing to fear. Not now."

In every direction, people edged away from a nut-job, yelling at no one, for the entire world to hear. A Sheriff's cruiser issued one short chirp of its siren. Flashing lights were a serious problem for Charanya.

Two linebackers, running towards her from the waterfront, jerked to a halt.

Charanya hit full speed in a single stride, running across Aselton Park to the lawn behind Town Hall. McGettigan lost her in less than five seconds. The linebackers split up: One followed Charanya; the second entered the Park.

On the circumference of the orchestra's hardscape, Hub Durant and Sanun Nantakarn sat in contentment enjoying the salt air. Saltwater taffy chewed, they wouldn't be taken for men selling girls to a slaughterhouse. Returned to his roots as a money grubbing, amoral prick, Hub was the definition of a perfect partner. Nantakarn wasn't opposed to expansion of the Thai sex trade, as long as he shared in its profits.

But Charanya?

For the first time McGettigan believed she was out of Nantakarn's control, and declared her independence during the episode at the Canal. If past was prologue, a large yacht was where Durant kept the newest girls, or stored corpses.

I reached Pleasant Street, where across the harbor's black water glowed the lights of Hyannis' largest marina.

In the marina's unpaved storage area, bloody shirt unbuttoned and flapping, face streaked with stone dust, McGettigan passed as a decrepit old Fool. Too tempted by boats and yachts beyond the dreams of ordinary folk, the old Fool muttered to himself, in a hangdog slouch, as he worked his way towards the docks. This plan was identical to the unworkable method rescued by luck at Chick's, in Ogunquit, half a lifetime ago.

Movement on the yacht furthest to my left jerked me to a halt: Seven shadows jumped from the stern and ran along the finger-pier towards a fifty-foot sport fisherman hanging from dual straps of a travel-lift. Charanya somehow must have beaten me here. On one knee, I rose to better scrutinize the girls' liberation.

"Whatcha doin' you old bastard?" The goon made no pretense of representing the Chamber of Commerce.

At the rear fender of a panel truck, Hub's foot soldier hadn't drawn his weapon. McGettigan saw the conclusion on his malevolent mug: Shitfaced old fart isn't worth it.

"Sorry, sir. Didn't hurt nothin'. Just lookin' thas all."

Straggled in his direction while the apology fumbled from my lips, the Organism bent over in a coughing fit. True to his nature, he kicked me in the ribs. The Organism coughed blood on the mug's boot, while McGettigan gagged for breath.

Grabbed under my right armpit, he ordered, "Get up, you disgusting old bugger."

No ladder. No noise. Charanya and her escapees were hiding themselves in plain sight.

Already leaning forward to drag me upright, my abuser was unable to resist when I windmilled my left towards the back of his exposed skull. A rusted, eight pound mushroom anchor gained centripetal force at the square of my arm's velocity; doing the calculation allowed me to reduce guilt for the damage. Unconscious and bleeding rather more than I'd hoped, a fractured skull wasn't out of the question. Diagnosis ill-informed at best, McGettigan wasn't the kind of doctor he needed. I tossed his 9mm into the evil thorns of Rosa Rugosa growing wild along the chain-link fence.

The third to last floating dock held a large ketch—the second to last a fast Italian cruiser. On the last pier, where female shadows first materialized, an older hundred-foot vessel seemed abandoned.

Noise from the road pushed McGettigan back into shadow.

Where Durant and Nantakarn were expected, the arrival of five wasn't a total shock. A linebacker led the way followed by Hub, Connie, Kristian and the Thai Colonel.

As they passed McGettigan's hidey-hole, Kristian said, "In the morning, we'll transfer the girls to the truck...then send the boat on its way. You've arranged delivery, Hub?"

"New place. New people. It's all good."

McGettigan could do nothing but wait for the inevitable. As they made their way along the pier, complete sentences faded to snatches of conversation and, finally, to indecipherable sounds. Nearer, yet unseen, was where I needed to be. Tied-up at an auxiliary dock, an old launch powered by a venerable diesel, steered by a tiller and armed with a massive knotted-rope bow fender, was a prayer answered.

Linebacker was first to board the big yacht. When he rushed back on deck, his words threw their calm demeanor into turmoil. "Girls are gone. Captain's gutted...the other crew are dead in a rope locker."

Durant turned to Kristian. "Can you drive this thing?"

Kristian was exasperated by Hub's asinine question. "Drive it where? We should charter a plane."

Hub stated what should've been obvious. "Boat's full of evidence. Best if it sinks."

Kristian started to walk away.

Durant extended his arm. A gun wasn't visible from my distance, but it was there.

In the distance *M/V Eagle*, two hundred fifty feet of massive ferry, barreled down Lewis Bay at fourteen knots, headed our way.

The very idea Hub Durant could avoid arrest and prosecution was an abomination: McGettigan started the little diesel. Eased along the pier, McGettigan turned to port, slipped past the two other yachts before easing up to the starboard bow of *Priceless*. In a blind spot obscured from the helm, McGettigan looped a line over the anchor's fluke.

Dead Reckoning was imprecise, a mixture of art and science. McGettigan's audacity and finesse were about to be tested.

MV Eagle displaced thousands of tons. Her freight deck and pilothouse may have looked awkward to a casual observer, but a bulbous bow, sponsons and bustle bludgeoned waves in Nantucket Sound's worst weather. Now a quarter mile from the narrow inner harbor entrance, where maneuvering room was less than a hundred feet, her speed would be plus or minus five knots.

McGettigan knew Kristian was a yachtsman, but an effort to pass the ferry in the narrows was low percentage at best and suicidal at worst.

Priceless began to move.

Kristian was experienced. In a high-risk situation he'd be tentative and slow, not ideal for McGettigan's purpose.

Eagle entered the narrows.

Priceless moved at headway speed.

Maritime rules required vessels to pass each other port-to-port. Kristian positioned *Priceless* in the proper location for the maneuver. When *Eagle* passed, *Priceless* would exit the inner harbor pretty as you please.

Twelve feet a second was an engineer's reckoning of *Eagle's* closing speed. Five seconds—how long Kristian would be ultra-cautious. Ten seconds, McGettigan calculated, to push the bow of

Priceless in front of *Eagle*. Throttle jammed forward, tiller pushed hard to starboard, the little diesel groaned. White water streamed from the launch's stern; any movement in the bow of *Priceless* a figment of my imagination.

Eagle's horn blasted.

The bow of *Priceless* began to move faster.

Kristian must be panicked. He couldn't see McGettigan's launch, and his yacht's misbehavior was without a rational cause. His choices were full emergency reverse or collision.

In seconds the launch would be crushed between the two vessels. Reverse wasn't an option for McGettigan.

Wait.

Wait.

A Fool instructed the Organism: Yank the tiller to port, and pray not to be jelly in this maritime sandwich.

Looming out of darkness, the ferry filled my vision.

The launch skidded off *Priceless's* bow and gained momentum. Lifted and rolled over by the ferry's bow wave the launch was struck by its steel hull.

Black water enveloped me.

In an unforgiving nightmare, I heard the whoosh, whoosh, whoosh of propellers and the screeching sound of metal crushing metal.

Eagle rammed *Priceless*.

Blessed silence enveloped McGettigan.

Am I dead?

CHAPTER 29

McGettigan understood—not as a faint superstition, but at the cellular level—the last weeks of serenity would today be broken in some hellish fashion. To understand wasn't knowing, not really, it was a combination of wanting, wishing, fear and anticipation.

Receipt of the invitation made no particular sense, unless order in the universe demanded resolution. Why else would Astor and Jill Lawrence invite James McGettigan to the topping-out for Rivers Nest Towers II.

To taunt me?

Patrick suggested he keep me company, a little boy's chance to visit a construction site with his daddy, play on the crane, hold a rivet gun, wear a safety harness, venture on a high-steel tightrope with no safety net, to never tell mom, to exaggerate to his sister, to eat hamburgers and drink milkshakes until the lone danger to conquer was indigestion.

How could 'no' have been my response?

***

Construction sites were, by their nature, dangerous.

Dust mixed with sweat covered brushed-clean, steel-toed, work boots, when I craned my neck to see the top floor. Not here to be a faux socialite, or to worm my way into anyone's good graces, I *was* here to be finished with feelings I couldn't put aside. Where the invitation called for *business attire*, a light blue work-shirt and khaki work-pants were a Fool's rebellion.

Why hadn't Ellen Harding lost her position of authority and power? Why no arrest? Where was the hue and cry for Senator Harding's resignation?

How was it possible neither Astor Lawrence nor Kristian Solberg had been questioned or charged? They were guilty as sin, wealthy as Croesus.

Beyond obvious injustices, the cosmos decided McGettigan must be crushed for a petulant uprising against the way things were and would be forever and ever. Amen.

Started with sunrise, gray men with wary eyes and twitchy hands crossed my vision in a never-ending procession. As we left the cottage's driveway, one gray man stood on my neighbor's porch. At the gas station the kid with a straggly goatee put his hand on his holster. Twice, cars with gray men in dark gray suits pulled even with us. At a quick breakfast stop, the woman with two teenagers hid her weapon in a gray bag of Lacrosse sticks.

McGettigan wasn't fooled.

In Jersey City, things were worse. I made Patrick walk in the street in case we were targeted by falling debris from above. We circled the building looking for glinting sunlight on gunmetal. Waiting by the elevator's rusted cage, we were exposed. With immense restraint, I refrained from pointing out the man staring at us from Rivers Nest Towers I. Upon our arrival at the topping-out platform, my diligence escalated. Patrick was embarrassed, but temperate in his condemnation of unreasonable negativity.

Topping-out occurred when the last beam was placed on a building. Today an evergreen tree was fixed to the ceremonial last beam, a symbol of growth and good fortune. Painted white and signed by the entire crew, Stars & Stripes would stream in the breeze as Chinese steel was hoisted into position. A toast would be drunk. Ironworkers would be treated to a meal alongside architects, engineers and all varieties of VIPs.

Ironworkers drank coffee, impatient while a single painter gussied-up the beam for photographers. Later it would be fixed in its permanent position—double the work for the ironworker's regular paycheck. When champagne no longer flowed, suits and dresses would depart in a hurry, moving on to more important duties. Paid by the hour, the not-as-swell would go back to their jobs.

Jersey City's Mayor was bombastic, shaking hands and shaking-down the well to do.

Immune to scandal, Ellen Harding, still an Assistant US Attorney, held hands with Kristian. Her Senator father backpedaled from a run for President, citing devotion to family.

Ingrid was resplendent standing with Anna, who loved her children through thick and thin. Rand Jellenek was on Anna's opposite side, looking morose. Rand had been arraigned and a trial date set for next year.

Meredith Lawrence was accompanied by her newest best friend, Gayle Swain, both prideful in appearance. Meredith's delight was special, since Astor's success was his first. Asking Meredith about her personal security seemed loutish; an old lady was entitled to her *ignis fatuus*.

Henry Linney and Connie Durant were the picture of blissful siblings. How Henry would suck additional money from a stone, eluded me.

Granville Proost represented BGFH's subsidiary. His presence offered an opportunity to demonstrate the Queen's fall from grace. Had she been beheaded, it would've been more to his taste.

Astor Lawrence beamed with imperious arrogance, betrayed by damning his mother with faint praise. Astor still planned to accelerate Meredith's death; McGettigan could smell it. Jill Stoddard Lawrence was animated and beautiful, moving among her guests like the well-groomed hostess she'd been brought up to be. Wilson basked in reflected glory. As at their wedding, oddities stood out like sore thumbs. Not just the McGettigan boys, but Julian and Ryan Rommery, Martin Cardillo and Phil Spazutta shifted foot to foot. Hub Durant wasn't in sight; was he camouflaged with James McGettigan in his gunsight?

Representatives from the serious financial press awaited speeches.

McGettigan focused on lines of sight. As Patrick circulated, there was a Jesuit to be foiled. Charlie assured me a kill shot from an adjacent building would be kindergarten stuff for a man of Timothy's legerdemain. In bright sunshine mirrored reflections were the rule, contrast being non-existent. Whatever would befall McGettigan was unknowable.

Behind me I heard, "Delivery of the original ledger was a complete surprise…good as gold. Never thought you'd send it."

"Why wouldn't I keep my word, Bazel? You've no faith. Why no diligence in pursuing the privileged?" Bazel moved away, unconcerned with my insult.

Working my way through the crowd, my hand closed on Phil's shoulder. "To what do the owners of Rivers Nest owe the honor?"

"Helping the wealthy calculate their tithe. And by the way you SOB, who owes who?"

"Who owes *whom*, Phil? Learn to speak the language."

"Fuck you, James." Phil wanted me to know I'd never live the sex video down, not with him.

Astor held the microphone in manicured fingers.

McGettigan kept his eyes on Meredith. There was a chance I could keep her out of harm's way, when the threat came clear.

"Welcome all of you to my first official act as CEO of Lawrence Foods."

A smattering of applause proved laconic. A look of minor irritation crossed Astor's face, replaced by a smile laden with snark.

"As we celebrate Rivers Nest II, it's with pleasure I announce our acquisition of Cardillo Crystals Corporation. I'll ask Martin Cardillo to join me at the microphone."

Astor sounded like a CEO. What would he sound like, if McGettigan released the safe room audio between he and Kristian?

Martin spoke in subdued tones.

"After the recent death of my father, I was forced to reevaluate the path of my life. There is no logical heir to the family business, and my interests have always been elsewhere." Martin looked straight at James. "My father was a giant. I pray he'd approve of the sale's structure. Lawrence Foods has acquired the sugar mills and a portion of associated acreage. Eco-Waste, in which the Lawrence Family holds substantial shares, has purchased a large, but separate tract for which they'll seek permits to develop a new garbage landfill. All the Cardillo interests in Cuba, disputed though they may be, have been retained by the Cardillo family."

Martin smiled a gracious look of delight for the photographers.

Astor didn't like being upstaged.

Julian Rommery was red-faced. I'd bet the County was thrilled to now own the old Eco-Waste landfill, where economic value was limited and more bodies were buried than just Gideon's.

Astor said, "I'll take questions from the Press before we officially *Top-out.*"

"When will your mother retire as Chairman of the Lawrence Board?"

"Whenever she wants. Mother *is* Lawrence Foods."

"Is the white-slavery scandal a concern to you?"

Astor sported his now perfected sneer. "Not today. Not ever. One last question and we'll get on with it."

"Mr. Cardillo, will you be staying on at Lawrence Foods?"

"No. I'll be joining close friends in funding an education foundation for at-risk children. As well as running a charter fishing business."

Astor signaled.

The crane's trolley lifted the painted beam. The slewing unit rotated the immense length of the jib arm into position as the operator lowered the steel into position between two columns. To the uninitiated, the crane jib appeared ungainly and certain to be pulled over by the weight of its burden. Too short in its counterweight's protrusion, the machinery seemed overmatched.

Despite radio communication available to the operator above and steelworkers below, hand signals prevailed.

While the beam dropped, I herded Patrick to an interior cluster of columns where protection was offered versus either a bullet or falling steel. McGettigan eyeballed Rand Jellenek: Concluded a crane accident, perhaps a failure of the ceremonial beam, wasn't his intent.

Dropped ten feet into a near final position, the beam crept to a stop. Four bolts were inserted and secured.

Relief showed on uninitiated faces wearing suits and dresses. Mild disorientation prevailed while high society and working stiffs milled around consuming champagne, finger sandwiches and Petits Fours. On his own, wearing a smile and acting relaxed, Patrick was outside my feeble protection, and still subject to a father's unbearable premonition.

The celebration's half-life of fifteen minutes, consisting of one or two glasses of bubbly, a sandwich and a delicate bite of pastry, evaporated.

A few made their way to the elevator, eager to be safe, out of the heat and increasing wind, and on Terra-Firma. Each expression told an identical story; humans were meant to be inside buildings.

For the most part, the construction crew was left to ensure no crumbs would be left behind. A tub of beer appeared. Last to belly-up to a makeshift bar was the crane operator, whose climb from his high perch left his machine at idle.

A line formed for a second trip on the eight-passenger elevator.

Patrick and Martin were deep in conversation. If they'd planned to surprise me, their success was complete. My son and my friend, working together, held strong appeal. Three or four media types pestered them for details.

Hunger prodded McGettigan the Ravenous. Relaxed, sitting on the painted beam, the panoramic view reflected satisfied contentment. The Organism enjoyed the beer. Relaxation, though a foreign emotion, was welcome. An entire sandwich stuffed in my mouth, James watched Connie and Ellen join Meredith, Jill, Gayle and a few other women.

Swain waved her cigarette at me.

James looked for Anna, who might never speak to me again. I saw her in the center of the elevator, arms locked with Ingrid. Astor, Henry, Phil and two financial reporters made fun of their fear of heights.

Julian and Ryan Rommery stood in line for the next trip.

With a grunt, the crane operator settled next to me, plate piled high. "Can't refuse a free feed."

"Something's wrong," the Ghostly One revealed in a whisper no one should have heard.

Crane Operator said through a mouthful, "Whassat?"

I heard her heartbeat everywhere.

Phil Spazutta caught me looking his way as the elevator began its descent. He gave me the finger, holding it for emphasis when everyone's ears were assaulted by two successive percussions: Boom; Bang. Muffled, but too loud for bullets, I hunted for the source. Watched in horror as the elevator detached from its rails, secured now by steel traction ropes swaying on the wind.

Screams and panic filled the air.

Where was Rand Jellenek? Eyes swept the deck. I couldn't see him: Ingrid's death would be good for Rand.

No time for who, when or why, the elevator dangling in space wasn't the idea of this sabotage: Falling was. So traction ropes would fail next. When whomever exploded the car from the rails, detonated the pulleys off the car, it would fall for a grim few seconds.

Rand stood by the base of the crane, trying to cut the slings. Knee or no knee, I'd have to run.

Patrick passed me, launching himself at Jellenek. Both men collided with the frame of the machine and were, for a few moments, groggy. McGettigan kicked Jellenek in his ribs—tore the heavy sling from his grip. Cut part way across its width, it wouldn't serve as a substitute cable.

Where was the second sling?

Patrick and I saw it at the same time. Never showing hesitation, my precious son grabbed the sling and, headed for the elevator, yelled back at me.

"Get the crane, Dad."

I expected the crane operator to be on the climb back to his cab. Nowhere in sight, a conclusion took no leap of insight.

Climb, James—the order given to the Organism.

Five steps up, I heard "Oohs" and "Aahs" from those who were safe, mingled with screeches of dread from those whose fate lay hundreds of feet below. A quick, desperate, look and I saw Patrick, heavy sling around his shoulders, leap from the building's edge to the elevator's roof more than a floor below. My boy's fingers locked in the cage's steel mesh, when he missed the landing. Progress excruciating, Patty scrambled to pull himself upright.

Legs implored to push harder, knee pain crippled progress. McGettigan pulled the Organism upwards with his arms. One eye on the climb, one on Patrick, I reached the crane's cab.

Patty positioned the sling through the car's cross-braces. He waited, dependent on his father to save him a second time in the same year.

Crank it up, James.

Controlling my heart rate was next to impossible as the Organism's focus turned to the crane controls; a newer layout needed examination.

"Nudge the joystick, James. Slow now…don't overshoot."

The sound of the Organism's voice was reassuring; McGettigan wasn't alone. Jib gliding into position, James moved the trolley's rugged hook to where Patrick could attach the sling's loop ends and secure the car's rescue.

High above the melee, McGettigan's straight-line vision encompassed Patrick, the street below and the roof of the opposite tower. Movement over there miniscule, but not inadvertent, with the hook more than twenty feet above Patrick's head I saw Timmy, hand in the air, performing a lousy imitation of Lady Liberty.

Two heartbeats later I identified a cell phone in his outstretched hand.

Four heartbeats and McGettigan digested his wicked expression: Timmy would tease McGettigan, allow the hook to reach Patrick, then and only then would he trigger destruction.

Six heartbeats and from too far a distance I guessed what Timilty mouthed. At eight heartbeats, certainty struck me down.

Choose.

Ten heartbeats and a father flung open the crane cab door and howled. "Jump for the hook, Patrick. Now!!" *Reverse the trolley's direction, you stupid Fool. Raise the hook faster.*

When Timmy blew the pulleys, traction ropes would react in a violent, whip-like, motion, lashing the elevator car, its roof and Patrick. When it happened, Patrick must be high enough, must be clear of this lunacy. No other option existed for McGettigan: The crane must lift him.

Twelve beats of my heart, six seconds—whoompf—such a small sound, a puff of smoke.

Chaos enveloped my world. The elevator's crash could be heard for blocks. Cries of pain told of steel traction ropes which sliced and diced unsuspecting onlookers.

McGettigan, head in his hands, wept.

"Lower him before he falls." Daniel Bazel's interruption was so very welcome.

A few touches of the controls and Patrick stared up at me—in shock from serious injury and motivations he'd not begun to comprehend.

In my aerie, the world was at peace. Sirens failed to intrude, nor the cacophony of accusations hurled in my direction. The rest of life would be available to examine McGettigan's prejudice, selfishness and weakness.

It was true: I made a life and death choice.

I wasn't sorry.

Not for a nanosecond had consequences been an influence.

Second-guessers were welcome to replay my decision. When they carped and offered uninformed criticism, by what measure would they calculate my guilt or innocence? Were they familiar with the thin line separating sanity from its opposite?

Three things were clearer than either an eternity or less than a minute ago would enlighten: Patrick was alive; one particular Jesuit exceeded the cruel, harsh expectations of the worst of his predecessors; and James McGettigan had been so very wrong about Meredith Lawrence.

***

Three hours passed before Jersey City Fire/Rescue triaged the injured, tagged the dead and coordinated everyone's removal from the rooftop down to the street. McGettigan, by choice and necessity, was the last one down after operating the crane to assist the rescues.

Gayle Swain waited at the bottom, holding her phone for me to see. It showed Patrick swinging from the hook; nothing but his left arm prevented death. I cringed—searched her face for anything other than honest relief.

Satisfied Meredith's arrangement with Timmy involved no co-conspirators, I should've known an old lady, who'd outlasted all-comers, relied on naught but her inner strength.

Anna Solberg, Astor Lawrence and a writer for the *Wall Street Journal* perished on impact. The second journalist passed away minutes later. Ingrid Solberg, Henry Linney and the victim I prayed for, Phil Spazutta, were listed as critical. Four onlookers would survive surgery with unpleasant dreams of a bad day.

Timmy was a creature not given to patience or acceptance of the status quo. Our uncodified bargain required me to wipe away Brendan's risk of scandal or blame. With McGettigan moving like a tortoise, if at all, and Brendan still at risk of Henry's blackmail, the elevator had been opportunity blended with justice meted out in broad strokes of an archangel's sword.

When I found Patrick at the hospital, there were more tears. His leg encased in pressure bandages, being prepped for surgery on a broken, battered limb, hindered by pre-op drugs, he sought a single answer.

"How did you know?"

A remnant of childhood emerged, from when his mother would explain unanswerable questions with a whisper. "Your own special angel told me."

After Patrick emerged from surgery, I begged a ride to Phil's hospital from a cop who wanted to question me. My vague responses were truthful, for as time passed McGettigan was less certain of what happened, or why. I sat all night waiting for news. Kicked out, along with Phil's children, the next morning I returned to Julia and Patrick.

At lunchtime, Meredith and Jill poked their faces into Patrick's room.

Meredith spoke to Patrick. "You poor child. Jill and I just wanted you to know...you're in our prayers. Get well and we'll talk about how I can support this foundation of yours."

A Fool was tempted to spit on kind words. "Your prayers seem to receive high priority, Meredith. We appreciate them."

Ryan Rommery could be seen outside Patrick's room. Jill would mourn Astor for an appropriate period; proprieties would be maintained. Ryan and Jill would be together, since they were never apart. Jill would be installed as CEO of Lawrence Foods; McGettigan remembered every glowing word Meredith spoke about her. The Lawrence Empire would be passed-on as determined by its primal force. Astor died to preserve the corporation, not for his crimes against young girls, the laws of several States or God's law. Should a mother so callous be condemned? It mattered not at all; forgiveness wasn't on Meredith's bucket-list.

Meredith and James held each other in continuous appraisal. Something needed saying about Astor. It needn't have been sloppy or sympathetic, for we two abhorred his hubris and sadistic nature. I twisted a quotation about fathers and sons to suit.

"A queen, realizing her incompetence, can either delegate or abdicate her duties. A mother can do neither. If Astor could have comprehended the paradox, he would've understood your dilemma."

Without doubt one sociopathic ex-priest enjoyed Astor's passing to a place Timmy would inhabit throughout eternity. If one chose to believe religious rants of the overly righteous.

***

Patrick came home today.

Ingrid, too injured to survive, slipped from this world within hours. I prayed for Ingrid.

Robert Linney's home was in the process of becoming the offices of Patrick's foundation, the endowment of which soared past a hundred million dollars heading for a much bigger total. When Meredith pitched a charity to her buddies, well, good things happened. Paradox indeed.

Henry Linney would soon be resident in Robert's home. A broken body may heal with time, massive brain injury would not. Gwyneth's love demanded Henry's care be impeccable; impeccable it would be. Connie signed the papers. Not a word passed between us about visiting her brothers. Bitterness would be our collective harvest.

Hub was missing.

Martin lived aboard *Sugar Daddy*. Now a multi-billionaire without a *real* job, he told me a baseball team would make a fine investment.

Marianna found her way back to Cuba, with Martin's assistance.

I mailed the original, un-doctored ledger back to Mama-san.

I sold the Marsh Landing property to Gayle Swain.

Anton Petrovsky was too busy to call. Granville Proost e-mailed to say Preston recovered nicely, and would be cared-for during his mother's incarceration. Granville and the ways of the world would continue apace.

Summer lingered on Cape Cod. Charlie visited with his wife and daughter.

CHAPTER 30

Stephen Lincope stared at me in anticipation.

For a second time, James McGettigan attended a Grand Jury session in Barnstable Superior Court, this time as a witness with full immunity.

Lincope established my background for the jurors. From earlier testimony, they'd heard an outline of charges pending. Months may have slid by since our prior encounter, but his ego was still bruised.

"What is your relationship to Mrs. Durant?"

"Connie Durant is the sister of my best friend from boyhood, Robert Linney."

"So you know her well."

"No. Until recently, I hadn't seen or spoken to her for years."

"Are you responsible for the long-term care of Mrs. Durant's two adult brothers: Robert and Henry Linney?"

"Yes." I could quibble, if irritating Lincope would provide comic relief. McGettigan was responsible for the loving care of Robert. I paid Henry's bills—an important distinction to no one but James.

"Mr. Kristian Solberg has been indicted by the Grand Jury on several felony counts involving kidnapping of underage citizens of Thailand for the purpose of sexual crimes and, ultimately, murder. Would you, please, describe Mrs. Durant's involvement in those crimes?"

"No."

Lincope sighed: *Not again, please.*

Sitting in a corner, Brendan Timilty suppressed his urge to laugh.

Amateur video of *Eagle* ramming *Priceless* went viral within two hours. *Eagle*, undamaged beyond scraped paint, continued on her way to the wharf at the direction of the Harbormaster. *Priceless* sank slowly, sliced opened and squashed just forward of the helm. All seven of her living occupants abandoned ship and were dragged from the water within minutes. By midnight, Hub and his three Agency handymen left Hyannis in black SUVs. An Air Force Major from Otis arranged a similar result for Colonel Sanun Nantakarn of the Royal Thai Police. Nantakarn returned home with an official apology from the State Department.

Tom Nichols, in full Massachusetts State Police regalia, discovered six Thai women huddled together on the property of Lewis Bay Marine. Over several days, each of the women, speaking through translators, with the exception of one who spoke in an educated British accent, provided statements. Based on their testimony, Mr. Kristian Solberg had been indicted for the aforementioned felonies.

"Again, I ask you Mr. McGettigan, please describe Mrs. Durant's crimes?"

Lincope hadn't meant to misspeak. Regardless, he invited the testimony I was here to provide.

"Mrs. Durant murdered her mother, Mrs. Gwyneth Linney."

"What..." Lincope struggled to rearrange his notes for a disrupted interrogation.

"In an attempt to gain control over Robert Linney's wealth, Connie Linney Durant murdered her mother at the kitchen table of Gwyneth Linney's home."

McGettigan and the launch had been brushed aside by *Eagle*, like popcorn in a strong wind. Both washed up on a strip of beach, neither the worse for wear.

"Well...really...murder isn't..." Lincope glanced at Brendan, who nodded in affirmation.

McGettigan said firmly. "Yes. That is precisely what she did."

"Well...how would you know?" Lincope was in uncharted waters.

"Because no one but a daughter knows where her mother hides the sterling silver. No man would strangle an old woman, tear the house apart for a sterling silver tea service and set a table for two...all to suggest a different killer."

For twenty minutes thereafter, Lincope followed Brendan's alternate script to the letter. All McGettigan's testimony would be provided to the District Attorney for Framingham. Would it result in Connie's indictment and conviction? Who could say?

***

McGettigan was no longer in therapy.

Should he be considered sane?

Thirty-six years of marriage said yes; whether *she* was dead didn't count. Till death do us part wasn't the limit of James McGettigan's vow. It filled me with sorrow to admit forever would never last, not on this earth. Having two children who loved me should keep me grounded. There were a few friends about whom I gave a tinker's damn.

Business was a shambles—my reputation so recently off life-support.

I was over sixty with a history of cancer.

Most of the time for the better, though occasionally for a bit less, Lucifer remained the sole companion in my bed.

Gwyneth's heartbeat settled into fond remembrance.

The phone message after my latest Grand Jury appearance made me laugh out loud.

"Crudelius est quam mori semper timere mortem," it said succinctly: *It is more cruel to be always afraid of dying than to die.* Not that Timmy would know, since his was the delivery side of death, not the receiving end. But Timmy had, all those months ago, been correct about one thing: Life could deal out some twisted shit.

ABOUT THE AUTHOR

John Hayden has spent a career in engineering/construction, advising politicians and high ranking officials across the USA, Europe and the Middle East. Having met the best and worst of people, often involved in a stew of corruption and crime, his novels reflect flawed lives intervened upon by unexpected disasters.

John earned a Ph.D. in engineering from the University of Pennsylvania. Married with three adult children, John and his wife, Janet, live on Cape Cod.

www.ingramcontent.com/pod-product-compliance
Lightning Source LLC
Chambersburg PA
CBHW022257190626
46812CB00014B/2197